Emma; or, The Unfortunate Attachment

A Sentimental Novel

Emma; or, The Unfortunate Attachment

A Sentimental Novel

Georgiana, Duchess of Devonshire

Edited and with an Introduction by
Jonathan David Gross

STATE UNIVERSITY OF NEW YORK PRESS

Published by
State University of New York Press, Albany

© 2004 State University of New York

For information, address State University of New York Press,
90 State Street, Suite 700, Albany, N.Y., 12207

Production by Kelli Williams
Marketing by Fran Keneston

Library of Congress Cataloging-in-Publication Data

Emma; or, The unfortunate attachment: a sentimental novel / Georgiana, Duchess of
    Devonshire; edited and with an introduction by Johnathan David Gross.
        p. cm.
    Some authors have attributed this anonymous work to Georgiana, Duchess of Devonshire.
    Includes bibliographical references (p.   ) and index.
    ISBN 0-7914-6145-9 (alk. paper) — ISBN 0-7914-6146-7 (pbk.: alk. paper)
        1. Arranged marriage–Fiction. 2. Runaway husbands–Fiction. 3. Married
    women–Fiction. I. Title; Emma. II. Title: Unfortunate attachment. III. Devonshire,
    Georgiana Spencer Cavendish, Duchess of, 1757–1806. IV. Gross, Jonathan David, 1962–

PR3291.A1E37 2004
823'.6—dc22   2004045336

10 9 8 7 6 5 4 3 2 1

For my father

Contents

*A*cknowledgments

I WOULD LIKE TO ACKNOWLEDGE the generous assistance of DePaul University, which provided research support in the form of a University of Research Council grant as well as a spring quarter leave in 2003 that enabled me to complete this edition. My thanks to Mike Mezey, Dean of the College of Arts and Sciences, and Helen Marlborough, Chair of the Department of English, for making this possible.

Professor Peter Graham set high standards for what an edited volume should be. His generous suggestions and helpful advice guided my research at every stage. Professor James Murphy at DePaul answered numerous genealogical and historical questions related to the Spencers and Camdens. His timely and gracious help saved me from numerous errors. My thanks also to my three research assistants. David Bachmann located reviews of *Emma* and other periodicals at the Newberry. Shannon Siggeman proofed the introduction, created files for the notes, and helped locate other copies of *Emma*. She also assisted in preparing the manuscript for publication. Linda Neiberg assisted with the collation of the 1784 and 1773 editions at the University of Bristol library and obtained periodicals at the New York Public Library; her work in England helped make the 1784 collation possible. Students in my M.A. in English, English 471: Bibliography and Literary (Winter 2002) found clues and sources for several allusions in the novel. I am particularly grateful to Jennifer Parrott, Matthew Infantino, and Randi Russert for their work in this area. Frank DeConstanza and Darren Trongeau gathered valuable information on *The Sylph* in the electronic edition they prepared in Winter 2001 that proved helpful in drafting the introduction to this volume.

This project would not have been possible without the assistance of the following librarians and curators who were kind enough to set up visits to their archives: Peter Day of Chatsworth; M. T. Richardson of the Rare Books Room at University of Bristol; Peter Berg of Michigan State University, East Lansing; curators at the University of Pennsylvania, Van Pelt Library (who produced a microfilm copy of *The Married Victim* on short notice); Kathryn DeGraff of Special Collections at DePaul University; the staff at the Newberry Library, Chicago; Stephen Jones of Yale University library; and the staff at the Rare Books Room at University of Chicago Library.

I am grateful to James Peltz, along with the two readers of this manuscript, who provided crucial suggestions that improved the final draft. The professional staff at the State University of New York Press has been a joy to work with.

My sister, Donna, and wife, Jacqueline, helped me see my way to the end of this project. Shiri, my daughter, continues to inspire my interest in women's writing. A final thanks is due to my father, my own model of scholarship, who read the entire manuscript at a late stage, and to whom this book is dedicated.

Preface

LADY GEORGIANA SPENCER WAS a patron of the arts, a writer, a musician, and an amateur scientist. Art historians know her as the subject of eighteenth-century portraits by Sir Joshua Reynolds that feature her sometimes outlandish innovations in fashion, hairstyle, and taste. Thrown into what she later described as the "vortex of dissipation" at a young age, Lady Georgiana used her charisma to aid the cause of the Whigs. Her circle at Devonshire House inspired Richard Sheridan's *School for Scandal,* which she saw on its opening night; later she helped launch Sheridan's political career as MP for Stafford. Her most visible political success, however, occurred when she undertook a massive public relations campaign that secured Charles James Fox's reelection in 1784. She solved various crises in the government connected with the Prince Regent's marriage to Maria Fitzherbert, and Devonshire House soon became the *de facto* meeting place for the Whig party during their long period in the political wilderness under George III. One French diplomat complained that her pregnancy in the late 1780s interrupted the flow of political business in the English capitol.

At Althorp and Spencer House in London, Lady Georgiana was fêted, on various occasions, by David Garrick, Samuel Johnson, and Laurence Sterne. They wrote odes in her honor, visited her soirées at Chatsworth, and Sterne even dedicated the sixth book of *Tristram Shandy* to Lady Georgiana's mother. Lady Georgiana continued her mother's tradition of patronizing writers by supporting the talents of Mary Robinson, Joanna Baillie, Ann Yearsley, and Charlotte Smith; a long line of actresses, including Dorothy Jordan, Mrs. Nunns, and Sarah Siddons owed their London triumphs, in part, to Lady Georgiana's active endeavors on their behalf. Though readers have become familiar with Regency society through the works of Jane Austen and the reprinting of works by Mary Robinson and Charlotte Smith, the perspective of the aristocratic class on the period just before this time—contemporaneous with the American Revolution—has not received as much attention. "What is the history of rich, powerful and establishment women?" Linda Colley asked in the *Sunday Times* (April 17, 1994). "Few people write it, so the question is rarely asked." This edition of *Emma, or The Unfortunate Attachment* builds on Amanda Foreman's award-winning biography of Georgiana, Duchess of Devonshire (1998) and seeks to provide a literary response to Colley's important question.

Lady Georgiana was the likely author of two novels. The first of these, *Emma; or The Unfortunate Attachment* (1773), appeared when she was only sixteen and anticipates many of the major events of her life. The second, *The Sylph*, advertised with Fanny Burney's *Evelina*, reached a London audience in 1779, when Lady Georgiana's reputation as an arbitress of fashion was already secure. Because she published her novels anonymously, Lady Georgiana's authorship cannot be definitively determined. By examining the circumstances that led her to write them, however, the reader can learn much about the outlook of aristocratic women in the late-eighteenth century.

Emma's complex depiction of an arranged marriage, which borrows at times from Richardson's *Clarissa* and Rousseau's *Julie, ou La Nouvelle Héloïse*, adds a woman's voice (complementing Fanny Burney's, Frances Sheridan's, and numerous others) to the history of the epistolary novel. In its reliance on ellipses and italics to convey heightened emotion, *Emma* is very much a work of its day: its subtitle, after all, is "a sentimental novel." As such, it reflects the influence of Laurence Sterne's *A Sentimental Journey Through France and Italy* (1768) and Henry Mackenzie's *The Man of Feeling* (1771). At the same time, *Emma* anticipates Jane Austen's *Sense and Sensibility* (1811) in several ways, reflecting a more ironic treatment of unbridled feeling. Before Mary Wollstonecraft and Mary Hays, Lady Georgiana took up the subject of feckless husbands and dandies, satirizing the "strutting boobies who would be the supreme rulers of it [this world] in everything," as Kitty Bishop puts it. More tentatively, she broached feminist themes explored by Charlotte Smith's *Desmond* (1792). She sympathized with Robinson and Smith's perspective enough to assist them actively in publishing their works.

What becomes clear from actresses' diaries and press accounts of Lady Georgiana's patronage is that the boundaries between Whig politics, fashion, and musicianship were quite permeable. For this reason, it would be a mistake to view Lady Georgiana solely as a professional writer. Her social milieu made her, like her mother, a patroness of the arts in a broader sense. "Personal displays of refinement and elegance in dancing led to an etiquette and fashion that shaped polite society in a golden age of social dance, which, at this period, was closely connected with theatrical dance," Anne Bloomfield writes.[1] Aristocratic women who attended the opera also paid dancing masters for their own personal needs. Lady Georgiana studied dance with Gaetan Vestris (1729–1808), who introduced the Devonshire minuet in her honor. When the prince's official debut took place on New Year's Day, 1781, the prince used the occasion to snub his father and dance with a leading member of the opposition. "The Court beauties looked with an eye of envy on her Grace of Devonshire, as the only woman honoured by the hand of the heir apparent, during Thursday night's ball at St. James's," the *Morning Herald* noted on January 19, 1781.[2] In 1782, Fox sought to capitalize on Lady Georgiana's popularity by asking her to help organize his re-election campaign. "Milliner's shops began making fans bearing Lady Georgiana's portrait, which sold in [the] hundreds; Charles J. Fox and the Prince of Wales also became fashionable subjects" (Foreman 93). The same year she celebrated Fox's victory in 1784, which she had quite visibly helped to engineer, Lady Georgiana saw *La Reine de Golconde*, an opera that included a small piece she had composed.[3] Clearly, Lady Georgiana felt comfortable on both sides of the stage. Her cultural influence led her to become an important force in shaping Whig political and social life, but she did much of her work anonymously, when the press would let her.

Partly because of her role as a cultural leader, Lady Georgiana's literary efforts were sometimes trivialized. "I have seen an *Ode to Hope* by the Duchess of Devonshire and Hope's Answer," Horace Walpole wrote on January 3, 1782. "The first is easy and prettily expressed, though it does not express much. The second is the genteelest sermon I ever saw and by much the best-natured, and the expression charming."[4] But Horace Walpole continued to collect Lady Georgiana's poetry even as he disparaged it. Throughout his life, he watched Lady Georgiana,

1. Anne Bloomfield, "Patroness of the dance," *Dancing Times.* (January 1996), pp. 361, 363.

2. Amanda Foreman, *Georgiana, Duchess of Devonshire* (London: HarperCollins, 1998), p. 40.

3. Earl of Bessborough, ed., *Letters of Georgiana* (London: John Murray, 1955), p. 77. Hereafter cited as Bessborough.

4. Horace Walpole, *The Yale Edition of Horace Walpole's Correspondence*, ed. by W. S. Lewis et al. 48 volumes (New Haven: Yale UP, 1937–1983), 25:179n. Cited hereafter as Walpole.

Lady Melbourne, and the talented Anne Damer from the sidelines, re-
cording, often enviously, his acerbic commentary. Acknowledging Lady
Georgiana as a "phenomenon" in February 1, 1775, Walpole took some
malicious delight in concluding that she was "no beauty at all" and
"verges fast to coarseness" by 1783 (Walpole 25:411).

Emma and *The Sylph* chart the early stages of her disillusionment that
led to this decline. The overwrought feelings that receive so much attention
in Lady Georgiana's first sentimental novel give way to a withering portrait
of her own unhappy marriage to a neglectful husband in her second. "My
person still invites his caresses," Julia Stanley complains in *The Sylph*, "but
for the softer sentiments of the soul . . . that ineffable tenderness which
depends not on the tincture of the skin . . . of that, alas, he has no idea.
A voluptuary in love, he professes not that delicacy which refines its joys.
He is all passion; sentiment is left out of the catalogue."[5] As this passage
from *The Sylph* would suggest, *Emma* has all the benefits, and some of the
drawbacks, of a sentimental novel. Almost forty years before the much
greater achievement of Jane Austen's *Sense and Sensibility* (parts of which
were drafted in the 1790s as "Elinor and Marianne"), Lady Georgiana
portrays her own perspective on the tension between the head and the
heart. Thomas Jefferson's famous letter to Maria Cosway (October 12,
1786), along with his literary scrapbooks, remind us that Lady Georgiana
was not alone in her interest in sentimental fiction. While ambassador to
France, Jefferson carried a copy of Sterne's *Sentimental Journey* on his
vacations, so he might have it for moral consultation and amusement.

Unlike Mackenzie and Sterne, Lady Georgiana did not seek literary
celebrity. In fact she shunned it. Nevertheless, her first novel went into
four editions; her first published poem inspired a response by Coleridge.
Despite her best efforts to keep her novel anonymous, a new generation
now has the opportunity to appreciate her talents. Ideally, she will escape
the fate Byron thought Horace Walpole faced: "It is the custom to
underrate Horace Walpole; firstly, because he was a nobleman, and secondly, because he was a gentleman."[6] Lady Georgiana's writings should
not be read solely because of her social position, but they should not be
ignored for that reason either. In seeking a publisher to reprint this
novel, I have been inspired, in part, by Amanda Foreman, who once
dreamed she heard Lady Georgiana reading her poems on the radio.

---

5. Georgiana, Duchess of Devonshire, *The Sylph*, with an Introduction by Amanda Foreman (York: Henry Parker, 2001), p. 84.

6. George Gordon, Lord Byron, *The Complete Poetical Works*, ed. by Jerome McGann. 5
vols. (Oxford: Oxford UP, 1980–1986), 4:305.

Introduction

beware then how you chuse, for your first preference makes your destiny

Emma; or, The Unfortunate Attachment

WHEN GEORGIANA SPENCER MARRIED the duke of Devonshire on June 4, 1774,[1] she fulfilled her mother's greatest hope and fear. "My dread is that she will be snatched from me before her age and experience make her by any means fit for the serious duties of a wife, a mother, or the mistress of a family," her mother wrote in January 1774 (Masters 12). Despite her belief that she was facilitating a love-match, Lady Spencer's prophecy proved correct. "Lady Georgiana's marriage was one *de convenance*," her niece Lady Caroline Lamb wrote with typical hyperbole. "Her delight was hunting butterflies. The housekeeper breaking a lath over her head reconciled her to the match. She was ignorant of everything."[2] In fact, Lady Georgiana received an "exemplary education"[3] from her mother. She was a proficient musician, poet, and writer who knew her future husband as early as 1765 and 1766, for he visited Althorp House on frequent occasions (Masters 12).

The difference between Lady Georgiana and her husband is perhaps best shown by a perfunctory note the duke wrote shortly after their marriage. "I am going to sup in St. James's Place and have sent you the carriage that you may come in it if you like it." On the back, Lady Georgiana allowed her high spirits to overflow in verse.

> J'aime, je plais, je suis contente,
> Tout se joint pour mon bonheur.
> Que peut on plus, je suis amante

Et mon Amant me donne son coeur.
Il est si digne de ma tendresse,
Il est mon amant, mon ami.
Loin de lui rien ne m'interesse
Et tout m'enchante auprès de lui.
[I love, I please, I'm full of joy,
All things conspire toward my happiness.
What else is there to do? For I'm in love,
And my beloved gives his heart.
He is so worthy of my tenderness,
He is my lover and my friend.
I care for nothing when away from him
And everything charms me when with him][4]

The duchess turned the duke's prose into poetry, as if she could speak for the two of them. But Lady Georgiana's more reticent husband seemed oppressed, at times, by her high spirits. On one occasion, when she sat in his lap in front of company, he pushed her aside and walked out of the room.[5] Lady Spencer, who witnessed this event, wrote countless letters advising her daughter on how to handle the fifth duke. "When a husband will speak his wishes a wife who loves him will find it by no means difficult to sacrifice her inclinations to his," her mother wrote on April 14, 1775. "But where a husband's delicacy and indulgence is so great that he will not say what he likes, the task becomes more difficult."[6] Lady Spencer tried to make her daughter more attentive, urging her to learn "his sentiments upon even the most trifling subjects" (Bessborough 22).

HISTORICAL BACKGROUND

The object of all this concern came from one of the first families in England. He could trace his ancestry to William Cavendish, who had been fortunate enough to marry Bess of Hardwick, the richest woman in Elizabethan England after Elizabeth I. Sir William Cavendish advised Henry VIII on the dissolution of the monasteries. He was her favorite husband and the only one by whom she had any children. Bess of Hardwick had fallen out with members of her own family, and bequeathed her enormous wealth and estates to the Cavendishes. Her son, William Cavendish, inherited Chatsworth, Hardwick, and Oldcotes, in Derbyshire, while Welbeck went to another son, the ancestor of the duke of Portland (Masters 16). The defining moment of the Cavendishes' political fortunes came on June 30, 1688. The fourth earl of Devonshire joined seven Whigs and Tories in inviting William of Orange (William III) to take the throne from the Catholic James II, a man they believed intent on curbing parliamentary privileges. Upon William's arrival in England, the fourth earl accompanied him through the Midlands, suppressing resurrections in Derbyshire and Chesire; for his labors, William III granted him the dukedom of Devonshire in 1694, the same day his political ally William Russell was created duke of Bedford (Masters 17). When George III came to the throne over fifty years later, William Cavendish lost his position as Lord Chamberlain, thus beginning a long period of opposition for the fifth duke of Devonshire and his young wife (Foreman 15).

The fifth duke of Devonshire's father served as prime minister for six months in 1756–1757 which nearly killed him. The son shared his father's political connections and his disinclination to use them. "He was undoubtedly very well read, deeply versed in Shakespeare, and he possessed a shrewd political sense," Lees-Milnes notes of the fifth duke.[7] He showed a charming side in 1782, when he read portions of *Hamlet*, *A Midsummer's Night Dream*, and *The Tempest* to Lady Elizabeth Foster and the duchess, making them all "Shakespeare mad" (Bessborough 55). Yet to those who did not know him, he did not cut a great figure. "Constitutional apathy formed his distinguishing characteristic," Nathaniel Wraxall observed (Foreman 17). To stimulate his torpid disposition he played whist and faro at Brooks and would conclude the evening at four o'clock by ordering a plate of boiled mackerel. To some, the duke's phlegmatic nature must have seemed a dandiacal affectation; his almost morbid incapacity for enthusiasm, however, became a severe trial to his young wife who found him to be one of the few men she could not charm (Masters 17). With the exception of his penchant for gambling, he could not have been more different than the duchess of Devonshire.

Georgiana was eight years old when she became Lady Georgiana Spencer, due to the enoblement of her father, John Spencer in 1765 (Foreman 4). An avid book collector, he served as tutor to the duke of Cumberland, a privy councillor, and friend of the dukes of Devonshire (Pearson 92). The first earl of Spencer built his considerable library at Althorp in Northamptonshire, while also enjoying residences at Wimbledon Park and Spencer House, St. James's Place, "one of the finest houses in London."[8] Lady Georgiana's father made his mark on his eldest daughter when the family and an entourage of servants had set out on a grand tour from Wimbledon in 1772, visiting Calais, Brussels, and Spa, where they met the duchess of Northumberland and Princess Esterhazy. Lady Georgiana and her sister accompanied their father on a boar hunt in Liège, following behind on ponies; they were also instructed in religious tolerance and encouraged to sleep on the floor to become accustomed to privations. In April 1773, they passed through Lyons and then back to Paris, observing Marie Antoinette at the theater at Versailles. As the highest ranking Englishman in Paris at the time, Lord Spencer took it upon himself to hold a ball for the queen on her birthday that lasted until six in the morning. By June 12, 1773, the grand tour for ladies had been an apparent success. As for "Georgine," Madame Du Deffand wrote, "sa taille, sa physiognomie, sa gaite, son maintien, sa bonne grace ont charme tout le monde" (Masters 12). The family returned to Spa and then England in June 1773, having been away from England for a full year.

Lady Georgiana most likely completed her novel at the same time as her younger sister, Harriet, was taking copious notes during the Grand Tour. Verse letters between the two sisters give evidence of their literary inclinations. Several years after her father died in 1783, Lady Georgiana wrote "The Crowning Monuments of Spencer's Fame" (May 1787), so "That Strangers & posterity may know/ How pure a Spirit warm'd the dust below."[9] In awe of her father, Lady Georgiana was almost inseparable from her mother, penning a poem on the latter's seventy-third birthday. "The muse must weep to think how few shall bear / Fruit like the Parent Stem as rich as rare / Feelings unite with reasons strong controul / A Mind inlarged & heaven directed soul," she wrote.[10] Though she sometimes reinforced a sense of unworthiness in Lady Georgiana, her mother was by her side at her most trying moments: her miscarriages, the births of her two daughters and son, and her marriage to the diffident fifth duke of Devonshire. "I think I shall never love another so well," Lady Spencer wrote on September 30, 1758. Lady Georgiana clearly reciprocated the feeling. "You are my best and dearest friend," the seventeen-year-old Georgiana informed her mother. "You have my heart and may do what you will with it" (Foreman 4).

Lady Georgiana's mother was daughter and co-heiress of General Lewis Mordaunt; her father, Stephen Poyntz, was an upholsterer who became a courtier, diplomat, and favorite of George II. George II served as godfather to the bride. An amateur musician, Lady Spencer married her future husband when he was only twenty-one and wrote that she never regretted the decision. She wore diamonds from the old duchess of Marlborough worth 100,000 pounds; her husband's shoebuckles, also set in diamonds, were worth 30,000 alone (Cash 81). She was "remarkable in any age for her liberal views, strong sense of *noblesse oblige,* and philanthropic activities," Hannah More's biographer notes.[11]

One of these activities was education. "[S]he founded schools wherever she might be living," Georgina Battiscombe observes, "supervising and sometimes teaching in them herself, and she assiduously visited schools run by other people so that she might study the new methods practised by such pioneers as Hannah More."[12] Her school at St. Albans was a particular source of pride (Jones 152). As a teacher, she was well equipped for the task, for she could read Greek, French, and Italian (Lees-Milnes 43). She passed the French, if not the Greek and Italian, on to her daughter.[13]

Lady Georgiana benefited from her mother's friendships and literary patronage. David Garrick was a favorite who performed privately at the house; Countess Spencer kept up a correspondence with his wife, sending her a turkey on one occasion. The friendship extended to Lady Georgiana, for in 1778, Garrick wrote an ode to the duchess on learning that she was ill.

> When to the Fever's rage, which Art defies,
> Georgiana's Charms become the Prey,
> When the Mother Ev'ry Virtue sigh's,
> And Ling'ring Hope still keeps away:
> Shall you alone not feel the gen'ral Woe,
> Nor sing the Beauties you adore?[14]

This unpublished poem reflects the tone of another that appears in his complete works, mildly rebuking the duchess for waking up at midday. Lady Spencer would have agreed. She rose at five and frequently faulted her daughter for her late hours. Nevertheless, it was the theatrical world rather than evangelical religion that left its greatest mark on Lady Georgiana's imagination. Her exposure to Garrick finds its way into *Emma; or, The Unfortunate Attachment* in many ways. One of these, perhaps, occurs when Kitty Bishop quotes Calista's famous speech from Nicholas Rowe's *The Fair Penitent*, a role David Garrick performed as Lothario in London (see annotations). Another becomes apparent in Lady Georgiana's successful depiction of her characters' visually observable responses to tragic news, a stage technique she employs effectively in her novel, anticipating Elizabeth Inchbald's method in *A Simple Story*.

As a young girl, Lady Georgiana heard Laurence Sterne read privately at Althorp House. Sterne dedicated the "Story of Le Fever" in Volume VI of *Tristram Shandy* to Lady Spencer, "for which I have no other motive, which my heart has informed me of, but that the story is a humane one" (Cash 108). In this section of the novel, Toby and Trim care for a dying officer and his boy. Spencer granted his permission that the whole novel be dedicated to him and Volume VI to his wife. Shortly after, Sterne boasted to assembled guests of Sir Joshua Reynolds. Samuel Johnson was unimpressed.

Tristram Shandy introduced himself; and Tristram Shandy had scarcely sat down, when he informed us that he had been writing a Dedication to Lord Spencer; and sponte suâ he pulled it out of his pocket; and sponte suâ, for nobody desired him, he began to read it; and before he had read half a dozen lines, sponte meâ, sir, I told him it was not English, sir. (Cash 109)

Stung by Johnson's rebuke, Sterne allegedly showed Johnson a pornographic picture. Johnson refused to return to Reynold's home because he had been "much hurt by the Indelicate conversation of Laurence Sterne," that "contemptible Priest" (Cash 109).

That the Spencers could encourage the literary efforts of men with such markedly different sensibilities might seem surprising. In fact, it was characteristic. The Spencers kept a Bible on the table and play cards in the top drawer, as one caustic observer noted. Whatever her true principles, Lady Spencer admired Johnson as "one of the first geniuses we have" (September 16, 1784; Bessborough 93). "By Johnson, I take it for granted he means Dictionary Johnson," Lady Spencer wrote to her daughter on October 11, 1774, "and if he does I am with the Doctor in thinking him a very extraordinary man, he is possessed of an uncommon share of learning, has great talents and ingenuity, and what is very unusual in this age among what are call'd the great men, is a most zealous Christian," vitiated by a "ruggedness and brutality of manners" (Bessborough 17). Lady Georgiana also noted the lapse in decorum when Johnson visited Chatsworth at the age of seventy-five. "He din'd here and does not shine quite so much in eating as in conversing, for he eat much and nastily" (September 4–10, 1784; Bessborough 90).

Like Dr. Johnson, Lady Georgiana was both a writer and patroness. She had nine novels dedicated to her, more than most other women in late eighteenth-century England (Raven 56); only the queen and the prince regent's wife had more. Lady Georgiana owed such flattering attention to her rank, no doubt. On the other hand, her interest in the literary labors of others is more understandable in light of our renewed appreciation of her own.

Lady Georgiana began writing at an early age. At Althorp, she wrote poems and playlets to amuse her family after dinner (Foreman 9). Sometime before the age of fifteen, she penned a drama called *Zyllia*, in which a child discovers that her closest friend is her mother (Foreman 104). On April 14, 1773, her brother George circulated his sister's verse letters at Harrow and proposed that she publish them under the title, "An epistle from a young lady of quality abroad to her Brother at School in England" (Foreman 10). She wrote verses praising her father that inspired

Lord Palmerston's "On Reading Some Poetry of Lady Georgiana Spencer's, Wrote at Althorp–1774." Palmerston praised her "artless song" and concluded by connecting her to her ancestress on her father's side, the countess of Sunderland (d. 1684), who Edmund Waller unsuccessfully wooed as "Sacharissa" in his poetry. Walpole thought enough of Lady Georgiana's verse to collect them in a volume entitled "Ladies and gentlemen distinguished by their writings, learning, or talents in 1783."[15] Various poems by Georgiana, mostly unpublished, can be found at Yale and the British Library: two of these, "The Butterfly," and "The Table," give a sense of her style and are included in Appendix 3.

In 1799, Lady Georgiana composed a prose work entitled *Memorandums of the Face of the Country in Switzerland* (1799)[16] and *The Passage of the Mountain of St. Gothard,* which appeared in a pirated edition in the *Morning Chronicle* on December 20, 1799. Coleridge praised "The Passage" in "Ode to Georgiana," which appeared in the *Morning Post* on December 24, 1799.

> Splendor's fondly fostered child!
> And did you hail the platform wild,
> Where once the Austrian fell
> Beneath the shaft of Tell!
> O Lady, nursed in pomp and pleasure!
> Whence learn'd you that heroic measure?

Coleridge celebrated the duchess, but not without some condescension mixed with envy. "Rich viands and the pleasurable wine/Were yours unearned by toil," he wrote. What he did not consider, perhaps, was the pathos that produced the work. Forced to travel the continent by her husband, the fifth duke, because of her affair and child by Charles Grey, Lady Georgiana's separation from her children at this time found expression in her poem. Delivering her child by Charles Grey in France, later named Eliza Courtney, Lady Georgiana wrote what she believed to be her last letter to her son, Hart, in her own blood. Lady Georgiana may have had a taste for melodrama in her life and fiction, but she suffered for every day she had been nursed in pomp and pleasure.

Lady Georgiana learned her "heroic measure," in part, from her friendship with actors and playwrights, who asked her to contribute to or patronize their works. She composed a song for Sheridan's *Pizzaro* in 1799, for example, that was very well received and went into a print run of 30,000. The play was adapted from Kotzebue's *Die Spanier in Peru,* though Lady Georgiana's song title is not known. Sounding a patriotic theme at a time when Britain was at war with the American colonies and the French, the play opened on May 24 and ran for thirty-one nights. Sheridan's biographer notes that the song was a success in its own right (Foreman 414). When Sheridan wrote *The Stranger*—adapted from Kotzebue's drama of the same name—he called on the duchess's talents once again and she produced "The Favorite Song," for which Sheridan provided memorable lyrics.

> I have a silent sorrow here,
> A grief I'll ne'er impart.
> It breathes no sigh, it sheds no tear,
> But it consumes my heart.

The play treated a woman who deserts her husband and children for a lover and then reunites with her husband, a situation very close to Lady Georgiana's own.

In almost every activity she engaged in—even in her romantic adultery—Lady Georgiana caught the temper of the time. It is worth noting that the German drama of Kotzebue became enormously popular between 1796 and 1801—later adapted and translated by Elizabeth Inchbald as *Lover's Vows*. The play then became notorious as the drama proposed by Sir Thomas Bertram in Jane Austen's *Mansfield Park*.

While cartoonists like Rowlandson and Cruikshank questioned her morals—particularly her gambling and late-night carousing—actresses were indebted to Lady Georgiana for her patronage. She arranged Mary Robinson's appearance as Juliet in 1776 and had a hand in launching Sarah Siddons's career in 1784. "My good reception in London I cannot but partly attribute to the enthusiastic accounts of me which the amiable Duchess of Devonshire had brought thither, and spread before my arrival," Siddons noted. "I had the honour of her acquaintance during her visit to Bath, and her unqualified approbation at my performances" (Foreman 169). Mrs. Nunns served as Lady Georgiana's protégée. *The Morning Herald* reported that "the Duchess of Devonshire, in her patronage of Mrs. Nunns, had behaved with her accustomed liberality. Her Grace not only introduced her to London, and supported her very powerfully on the first two nights of her appearance, but corrected her dress in the Confederacy as directed and gave the dress in the Jealous Wife" (July 4, 1785; Foreman 174). Even after her eye surgery—when she ventured less often in public—she offered Mrs. Dorothy Jordan two stage boxes on her benefit night in September 1802.

Lady Georgiana responded to the generation of actresses she helped shape by composing songs and epilogues for their works. As early as March 17, 1784, she wrote the concluding march to the opera *La Reine de Golconde* (Bessborough 77). Her artistic activity continued well into the 1790s, even after she had supposedly retired from public life. "I am guilty of having wrote the epilogue to [Joanna Baillie's] Montfort to be spoken by Mrs. Siddons tomorrow," she wrote with characteristic self-effacement to her brother on April 28, 1800. "I did not mean that it should be spoken but Mrs. Siddons had taken a liking to it" (Foreman 331). In 1802, she collaborated with her sister Harriet on a tragedy based on the character of Count Siegendorf in *The German's Tale*, from the fourth volume of Harriet Lee's (1757–1851) popular novella, *The Canterbury Tales*. Lady Georgiana's play (her sister admits she had the principal hand in the production) existed until 1822 but by 1899 all manuscripts were lost or destroyed.[17] Lady Georgiana's grandson charged Byron with basing *Werner* on this adaptation, claiming that Lady Caroline Lamb showed the work of her aunt to the poet in 1812 (Foreman 331, 431n8).

Lady Georgiana's literary interests and extravagant, extroverted behavior attracted the attention of Richard Sheridan, William Combe, and Samuel Taylor Coleridge. Sheridan was inspired by the conversation of the duchess and her close friend, Lady Melbourne, to write *The School for Scandal*, which he dedicated to Anne Crewe, a member of the Devonshire House circle. Combe, or possibly Lord Carlisle, composed *The Duchess of Devonshire's Cow*, admonishing the duchess for her extravagant behavior. She became something of a favorite with Combe, who wrote long, admonishing letters, encouraging her to mend her ways (Walpole 28:313n4). Her passion for "deep play," inherited from her mother, attracted special comment. The ruin of William Walpole in *Emma*, gambling, also became the main subject of her second novel, *The Sylph*. "You have not as yet, I trust, acquired a taste for gaming," her mother wrote on May 8, 1775. "Play at whist, commerce, backgammon, trictrac or chess, but never at quinze, lou, brag, faro, hazard or any games of chance, and if you are press'd to play always make the fashionable excuse of being tied up not to play at such and such a game," she wrote when it was already too late (Bessborough 24). A year after her marriage, and shortly after her first miscarriage in September 1775, Lady Georgiana accrued gambling debts of 3,000 pounds (the equivalent of $270,000 today) (Foreman 42). The Spencers immediately paid them, but tried, in vain, to end their daughter's fashionable activity. A decade later, Lady Georgiana assumed the trait was "innate, for I remember playing from seven in the morning till eight at night at Lansquenet with old Mrs. Newton when I was nine years old" (January 21, 1784; Bessborough 71). Her mother gambled until six in the morning, Lady Georgiana's sister remembered in her diary. Despite her mother's somewhat hypocritical injunctions, Lady Georgiana could not avoid her addiction. In

1804, Lady Georgiana confessed to gambling debts of 50,000 pounds (Foreman 380). After her death, in 1806, her husband found her total indebtedness was 109,135 pounds.[18]

Lady Georgiana's anxiety about sharing her gambling debts with her husband plagued her for more than twenty years. She often delayed her confessions to coincide with her pregnancies, hoping against hope that when she produced a male heir all would be forgiven. That her husband was living under one roof with Lady Elizabeth Foster and his own wife at Devonshire House does not seem to have compromised his authority over her. Lady Georgiana's proclivity for pleasing those around her may well have led her to consent to the ménage à trois that characterized her marriage from 1783 to her death in 1806. Under laws of coverture, she had little choice. Yet Lady Georgiana seems to have preferred the company of Elizabeth Foster (at least in the early decades) to her own husband; the loneliness of an aristocratic and arranged marriage is abundantly clear in Lady Georgiana's letters, where she pleads with her mother to allow her to retain Foster as a close friend.

Lady Georgiana had a complex relationship to her social class. An intellectual woman who collected fossils and minerals later in life, she nevertheless had a reputation for flightiness and superficiality as the young wife of the fifth duke. Surrounded by material wealth, she wrote against its dangers. Lady Georgiana portrays her heroine Julia Stanley as a victim of French hairstyles that Lady Georgiana herself popularized. In both *Emma* and *The Sylph*, she criticizes the bon ton, though she was its most prominent member. Her moral critique of her contemporaries succeeded because she exposed their chief failing: a lack of heart. Lady Georgiana exhibited an excess of sensibility in an age of good sense. Caught up in what she characterized as a "vortex of dissipation," she would have agreed with the narrator of Byron's *Don Juan*, who dismissed society as "one polish'd horde, / Form'd of two mighty tribes, the *Bores* and *Bored*."[19] Emma, like Julia Stanley of *The Sylph*, longs desperately to escape such a world. Perhaps novel writing provided the author with one means of doing so.

THE QUESTION OF AUTHORSHIP

Since Lady Georgiana never acknowledged, or denied, being the author of *Emma* or *The Sylph* in print,[20] one of the more compelling questions regarding *Emma* is whether she actually wrote it. Seven independent sources list her as author,[21] including the most recent and definitive work on the subject, *The English Novel*, which attributes the novel to her with a question mark. "If *Emma* was indeed by the Duchess of Devonshire then it was published when she was sixteen," James Raven concludes. "Only a year older was Elizabeth Todd when her *History of Lady Caroline Rivers* (1788) [appeared], and Margaret Holford when she published *Calaf: A Persian Tale* (1798)" (Raven 45). "Youth was no bar [to authorship]" at this time, J. M. S. Tompkins explains, "for in 1779 Dodsley issued *The Indiscreet Marriage* by Miss Nugent and Miss Taylor of Twickenham, whose ages together do not exceed 30 years."[22] The *Monthly Review* believed *The Fortunate Blue Coat Boy* (1769) by Orphan Otrohian was really the product of Christ's Hospital; and in 1793, Anna Maria Porter completed *Artless Tales* at the age of thirteen.

The fact that *Emma* appeared with no name appended to its title page is no argument against Lady Georgiana's authorship either, for over eighty percent of novels in the 1770s and 1780s were published anonymously (Raven 91). Authors feared public ridicule and the wrath of their families (Raven 41): a woman about to marry England's most eligible bachelor had more to lose than most by displaying her anxieties about marriage for public inspection. And then there is the question of aesthetic judgment. "The public evaluation of almost all new novels by the periodical reviewers was itself a leading cause of title page disguise and the publication of works anonymously," Raven notes (43).

Far from being unusual, *Emma* is very typical of novels written for circulating libraries, that "evergreen tree of diabolical knowledge" that Richard Sheridan mocked in *The Rivals*.[23] There were twenty circulating libraries operating in London by 1770 (Raven 84) and they existed to "rent out" books, hence the three-volume format. Many novels were published in editions of 500, expressly for libraries run by the Noble brothers, T. H. Lowndes (publisher of Lady Georgiana's *The Sylph*), William Lane, and T. H. Hookham (Lady Georgiana's publisher for *Emma*). *Emma* is unusual because it went into four editions (only forty-two percent went into a second edition) and because it included a frontispiece (Raven 35). "The fashionable novel remained the luxury of a narrow section of society," Raven observes (111). It is hardly surprising that an arbitress of sartorial fashion would also participate in the fashionable activity of novel writing. "A novel by a lady of quality seems to be now almost as common, and often I believe as bad, a thing, as *verses by a person of honour* was in the last age," Hannah More wrote disapprovingly on July 20, 1788 (Walpole 31:274): Lady Georgiana may well have set this fashion. On May 8, 1777, the duchess of Devonshire's circle attended the opening of Richard Sheridan's *School for Scandal* and were delighted to find themselves lampooned: the dedicatee was Lady Anne Crewe, Sheridan's current infatuation, while Lady Melbourne and the duchess appeared, alternately, as Lady Sneerwell and Lady Teazle. Sheridan's character, Charles Surface, stole witticisms from James Hare and Charles James Fox, while Samuel Johnson's love of paradox was suggested in a line that might serve as the play's epigraph: "there's no possibility of being witty without a little ill nature" (Masters 65).

The evidence that Lady Georgiana wrote *Emma* is both external and internal. Unfortunately, the correspondence of her publisher, T. H. Hookham, does not exist for the 1770s, though a pirated Dublin reprint of 1784 states that the novel is "by the author of The Sylph" (the only external evidence we have). While this may be untrustworthy—a mere effort to attract more readers to an anonymous novel—the work itself is dedicated to Lady Camden, whose husband was a friend of the family as early as 1774 (Bessborough 292; Foreman 78). Here again, however, evidence is inconclusive. Another writer might have dedicated the novel to Lady Camden in order to give the work cachet. "A particular attraction for the novelist seeking subscribers was association with an illustrious dedicatee," Raven notes (55). Of the 315 novels published in the 1770s, for example, forty-two carried dedications (or thirteen percent of the total) (Raven 56). What makes *Emma* different is that many of the subscribers were close friends of Lady Georgiana, Lady Melbourne being the most prominent. Other members of the subscription list, especially the duchess of Manchester, the countess of Thanet, and the dowager of Westmoreland, have demonstrable connections to Lady Georgiana (Foreman 45, 184, 78). Finally, the subscription list seems to point to a female author. "The gender division of these public supporters was often extreme," James Raven notes. "*Emma; or, The Unfortunate Attachment* (1773:28) listed 16 men and 100 women" (55).

So autobiographical is the novel that it can be read as a *roman à clef.* William Walpole resembles the fifth duke in his fastidious tastes and uncommunicative nature; the previous mistress of Walpole recalls Charlotte Spencer, by whom the fifth duke had a child before marrying Lady Georgiana (who appears as a composite of Emma herself and Harriet). Colonel Sutton could be anyone, but surely Mathilda is Lady Harriet, Lady Georgiana's sister, for this young lady comforts Priscilla in times of grief, showing the warm heart and sensibility that Lady Melbourne sometimes lacked. The kind-hearted father recalls Lord Spencer, whose eccentric ideas about female education resemble Emma's wayward father whose paternal authority destroys his daughter's happiness. Emma experiences life as a series of crises, which she communicates to Frances Thornton (Lady Melbourne), on whom she relied for her good sense and referred to as "the Thorn" because of her sharp tongue. In *Emma*, Lady Noel (Thornton's married name) observes that "she who shows an indifference to the opinion of the world deserves the censures of it" (118), a line very similar to one Lady Melbourne actually penned to Lady Caroline Lamb on April 13, 1810.[24] Lady Melbourne's cynical comments on marriage appear to humorous effect again in *The Sylph* and, most likely, in Richard Sheridan's *School for Scandal,* which records remarks he heard at Devonshire House (Masters 62–64).

Both *Emma* and *The Sylph* treat similar themes, such as the corruption of London high society, the neglect of tradesmen's bills, and the arrogance of foppish men. These topics recur, with similar political inflections, in Lady Georgiana's letters. The editor of Lady Georgiana's letters, the earl of Bessborough, attributes *The Sylph* based on its inside knowledge of the bon ton (3, 35). In *Emma,* a reference to the word "sylph" appears, which anticipates the title of Lady Georgiana's second novel ("He is Emma's sylph, and cannot afford to attend to me" [150]). In addition, both novels make coy references to a "Georgina" or duchess of Devonshire. Emma notes that "Lady Georgina, not so completely beautiful, is infinitely more charming and the laughing Graces sport in her countenance" (131); in *The Sylph,* William Stanley alludes to a French hairdresser who must "disoblige the Duchess of D—— by giving radishes (meant to adorn her hair!) to Lady Stanley."[25] Lady Georgiana did more than anyone else to make French hairstyles fashionable in London, as the cartoonists were fond of noting (Foreman 208). Lady Georgiana's unconventional beauty is also suggested in both works. Emma's husband describes her attractions "as much out of the usual style as the rest of her perfections. . . . I have seen features more exactly regular, forms more striking; but never was there such an assemblage of the graces to be found in one person! Her whole soul is to be seen in her countenance, which in every turn expresses all that is desirable in woman" (58). In *The Sylph,* Lord Stanley offers the following assessment of his wife Julia. "She is not a perfect beauty: which, if you are of my taste, you will think rather an advantage than not; as there is generally a formality in great regularity of features, and most times an insipidity. In her there are neither. She is in one word *animated nature*" (20), a phrase Maria Cosway used when she painted the duchess of Devonshire as Diana, bursting through the clouds.[26]

Like Lady Georgiana, who studied violin under Giardini and dancing with the Italian master Vestris, Emma is musical (Foreman 86). She plays the harpsichord (like Richardson's Clarissa), and her failure to do so after she leaves her father's home is uncharacteristic enough to become a sign of her romantic unhappiness. (She begins to play again, strangely enough, after her father's death and her ill-fated decision to marry William Walpole.) Both Lady Georgiana and her literary creation link their pursuit of culture and self-improvement to a political outlook: "mortals who are indebted to the dexterity of their taylors alone for all their consequence, are not subjects in which my pen can dwell with any chance of pleasing you or myself," Emma notes of the men she surveys at a ball (3). The frequent references to Whig politicians—including the Spencers (her own family name)—also point to Lady Georgiana's authorship, especially the tendency to apply Whig principles to women's rights (as Kitty Bishop tries to do). The novel appears to have been written by Lady Georgiana, but cannot be conclusively proven to be by her.

THE RECEPTION OF EMMA

In 1773, *Emma; or, The Unfortunate Attachment* appeared in three volumes. It was soon successful enough for a Dublin pirated edition to appear in 1784, for *The Minstrel* to advertise it in a "new edition" with illustrations (1787), and for a third and fourth London edition to appear in 1789 and 1793.[27] Any effort to assess its aesthetic value, however, cannot be easily separated from the politics of its reception: the fact that it was written by a woman and published for a circulating library. "Innocent, but not excellent:—yet not contemptible," *The Monthly Review* noted in 1773. "We have characterised fifty such; and are sick of repetition" (Raven 203). The sheer volume of novels may explain the patronizing reviews they often received. "We heartily recommend the perusal of these three volumes to those who are in want of a soporific," the rival *Critical Review* announced, "and we do it very confidently, as we have experienced its effects. The story of *Emma* is told in a series of letters; a mode of writing which Richardson and Rousseau have indeed practised with the greatest success, but which requires too great a share of talents for every dabbler in novel-writing to adopt" (Raven 203).[28] This telling comparison between a "dabbler in novel-writing" and Richardson and Rousseau appears, more favorably cast, in *The Universal Catalogue's* notice: "the different characters are well drawn and highly coloured, and there is one, a sprightly young lady, sensible and witty, little in any thing inferior to Richardson's Miss Howe, in his *Clarissa*, or Lady G. in his *Sir Charles Grandison*."[28] Modern assessments accord with this review, stating simply that Lady Georgiana wrote "two fine epistolary novels" (Blain 288).

Though the critics seem harsh in their estimate of *Emma*, they faced an almost unprecedented growth in the novel market in the 1770s, which tapered off significantly in the period shortly after the American Revolution. And their opinions mattered: "a novel is a dish I never venture upon without a taster, or some knowledge of the cook," Hannah More confessed to Horace Walpole (35:41). Reviewers complained that "novels spring into existence like insects on the banks of the Nile, and if we may be indulged in another comparison, cover the shelves of our circulating libraries as locusts crowd the fields of Asia. Their great and growing number is a serious evil, for, in general, they exhibit delusive views of human life; and while they amuse, frequently poison the mind" (Raven *JNW* 68). The Nobles, prominent and somewhat notorious publishers of novels for circulating libraries, accused the "Impartial" *London Review* of "damning every novel we publish and as we have reason to believe, frequently without reading them" (101). This may well have been the case, for novels were reviewed anonymously by six male editors at *The Monthly Review*, including Ralph Griffiths, John Cleland, William Rose, and John Hill,[30] whose names were not known at the time. *The Critical Review* made a point of altering the practice of anonymous reviews, but never did, only infrequently appending the initials of reviewers to some, but not all, notices.

In *The Sign of Angelica*, Janet Todd questions why novels such as *Emma* have not been considered part of the literary canon. "Is it a reaction to a literature that constantly declares that it exists to make money? Or is it because our critical assumptions have been fashioned through a particular body of male literature and literary criticism? My answer to both of these questions is a qualified yes," she concludes.[31] Certainly the predominance of male reviewers may have helped marginalize novels written for the circulating libraries. But does *Emma* deserve to be classified as a novel written for the marketplace? Clearly, Lady Georgiana did not write the novel because she needed money. Self-expression, even fashionable self-expression, seems a more likely motive.

Despite Lady Georgiana's social position, her novel still had to justify itself on moral grounds, especially to evangelical critics like Hannah More. In a perceptive essay written on the sentimental novel, and published fourteen years after his own *The Man of Feeling*, Henry Mackenzie described "The principal danger of Novels, as forming a mistaken and pernicious system of morality, which seems to me to arise from that contrast between one virtue or excellence and another, that war of duties, which is to be found in many of them, particularly in that species called the *Sentimental*."[32] *Emma* was lucky enough to escape such censure from *The Universal Catalogue*, which found the subject "excellent, the style is easy and unaffected, and the whole abounds with such noble sentiments, as if properly attended to, must certainly correct the human heart."[33] Perhaps Lady Georgiana's decision to reconcile Emma and William Walpole garnered this favorable review from an editor. He may well have appreciated the novelist's tendency to uphold the system of primogeniture, even if it did so in such a strained and improbable manner as to invite an ironic reading.

In *Emma*, William Walpole, a macaroni and fop, indicates the dangers of what Henry Mackenzie called "refined sentimentalists, who are contented with talking of virtues which they never practice, who pay in words what they owe in actions; or perhaps, what is fully as dangerous, who open their minds to *impressions* which never have any effect upon their *conduct*, but are considered as something foreign to and distinct from it" (*Lounger* 34). *Emma* might be regarded as a critique of the traditional sentimental novel, much in the terms that Mackenzie outlines. In *Emma*, Walpole's vanity outweighs his compassion; he is so mortified to discover his wife had a previous lover that he misses the first six months of his infant's life, providing no support to the woman who has borne his child. When he realizes his error, he has scruples about returning to his wife until he recoups his fortune (232). George Sutton warns William about "souring your own disposition by imaginary affronts" (125). Unfortunately, he suffers from the same flaw. Both men call themselves feeling but fail at key moments to exhibit true compassion. Thus Walpole complains of Emma's attachment to her father when he is dying, for example, and Sutton complains of Priscilla Neville's care for her sister Mrs. Wentworth: "Amiable as her motives for her slighting me were, and thoroughly acquainted as I was with them, I could not help being wounded by her indifference" (107). Not only do these men behave selfishly, but they interfere with women's roles in caring for their sick or grieving relatives. Foppishness is not only ridiculous, it is socially disruptive.

William and Emma are prone to high feeling, a quality roundly ridiculed by both men and women. Kitty Bishop and George Sutton dismiss William's "fine scruples" about women's chastity, while Emma's reticence leads her husband to misunderstand her as cold. Characters like Kitty Bishop and Lady Noel, on the other hand, use their minds to control their feelings and are happier for this reason. But not without a struggle. Many suffer from an excess of sensibility that leads them to become depressed, if not morbid. Mathilda has withdrawn from society; Emma cultivates her own melancholy after the birth of her daughter (though, with an absentee husband, she has good reason to do so): "That creation of refined and subtile feeling, reared by the authors of the works to which I allude, has an ill effect, not only on our ideas of virtue, but also on our estimate of happiness," Mackenzie concludes. "That sickly sort of refinement creates imaginary evils and distresses, and imaginary blessings and enjoyments, which embitter the common disappointments, and depreciate the common attainments of life." Lady Spencer warned her daughter against precisely this sort of overwrought feeling.

Throughout the novel, Walpole's foppishness betrays his "sickly sort of refinement." Emma notes how her husband takes an excessive interest in her wardrobe: "he was in my dressing room twice or thrice during the time allotted to the toilet, " Emma notes. "He did not like this colour—that ornament would best suit my face,-I must put on my *petit-gris*" (131). Such attention to feminine finery bespeaks an effeminacy in Walpole, perhaps a product of his Italian travels, which contrasts with Augustus Sidney, who educates Emma's mind and pays little attention to cosmetics. (The theme recurs in *The Sylph*, when Lord Stanley repulses Lady Stanley by correcting her conduct in court—much as the duke of Devonshire did when first presenting his wife to Queen Charlotte). He is not a coxcomb, he suggests (105), and Emma agrees (thus showing her lack of insight). Catherine Bishop, by contrast, satirizes a guest who tries to instruct her on the distinction between coxcombs and macaronis: "The common coxcomb has taste enough to like one person better than another, to have his clothes cut fashionably, to frequent the company of the ladies; good humor enough to be easy, and is vivacious enough to amuse: not a melancholy, woe-begone, self important prig, puffed up with affectation of pre eminence in knowledge; too proud for content, too high for ease" (158). In writing about such foibles in her novel, Lady Georgiana anticipates Mackenzie's fears about "a mistaken and pernicious system of morality"; in fact, she turns the tables on her mother's favorite, Hannah More, who thought the genre of the novel would corrupt "young ladies" by writing one that exposes the shortcomings of young men.[33] In this sense, *Emma* can be read as a conduct book for men that rivals and perhaps updates Lord Chesterfield's.

One example of Lady Georgiana's palpable design occurs through the device of complementarity. Colonel William Sutton, a straightforward if somewhat obtuse man, corrects the excesses of the overly-refined William Walpole. Yet the novel does not blindly prefer English virtue to European cosmopolitanism. Lady Noel, perhaps the most sophisticated of the novel's heroines, enjoys her visit to Paris and comments on the city's attractions. Her letters recall Emily Cowper's to Lady Melbourne, who suspected English jingoists who could not acknowledge the improved Simplon Pass because they despised Napoleon (September 8, 1816; 45549, f. 79; Gross 56). They also remind us that Lady Georgiana befriended Marie Antoinette (for whom she used the code name Mrs. Brown [Bessborough 54]) as a young girl, and understood the attractions of Parisian fashion even as she parodied French excesses in *The Sylph* (1779). Lady Georgiana's tour of France, shortly before *Emma* was published, did much to shape these views.

During her continental tour, Lady Georgiana imbibed moral instruction from her somewhat didactic father, which may have found its way into *Emma*. If so, such passages take up political topics Henry Mackenzie also made fashionable through the character of Harley in *The Man of Feeling.* "You tell me of immense territories subject to the English," Harley exclaimed, two years before *Emma* appeared. "I cannot think of their possessions without being led to inquire by what right they possess them . . . what title have the subjects of another kingdom to establish an empire in India? . . . The fame of conquest, barbarous as that motive is, is but a secondary consideration [to wealth] . . . . When shall I see a commander return from India in the pride of honourable poverty? You describe the victories they have gained; they are sullied by the cause in which they fought: you enumerate the spoils of those victories; they are covered with the blood of the vanquished."[35] Though Mackenzie was partly exposing his character's naivete in 1771, Edmund Burke and Richard Sheridan used similar arguments to prosecute Warren Hastings, director of the East India Company, in 1783 and 1785. In *Emma,* poverty and a lack of worldliness are also "honourable" virtues. Walpole expresses his outrage that his political rival, a "nabob," can spend a fortune earned in corrupt colonial practices to win an English election. That Lady Georgiana, Duchess of Devonshire, sympathized with such a political outlook can be shown, in part, by the fact that she helped launch Sheridan's career as MP for Stafford.

In *Emma,* Walpole reveals his prejudices against opportunistic Englishmen, suggesting that money made in India is somehow tainted. This response to an increasingly globalized economy pits English virtue against more cosmopolitan standards: the old Whigs who protected the country from James II in the Glorious Revolution have been replaced by commercial agents who make ill-gotten gains in foreign countries. They then return to England to corrupt the political process. Emma frequently contrasts the Whigs who opposed royal tyranny with the trivial pursuits of the debased generation of fops and macaronis who have succeeded them. Burke's claim that the "age of chivalry is over" would be uttered almost twenty years later. *Emma* offers a similar, though more muted, account of dissipated male virtue by portraying William Walpole as unable to understand his own political opportunism.

At times, Emma exhibits a rather conventional moralism. A series of set speeches, for example, recall favorite themes of Lady Spencer (learned, no doubt, from her mentor, Hannah More): the importance of filial devotion (140), the limits of despair and mourning (155), and the dangers of gambling (194). Others reflect Lady Georgiana's responses: the importance and danger of sensibility (82, 148), the happy state of the unknowing (130), the importance of friendship (113), of keeping appearances (130), and the uselessness of money (27). The rational tone of these Christian homilies resembles More's *On the Manners of the Great* and other works. Some monologues prompt debate: George Sutton and William Walpole's remarks on female honor, for example, or Frances Thornton and Emma's comments on whether there "are women inhuman enough to enjoy the pain they inflict" (130). Others may be ironic: Kitty Bishop and the newly married Frances Thornton discuss whether women should contradict their husbands (138), or, to put it differently, on whether there are more pleasures in commanding or obeying. Often these debates contribute to the artistry of the epistolary novel, as they form a running correspondence between two characters. Inspired by Lady Clarendon choosing Lord Clarendon over Mr. D'Arcy, Sutton and Emma discuss whether "women are oftener biased by ambition, than by love in chusing" (153). The importance of making such a choice, however, is never in doubt: "You, Priscy, may be rendered miserable by the carelessness, by the almost unavoidable failings of men," Priscilla's mother warns her (in a letter that Emma, ironically enough, quotes): "beware then how you chuse, for your first preference makes your destiny" (208).

In *Emma*, as in many of the novels that appeared in circulating libraries, men rather than women are held up for moral scrutiny and found wanting (this may be why one reviewer found the novel "insipid"); the women who exhibit admirable conduct are not sanctimonious or priggish, but experienced mothers and wives who must manage their husbands; they do not have the privilege of forsaking them. Though chaste and modest, these same women articulated their views of men with surprising candor (a candor *Emma* exploits, perhaps, more than its predecessors). Emma and Frances's letters exhibit some of this freedom, for they are filled with minute examinations of the visitors to their estates. The justness of their delicate, though pointed, observations on men's shortcomings (the reticence of Augustus Sidney; the self-conceit and narcissism of Walpole) are only reinforced by Kitty Bishop's unbridled responses. Emma, Priscy Neville, Lady Noel, and Kitty Bishop form a continuum in this regard: each letter writer is more self-confident and dismissive of men than the last. Where Walpole or Sutton correct each others' misogyny, Kitty's critique of men remains unanswered—the moral impetus of the novel is toward reforming the "strutting boobies" (168) who believe that they are indispensable to their country's well-being.

EMMA AS AN EPISTOLARY NOVEL

Like other epistolary novels of the period (*Clarissa*; *Julie, ou La Nouvelle Héloïse*; and *Sir Charles Grandison*), Emma explores the familial tension that arises from arranged marriages. "The heroine of *Emma: or, the*

Unfortunate Attachment (1773) by Georgiana Spencer, late Duchess of Devonshire, actually transfers her affections, as Clarissa could not, at the command of her father," Isobel Grundy notes. In addition, Emma imagines her husband 'covered with the blood of Sidney,' coming to stab her with the same sword, just as Clarissa has a dream of being "stabbed . . . to the heart," by Lovelace (Grundy 227–228), "and then tumbled . . . into a deep grave ready dug."[36]

A more powerful influence still may be Rousseau's *Julie, ou La Nouvelle Héloïse* (1763), which Lady Georgiana had read and enjoyed (Masters 68). In the same way that Julie and her tutor St. Preux become intimate by inhabiting the same domestic space as brother and sister, Emma and her instructor Augustus Sidney are raised as siblings, with Emma's father adopting Augustus Sidney after the death of Sidney's father. In both novels, Julie and Emma sacrifice their lover for an arranged marriage dictated by their father. Julie and Emma transform themselves by obeying their father's dictates. Monsieur de Wolmar and William Walpole are comparable characters, whose fastidiousness helps their wives improve their conduct, though Walpole learns from his passive wife in a way that Wolmar never does. Finally, both novels explore a woman's moral development through marriage and child-rearing.

Rousseau was much influenced by Richardson. In Richardson's novel, Clarissa's virtue seems inseparable from "the dairy-house" of Harlowe Place where she is reared. Nicknamed "The Grove," as if to emphasize its rural location, Clarissa's home (and sense of rootedness) forms a marked contrast with the whorehouse in London where she resides, unknowingly, after Lovelace abducts her. *Julie, où la Nouvelle Héloïse*, and *Emma* follow a similar trajectory. Both novels contrast country and city. Julie's generous nature seems to arise, organically, from Clarens, which St. Preux is pleased to contrast, favorably, with the dissolute city of Paris. Emma's virtue and "reticence," which she shares with Augustus Sidney, are also attributed to her country origins (Kitty Bishop's brashness, which William Walpole enjoys, seems an urban quality by contrast). *Emma* celebrates pastoralism as surely as Rousseau, including a portrait of a grey-headed gardener who becomes a metonymy for lost English virtue: "There is a simplicity and heartiness in him, that charms me prodigiously," Emma writes (114). Walpole owns estates at Spring Park and Rose-Court in Yorkshire; Frances Greville (later Lady Noel) lives at Noel Castle; Priscy Neville lives in London on Sackville Street (then Park Street), where she is miserable, before retiring to Rose-Court; Harriet Courtney resides at Milfield. The residences seem arbitrary, but virtuous characters migrate toward the northern countryside or Yorkshire, while romances unravel in the bustle of balls and masquerades in London

(Walpole's at Grosvenor Square and Sutton's at Park Street) and these locations are inscribed in the letters themselves.

Though derivative in some respects, *Emma* does make use of its epistolary form with more art than other novels in T. H. Hookham's circulating library, even as it betrays an acute sensibility. Advertised on the last page of the first volume of the 1773 edition of *Emma*, for example, was *The Married Victim; or the history of Lady Villars, a narrative founded on facts* (1772). This epistolary novel forms a complement of sorts to *Emma* since it portrays a man victimized by his wife's cruel treatment. Where *Emma* explores how Walpole neglects his wife after her pregnancy, *The Married Victim* examines how a stepmother can mistreat her own children, hiding her coldness under a veneer of good manners (Madame de Staël's theme in *Delphine*). *The Married Victim* presents a world of heroes and villains, however, while *Emma* exploits its epistolary form to delineate character and exhibit the pathos of human shortcomings. One work is a "history," depending in part on salacious gossip for its appeal; the other is a sentimental novel that explores the genre Henry Mackenzie helped make fashionable.

Emma also differs from the work of other authors writing for circulating library novels to which it has recently been traced. James Raven questions whether Sophia Briscoe wrote Lady Georgiana's second novel (1:277) based on a letter of payment from T. H. Hookham on October 29, 1778 to S. Briscoe. In the introduction to his study, however, he notes the more likely possibility that Briscoe "collected the money for *The Sylph*" (53n119) on Lady Georgiana's behalf, an arrangement Lady Georgiana made with Joseph Johnson when she contemplated publishing a children's story and sacred drama (Foreman 336). Also against Briscoe's authorship is her writing style, which is serviceable but flat, far less graceful or psychologically incisive than either *Emma* or *The Sylph*. The first of Briscoe's novels is a hasty effort to capitalize on the success of Richardson's *Clarissa*, including a scene where a woman is drugged; the second exploits the taste for domestic histories that are by turns sensationalistic and sentimental. The resolution of Louisa Somerville's problems in *The Fine Lady* is straightforward, uncomplicated, even melodramatic (which actually bears some resemblance to *Emma*).

In its artful use of the epistolary form, however, Emma is quite different. Letters highlight misunderstandings (as when the reticent Sidney thinks Emma loves Walpole) and delayed recognition scenes (as when Emma discovers through a letter that Augustus Sidney loved her all along) and provide insight into a character's psychology (as when Kitty reports on Emma's distressed appearance during her marriage). In *Emma*, the epistolary form also underscores moments of dramatic irony. Thus

Emma loves Augustus Sidney, but fears her love is not reciprocated; Augustus Sidney's letter to Lady Noel clarifies the misperception, but not before Augustus Sidney has precipitously joined the army. George Sutton mistakes Priscy Neville's attention to her sister for neglect of him; Emma corrects the impression but not before Sutton compromises his reputation in Priscy's eyes by flirting with Harriet Courtney. "Reading, we confront the psychological consequences before the event which produced them, which is then revealed in the text of the letters Emma has read," Isobel Grundy notes (228).

Two of the most important scenes of the novel, Emma's marriage and Walpole's abandonment of her, are told through the novel's most caustic correspondent, Kitty Bishop. Bishop's insight into Emma's state of mind makes Emma's efforts to comply with her father's injunction to marry William Walpole that much more poignant. The technique is multiplied throughout the novel, underscoring the letter writer's dependence on appearance. Walpole reads Emma's reticence and reserve as coldness, especially when Mrs. Bromford encourages such a misreading; Sutton similarly misreads Priscy Neville's care for her sister, Mathilda, as neglect of him until it is explained (not to Sutton but to Emma). Through the letter form, characters give a moral accounting of themselves to their friends that indicate their spiritual growth, though this growth is rarely noticed by their lovers. Delayed recognition scenes between these lovers conclude in the happy marriages of Lady Noel, Emma Walpole, and Kitty Bishop, all of which are "blessed" by the birth of male heirs.

Lady Georgiana also shows her skill as a novelist by matching each correspondent's language to his or her character and gender (in Briscoe's novel, by contrast, the characters speak in a voice that is too similar stylistically). Thus Emma's puns, which suggest her playful wit, innocence, and moral earnestness, also reveal her somewhat girlish (or is it rural?) tendency to rely on and offer moral homilies. "Contented *minds* are capable of supplying more precious treasures than Peruvian *mines* can do," Emma reminds herself on one occasion (75); "so much respect does the world pay to quality than to qualities" (131), she writes, deflating obsequious praise she has heard of Lord Surry. Lady Noel rarely quotes such lines. These contrasting styles function dramatically as well because the latter (as advisor to Emma) has more successfully internalized the social behavior expected of her. Lady Noel demonstrates her poise by not immediately answering her husband's summons; instead, she continues to write to and advise her friend Emma. She describes her engagement to Charles Noel (and his impetuous conduct) with wit and irony. Clearly, she considers herself free to criticize her husband as well as praise him. When he arrives drunk one evening, for example, and proposes that she take a ride in a carriage with him, she refuses. This sets the tone for their marriage. In fact, the bon ton ridicule him when he refuses to leave her side at a gaming table in London; being seen in public too often with one's spouse was considered bad form.

Kitty Bishop's satirical tendencies sometimes get the better of her. She explains how she inflicted herself on an unwitting misogynist who advanced the other day that "*we* were vain, fantastic, and froward; insolent in power, abject without it." She responds by calling him an "oddity." "Had you been husband, or father, you might have had a more honorable denomination: but, according to the Roman edict, you can have none as you are—not a citizen; for you do not contribute to the benefit of any place, by adding to the number of its inhabitants—not a man; for you have no social principle in your nature.—*An oddity* then you must be; and my award is ratified by the authority I quote" (151). That this letter is written to Lady Noel is fitting, for Lady Noel admires Kitty's self-confidence. Conversely, she becomes exasperated with her friend Emma's passivity: her willingness to live in Rose-Court in a squalid cottage, to accept her husband's abandonment of her, to refrain from speaking ill of him, and to befriend the even more retiring and reticent Priscy Neville.

Lady Georgiana expressed opinions in her novel that she never could share with her taciturn husband. Unlike Richardson, she presents a sexually mature heroine who complicates her husband's ludicrous ideas about female chastity. In contrast to her character, Kitty Bishop, however, Lady Georgiana was a woman "in whom good breeding and sincerity are so happily blended, as to form at once the woman of fashion and the best of friends." Like Emma and Rousseau's Julie, Lady Georgiana "endure[d] daily mortification for the sake of being reckoned well bred" (140). Her frequent rebellions against the appearances she maintained—her reckless gambling and outrageous fashions—suggest that the act of conformity came at a high price.

Neither a Bluestocking nor Jacobin Novel

As its publication date of 1773 might suggest, *Emma; or, The Unfortunate Attachment* lies between Sarah Scott's bluestocking novel, *Millenium Hall* (1762), with its utopian idealism, and Charlotte Smith's *Desmond* (1792), which is a more overtly political response to the French Revolution. *Millenium Hall* uses inset narratives but is straightforwardly historical in its account of the lives of Mrs. Trentham, Harriot, and other protagonists who come to live in a Christian version of the classical arcadia. *Millenium Hall* revises the emphasis of Milton's *Paradise Lost* to note how men, not women, despoil companionate marriage through their selfishness, corruption, and tyrannical behavior. *Desmond*, like Mary Wollstonecraft's *Maria, or The Wrongs of Woman* (1797), turns historical narrative into an extended advertisement for the virtues of the self: in both cases, Smith and Wollstonecraft use the novel form to note their unjust treatment at the hands of a husband and married man. The background to these works of "boundless vanity" (in the words of Anna Seward) was the French Revolution, which promised to do away with over 100 years of patriarchal law. The law most problematic for women in the late eighteenth century was coverture. Under coverture, a woman was literally the property of her husband and had no legal identity, but was a commodity to be purchased, a vessel to extend his fortunes and safeguard his property. Women had no right to divorce and were often married so young that their choice in a spouse was nominal.[37] Smith was sixteen when she wed, the same age as Lady Georgiana.

Though critical of social mores in England, first- and second-generation bluestocking writers such as Sarah Scott and Hannah More rejected the revolution and its British sympathizers. "They were shocked by the kinds of direct political activism and explicit feminism promoted by Wollstonecraft and others," Gary Kelly notes.[38] Lady Georgiana's mother had much in common with the bluestocking circle, though she also had fashionable friends as a young woman. Her daughter is a more difficult case to discern.

Lady Georgiana differs from writers like Wollstonecraft and Smith who suffered more directly at the hands of English institutions. A personal friend of Marie Antoinette ("Mrs. Brown" in Lady Georgiana's letters), Lady Georgiana must have also been horrified by the violence perpetrated against aristocrats in France. Her two novels are sprinkled with sympathetic references to tradesmen; in her own life, however, Lady Georgiana was notoriously behind in her debts and not above using Thomas Coutts's social aspirations for his daughter to arrange shady loans to cover her gambling debts. Like Lady Melbourne and Charles Grey, Lady Georgiana viewed the French Revolution more sympathetically than such social activists as Hannah More. Lady Georgiana followed the example of Charles James Fox—a "man of the people" who never doubted that an aristocratic class should lead the common people. Like Fox, she favored the French Revolution and the liberalization of English domestic laws. She could also be intensely patriotic, however, and organized a female brigade at Coxheath in Kent when her husband was engaged in military exercises in June 1778. She set a good example for the English aristocracy, for she was sympathetic to the physical and

emotional suffering of the poor, voting and campaigning in their interest.[38] At times, her "common touch" may have made her appear more
supportive of their plight than her actual conduct would indicate. But
she remained a Whig to the end. In 1806, she was delighted by (and
apparently did something to arrange) Charles James Fox's participation
in the Grenville coalition, which alleviated the social distress created by
Pitt's harsh wartime policies.

In 1798, Richard Polwhele published *The Unsex'd Females: A Poem.*
This poem distinguishes between vindicators of women's rights (Anna
Laetitia Barbauld, Mary "Perdita" Robinson, Charlotte Smith, Helen
Maria Williams, Ann Yearsley, Mary Hays, Angelica Kauffman, and Emma
Crewe) and models of "female genius" (Mary Wortley Montague, Eliza-
beth Carter, Anna Seward, Hester Thrale Piozzi, Fanny Burney, and Ann
Radcliffe). Some of these distinctions are difficult to maintain. Lady
Georgiana was a patron of Mary Robinson and Charlotte Smith, but her
second novel was advertised with Fanny Burney's *Evelina* (a more con-
servative novel of manners). Lady Georgiana's work thus reflects the
tension between her education at the hands of a bluestocking mother
and her role as an arbitress of fashion during the period of the American
Revolution. Her concerns are different from the "Jacobin" politics of
feminist writers in the 1790s, though she anticipated their efforts to
foreground the political dimension of the sentimental novel. "For these
writers of the 1790s sentimental or domestic fiction was not just about
courtship, love, and romance," Ty explains, "but also about interrogating the structures of the society, criticizing and making relevant the
connections between the personal and the political, the domestic and the
public spheres."[40] Significantly, *Emma* was reprinted three times just
before, during, and after the French Revolution; this suggests that she
had as much relevance to the readers of Inchbald's *A Simple Story* and
other novelists of the 1790s as she did to a previous generation that
enjoyed Sterne and Mackenzie's sentimental fiction in the 1770s.

Though it is tempting to read Lady Georgiana's novel as an ironic
send-up of the sentimental novel, Emma Walpole is sincere in her struggle
to obey her father's selfish desire that she marry a man with absurd
notions of female chastity. In this sense, the sixteen-year-old author aimed
to be a "proper lady," in Mary Poovey's sense of the term.[41] "One of the
essential qualities of a 'proper lady' is her subordination," Eleanor Ty
observes. To explain the teleology of English feminist thought in the
nineteenth century, Elaine Showalter divides women's literary history
into three distinct phases: "the feminine phase, in which women 'inter-
nalize the male culture's assumptions about female nature'; the feminist
phase, in which women are able to 'dramatize the ordeals of wronged

womanhood'; and the female phase, when women 'turn . . . to female experience as the source of an autonomous art.'"[42] I would locate Lady Georgiana's novel between the first and second stage, with a strong sense of the "wrongs of women" without Wollstonecraft's willingness to write, except obliquely, on such wrongs. Lady Georgiana was very much her mother's daughter. What Hannah More suggests about women's education in 1799 rings true of the heroine Lady Georgiana created in Emma Walpole:

> An early habitual restraint is peculiarly important to the future character and happiness of women. They should when very young be inured to contradiction. . . . They should be led to distrust their own judgement, they should learn not to murmur at expostulation; but should be accustomed to expect and to endure opposition.[43]

More's views reflect conduct books written thirty years earlier, such as Fordyce's *Sermons to Young Women* (1766), which recommended that women avoid competing with men in the fields of philosophy or literature. "For my part, I could heartily wish to see the female world more accomplished than it is," Fordyce wrote, "but I do not wish to see it abound with metaphysicians, historians, speculative philosophers, or Learned Ladies of any kind. I should be afraid, lest the sex should lose in softness what they gained in force; and lest the pursuit of such elevation should interfere a little with the plain duties and humble virtues of life."[44]

Fordyce bored Lydia Bennet, who reads him in Austen's *Pride and Prejudice*.[45] Yet in her own *Strictures*, More echoes his belief that "a girl who has docility will seldom be found to want understanding sufficient for all the purposes of a useful, a happy, and a pious life" (1:159). Lady Georgiana's saucy character, Kitty Bishop, represents precisely the type of wife that Coelebs (the hero of a novel by Hannah More) finds unappealing. They are "either too frivolous, not religious enough, too learned or 'accomplished' in useless arts, or unable to cook. . . . The superiority and judiciousness of patriarchal authority are reinforced in the novel as Coelebs's 'choice' of partner turns out to be one whom his father had desired from the beginning" (Ty 18). Lady Georgiana's *The Sylph*, with its epigraph from Alexander Pope, reinforces More's ideas that male authority is sacrosanct. Horrified by her husband's immorality, Julia Stanley turns not to herself but to Baron Tonhausen for moral guidance (Tonhausen turns out to be Julia's close friend from childhood). The novel's Rosicrucian theme reminds us that Lady Georgiana's religious convictions were heartfelt, with a tendency toward Christian mysticism.

Apparently, Lady Georgiana never read Mary Wollstonecraft's *Vindi-cation of the Rights of Woman* or knew of the writings of such early feminists as Mary Hays and Catherine Macaulay. "Georgiana was more interested in practical political issues than with philosophical debates about women's rights and social equality," Amanda Foreman explains. Women should shun the spotlight, limiting their activity to that of "moderators." If they did this, they would "do good instead of mischief" (Foreman 292). Lady Georgiana's tension between the bluestocking values of her mother and Hannah More and the feminist implications of *Emma; or, The Unfortunate Attachment* is nowhere more apparent than in her work as a patron. Sometimes mother and daughter acted together. When Lady Spencer subscribed to Ann Yearsley's first collection of poems (at Hannah More's emphatic suggestion), the duchess also sent Yearsley a package of books as a gift (Jones 108). Yearsley notoriously rebelled against More's social conservatism, accusing her patron of absconding with the money she had earned; for her part, as Mona Scheuerman has shown, More believed Yearsley, the milkwoman of Bristol, should remain a milkwoman, and not rise above her social class.[46] It is not clear that the duchess shared such beliefs: certainly her financial aid to Mary Robinson and Charlotte Smith suggests a more aggressive, perhaps progressive, approach to patronage, for which she had already acquired a reputation by 1775. Proofs of Lady Georgiana's generosity toward aspiring authors were strong enough to encourage Mary Robinson to send "a neatly bound volume of my Poems," through her brother, to Chatsworth in 1775 while Robinson was living in debtor's prison with her husband and young girl. Lady Georgiana then invited the eighteen-year-old woman to her estate with her child on several occasions and supported her financially with small gifts. "Frequently the Duchess inquired most minutely into the story of my sorrows," Robinson writes, "and as often gave me tears of the most spontaneous sympathy."[47] When Mary Robinson ended her fifteenth-month incarceration, Lady Georgiana sent a congratulatory note from Chatsworth (83); she did the same when Robinson made her debut with Garrick at Drury Lane (87).

After meeting Charlotte Smith at a small party in 1789, the duchess assisted Smith's literary career as well, collecting "subscriptions for her second volume of sonnets and for a play the Duchess encouraged her to write" (Fletcher 238). With the duchess's permission, Smith dedicated *Rambles Farther* to Lady Georgiana's twelve-year-old daughter. Even more directly, she served as a *de facto* literary agent for Smith, writing Smith's publisher, Cadell and Davies, and asking them to come and see her. Her willingness to associate herself with Smith's novel was instru-mental in securing its publication. "The day after we were favoured with your Letter of the 17th," they wrote after discouraging Smith for weeks, "we received a Note from the Duchess of Devonshire desiring to know when she could see us on the Subject of two more Volumes of `Rural Walks' in answer to which we informed her Grace that we would wait upon her whenever she would be pleased to direct. . . . We are surprised to find that some Misapprehension had led you to understand that we declined the Purchase of your new Volumes . . . we are ready to undertake if it meets with your Approbation to pay you *fifty pounds* for the Copyright of them the Instant we receive the Mss. Compleat" (Fletcher 256). These activities suggest that Lady Georgiana supported, however indirectly, a more radical political agenda than her social class may have allowed; though she kept the appearance of a "proper lady," her role as an arbitress of fashion—in clothing and in literature—helped her to shape, rather than merely follow, current tastes.

Though a less accomplished writer than the generation that followed her, Lady Georgiana may nevertheless have influenced them. One astute reader of *Emma* notes how Priscilla's sister, who is ruined by a love match with a young naval officer, Mr. Wentworth, prefigures Jane Austen's Anne Elliot, who refuses a similar match with *her* Colonel Wentworth in *Persuasion*. The masquerade episode with Lady Wilmington as Diana is echoed in a similar scene in Elizabeth Inchbald's *A Simple Story*, both may well reflect Briscoe's *The Fine Lady*, which includes a similar scene. Inchbald recalls Lady Georgiana in portraying a fanatical and self-righteous husband/father who abandons the heroine. *Emma* also resembles Charlotte Smith's *Desmond* (1792), Wollstonecraft's *Maria* (1797), and Anne Brontë's *The Tenant of Wildfell Hall* (1848), novels that focus on "injustices experienced by women as victims of the unjust patriarchal institution of marriage that gives complete control to profligate and totally unworthy husbands."[48] *Emma's* father is unworthy, for example, because his profligate spending prevents her from marrying the man she loves. Walpole proves equally hapless, using his jealousy of a "dead man" (as Kitty memorably puts it) to justify squandering his fortune and abandoning his wife and newborn child. Two decades before Wollstonecraft and Hays, Lady Georgiana framed the marriage question from the perspective of a different social class (aristocratic women), exposing the "wrongs of men" and the ways in which primogeniture supported such unjust treatment.

SOCIAL AND POLITICAL ALLEGORY

Lady Georgiana's discomfort with the restrictions placed on aristocratic women in the late eighteenth century finds expression in the letters of

Kitty Bishop. Though unsuccessful in her own romantic life (and there is deliberate irony here), Kitty Bishop advises Lady Noel against submitting, passively, to the conduct of her husband.

> As I have addressed you as a bride, my dear Lady Noel, I shall now talk to you as a wife. Are you impatient to hear *my sage* instructions?—I begin then by caviling at the conclusion of your last letter to Emma, in which you *piously* purpose never to contradict *your spouse*, merely because he is such. I never thought such doctrine would have been broached by you; it was worthy only of the non-resisting gentleness of our meek friend, who, born "to be controuled," does not find any hardship in obeying. For my part, the *jus divinum* of husbands seems to me full as oppressive as that of kings; and, had our parliament been properly *mixed*, both would have been abolished together; but, *excluding us* from taking any part in the formation of the laws, like all usurpers they tyrannise, to ensure by tenure what they do not hold by justice. Our men are not only the sons, but *heirs* of liberty, and, like the eldest-born, run away with all the inheritance from us defenceless beings.—"Wherefore are we born with high souls, but to assert ourselves, shake off this vile obedience they exact, and claim an equal empire o'er the world?"—Wherefore indeed! I'll answer for it, there never was an Hampden, a Selden, or a Russel, who had a greater aversion to *passive-obedience* than myself: and why should I be more obliged to it by the laws of my country than they were?

To drive her point home, Kitty Bishop quotes Calista's speech from *The Fair Penitent* ("Wherefore are we born . . . "). In this, she resembles Mary Robinson, Lady Georgiana's protégée, who later used the same quotation from Nicholas Rowe's drama as the epigraph to *Thoughts on the Condition of Women, and on the Injustice of Mental Subordination* (1799). Kitty Bishop sees herself in the tradition of the Whigs who led the Glorious Revolution of 1688; though defenseless, Kitty, through her wit, is anything but "passive."

Other characters in the novel (William Walpole, for example) recall the great but corrupt Whig statesman, Robert Walpole; the name of his rival, Augustus Sidney, alludes, perhaps, to Algernon Sidney (1622–1683), an extreme Republican who opposed Charles I and regarded Cromwell as a usurper. In June 1683, when the Rye House plot was announced, Lords Russell, Essex, Howard, and Sidney were sent to the Tower. In November, Sidney was tried for high treason before Jeffreys and be-

headed on December 7, 1698. Augustus Sidney resembles Algernon in
his military activity (Algernon Sidney was wounded in battle in Ireland),
unfortunate demise (in war and, perhaps, in the name of Rye Farm in
Yorkshire where the virtuous Priscilla Neville retreats and Emma finds
her), and martyrdom. They differ in disposition, for Algernon Sidney
was, by most accounts, rather "bellicose."[49] Both Emma and Priscilla
undergo an emotional exile from London; like Sidney's retreat to France
and his persecution by a corrupt English government (represented perhaps by Walpole's electioneering practices in London and mistreatment
of Emma), Augustus travels to Russia and continues to hold the allegiance of Emma, even though he no longer resides in the country. This
situation echoes that of the Spencers who were forced to show their
patriotism while resenting the rule of a foreign king, George III, who
behaved as tyrannically, and as capriciously, as William Walpole does as
a husband. That Walpole's name also suggests the Whig prime minister,
Robert Walpole, only heightens the interest of this Whig allegory, though
Sidney anticipates the formation of a Whig party by more than fifty years.
Colonel Sutton's rebuke to William Walpole regarding his effort to
purchase votes might be applied more broadly to the use of patronage
in eighteenth-century political life: "Your freeman knew the general interest would be betrayed as soon as you got into parliament. They,
therefore, as individuals, were for making as much as they could of you"
(203). Lady Georgiana would have taken particular pride in the Spencer
family's connections to the Sidneys: Lady Dorothy Sidney, daughter of
the second earl of Leicester and the "Sacharissa" of Waller's poetry,
eventually married Henry, third baron of Spencer, and first earl of
Sunderland (Walpole 28:203); Philip Sidney and Algernon Sidney are
thus related through the Leicester line.

Lady Georgiana became involved in many of the activities she attributes to William Walpole, anticipating the crises that marked her life.
In 1784, for example, she helped to elect Charles James Fox to the
House of Commons. "The proceedings ended with a procession to
Devonshire House, closed by the coaches and six of the dukes of
Devonshire and Portland," the earl of Bessborough notes, and "The part
played by Georgiana was recognized by a flag bearing the legend 'Sacred
to Female Patriotism'" (82). Walpole's venture into politics is less successful and his loss of a parliamentary seat to an East Indian with a bag
of rupees may well reflect British anxiety about the East India Company.
The issue came to a crisis when Lady Georgiana's close friend Charles
James Fox was caricatured in the press as Carlo Khan.[50] Other autobiographical parallels also suggest themselves. When he believes Emma has
been unfaithful, for example, William leads a dissipated life in London.

He flirts with, but does not seduce, Lord Clarendon's wife. The duke of Devonshire, on the other hand, needed no provocation to have a child by Charlotte Williams before he married Lady Georgiana; for her part, Lady Georgiana remained faithful to her husband until after she gave birth to a male heir, when she had a brief affair with Lord Grey (the "Mr. Black" of her letters to Lady Melbourne). Emma never repeats the conduct of her philandering husband, which gives her a moral authority that, at times, strains belief.

Lady Georgiana portrays the decline of male virtue by focusing on macaronis and dandies who attended clubs in St. James. Included among these were her future husband and friend, Charles James Fox, both of whom frequented Boodle's, at 28 St. James Street (the haunt of Lady Georgiana's fictional character, William Walpole). Other dandies drawn from personal knowledge include the husband of Anne Damer (1749–1828), one of Lady Georgiana's closer friends. John Damer shot himself in a London tavern on August 15, 1776, when the extent of his gambling debts became clear. Damer's wardrobe alone was assessed at over 15,000 pounds, but he left no political accomplishments behind to compare with those of his illustrious Whig predecessors. Damer wrote a fashionable novel entitled *Belmour* [1801] that makes no mention of the incident, for Damer's life was more extraordinary than any novelistic reenactment could make it appear. "Has Lady Greenwich told you of the Duchess of Devonshire, Lady Melburn, and Mrs. Damer all being drawn in one picture in the Characters of the three Witches in Macbeth?" Coke asked an unnamed friend (July 14, 1775; Birkenhead 13; Gross 20). Lady Georgiana's friendships with Lady Melbourne and Anne Damer may well have inspired the portraits of witty (Catherine Bishiop) and victimized (Priscy Neville) women who appear in *Emma*. Certainly their high living provoked the ire of Horace Walpole and Damer's father-in-law, Lord Milton, who ordered Anne Damer out of Milton Abbey after his son's death. Lady Georgiana's novel, far tamer than Gardner's portrait, anticipates some of the events she would experience a year after her marriage, including her own indebtedness.

Lady Georgiana seems to have gained more from the love of women than men. She found herself continually tormented by the emotionally stunted duke of Devonshire and Charles Grey, while relying on close friends like Lady Melbourne and Lady Elizabeth Foster to explain their inscrutable conduct. When separated from her husband in France, Lady Melbourne conducted a correspondence with Lady Georgiana about her lover, Charles Grey, and did so without her own sister (and traveling companion!) Lady Bessborough or mother knowing. A similar situation arises in her novel. Emma's friendship provides Lady Noel and then

Priscy Neville with great comfort, while her husband tortures her to such an extent that she almost loses her life after giving birth. Similarly, Sutton and Walpole obtain more understanding from each other than they do from their future spouses. Yet Lady Georgiana dissects womens' characters as minutely as mens'. The designing Mrs. Bromford (who becomes a fanatical Methodist), the passive Emma, the cynical Kitty Bishop, and the shrewd Frances Neville provide the reader with several competing strategies for navigating a hypocritical world without becoming hypocritical oneself.

NOTES

1. Brian Masters, *Georgiana* (London: Hamish Hamilton, 1980), p. 9; hereafter cited as Masters.

2. Sydney Owenson, *Lady Morgan's Memoirs: Autobiography, Diaries and Correspondence* (London, 1862), 2: 199. Quoted in "Duchess of Devonshire," *Romantic Women Poets: An Anthology*, ed. Duncan Wu (London: Blackwell, 1997), pp. 170–171.

3. *European Magazine* 11 (1787): 219.

4. John Pearson, *Stags and Serpents* (Chatsworth: Chatsworth House Trust, 2002), p. 94.

5. Amanda Foreman, *Georgiana, Duchess of Devonshire* (London: HarperCollins, 1998), p. 40; hereafter cited as Foreman.

6. Bessborough, Earl of, ed. *Letters of Georgiana* (London: John Murray, 1955), p. 22; hereafter cited as Bessborough.

7. James Lees-Milnes, *The Bachelor Duke* (London, 1991), p. 16; hereafter cited as Lees-Milnes.

8. Arthur H. Cash, *Laurence Sterne: The Later Years* (London: Methuen, 1986), p. 81; hereafter referred to as Cash.

9. May 1787; Osborn Mss.

10. May 1787; Osborn Mss.

11. Mary Gwladys Jones, *Hannah More* (Cambridge: Cambridge University Press, 1952), p. 108; hereafter cited as Jones.

12. Georgina Battiscombe, *The Spencers of Althorp* (London, Constable, 1984), p. 79.

13. October 9, 1774; Bessborough, p. 16.

14. Garrick's Poem, Osborn Mss.

15. Horace Walpole. *The Yale Edition of Horace Walpole's Correspondence.* Ed. by W. S. Lewis et al. 48 volumes (New Haven: Yale University Press, 1937–1983), 28:203n7; hereafter cited as Walpole.

16. This manuscript is in the John Rylands Library in Manchester (Foreman, 414n53).

17. This play has been recently discovered by Prof. Bewley at the Huntington Library.

18. David Cannadine, *Aspects of Aristocracy: Grandeur and Decline in Modern Britain* (New Haven: Yale University Press, 1994), p. 167.

19. George Gordon, Lord Byron. *The Complete Poetical Works*, ed. by Jerome McGann. 5 vols. (Oxford: Oxford University Press, 1980–1986), 5:13.95.7–8.

20. Foreman, pp. 59–61; Masters, p. 70; Masters, following Bessborough (33), states that she never denied authorship; Foreman states that she admitted it in private; no documentary evidence exists for these claims.

21. The following sources list her as author of both works: *The Feminist Companion to Literature in English: Women Writers from the Middle Ages to the Present*, ed. Virginia Blain, Patricia Clements, Isobel Grundy (New Haven: Yale University Press, 1990), p. 288 (hereafter cited to as Blain); Duncun Wu, *Romantic Women Poets: An Anthology* (London: Blackwell, 1997), p. 170; Cheryl Turner, *Living by the Pen: Women Writers in the Eighteenth Century* (London: Routledge, 1992), pp. 103, 168; Dale Spender, *The Europa Biographical Dictionary of British* Women (Detroit: Gale, 1983); and *The English Novel 1770– 1829: A Bibliographical Survey of Prose Fiction Published in the British Isles*, vol. 1, *1770–1799*, ed. Peter Garside, James Raven, and Rainer Schowlering, 2 vols. (Oxford: Oxford University Press, 2000), 1:203; hereafter cited as Raven; Isobel Grundy, "'A novel in a series of letters by a lady': Richardson and some Richardsonian novels," *Samuel Richardson: Tercentenary Essays*, ed. by Margaret Anne Doody and Peter Sabor (Cambridge: Cambridge University Press, 1998), 223–236; 227–228. Though *The Sylph* has been attributed to Sophia Briscoe, author of *Miss Melmoth* (1771) and *The Fine Lady* (1772), also published by Lowndes, internal evidence, and a contrasting style, suggest that Georgiana is the author.

22. J. M. S. Tompkins, *The Popular Novel in England: 1770–1800* (1936; Lincoln: University of Nebraska Press, 1961), p. 21; hereafter cited as Tompkins.

23. James Raven, *Judging New Wealth* (Oxford: Oxford University Press, 1992), 55; hereafter cited as Raven, *JNW,* with a page number.

24. "when any one braves the opinion of the World, sooner or later they will feel the consequences of it" (April 13, 1810), Lady Melbourne wrote to Lady Caroline Lamb, shortly after she became aware of her daughter-in-law's affair with Sir Godfrey Webster. *Byron's "Corbeau Blanc": The Life and Letters of Lady Melbourne*, ed. Jonathan Gross (Houston: Rice University Press, 1997), p. 107.

25. Georgiana, Duchess of Devonshire, *The Sylph*. With an Introduction by Amanda Foreman. (York: Henry Parker, 2001), p. 34.

26. Stephen Lloyd, *Richard and Maria Cosway: Regency Artists of Taste and Fashion, with Essays by Roy Porter & Aileen Ribeiro* (Edinburgh: Scottish National Portrait Gallery, 1995), p. 25.

27. See also Montagu Summers, *A Gothic Bibliography* (London: The Fortune Press, 1941), Tompkins describes the 1793 London edition, advertised by T. H. Hookham, which I have not been able to locate (13n1); the British Library Catalogue lists the 1784 Dublin edition, which I have consulted in the Bristol Early Novels collection, and the 1787 London edition, which I have consulted at the British Library and the University of Michigan/East Lansing.

28. The original reviews are *Monthly* Review 49 (July 1773) 69; *Critical Review* 35 (June 1773): 475.

29. *Universal Catalogue* [2] (1773) art. 733.

30. Antonia Forster, *Index to Book Reviews in England, 1775–1800* (London: The British Library, 1997), 6.

31. Janet Todd, *The Sign of Angelica* (New York: Columbia University Press, 1989), p. 6.

32. Henry Mackenzie, "Untitled Article in *The Lounger.*" No. 20 (Sat. June 18, 1785).

33. *Universal Catalogue* [2] (1773) art. 733.

34. Hannah More, "On the Danger of Sentimental or Romantic Connexions" (1778). In *Works.* 6 vols. (London, 1810), 6:295–307.

35. Henry Mackenzie, *The Man of Feeling,* ed. Brian Vickars (New York: Oxford University Press, 1970), p. 103. See Maureen Harkin, "Mackenzie's Man of Feeling: Embalming Sensibility," *ELH* 61, No. 1 (1994): 317–340, who discusses this passage, noting "the conflicts between the man of feeling and the age of commerce" (320).

36. Samuel Richardson, *Clarissa, or the History of a Young Lady,* ed. Angus Ross (London: Penguin, 1988), p. 342.

37. Janet Todd, introduction to *Desmond,* ed. Antje Blank and Janet Todd (London: Chatto & Pickering, 1996), p. xiv. As Todd states, "the concept of the feme covert, the legal notion of the unity of person, denoting that the very being and essence of the woman was suspended during the coverture, meant a woman had no legal personality in common law, was unable to enter into contracts, sue or be sued, or instigate legal actions." See also Alicia Browne, *The 18th Century Feminist Mind* (Detroit: Wayne State University Press, 1989), chapter two.

38. Gary Kelly, *Women, Writing, and Revolution: 1790–1827* (Oxford: Clarendon Press, 1993), p. 18.

39. Charles Spencer, *Althorp: The Story of an English House* (New York: St. Martin's Press, 1998), p. 9. "Georgiana Spencer, later duchess of Devonshire" was "one of the most glamorous figures in eighteenth century England," Charles Spencer has written. She "used to cause similar reactions among the people of London during her public appearances, as Diana did, 200 years on." Both women engaged in humanitarian work and used their social station to reach out to the disadvantaged; both were enormously popular individuals preferred by the public to their more reserved spouses. By humanizing the aristocracy, they helped legitimize it in times of social upheaval.

40. Eleanor Ty, *Unsex'd Revolutionaries: Five Women Novelists of the 1790s* (Toronto: University of Toronto Press, 1993), p. xii. Hereafter cited as Ty.

41. Mary Poovey, *The Proper Lady and the Woman Writer: Ideology as Style in the Works of Mary Wollstonecraft, Mary Shelley, and Jane Austen* (Chicago: University of Chicago Press, 1984), pp. 56–68.

42. Elaine Showalter, "Towards a Feminist Poetics" and "Feminist Criticism in the Wilderness," in *Feminist Criticism: Essays on Women, Literature, and Theory* (New York: Pantheon, 1985), pp. 125–143, 243–270, quoted in Ty, p. 14.

43. *Strictures on the Modern System of Female Education, with a View of the Principles and Conduct Prevalent among Women of Rank and Fortune*, 2 vols. (London, 1799). 1:108.

44. Fordyce, *Sermons to Young Women*, 3rd edition, corr., 2 vols. (London, 1766), 1: 201–202, quoted in Gary Kelly, *Women, Writing, and Revolution: 1790–1827* (Oxford: Clarendon Press, 1993), p. 12.

45. Loraine Fletcher, *Charlotte Smith* (London: Macmillan's, 1998), p. 236.

46. Mona Scheuerman, *In Praise of Poverty: Hannah More Counters Thomas Paine and the Radical Threat* (Lexington: University of Kentucky Press, 2002), p. 215.

47. Mary Robinson, *Perdita, or the Memoirs of Mary Robinson*, ed. M. J. Levy (London: Peter Owen, 1994), p. 81.

48. I quote from a reader's report that helped me situate this novel in the decade of the 1790s and noted the comparisons with Austen and Inchbald mentioned earlier in this paragraph.

49. Sidney himself was never a Whig, for he was a product of a different age, as Jonathan Scott explains in *Algernon Sidney and the English Republic, 1623–1677* (Cambridge: Cambridge University Press, 1988), pp. 2–3.

50. Nicholas Penny, *Reynolds* (London: Royal Academy of Arts, 1986), p. 145.

References

Archives

Chatsworth Archives; Journal of Lady Spencer (1768–1792)

British Library, Add'l ms. 45546–9, Letters of Emily Cowper, Georgiana, Duchess of Devonshire

Bodleian Library, Oxford University; Lovelace Ms.

Bessborough Papers, Osborn Collection, Yale University

Special Collections

Early Novels Collection, University of Bristol

Special Collections, Michigan State University, East Lansing

Van Pelt Library, University of Pennsylvania

Editions of The Sylph

The Sylph; a novel. 2 vol. London, T. Lowndes, 1779.

Editions of Emma; or, The Unfortunate Attachment

Emma; or, The Unfortunate Attachment. 3 vols. London: T. Hookham,1773 (University of Chicago).

——. 2 vol. Dublin: printed by S. Colbert, 1784 (Early Novels Collection, Bristol).

——. 2 vol. London, T. Hookham, 1787 (Michigan State University).

——. 2 vol. London, T. Hookham, 1789.

Novels

[Anonymous]. *The Married Victim, or the History of Lady Villars.* London: T. Hookham, 1772.

Briscoe, Sophia. *Miss Melmoth.* London: T. Hookham, 1771.

——. *The Fine Lady.* London: T. Hookham, 1772.

Richardson, Samuel. *Clarissa, or the History of a Young Lady,* ed. by Angus Ross, London: Penguin, 1988.

Periodicals

European Magazine 11 (1787): 219.

Reviews of Emma: *Monthly Review* 49 (1773): 69; *Critical Review* 35 (1773): 475; *London Magazine* 42 (1773): 249; *Town & Country Magazine* 5 (1773): 378; *Universal Catalogue* [2] (1773) art. 733 (Forster 95).

Reviews of *The Sylph: Monthly Review* 60 (1779) 240: *Critical Review* 48 (1779) 319; *London Magazine* 48 (1779) 37-8; *Town and Country Magazine* 11 (1779) 568.

Review of "Passage of St. Gothard." *Literary Journal* 1 (10 March 1803) 313–14.

Secondary Sources

Armstrong, Isobel. "Richardson and some Richardsonian novels," in *Samuel Richardson: Tercentenary Essays,* ed. by Margaret Anne Doody and Peter Sabor. Cambridge: Cambridge University Press, 1988.

Battiscombe, Georgina. *The Spencers of Althorp.* London: Constable, 1984.

Bessborough, Earl of, ed. *Letters of Georgiana.* London: John Murray, 1955.

Blain, Virginia, Patricia Clements, and Isobel Grundy, ed. *The Feminist Companion to Literature in English: Women Writers from the Middle Ages to the Present.* New Haven: Yale University Press, 1990.

Bloomfield, Anne. "Patroness of the dance." *Dancing Times.* London (January 1996) 86:1024, pp. 361–364.

Byron, George Gordon, Lord. *The Complete Poetical Works,* ed. by Jerome McGann. 5 vols. Oxford: Oxford University Press, 1980–1986.

Cannadine, David. *Aspects of Aristocracy: Grandeur and Decline in Modern Britain.* New Haven: Yale University Press, 1994.

Cash, Arthur Hill. *Laurence Sterne: The Early and Middle Years.* London: Methuen, 1975.

———. *Laurence Sterne: The Later Years.* London: Methuen, 1986.

Complete Peerage of England, Scotland, Ireland, Great Britain, and the U.K., by *GEC[ockeyne],* ed. The Honorable Vicary Gibbs. 2 vols. London, 1912.

Craciun, Adriana, and Kari E. Lokke, eds. *Rebellious Hearts: British Women Writers and the French Revolution.* New York: State University of New York Press, 2002.

"Duchess of Devonshire." *Romantic Women Poets: An Anthology,* ed. by Duncan Wu. 170–171. London: Blackwell, 1997.

Fletcher, Loraine. *Charlotte Smith: A Critical Biography.* London: Macmillan, 1998.

Foreman, Amanda. *Georgiana.* London: Harpercollins, 1998; New York, Random House, 2000.

Forster, Antonia. *Index to Book Reviews in England, 1775–1800.* London: The British Library, 1997.

Garside, Peter, James Raven, and Rainer Schowlering, eds. *The English Novel 1770–1829: A Bibliographical Survey of Prose Fiction Published in the British Isles.* Volume I: 1770-1799. Oxford: Oxford University Press, 2000.

Gray, Thomas. *The Odes by Mr. Gray.* Strawberry Hill: R. and J. Dodsley, 1757.

Grundy, Isobel. " 'A novel in a series of letters by a lady': Richardson and some Richardsonian novels,' " *Samuel Richardson: Tercentenary Essays,* ed. by Margaret Anne Doody and Peter Sabor. 223–236. Cambridge: Cambridge University Press, 1998.

Harkin, Maureen. "Mackenzie's Man of Feeling: Embalming Sensibility." *ELH* 61:1 (1994): 317–340.

Kelly, Gary. *Women, Writing, and Revolution: 1790–1827.* Oxford: Clarendon Press, 1993.

———, ed. *Millenium Hall,* by Sarah Scott. Peterborough: Broadview Literary Texts, 1995.

Kelly, Linda. *Sheridan.* London: Pimlico, 1998.

Lloyd, Stephen. *Richard and Maria Cosway: Regency Artists of Taste and Fashion,* with Essays by Roy Porter and Aileen Ribeiro. Edinburgh: Scottish National Portrait Gallery, 1995.

Lees-Milnes, James. *The Bachelor Duke.* London: 1991.

Mackenzie, Henry. *The Man of Feeling,* ed. by Brian Vickars. New York: Oxford University Press, 1970.

——. "Untitled Article in *The Lounger.*" No. 20. Sat. June 18, 1785.

Masters, Brian. *Georgiana.* London: Hamilton Hamish, 1980.

More, Hannah. *Strictures on the Modern System of Female Education, with a View of the Principles and Conduct Prevalent among Women of Rank and Fortune,* 2 vols. London, 1799.

——. "On the Danger of Sentimental or Romantic Connexions" In *Works.* 6 vols. London, 1810. 6:295–307.

——. *On the Manners of the Great.* London, 1802.

Owenson, Sydney. *Lady Morgan's Memoirs: Autobiograhy, Dairies and Correspondence.* 2 vols. London, 1862.

Pearson, John. *Stags and Serpents.* London: Chatsworth House Trust, 2002.

Penny, Nicholas. *Reynolds.* London: Royal Academy of Arts, 1986.

Poovey, Mary. *The Proper Lady and the Woman Writer: Ideology as Style in the Works of Mary Wollstonecraft, Mary Shelley, and Jane Austen.* Chicago: University of Chicago Press, 1984.

Raven, James. *Judging New Wealth.* Oxford: Oxford UP, 1993.

Robinson, Mary. *Perdita: The Memoirs of Mary Robinson,* ed. M. J. Levy. London: Peter Owen, 1994.

Scott, Jonathan. *Algernon Sidney and the English Republic, 1623–1677.* Cambridge: Cambridge University Press, 1988.

Scheuerman, Mona. *In Praise of Poverty: Hannah More Counters Thomas Paine and the Radical Threat.* Lexington: University of Kentucky, 2002.

Showalter, Elaine. "Towards a Feminist Poetics" and "Feminist Criticism in the Wilderness." In *Feminist Criticism: Essays on Women, Literature, and Theory,* ed. by Elaine Showalter. New York: Random House, 1985.

Spencer, Charles. *Althorp: The Story of an English House.* New York: St. Martin's Press, 1998.

Spender, Dale, ed. *Dictionary of British Women.* London: Pandora, 1989.

Summers, Montagu, ed. *A Gothic Bibliography.* New York: Russell & Russell, 1964.

Todd, Janet. *The Sign of Angelica*. New York: Columbia University Press, 1989.

——. "Introduction" to *Desmond*, ed. by Antje Blank and Janet Todd. London: Chatto & Pickering, 1996.

Tompkins, J. M. S. *The Popular Novel in England: 1770–1800*. Lincoln: University of Nebraska Press, 1961.

Turner, Cheryl. *Living by the Pen: Women Writers in the Eighteenth Century*. London: Routledge, 1992.

Ty, Eleanor. *Unsex'd Revolutionaries: Five Women Novelists of the 1790s*. Toronto: University of Toronto Press, 1993.

Walpole, Horace. *The Yale Edition of Horace Walpole's Correspondence*. Ed. by W. S. Lewis et al. 48 volumes. New Haven: Yale University Press, 1937–1983.

Ward, William S., compiler. *Literary Reviews in British Periodicals: 1789–1797, A Bibliography*. 4 vols. New York: Garland, 1979.

Watson, George, ed. *The New Cambridge Bibliography of English Literature*. 2 vols. Cambridge: Cambridge University Press, 1971.

Wollstonecraft, Mary. "The Wrongs of Woman: or, Maria," In *The Works of Mary Wolstonecraft*, ed. by Janet Todd and Marilyn Butler. 7 vols. New York University Press, 1989. 1:81–184.

Note on the Text

THIS TRANSCRIPTION HAS BEEN TAKEN from the three-volume, 1773 London edition of the novel at Special Collections, University of Chicago Library. Illustrations for this edition have been taken from the two-volume, 1787 London edition at the British Library.

The 1773 edition has been chosen as the copy-text for this reprint. The 1773 edition has more dramatic immediacy, fewer errors, and seems closer to the author's intention; there is no evidence that Lady Georgiana supervised the first or subsequent editions of her novels. The 1773 edition relies, to a greater extent, on italics for expressivity. In the absence of a fair copy of the manuscript, I have elected to retain what I assume to be Lady Georgiana's irregular punctuation, including the use of commas for dramatic emphasis and dashes to replace full stops. I have also retained "original" spelling and the idiosyncratic use of capital letters. In the rare instances when the 1787 version corrects an obvious mistake in the 1773 edition, I have incorporated it. This is indicated with an asterisk; a collation of the three editions (1773, 1784, 1787) appears at the end of this volume.

Volume 2:254 of the 1787 edition includes a printer's error that numbers letters in an incorrect sequence (82, 84, 73, 85) before resuming a normal numbering pattern. Volume 2 of the 1787 edition also includes omitted text on p. 212. Collating the British Library's 1773 and U. Michigan/ Lansing's 1787 editions, I have found approximately 690 differences, the great majority of which can be ascribed to punctuation, hyphenation [239 Rye-Farm/RYE FARM (236)], and altered usage.

There are 1,175 differences that exist between the 1784 Dublin pirated edition and the 1773 edition. "Some three-quarters of all novels of the period were reprinted in Dublin," Raven notes, "and design differences between London and Irish versions were often extreme" (107). The phrase, "by the author *The Sylph*," appears on the title page of the 1784 edition, which I have consulted in the Early Novels Collection at the University of Bristol. Because the 1784 edition was pirated, my comments compare the 1773 and 1787 London editions. Before turning to that collation, I should say that differences between the 1773 and 1784 editions refer primarily to italics, which occur more frequently in the 1773 edition (names of places at the beginning of letters are italicized in the 1784 edition). Differences of spelling can be observed (honor/honour), use of semicolons versus colons (comfort/comfort: or promising;/promising), ellipses versus long dashes (sickness . . . . . /sickness———). It is tempting, and perhaps not inaccurate, to conclude that the 1773 edition reflects the unbridled use of punctuation popularized by Sterne and Henry Mackenzie; by 1784, use of punctuation to express sensibility had somewhat tapered off. I have retained Emma's expressive use of italics, punctuation, and dashes: the sentimental novel depends on such devices, as surely as it depends upon an historically specific form (the 1773 version of the epistolary novel).

One particularly noteworthy distinction between the 1773 and 1784 editions occurs in the references to Whig heroes. The 1773 edition reads as follows: "a Portland, a Manchester, a Buccleugh, a Thanet, an Abingdon, more than one Spencer, a Delaware, a Torrington, a Wenman, and innumerable others, whose beauty adds the highest lustre to their prudence" (2:29). The 1784 edition, written two years after an Irish parliament was established, reads: "a Rutland, a Leinster, a Temple, an Antrim, a Carrick, a Moira, an Arran, a Charlemont, a Mountgarret, a Kingsborough, a Lissord, and innumerable others whose BEAUTY adds the highest LUSTRE" (2:145).

As a rule, there are more hyphens, ellipses, and italicized words in the 1773 edition, thus showing greater expressiveness and, perhaps, authorial intention. In the 1787 edition, italics have been removed and sentences repunctuated, sometimes altering the sense, often for the worse. Punctuation changes include altered placement of commas; hyphenation and capitalization frequently occur in titles of letters and places (Rose-Court vs. ROSE COURT; honor/honour; favorable/favourable) and changes in capitalization (Bruton-Street/Bruton-street). Since every subsequent edition seems to take us further away from the text that the Duchess submitted and often introduces new errors of punctuation (while modernizing spelling), I have chosen the 1773 edition. The 1773 edition has the merit of situating the novel in the time in which it was written. Where the 1787 corrects the 1773 edition, I have indicated this: in choosing between "visiters" (1773) and "visitors" (1787), for example, I have preferred the latter, since it conforms with modern usage. Finally, I have followed Margaret Doody's edition of Charlotte Lennox's *The Female Quixote* in listing all changes at the end of the volume and Gary Kelly's reasoning in his edition of Sarah Scott's *Millenium Hall* and Pamela Clemit's edition of Inchbald's *A Simple Story* in preferring an early to a later edition of a novel.

The fact that this novel was written for subscription is an important part of its publication history. A novel that appeared with a long list of subscribers could add cachet to the work, boosting circulation and sales. For this reason, I have retained the list of subscribers for the 1773 edition that appears, verbatim (though single spaced), in the 1787 edition. I have also retained the list as possible evidence for Lady Georgiana's authorship. Of the list of subscribers, for example, the following names appear in Lady Georgiana's letters or biography: Hon. Mrs. Bouverie (Edward Bouverie her husband, appears as an acquaintance between 1776 and 1778 in Bessborough 84; Foreman 48); Mrs. Graham, possibly Mary Graham, apparently met Lady Georgiana in October 1777 (Foreman 51); Lady Melbourne corresponded with Lady Georgiana (Bessborough 54; Gross 19), Lady Elizabeth Hamilton (Bessborough 102). Conspicuously absent are Lady Crewe, Lady Jersey, Lady Derby, and Lady Douglas, friends acquired at a later date, but who she might have known by 1773. Some names appear after the 1773 publication date of *Emma*, but this does not necessarily mean that Lady Georgiana did not know them then. Lady Mary Coke provides evidence of Lady Melbourne's friendship with Lady Georgiana as early as July 14, 1775, for example, though the first surviving letter between Lady Georgiana and Lady Melbourne does not occur until August 1776 (Gross 96).

In terms of the physical appearance of each text, the 1773 edition has seven words to the line and nineteen lines per page with $3/4$" side margins, 1" top margin and 2" bottom margin; the page size is 7.25" × 4.25"; the 1784 edition has seven words to the line and thirty one lines per page and appears with $1/2$" left margins and $1/2$" right margins, $1/2$" inch top and $1/2$" bottom margins; the page size is 6.25" × 3.75". The 1787 edition has ten words to the line and twenty six lines per page and appears with $3/4$" left margins and 1" right margins, $3/4$" top margins and $3/4$" bottom margins; the page size is 8" × $4^{3}/4$".

The pagination for the 1773 volume is: I.274 p; II.295 p.; III. 330 p. 12 mo. 9s, 7s 6d sewed or 9s bound; the pagination for the 1787 edition is: I. 250 p.; II. 292 p.

To
THE RIGHT HON.
LADY CAMDEN

MADAM,

In presuming to dedicate this Novel to your Ladyship, I am
influenced only by the general respect paid to the name of Camden,
and my own veneration of your Ladyship's character. The one, I
flatter myself, will procure the book a favorable reception, by preclud-
ing all suspicion of its containing sentiments inconsistent with the
wisdom and virtue implied in such congenial patronage; and by the
other I am prompted to embrace every opportunity of adding my
mite to the tribute of public praise, spontaneously paid to your
Ladyship's conduct, whether supporting your exalted station by the
easy dignity of your deportment abroad, or adorning it with those
domestic virtues and Christian graces that constitute the chief beauty
and glory of a woman. It is peculiar to good minds to receive tokens
of respect and kindness, not for the importance of the gift, but for
the good-will of the giver. This trifle your Ladyship will condescend
to receive as a testimony of the unfeigned esteem of,

                          Madam,
                          Your Ladyship's
                          Most Respectful
                          And obedient servant.

ℒist of Subscribers

(1773 Edition)

Ancaster, Duchess of
Argyll, Duchess of
Ailesbury, Countess of
Ashburnham, Countess of
Agar, Mrs.
Ashley, Miss

Bampsylde, Lady
Beauclerke, Lady Catherine[1]
Beauclerke, Hon. Miss
Blessington, Countess of
Bateman, Hon. Mr.
Bagot, Miss
Boscawen,Mrs.
Boscawen, Hon. Miss
Bever, Mrs.

Baten, Mr. Peter
Barrel, Miss
Bland, Mrs.
Boone, Mrs.
Boone, Miss
Bouverie, Hon. Mrs.[2]
Brudenell, Hon. Mrs.
Brudenell, Miss
Brown, Mrs.
Bryet, Mr.

Camden, Lady
Champness, Lady
Cope, Lady
Conolly, Lady Anne
Cornwallis, Countess Dowager

The names with footnote numbers suggest biographical connections to Georgiana, Duchess of Devonshire. They are mostly speculative, with the exception of number 7, and are offered in the interests of further historical research.

1. Georgiana's cousin Lady Diana Spencer committed adultery with Topham Beauclerk in order to provoke her violent husband Lord Bolingbroke into divorcing her (Foreman 48).

2. Mrs. Bouverie, whom Reynolds painted to much acclaim, was part of Lady Georgiana's inner circle between 1776 and 1778 (Foreman 48). [Edward Bouverie, d. 1810, informed the duchess of the Prince of Wales had run himself through with his sword; she then visited him, trying to forestall his marriage to Mrs. Fitzherbert] (Bessborough, 83).

Cornwallis Hon. Mrs.
Cranstoun, Lady
Chetwynd, Hon. Mrs.
Cranston, Hon. Mr.
Campbell, Miss
Calvert, Mrs.
Churchill, Miss
Clarges, Mrs.
Clarges, Miss
Chambers, Mrs.
Clive, Mrs.
Chute, John, Esq.
Cooper, Mrs.
Cooper, Miss
Cox, Mrs.
Cornish, Captain

Denbigh, Countess of
Donegall, Countess of
Dives, Hon. Mrs.
Duncombe, Miss
Diebbeg, Miss
Doig, Mrs.
Drummond, Miss

Evelyn, Mrs.

Fox, Lady Mary
Farmer, Captain
Fitzgerald, Mrs.
Fountaine, Mrs.
Fauquier, Miss

Fauquier, Miss Georgiana
Freeman, Mrs.

Gray, Lady
Graham, Mrs.[3]

Hamilton, Lady Elizabeth[4]
Harland, Lady
Howard, Lady Anne
Howard, Lady Juliana
Hulse, Lady
Hotham, Miss
Hutcheson, Mrs.
Hawkins, Mr.

Jefferys, Miss

Keene, Hon. Mr.
Kirkman, Mr. Jacob,

Lisbourne, Lady
Lyttleton, Lady
Lisle, Miss
Lloyd, Mrs.
Long, Miss
Long, Miss Emma

Manchester, Duchess of[5]
Melbourne, Lady[6]
Morton, Countess Dowager
Moyston, His Excellency General
Martin, Mr.

---

3. Possibly Mary Graham, with whom she became friendly in 1776 (Foreman 51–55).

4. Possibly the same Lady Elizabeth Hamilton mentioned in a letter of Dec. 10, 1785 by Lady Elizabeth Foster (Bessborough 102).

5. Lady Georgiana objected to the duchess of Manchester's social snobbery and seems to have known the duchess of Manchester between 1776 and 1778 (Foreman 45).

6. Lady Georgiana was close friends with Lady Melbourne as early as 1776 and earlier, though their first surviving letter only dates from 1780 (Gross 10); this list of subscribers is significant for it may indicate that their friendship dates back to 1773.

Martin, Mrs.
Mathews, Miss
Miller, Mr. Christopher
Montague, Mrs.
Morant, Mrs.
Murry, Miss

Osborne, Miss

Primrose, Lady
Pelham, Miss Mary
Palmer, Miss
Parsons, Mrs.
Plydell, Mr.
Plydell, Miss

Rice, Lady Cecil
Radcliffe, Lady Frances

Spencer, Lady Charles[7]

Scourfield, Mrs.
Sheldon, Mrs.
Stone, Mrs.
Stracey, Mrs.
Surman, Mrs.

Thanet, Countess of[8]
Thompson, Lady Dorothy
Thomas, Miss
Tilson, Mrs. Frances
Tryon, Hon. Miss
Twysden, Colonel

Westmoreland, Countess
   Dowager of[9]
Walke, Mrs.
Warner, Miss Sarah
Woodington, Mrs.

Zimmerman. Mr.

---

7. A friend of Lady Melbourne and mistress of the duke of Bedford (Foreman 333).

8. Lord Thanet and the duke of Dorset visited Georgiana, Duchess of Devonshire, on September 14, 1786 (Foreman 184).

9. Lady Georgiana records Lord Westmoreland's vote with Lord North on April 24, 1780 (Foreman 78).

E M M A;

OR, THE

UNFORTUNATE ATTACHMENT,

A SENTIMENTAL NOVEL.

IN TWO VOLUMES.

A NEW EDITION.

VOLUME THE FIRST,

LONDON:

PRINTED FOR T. HOOKHAM, NEW BOND-STREET.

MDCCLXXXVII.

1787 title page, by permission of the British Library.

E M M A;

OR THE

UNFORTUNATE

ATTACHMENT.

IN TWO VOLUMES.

BY THE AUTHOR OF THE SYLPH.

D U B L I N.

Printed by S. Colbert, (at the Eſtabliſhed Circulating Library) No. 135, Capel-ſtreet, oppoſite Abbey-ſtreet.
1784.

1784 title page: "by the author of The Sylph,"
by permission of the University of Bristol.

1787 frontispiece illustration to vol. 1,
by permission of the British Library.

Emma; or, The Unfortunate Attachment

A Sentimental Novel

MISS EGERTON TO MISS THORNTON
LETTER 1. SUNBURY.

Your absence, my dear Fanny, like that of the sun, has robbed our
little village of all its charms. I traverse, in vain hopes of discovering,
since you have left it, some of those beauties which heretofore
presented themselves to me in every step I took: but when I have
tired myself with walking, I sit down convinced how fruitless my
search has been; for every charm, alas! has fled with you; and the
peopled banks of the Thames present to me a prospect dull and
dreary as the deserts of Arabia.—It was your presence which enliv-
ened all the scene; and when I ceased to see you, nought else
remained which could give pleasure to my eyes.

Judge of the change in me when I tell you, that I have forsaken
my harpsichord, refuse to join the gay throng though courted to
return to it by all those who should have most interest with me, and
make so little use of my voice, that my father asked me seriously this
morning, "whether I had forgotten how to sing?" In answer, I
attempted our favorite song in the Padlock, but had not finished the
first verse when the recollection of past days deprived me of the
power of proceeding—I stopped—My kind father, perceiving my
distress, wiped off the trickling tear, and proposed a ride.—Glad to
quit the painful task I had undertaken, and happy always to comply
with his inclination, I instantly prepared myself to accompany him to
Burton, from whence we were not permitted to return until late in
the evening.

Lady Catherine, in whom good-breeding and sincerity are so happily blended, as to form at once the Woman of Fashion and the best of friends, omitted nothing that could help to dissipate the chagrin she saw me labouring under; whilst her lively daughter told me, with a frankness which commanded belief, that nothing should be wanted on her part to console me for the loss of my agreeable companion; but added at the same time, that Mr. and Mrs. Bridges were unreasonable creatures, if they imagined that Miss Thornton was to bury herself in their old mansion merely to please their humor.

When she had talked herself out of breath on this subject, she desired me to put on my *best looks*, and to prepare for *conquest*, as she meant to introduce me to some *smarts* who had promised to dine that day at Burton.

The little attention I paid to her *advice* was, I must flatter myself, the reason why her prediction was not verified. I passed the whole day without receiving any homage more than the rules of politeness required, and left the gentlemen in the evening in as absolute possession of their hearts as if I had never made my appearance. Out of the four who were there, but one of them was entitled to any degree of my notice, as he only had any thing extraordinary in his air and address; besides which, he is a near relation of Lady Catharine's. The other three did not rise above the rank of *beaux*, and owed all their gentility to the cut of their clothes: but mortals who are indebted to the dexterity of their taylors alone for all their consequence, are not subjects on which my pen can dwell with any chance of pleasing you or myself.

I quit these therefore for our worthy Sidney: yet I cannot say much of him either, as he seldom writes to Sunbury; but there is a pleasure in mentioning our friends, though we have nothing new to say of them. Have you heard lately of him? You know I always supposed him more partial to you than to me; which makes me now imagine that you are better informed of his situation. I confess myself somewhat curious to know how he passes his time at Newark. He told me when he left this, that he should not be able to return to us before the autumn; but I hope some change in their orders may bring his regiment nearer to us before that time; for it is too much to be at once deprived of my Fanny, and of this amiable tutor likewise. In losing you both I have lost all relish for any employment, but that of writing. Expect then to be frequently troubled with epistles from

Your ever affectionate,

Emma Egerton.

From the SAME to the SAME.
Letter 2. Sunbury.

Still my dearest friend, you will find me murmuring at your absence;
for time cannot lessen my regret for a misfortune which every hour
increases by furnishing me with new instances of my loss. If Mirth
comes with its smiling train, I sigh because my Fanny is not here to
partake of, and to insure its continuance; if Dullness intrudes, I
lament that she, who would have kept it at a distance, is no longer
here: thus in every turn your idea (all that now remains with me)
becomes my torment.

My kind, my indulgent father tries every art to make me forget
my grief, and is continually finding out some new amusement for
me. The whole neighbourhood at times is invited to the most
sumptuous entertainments at our house; at others we go to theirs.
Private balls are much in vogue with us; Cotillons and Allemands
prevail most, tho' we now and then admit of a few favorite English
country-dances for the sake of variety. I have had many partners,
but none of them equal to Mr. Walpole, who is polite enough to
tell me he finds no pleasure in dancing with any one but me. This
distinction has its charms, as he is universally allowed to have a fine
taste, and excels so much in this art himself, that I cannot help
supposing him a good judge.

I should have told you, that the name of Walpole belongs to the
gentleman, of whom I made such favorable mention in my last. He has
been ever since at Burton, where he is exceedingly caressed by the whole
family. Lady Catherine speaks highly of his munificence; Mr. Bishop
declares him to be the most accomplished young man he has seen lately;
and Miss Bishop, who flirts with all mankind without loving any one,
protests that her cousin would be the most enchanting fellow in the
world, if he was not so particular in his notions as to be a restraint upon
her vivacity sometimes, and so very refined in his sentiments as not to
leave himself a chance for happiness. My father says he is the *most
agreeable* man he knows. I do not say *quite* so much, though I allow
him to be uncommonly handsome, and very pleasing. He is just returned from his travels, and has acquired all the advantages which such a
tour can give, without having any thing of the coxcomb. His fortune is
large, and his connections noble. He is, in short, *tout comme il faut.* All
this I know, without having a wish to engage more of the notice of this
general favorite than just what is sufficient to give me a tolerable opinion
of myself; which I am convinced it is necessary to have, in order to
appear in public with any degree of ease.

You may remember how much trouble Sidney had, sometimes, to
make me overcome the *mauvaise honte* which made me so unfit to
shine in company, and which not all his flattery joined to yours could
make me get the better of. Should Mr. Walpole prove more successful, I doubt both you and Augustus will suspect that I pay more

regard to his words than to yours: but let me desire you rather to attribute my improvement to any other cause than to inattention to either of you; the last crime that can possibly be committed by

Your Emma

MISS THORNTON TO MISS EGERTON.
LETTER 3. THE GROVE.

The friend you so tenderly regret, my dear Emma, is not less sensible of your grief than of the misfortune you complain of. An equal sufferer with your self, I am equally afflicted, and mourn the necessity which caused our separation.

On my arrival at home I found my poor aunt, whose spirits had been affected by my long absence from her, much altered in her looks. This new proof of her affection drew severe reflections from me on my own ingratitude, and want of a proper regard for her; but she would admit of nothing that could depreciate me, and seemed to have lost remembrance of every thing disagreeable on seeing me again. My uncle, not less rejoiced at my return, begged me not to think of leaving them soon again, as neither he nor his wife enjoyed any happiness without me.

Indebted as I am to these affectionate friends, will you not call me ungrateful, Emma, when I tell you that I cannot find myself so perfectly happy at the Grove, as I used to be at Sunbury? I argue with myself on this subject to no purpose: reason has very little force when opposed to the ruling wish of our hearts; and I find myself dissatisfied after having repeated over and over again, that no situation can be more eligible than my present. But this is a secret which, you may assure yourself, I carefully conceal from every body about me.

Our neighbourhood is not in itself so well calculated to afford amusement as yours is. Most of the large mansions around us are deserted, either from the *nonage* or the *dotage* of their owners: I cannot therefore boast of the appearance of a Walpole among us, anymore than I can of the *peculiar* favor of a Sidney, not having had a line from Newark since I left you: but without this, I think, I can give a guess at "how he passes his 'time there,'" which for your *satisfaction* I will communicate in the next paragraph.

With his pretty person, embellished with a red coat and cockade, I hold it utterly impossible for him to remain long in any place without attracting the regards of every woman in it; and you know how far his politeness carries him towards the ladies: judge then whether he has not, in this case, employment enough to fill up every hour in the day, what with making parties with some for morning walks and rides, and attending others to the balls and tea-tables.

If this method of accounting for his silence does not please you, my sweet Emma, you must find out one more agreeable to you, and perhaps to him too. This I am convinced of though, that when you accuse him of giving me the preference to you in any respect, you wrong him, without persuading

Your affectionate

F. Thornton.

Mr. WALPOLE to Col. SUTTON.
Letter 4. Burton

I have been at this place ten days, my dear Sutton, during which scarce a moment has passed without some degree of *gaieté*. Would you believe, that amidst all this I have found leisure to fall in love? Yet it hardly amounts to that either; but there is not another phrase which offers itself at this instant to express what I feel for a little girl of seventeen, who visits here frequently, and who carries off all the admiration without knowing the meaning of the word. She is such an absolute novice in the ways of the world, that she does not understand the common language of it. When I am her partner in the dance, and squeeze her soft hand, she looks surprised, but shows no other emotion: if I compliment her beauty, she blushes without giving credit to a syllable I say. You will wonder, George, where this phenomenon has been bred. Faith, I did not imagine that such a being could exist in this age; but Emma Egerton has proved me mistaken. She is the only daughter of a sensible and worthy man, who is Bishop's intimate friend, and who has educated this darling child in a very different style from the generality of her sex: wrapped up in her, he has never lost sight of her since the death of her mother, who by all accounts was just as deserving of such a blessing as himself.

She is, they assure me, complete mistress of every accomplishment which can adorn a female: if her modesty was not as great as her merit, I might by this have been enabled to have spoken, from my own knowledge, of her uncommon qualifications; but I have not yet prevailed on her to discover more than her skill in music and dancing, in both of which I may venture to pronounce her superior to any English woman of my acquaintance. As to her person, I cannot attempt to describe it, as none of the terms made use of to express beauty will give you any just idea of hers, that being as much out of the usual style as the rest of her perfections. I have seen features more exactly regular, forms more striking; but never was there such an assemblage of the graces to be found in one person! Her whole soul is to be seen in her countenance, which in every turn expresses all that is desirable in woman.

If I was disposed to play the *inamorato*, this is just the object I would chuse; but as I do not fancy I should shine much in this character, I frequently quit her side to *flutter* about her less danger-ous companions. Amongst these Kitty Bishop is not the least charm-ing, though a very different creature from *la belle Emma*; but she is excellent too in *her way*. Never having seen her since she left the nursery until I paid this visit to Burton, her genius was not at all known to me; but it did not take much time to become acquainted with her: all life and spirit, she has no notion of confining herself to the dull forms established in this country, which make our women in general almost afraid of speaking to a stranger. This ease and affability render her easy of access, whilst her wit teaches us to keep at a proper distance; so that no girl is more liked, or more respected, than this.

When vivacity is thus happily tempered, it keeps the possessor safe from the bad consequences which sometimes result from an extraordi-nary flow of spirits, and contributes to the pleasure of those who converse with her. We now and then dispute about the propriety of an action, but she always gets the better of me by the keenness of her repartees.

Lady Catharine and Mr. Bishop are remarkably tender parents: this and one son are all the children they have; and between these they have immense riches to divide. Her Ladyship is the Best Sort of Woman on earth. Do not suppose that I mean, Colonel, she is insipid: she possesses, I give you my word, the highest merit, though that unfortunate expression does not imply so much: her heart is susceptible of the finest feelings, which she indulges freely, and makes, by so doing, the happiness of all around her. I do not know a more valuable friend, or one on whose judgement I would more firmly rely. She dotes on Miss Egerton with the fondness of a mother, and gives her a character which would enslave a heart less cautious than mine: it is not enough for me that she seems angelic; I must be sure of her being more so than any female I have yet met with, before I attach myself to her: her soul must be free from the least inclination to any other man; it must have been always so, or it will not, George, satisfy the delicacy of your friend. You have warned me against indulging this singularity; but it seems to be so interwoven in my nature, that no argument is able to remove it. But at present this is not a mate-rial point, as "I am not in haste to wed."

You are acquainted with Bishop: I shall not then say more of him, than that I join with you in esteeming him as he deserves.

I have already told you, that time passes in the most agreeable manner here; every body seems to be satisfied with it: I am so much so, as not to think of quitting Burton for some time, as I am pressed to continue as long as I can with these worthy people; but I am not permitted to remain longer in my room, as my wild cousin is thundering at my door, and insists on my joining the company, which has been assembled this hour, as she says, and has been impatiently expecting to see me.

Adieu! You never complain of me when I obey a Lady's orders, knowing me to be

Yours *per sempre*,
William Walpole.

MISS EGERTON TO MISS THORNTON.
LETTER 5. SUNBURY.

Fanny, my dear Fanny! Your Emma has been almost reduced to despair since you last heard from her. My beloved father has been on the brink of the grave: a violent fever attacked him a few days after I had written to you, and was near depriving me of the only support heaven has left me. For ten days, medicine proved ineffectual: during that time judge of my distraction by the cause of it. His head was hardly more affected than mine: his disorder was less cruel, from being confined to pain of body. . . . I sent an express to Newark; Sidney came, and brought back Hope to the dwelling it had deserted for many days. The sound of his voice, on his entering the house, was the first joy my heart had known for an age: I flew to receive him, and conducted him to my expiring father: he opened his eyes, and seemed to revive at the sight of the dear Augustus, who expressed all the tenderness of a son for him: his care and incessant attendance are rewarded by the recovery of that friend, to whose generosity the amiable youth owes all he possesses: the sense he entertains of his obligations to him is shown in every action of his life. . . . A dejection of spirits, which they assure me is the common effect of weakness, is all that now remains to disturb me on my dear father's account. We try every method that affectionate duty can invent to divert him: he smiles on our endeavours, though they do not seem as yet to have taken effect.

This alarming incident has broke up our late parties; but the absence of the *gay* world is amply made up to me in the company of two worthier men than any in it. Sidney entertains us with the many adventures, which from his profession he has been engaged in at every place he has been sent to: we pass whole days in my father's apartment, without wishing for any addition to our number, unless my Fanny could make a fourth.

Augustus tells me I am improved since he left me; that I am grown taller. He commends the progress I have made in music: that is now the only thing he gives himself any trouble about: he pretends that he cannot leave Mr. Egerton; but I suspect that he does not chuse to employ himself with one scholar only, and that not *the one* who promised to do him most credit. Beg Mrs. Bridges, my dear friend, to send you back to Sunbury, that I may stand a chance of knowing something more than my Alphabet: she does not guess what an injury she has done me by taking you away; make her sensible of it, and I am convinced she will grant my request.

A note is just brought me from Miss Bishop, containing an invitation for this evening: she will take no denial, and my good father adds his commands to hers. Sidney is to accompany me at his desire also; there is no choice left for me. I go, my dear Fanny; but I leave this pleasing employment with reluctance, though well-dressed beaux and harmonious sounds wait only the arrival of your

Emma Egerton.

MR. WALPOLE TO COL. SUTTON.
LETTER 6. BURTON.

Our pleasures have been damped, and every amusement has ceased, for some time: not a swain but hung his dog, and broke his pipe, during the absence of Emma, who had forsaken us for the last three weeks to immerse herself in her sick father's apartment, administering comfort to him during a long and dangerous illness. To save the rest of mankind from despair, the Fates have calmed his pulse, and restored his fair daughter to us: she made her appearance at Burton yesterday, and joy reassumed its empire. Confinement and anxious care have only faded the roses of her cheek, to show she does not owe her power of charming to the beauties of complexion. She has not yet forgot her apprehensions, though the faculty have positively declared him to be out of danger, and he is permitted to walk about the house: but never had she looked more lovely in my eyes than in this state; the sweet marks of an alarmed sensibility visible in her countenance, and increasing that softness which is so captivating in her. . . . She was escorted hither by a handsome young fellow—in *regimentals* too, George! I felt myself look *rather foolish* when, on going to hand her from the carriage, I perceived she had been better assisted by the lucky man who had the honor of being her companion from Sunbury. I lost no time in enquiring into his connexions with her: Lady Catharine, to whom I addressed myself, bid me, with a laugh, not to fear a rival in Mr. Sidney. As that was no reason for entering into particulars, and I was resolved not to lose the happiness I enjoyed in her presence, I took this advice: depending upon the hint, I banished all doubts, and begged the gentle Emma would favor me with her hand that evening; which she consenting to, I found no reason to envy any other man, as she made no distinction among us. . . .

No sooner had they left us, than, impatient to learn more of *this* Sidney, I engaged Lady Catharine to give me his story, which you shall have in her own words. . . .

. . . "His father, a man of more merit than fortune, was from his infancy the intimate of Mr. Egerton: near neighbours in the country, and educated at the same school, they were parted until Sidney (who was a younger brother) had a commission purchased for him, and went abroad with his regiment: Egerton about the same time went on his travels, and when he returned to England, found his friend had married contrary to the sordid maxims of his family, and was for that cause disregarded by it. Their friendship was now renewed with double warmth; and he who had been favored by fortune would have been happy to have shared his riches with the neglected worthy, had not the noble Sidney scorned to receive, even from the generous Egerton. Death very soon divided these kindred souls; and the survivor found no consolation for his loss, but in transferring his kindness to the unhappy widow and her infant son. . . . Mr. Egerton was on the point of marrying when his friend died; and as soon as he did, he carried home, with his bride, Mrs. Sidney and her boy: the two ladies soon formed an attachment as sincere as their husbands: the Inexorable Tyrant only could dissolve such bands; and Mrs. Egerton soon wept over the grave of her Euphemia, as Mr. Egerton had over Sidney's.————The young Augustus claimed all the tenderness of this worthy pair, and had not reason to lament the loss of his parents, caressed as he was, and treated in every respect as a child of the family.—He was sent to Westminster school, where he soon distinguished himself by his genius: his patron hoped to see him shine in one of the learned professions, and had actually destined him for the Bar; but the father's spirit prevailed, and nothing would satisfy the youth but a commission. Mr. Egerton remonstrated; but he talked in vain to a heart fired with the ambition of acquiring military fame, and much too warm to be confined to plod over lawbooks: finding he could not change the firm purpose of his soul, he at length consented to procure him a lieutenancy.

The little Emma, the youngest and only remaining child of five, was quickly deprived of her excellent mother, and became the sole darling of her father; nor was Sidney (who still remained under the hospitable roof at Sunbury, when he was not obligated to attend his new employment) less fond of her than if she had been his sister: all his leisure hours were dedicated to her improvement; he made her read, write, think, and speak, with propriety. Her father, equally attentive to her education, joined in finishing the accomplishments of a girl who does honor to her two preceptors."

So clear an account of their intimacy has destroyed every shadow of my late fears; and Sidney shall be dear to me, as the friend of Emma.

I am obliged to be at home next week: Digby, Parker, and Vernon, are to be with me. If after an absence of five or six weeks I still feel my heart disposed to return to Burton, I will come again, and try then to thaw the frozen bosom of Miss Egerton. I am not quite certain that I love her enough to be uneasy when I can no longer see her every day: yet the sensations I had on seeing her with Sidney yesterday, do not seem to prognosticate much *peace of mind* to me; I like not these symptoms—they must be ominous. . . . . . . But who can say what the air of Dorsetshire may produce? Absence has frequently been found a specific in such cases; nay, in much more violent attacks than that I sustain. Assure yourself however, that you shall be informed of every step I take.—But what business can you have again in Lincolnshire? It is but the other day you went from thence.—What's become of Miss Nevile? Is she gone down there?— You are reserved, Sutton; and this is no usual thing with you. . . . Take care of yourself—an artful woman will make a fool of you; an amiable one may make you still more unhappy: your temper will not bear you through, as mine will. Be advised by me; come to us at Spring Park, and be satisfied with the friendship of

Yours, W. Walpole.

COL. SUTTON TO W. WALPOLE, ESQ.
LETTER 7. MILFIELD.

It is no good sign with me, my dear Walpole, when you complain of my reserve: it is an infallible test of my being dissatisfied with my actions, when I wish to conceal them from you. Yet it is strange that I should not be satisfied, after having done what was meant to increase my happiness, and what I now think must do it.—Wherefore then have I expressed myself in doubtful terms?—Will not every wish of my heart be gratified in possessing the woman I love?—It must be so—I cannot have mistaken the means of bliss. . . . .

But I am mysterious—In good truth, I have no inclination to speak out; for I can hardly hope to find you a more partial judge, than I have been to myself.

After all however, if a man hurts no one by changing his mind, there can be no harm in it: fickleness of itself would not be criminal, unless its consequences were so; and this innocent failing is all I have to accuse myself of. But I have fallen into the *oracle style* again, which it is necessary I should quit, to enable you to comprehend what I would be at. Take then, in plain English, the account you extort from me. . . . .

True, it is not more than three weeks since I left Waterlands, in which time I have crossed several counties, and spent some days with Beresford at Milfield; and to-morrow I return again to Percy's: carried back by an irresistible impulse, and bound by solemn promise to be there the twentieth of this month. All this for the sake of a woman, and that woman not Miss Neville, though you suspect her to be the cause of my *journeying*. But she is too much engrossed by her sister's affliction to bestow so much attention on me; and she, who was for a long time my friend, my conductress, on whose counsels I could depend with safety, has resigned me up (at my own request, I acknowledge) to one not very capable of guiding even herself: but what she wants in *prudence* is amply supplied in "the sweet variety that's in her;" and then she loves me too, which, let me tell you, to a grateful heart is no small attraction. . . . . I sometimes indeed draw a parallel between the two *charmers*, which does not please me so much as I could desire: for instance, I throw into one scale Harriet Courtney's blooming youth, her beauty, vivacity, and ingenuous manner; into the other goes Priscilla Neville's merits—agreeable, generous, sincere, mild, sentimental: here I stop, lest my favorite nymph, with only her aërial attributes, should be found too light to preserve the balance. It is hardly fair to draw comparisons, since it is possible by so doing to injure very high characters. This is the case here. Harriet is lessened by the superiority of the other; but I do not wish her to be more perfect than she is; she would be less charming if she had fewer *formalities*. I renounce all this reflexion; it answers no end but that of breeding melancholy. To come back then to my story, I have engaged myself to meet this bewitching girl at Waterlands, where I first saw her; and when there, she is to dispose of me as she pleases: aye, should she even chuse to carry me to church with her, I am ready to attend her. . . . . So now, Walpole, you know as much of my destiny as I do myself. If you loved as much as I do, you would not hesitate about returning to Burton; but, I know not how it is, you do not in general appear to reason as I do on every point: yet you are less liable to be imposed upon, when your own *whims* do not throw you into the scrape; for when they predominate, I would not give a rush for all your sagacity. I approve of the description of your Emma; her softness will temper your violence: therefore pursue your *penchant,* and prevail upon her to go to Spring-Park, where I shall be very happy to pay my compliments to her as *Maitresse du Chateau.* Adieu!

Yours,

George Sutton.

Miss EGERTON to Miss THORNTON.
LETTER 8. SUNBURY.

At the conclusion of my last, I informed you, my dear Fanny, of our intention of going to Burton: we accordingly went, and spent the evening in dancing and other gaieties. Mr. Walpole fell to my lot, being a good partner: I own that, excepting our Augustus, I pre-ferred him to every other present: he was in higher spirits than ever I saw him in before, and appeared more agreeable than ever. . . . All the company seemed pleased but Sidney, who either sat with his eyes fixed on the floor in sullen silence or danced so inattentively that Miss Bishop (his partner) could not support his stupidity: she re-proached him continually with it; he did not listen to what she said, but still blundered on. When we got into the chaise to go home, I asked what had caused his uncommon gravity: he made no reply until, repeating the question, I added, that I believed he had left his heart at Newark: he then deigned to break silence, assuring me I was mistaken; but after that, until we got into my father's room, not another word escaped him.

Is not *your friend,* Fanny, much changed? I know not what to think of him. When I went down stairs the next morning, seeing the same discontent still in his looks, I ventured once more to enquire, whether he was well. "Yes, I am," was his short answer.——Have you seen my father to-day? Is he worse than he was? cried I, the last words followed by a shower of tears. He was visibly moved at this, and in the kindest manner begged me not to alarm myself unneces-sarily; that my father was just as well then, as when I saw him the night before, and he hoped there was not the least occasion for my fears. As he finished speaking, the object of my concern entered the room, and put an end to our further discourse on that subject, and to my anxiety—though not to Sidney's gloom, which has not suffered the smallest diminution these three days. He affects to treat me with the most distant respect; and if at any time he directs a speech to me, I am Miss Egerton, or Madam: the familiar name of Emma is never used now by him; one would suppose he had forgotten that I had such an appellation. He even takes such pains to shun me, that when my father goes out of the room where we are sitting, he gets up, walks a few turns about, then quits it in a hurry, as if afraid of being interrupted in his meditations by the impertinence of my conversation. As I perceive he wishes to avoid me, I have not lately attempted to offer to ride or walk with him. When he comes into humor again, he may not perhaps find me so complaisant as I have been.

We are engaged to Mrs. Talbot to-day: Augustus at first positively refused to go; but my father desiring him not to let me go alone, he at last consented.—If he does not make a more entertaining companion than he has been lately, I shall prefer going by myself another time...... I will finish this at my return: until then adieu!

Miss EGERTON in Continuation.

This is not to be borne! I shall never wish more to be accompanied by Mr. Sidney.—He has been ten times more stupid this evening than ever he was; not a syllable did he attempt to utter during our visit, nor was he more loquacious in going or coming from thence.—The vivacity of Mr. Walpole preserved me from the influence of this infectious melancholy, or I should have been horribly dull—but he sung, laughed, and chatted with so much good-humor and ease, that I found time pass away with unusual velocity, until he told me he should be obliged to go into Dorsetshire to-morrow; when the idea of our losing so great a help to our mirth, deprived me of much of what I might have enjoyed. Then, I said, he would be a loss to our Coterie: could he persuade himself that I really thought so, he would not be long absent, was his gallant reply.—I laughed at the speech, and left him to settle the point as he chose. I am apt to fancy he will do it to his own advantage; for, without having any extraordinary portion of self-conceit, he certainly has not the extreme diffidence of poor Augustus; he has, doubtless, been always taught to consider himself as a person of some consequence, and this would inevitably destroy much of that quality.

The clock has struck two; Wednesday morning has broke in upon me before I have done talking of Tuesday night.—Walpole departs to-day; Sidney remains in the dumps.——Alas! Your Emma cannot now hope for any amusement: even sleep forsakes her;—but friendship glows always with the same ardor in the breast of my dearest Fanny's

Affectionate

Emma Egerton.

Miss THORNTON to Miss EGERTON.
Letter 9. The Grove.

Really, Emma, I begin to suspect that you delight in drawing characters, by the sketch you have sent me of Sidney.—Know him again!
Not I truly; for how is it possible I should discover any thing amiable
through the gloom you have drawn him in?—I feel myself afraid of
the *goblin*; but as distance from danger inspires cowards with resolution, I shall venture, notwithstanding the *frightful tales* you tell, to
attack him upon the wonderful alteration of his behaviour. I shall
write to him by this post, and trust to his politeness for receiving a
more satisfactory answer than you have yet done: but should this be
fled with his other charms, and he should send me no more than an
Yes or a No, I shall lay up the letter in my cabinet of curiosities, and
keep it as a match for the Lacedaemonian *if*—which has hitherto
maintained an unrivaled glory among the Laconic answers.—I should
declare him to be in love, but I cannot accuse one of my sex of such
a crime as that of driving *him* to despair; there cannot be such
cruelty in a feminine form surely.

But to be serious, I cannot, my dear Emma, divine the cause of
this fatal change; yet I very sincerely pity the unhappy youth, who,
never having been known to act without reason, cannot now be
supposed to do so: from this I conclude that some heavy misfortune
weighs down his spirit. I have less right to demand his confidence
than you have; nevertheless, as I have often found it easier to write
than to tell a secret, I am not without hopes of prevailing on him to
entrust me with what he refuses to you. This benevolent design
forces me to conclude, with this only addition, that I am always

Yours, *F. Thornton*.

Miss EGERTON to Miss THORNTON.
Letter 10. Sunbury.

"What an enemy to beauty is sorrow! *It feeds*, "like a worm in the
body," on the damask cheek of Sidney: you would not suspect me of
exaggeration could you see him at this time. On his coming down to
breakfast this morning, so pale and unlike his former self, my father
was absolutely shocked at his looks, and asked with earnestness, what
was come to him: he complained of the head-ach, said the heat of
the weather had kept him awake the whole night: taking his hand,
my father protested he was in a high fever, and begged that a physi-
cian might be sent for, which the other absolutely refused consenting

to, saying he should be very well as soon as he went into the air; he
would walk, and that would infallibly restore him to health.—The
moment the breakfast things were removed, I proposed our walking:
he took up his hat to attend me; but his mind suddenly changing, he
desired me to excuse him, as he chose to ride.

I left him to pursue his inclination, and came up to acquaint my
dear Fanny with the unaccountable ways of *her* friend: he cannot be
mine, I am sure, or he would not act thus. . . . .

My dear father is not yet enough recovered from his late indisposition, to attend, as he used to do, to all the trifles that pass: he has
not observed any but the difference in the countenance of his once-
gay Augustus; and this is so well accounted for by his complaint, that
he is not tormented as I am, who see so much more, with a thousand uneasy thoughts about him.

From your letter, which I received to-day, I find you are equally
ignorant of the cause of his wretchedness—nay, then I should not
complain.—Yet, until now, I did not imagine Sidney had paid so
little regard to the rights of friendship: he always told me I should
be unreserved in my confidence, and that concealment became
criminal, when it made my friend unhappy. He speaks better than
he acts, and I am angry with him for teaching me a lesson which
he will not practise himself.—But he is unhappy; he is ill. Ah,
Fanny, how does my heart melt at his sufferings! Compassion has
subdued my resentment. . . .

He is returned: I see him enter the orange-walks, and go towards
the pavilion. I will follow him, I will beseech him to tell me his grief:
if he refuses, I renounce his friendship; it is become an empty name,
and I will no longer be the dupe of his false professions: it is now he
must prove himself sincere, for I will no more be put off with
evasions. * * * * * * * * * * * * * * *

O my friend! What has my indiscreet enquiry produced? Was it
not better to remain in suspense than to acquire the knowledge I
have done?—But whither am I rambling? What will you think of me
when I have repeated to you what I have just learnt from the most
amiable of men? How will you be able to reconcile the affliction I
have expressed, with the happiness of being beloved by Sidney? There
is no other way of doing it, than by recollecting that "Bliss goes but
to a certain bound; Beyond 'tis agony."

Let me, however, be more explicit, and proceed in order, from
the moment I quitted my room to join the dejected Augustus, until I
found myself again in the same place.

I laid down my pen, determined to know from him what had
thus long disturbed him, and followed him as fast as I could walk;
but before I could overtake him, he had turned into the pavilion,
and I saw him seated there in so profound a reverie, that he did not
look up even at my approach: the sound of my voice made him start:

I began by asking how his head was, and hearing *that* pain had been removed by his ride, Tell me, continued I, whether your head was not this morning an excuse for your heart? And when you have answered that, say, Mr. Sidney, how you can make your conduct and your doctrine agree together? Have I not been taught *by you*, that my friends have an indisputable right to partake in all that concerns me; and have I ever concealed a thought from you? Yet you have secrets which I am not allowed to know; you indulge a grief which consumes you, and *your friends* are not admitted to partake of it; and after numberless enquiries, I am still at a loss how to account for your late behaviour.

Do not, Miss Egerton, interrupted he, insist upon my telling you —I should but ill deserve the regard you show for me, were I to discover the cause of my unhappiness. It is not of a nature to be removed by your *compassion*.—Leave then, nor further urge me to reveal what—By heaven, Madam! I would not expose myself to your contempt. . . . . . .

This last word struck me with such astonishment, that, like Echo, I returned it back, and cried Contempt! Without knowing for an instant what to add, until, recovering myself a little, I proceeded to assure him, that it was impossible he should ever merit contempt— You distress me infinitely by supposing so—No, my dear Sidney, (laying my hand on his to detain him) you cannot. . . . .

Am I then dear to you, Emma? said he, taking my offered hand.

Indeed you are, replied I; nor have you ever had reason to doubt it, until your unkind reserve forced me to appear indifferent, for fear of being thought troublesome to you.

Oh! No Miss Egerton, pursued he, you have not *affected* indifference lately for *me*; you acted from your feelings: but I have no right to arraign your conduct; you are directed by principles which are not to be controverted. I am unhappy, I confess it, Madam, but so far from blaming *you* for it, I revere you the more. You have shown your judgement in loving Mr. Walpole. . . .

Mr. Walpole! Exclaimed I with new surprise; how have I behaved to make you accuse me of loving him? How can you be so unjust, Sidney? I did not expect such usage from you: he may be very deserving, but does it follow that I must love him?—So far from it, he is odious to me, since I find you suspect me of loving him. . . . .

Forgive me, my sweet girl, answered he with a voice softened into the tenderest accent, I did not mean to offend you; I only wanted to know whether your little heart had not been caught by the particular notice of an elegant man, who has distinguished you on every occasion, and who is himself universally admired. I am convinced now my Emma never loved him; but—there he stopped, as if he had repented having said so much, yet had more to say on the same subject . . . Impatient to hear the rest, I went on interrogating him. But what, Sidney?—this is not the secret you had to disclose; this has been invented only to draw off my attention: but I will not be so fooled. Why do you still look so dissatisfied, yet pretend it was because I loved Walpole? You say you are convinced now, that I do not love him, yet you still sigh. . . . .

Have I not cause to sigh, Emma? said he, again taking my hand:—can your being indifferent to *him* make me happy, unless it proceeds from your preference to——To whom? cried I (my patience quite exhausted by this delay)—speak, and I promise not to conceal a thought from you.

Your sincerity terrifies me: I dread, my Emma, to hear you pronounce your aversion to your once-favoured Augustus: as your friend you blessed me with an affection, which as a lover I may forfeit. This opened my eyes at once; and, shocked at the part I had played, I was going, without giving him time to add more; when, throwing himself at my feet, and preventing me from stirring out of the place where I was standing, he went on thus.—

You have forced this confession from me, my dear Miss Egerton: I have perhaps offended you by it; if so, I here entreat your forgiveness, and beseech you not to think of leaving me until you have spoke comfort to me—Indeed I am not angry, answered I in a tremulous tone; but let me go.

Now you have told me this, said the encroacher, you shall not leave me, until you have answered another question:——am I hateful to you?

You may guess, my friend, what reply I made; it was such as made Sidney happy, and procured me the liberty of retiring from the pavilion.

I had soon run the length of the garden, and had got half way up the stairs, when I met my father, who stopped and asked if I was well: yes, sir, said I, but with such agitation, that he grew more uneasy, and insisted on my going into the dressing room; where he and Wilson made me swallow a large dose of hartshorn drops. I do not think I ever stood more in need of them. The closeness of the weather was blamed again, and I was requested not to leave my room until the cool of the evening: glad to be excused from going down to dinner, I readily complied with my tender parent's desire; and have passed the time in scribbling to my dear Fanny, whose heart, I am convinced, is so much interested for her friends, as to enjoy their happiness. . . . . . Sidney will smile again, and joy will fill once more the soul of

Your

Emma Egerton.

Miss Thornton to Miss Egerton
Letter 11. The Grove

You may forgive Sidney, my dear Emma, because he put you into good-humor, I suppose, by saying he loved you. It must be owned there is something soothing enough in those words: but I, who have not such a veil thrown over my eyes, and whose anger (by the bye) will not break his heart—I may therefore indulge my vindictive temper. I then protest, that I resent, first, his unjust suspicions of you in regard to Walpole; and, secondly, his closeness in not sooner revealing to you the cause of his *moping*. I have no idea of his concealing from you a point, wherein you were equally concerned with himself: but he knew the gentleness of your disposition, and trusting to that, followed his own vagaries:—lucky was it for him that he had such a one to deal with . . . . . .

Read this to him, for I mean he should be lectured for his misconduct: it is necessary sometimes to let these blustering Lords of the Creation understand that we are capable of *correcting* and *directing* them.

As to the *shock* you felt on perceiving the part you had acted in the *comedy of the Pavilion*, I do not wonder at it; your invincible innocence having carried you much greater lengths than you could have imagined: but you have such an happy countenance, that there was no mistaking your artless intention; therefore there was no occasion for your blushing at what had passed. . . . . . . For the life of me, I could not have heard half of what you did, without having guessed all the rest:—this fore-knowledge would have embarrassed me, and instead of bringing on the declaration by *your leading* questions, I should have gulped and hemmed for an hour without getting out a word, and possibly might have left the garden without any more *delightful* sensation than that of disappointment.—Thus the ignorant frequently have the advantage over us knowing ones.

Having thus given my opinion of the commencement, let me now throw in a few instructions for your future proceedings: they consist chiefly in advising you to acquaint Mr. Egerton as speedily as possible with the situation of your hearts; it is a duty owed to every parent, and what he of all others is most entitled to from his extraordinary merits in that character: besides, the sooner such matters are adjusted, the better.

You may probably doubt my right to counsel in this affair, from my not having yet reached the *years of discretion* but after you have considered the advice, I do not think you can hesitate to allow I am as well qualified for that office, as any staid matron of forty-five.—This I am sure of at least, that no age can render me more sincerely interested in your welfare; which truth I shall subscribe my name at full length to.

Frances Thornton.

Captain SIDNEY to Miss THORNTON.
LETTER 12. Sunbury

Your censure, my dear Miss Thornton, is just: I was to blame in
suspecting my Emma; I was more so in hiding from her the source
of my uneasiness. Could I have been persuaded of this a week ago,
how many dreadful moments should I have escaped! But let me not
regret the past, since it has brought me to such delightful prospects.—Your charming friend repays all my sufferings, and bids me
expect happiness for the remainder of my days.—Yes, Fanny, her love
will ensure my felicity, and your esteem will increase it: this last I will
still hope for, since your *resentment* has only shown itself in the mild
correction of a friendly concern for my failings. . . . .

This passion, so newly discovered by our Emma, has long inhab-
ited the bosom of her Sidney, and seems to have been a native of the
place, so fixed and settled has it ever been. It had grown so powerful
for the last twelve months, that, fearful of betraying myself, I went
early in the spring to join the regiment, hoping that reason, assisted
by absence, would render my attachment less violent. Can you forget
how much it cost me to tear myself from the society at Sunbury?
You then expressed your surprise at the extreme concern I showed at
the thoughts of leaving my friends for a few months.—Ah, Miss
Thornton! You could not then conceive what I felt; will you not now
acknowledge that my distress was natural?—Emma had no need of
concealment; she was grieved at my departure, she did not hide her
emotions, and when I embraced her at going away, she sobbed aloud:
not capable of standing such a scene, I hurried from her, and flung
myself into the chaise. I passed hours in that journey, which even
now I shudder at recollecting: I endured all the tortures of despair.—
Time softened the horrors of it, but it could not destroy them; and I
was still unhappy, when the illness of Mr. Egerton recalled me to this
loved spot. Emma received me with the highest testimonies of joy:
soon after I came, Heaven restored her worthy father to her
prayers. . . .

'Till now, I had been of the general opinion of the world, which
supposed his only child, from the appearance he had always made,
would be entitled to a large fortune at his death: this circumstance had
entirely destroyed my hope; I would not for the creation have incurred
the suspicion of wishing to enrich myself by marrying the *heiress* of Mr.
Egerton, though I doated on his *daughter* to distraction.

At my arrival, I heard the physicians had pronounced the fatal
sentence, and that my friend, my generous benefactor, was thought
not to have many hours to live. Sensible of his own danger, the good
man had prepared to meet his fate with a fortitude consistent with
that character. One thought only embittered the pangs of death—his
little darling was to be left friendless and unprovided for, exposed to

all the hardships of a scanty fortune and disappointed expectations. He called me to his bedside the morning after I came, and then owned, for the first time, the real situation of his affairs, condemning the thoughtless prodigality he had been guilty of, and beseeching me to guard the sweet Emma from the snares that might be laid to betray her unsuspecting virtue, and to reconcile her to the misfortune of living on an income that would but barely supply the necessaries of life; a thousand pounds being all he could secure to her from the wreck of a considerable fortune: his place still furnished him with an handsome annuity; but as that would cease with his life, it made no provision for his daughter.

Pardon me if I say that at such a time I could feel joy: what I had just heard gave me, I confess, a sensation so near to it, that no other word will express my meaning; it was now I could first indulge a thought of her becoming mine. Small as my fortune is, it would preserve her from the wretchedness her father feared: the husband of his Emma would guard her from the wrongs, and by his tenderness soften all the miseries of life, repaying to her the obligations he owed to her parents.—Thus duty and love would unite in blessing the wretch, who until this hour had never dared to hope......

I did not then think it proper to declare my sentiments; but assuring my friend that I would be as good a guardian to his child, as he had been to me, I waited until I had sounded the heart of Emma, before I spoke more openly of my designs; for without her love nothing could be certain.—A favorable turn in the disorder put an end to our immediate apprehensions, and when time had strengthened our hopes, Mr. Egerton began to insist on our going into company again, dreading lest confinement and close attendance in a sick room should affect the health of his beloved girl.

At his request I attended her to Burton, and found that her return diffused a pleasure which her absence had robbed the party of: every one was eager to congratulate her on her father's recovery, and on her own releasement: Mr. Walpole (whom you know by character) was more violent than any one else in expressing his raptures. . . . The music being called for, the choice of partners became the next object; and I saw the envied Walpole lead my Emma to her place. Until that moment I had never felt the torment of jealousy: I became uneasy to myself, and disagreeable to the company. Miss Egerton was not struck with the change in my behaviour, till my lively partner (Miss Bishop) began to rally me unmercifully on my stupidity: she then asked me what ailed me: I hardly answered the question; and finding it vain to endeavour at assuming a chearfulness foreign to my heart, I bore with all they chose to say on my unusual dejection, without attempting to account for it.—After we broke up, Emma was scarcely seated in the chaise when she again renewed her enquiries: I now, unjust as I was! attributed the attention she paid to me only to Walpole's not

being by, who, I fancied, had engaged all her notice during the
evening: I therefore showed very little regard to the kindness she
then seemed to have for me, and did not speak to her until we got
to Sunbury.—The next day, and the next to that, passed without
our entering into conversation; for indeed I avoided her, unless
when Mr. Egerton was with us.—On the Tuesday following, the
same set of company met at Mrs. Talbot's: Walpole was even more
particular to Miss Egerton than he had been when I had seen them
together at Burton—his vivacity amused, his partiality, I thought,
charmed her: he spoke of leaving this neighbourhood in a few days
after: I heard the dear girl tell him, "He would be a loss—" I saw
his eyes sparkle with pleasure at the speech, and his answer
confirmed my suspicions. . . .

My wretchedness was not completed: I spoke not; I knew not
what was said to me. In the midst of my madness, I had however
honor enough to think it would be the height of injustice to reproach her: she had not deceived, she had not slighted me for him;
for she knew not that I loved her: there was no crime then in
preferring another; he was a man to be preferred to most others; and
I applauded the taste which doomed me to misery. . . . She saw
enough to find out that I was unhappy: she had asked the cause, and
I had refused to speak it: she grew angry at last, thought I treated
her with indifference, and showed so much resentment, that I imagined she hated me. This added new stings to my despair, and I
passed that night in agonies I had never known before.

When I appeared at breakfast, the kind Mr. Egerton was frightened at my looks, and the gentle soul of Emma seemed not less
moved. I complained of the headache, mentioned walking as a cure
for it: she condescendingly offered to accompany me. This was the
time in which I meant to prove myself worthy of her esteem at least.

She loves Walpole, cried I to myself: he can offer her a fortune
worthy of her merit—she will be happy—I will not disturb her felicity
by letting her know she has made me miserable—I will bury in
silence this luckless passion, and apply for leave to go into the
Russian Service—my dying in the field will spare her the regret of
having driven me to despair—her sensible heart shall not suffer an
unnecessary pang for me. . . . .

Knowing that, if I trusted myself with her, her softness would
undo my best-formed purpose, I begged she would excuse my
walking with her, as I thought riding would be most serviceable to
me. I did not stay out long, but came back, unperceived as I
supposed, and retired into the pavilion, intending to continue
there until I had summoned resolution enough to conceal my
disorder from the eyes of the family: I had just thrown myself on
a seat, when the musical voice of my angel roused me from the
dream I was in.

Her eloquence prevailed; I revealed to her all I felt, and was rewarded for the confidence I placed in her.

Come, my amiable friend! And witness our happiness: Emma is not quite satisfied without you; I am not *jealous* enough in my nature to quarrel with you, though so highly distinguished by her favor: come then, and be convinced you will always find a most sincere admirer in

Augustus Sidney.

MISS THORNTON TO MISS EGERTON.
LETTER 13. THE GROVE.

There are indispensable duties belonging to every connexion we form in life: those of a friend, my dearest Emma, are as numerous, and as obligatory, as any. It is in this light I venture to speak to you with a freedom which nothing else would authorise, but which this certainly will excuse: yet, should I exceed the limits which you prescribe me, let me entreat you to think the warmth only of my zeal for your welfare has drawn me into the fault; and your heart, I am sure, will pardon an error which springs from such a motive.

Taught from common report to consider your fortune as large, I enjoyed the idea of your bestowing on Sidney your hand, and by that means raising from mediocrity to affluence a mortal who would do credit to the highest rank, since only this was wanting to give lustre to his extraordinary merits.—It has ever been a maxim with me, that, if there be enough to provide decently for a family, it matters not which party brings the means. When a person loves, there is no great compliment in making the fortune of the object: it is done with a view of gratifying the passion; and therefore, if there is any obligation in the case, it is the receiver who confers it: and knowing the generosity of your temper, I was convinced your thoughts agreed with mine. Mr. Egerton is so indulgent a parent, and has such a liberal way of thinking, that I could not doubt his consent to your union with his beloved Augustus, although it would bring no increase of wealth with it.—Matters thus settled in my own mind, I encouraged an attachment which promised such happy consequences; but, undeceived by Sidney's letter, from which I learn that your expectations are reduced to a very small inheritance, I find my notions exceedingly changed in regard to you both: I tremble, my dear girl, at the dreary view which offers itself to me, when I reflect on the many disasters attending such imprudent matches. Do not hastily enter into engagements which will last when every inducement to them has fled: wait some years, at least until your lover's services shall have raised him in his profession. . . . I am at a loss what to advise, but my fears increase momently for you: they may however proceed from an excess of prudence, or from want of a thorough knowledge of things.

Let me hear soon from you; and, if you can dispel these troublesome mists of imagination, I shall rejoice to see the prospect brighten, as I am, believe me,

Most sincerely yours,

F. Thornton.

MISS EGERTON TO MISS THORNTON.
LETTER 14. SUNBURY.

The friendly manner in which my Fanny speaks to me, deserves the most candid dealing on my part. You are entitled to know every circumstance relating to me; even the basis of my future expectations shall not be concealed. . . . . .

You fancied, my dear friend, until you received Sidney's letter, that my father could bestow a large fortune on me, and your conclusions on the supposition were worthy of your noble character.—I never thought of the provision that might be made for me by the best of parents, who, I have always found, consulted my real interest in every instance: I did not know, until you informed me, that it would not be in his power to give me much. The knowledge of it caused no other regret, than that which arose from the thought of not adding to my lover's fortune. I told him this: he cursed his own folly in not enjoining you to secrecy on this head, as he never intended I should hear it. He rejoices at the circumstance, and bids me not to repine at what secures his bliss. Interested as I am in that, judge whether I am not already consoled for not being an heiress! He has not more than three hundred a year to offer me; but, my dearest Fanny, is not that enough, when people love as we do? I have no wishes which that sum will not supply; and Augustus swears he does not desire a larger but for my sake; if I am contented, he is entirely so. How many happy beings live on less!—The joys of possessing immense riches are all imaginary: with more confined desires one enjoys just as many with small possessions: it depends on ourselves, not on our wealth, whether we shall be happy or not.—Contented *minds* are capable of supplying more precious treasures than Peruvian *mines* can do.———I am not ambitious of eclipsing the rest of the world; nor does avarice tempt me to wish for gold to look at: what use then can I have for more?

You may say, perhaps, that with much money I might do much good. I will not satisfy myself with answering you in the common manner, by observing that few of those who are able, are willing to bestow benefits: I would not suppose my heart so bad, as to suspect it would feel less in any situation than it does now for the distressed. But let us examine who those are to whom we give that title, and we shall find that the demands on our purses are very trifling: the common objects of charity are relieved at a very small expence; the *scraps* and leavings of the most economical table suffice to feed numbers of those.—To the *unfortunates* of an higher class a tear dropt in sympathy is a more acceptable donation than an handful of gold; and it is for these I have always suffered most. But I have obviated the objections you might raise on both sides, and these are the only subjects on which I could possibly have been made uneasy with a moderate income.

Could wealth procure certain happiness, Mrs. West, whom you must remember to have seen here, would have been living at this time.—She gave up Mr. Lesley, to whom she had been solemnly engaged, for Mr. West, who offered her a large settlement and all the charms of affluence:—there was no great difference in the characters or persons of the two men; and her friends applauded her *discern-ment* in accepting of the highest bidder.—They married; the world pronounced her happy, and every appearance confirmed this sentence: yet this glittering beauty pined in the midst of splendor, and died two months ago of a broken heart, after possessing for four years the riches to which she had sacrificed every other consideration.—Mr. Lesley, on the contrary, with a more amiable woman, partakes of the highest happiness, though he has not as many hundreds a year as Mr. West has thousands.

It may not be fair, very likely, to draw a general conclusion from one example: my experience does not furnish me with more, and my heart does not require another to convince it of the inutility of money . . .

Sidney will speak to my father to-morrow: his content will sanctify my choice; he will approve the disinterested sentiments we both profess—sentiments which his own precepts have taught.—A doubt now and then arises, suggested by my *Fanny's fears*, and damps my joy; but I banish it instantly, and consider it as an insult on that kind father, who has never yet made me feel his power by contradiction, and who will not now show himself more averse to comply with the inclination of

Your Emma Egerton.

Captain SIDNEY to Miss THORNTON.
Letter 15.

It is all over, my dear Miss Thornton, and Sidney bids adieu to every faltering hope! Banished be every thought that cheated me with ill-founded schemes of happiness, the fond illusions of a distempered brain, destined as I was to the wretchedness I inherited from my birth!—It was madness to believe Mr. Egerton would give *me* his daughter; and his refusal brings death with it—

Oh, Miss Thornton, can you imagine distress equal to mine!—But you and—you, who are so well acquainted with my Emma, may guess what the loss of her must occasion—you will feel for my sufferings; and you alone shall hear the story of my woes.

Raised from my dejection by her kindness, my doating soul was carried beyond the reach of fears; and after hearing her say she loved me, I defied the malice of fate.—I told my love to Mr. Egerton, and besought him to bless me with her hand, not supposing he could deny a request which *my folly* called reasonable: he listened to me with a mixture of pity and surprise: I saw his countenance change, the instant he understood the purport of my speech; but my infatuated imagination could not be persuaded to suspect it could be unfavorable to me—its wildest sallies of fury now will not let me condemn him for his cruelty to me: he was not less affected than myself, when, after a heart-felt struggle, he spoke the following words. . . . "And would you, Sidney, ruin yourself and Emma? Would you entail beggary on your posterity?"—These fatal sounds gave me the first idea that I could yet be unhappy.—I was going to speak again, when he stopped me by saying, "Hear me, Augustus, not so much as the father of Emma, as the common friend of both . . . The ties of nature are not stronger in my breast than those of friendship; nor is your peace less dear to me than hers. I esteem your generous proposal; it is such as does honor to you: but the higher you are raised in my opinion, the more unwilling I am to involve you in misfortune. A large inheritance does not of itself constitute happiness, but a very small one is absolute misery. Could you bear to see a beloved wife and her helpless infants enduring all the hardships of poverty, and perishing in wants which you could not relieve?—Could your heart support horrors caused by your own imprudence? You are not aware, my dear Sidney, of the torment of leaving a family unprovided for!" His own situation for a moment checked his accents—I attempted again to speak, and was not more capable . . . Taking me by the hand, when he had a little recovered himself, he thus went on—"I would convince you that nothing but power is wanting to make me consent to your demand: could I give my daughter fifty thousand pounds, no other man should have her; but I cannot seal her ruin, and yours too, by consenting to your union.—I do not talk to your passions; it is your judgement I appeal to: and let that, in a calmer hour, decide the cause. . . . Take three or four days to consider of what I have said; argue the case with your usual candor; then tell me, my friend, my Augustus, tell me then, whether I have injured you in this refusal!—If you can help it, do not see my girl during the time I would have you take for consideration; your reason will not have fair play in her presence.—I will not add more; you are too much moved at this time to attend any longer to me;—but remember, Sidney, it is on your *honor* I depend."

It shall not disappoint you (exclaimed I to myself, for Mr. Egerton was gone): he who has dared to love thy Emma, dares not betray her into misery; satisfied to bear the whole weight of his own, provided she does not feel any part of it. . . Ah! Will she not feel it? cried I the next minute: there's the sting. She loves as well as I do, and her soul will be as deeply wounded by a separation; our sufferings must be mutual. What is this honor which Mr. Egerton depends on? A mere chimera, raised but to disappoint our views; there is more *real honor* in drying the tears of my love—Emma shall be mine. As I finished this, I was going to cast myself at her feet, to propose her going off with me. That thought, thank heaven! vanished as soon as I had formed it; the influence of virtue again enlightened my mind, and made me look with terror on the project. Shall I teach my lovely pupil a new lesson added I, and destroy the very charms I adore? Can I hope that her person alone will content me, after having deprived her heart of its most valuable qualities?—Is it by disobedience I would secure her love?—and is it by robbing my benefactor of his only child, that I would repay the debts I owe his bounty? The conflict now became too great to be endured, and in the transports of my frenzy nothing appeared too horrible to be attempted: quite overcome, at length I flung myself on the floor, and continued for some time in silent agony; then starting up, I rang the bell, and ordered my horses to be got ready, not clearly understanding what I meant to do; but after riding about for some hours, I determined on coming to London; where as soon as I arrived, I made application for leave to go into the Russian service: it cost me some trouble to procure it; but through the interest of Lord—it was at last obtained: and at the end of the week I dispatched a letter to Mr. Egerton, acquainting him, that his decree had been obeyed; that I submitted to his dictates; but that I could never bring myself to visit his house again; and as a proof of this, that a chaise then waited to convey me to Portsmouth, from whence I now write to my dear Miss Thornton; waiting only a change of wind to embark, quite indifferent as to what may befall me in a strange land, and firmly resolved never more to return to this.—

If I could give utterance to the pains that distract my heart, you might, my friend, conclude that they would find some mitigation.———Complaints are great helps to the unfortunate, but the ill-fated Sidney is not of the number of those who can waste their sorrow in murmurs.—Unhappy as he is, of whom can he complain?———Emma was too amiable not to be loved; her father too sensible of her worth, not to prize it highly.—Is then any fault to be found?—O Miss Thornton! Pity the wretch who is thus situated . . . . . Comfort your angelic friend; teach her to forget that lover, who would have sacrificed his life for her; who gives up his happiness in hopes of securing hers—who doats, who despairs! . . . . who retains no sense but of her loveliness, and of his own misery.—A signal calls us on board—Adieu for ever!

Yours, A. Sidney.

Mr. WALPOLE to Col. SUTTON
Letter 16. Spring-Park.

Positively I must go back to Burton: after an absence of three weeks, this Emma still dwells in my thoughts, and presents herself so constantly before me, that I can fancy nothing else: she has destroyed all those pleasures which heretofore delighted me—my friends wonder what has happened to me!—my flirts forsake me . . . but if she will love me, George, what need I care for any one else of the charming sex? She told me the night before I left Burton, "that I should be a loss to their Coterie:" she looked too as if she felt it—who knows, my friend, but she may have thought of me since? . . . If there is sympathy in our souls, she has not thought of another creature.—My company is still with me, and mean to stay some time longer.—You are by this happily arrived at Waterlands, and living on Miss Courtney's smiles: happy Sutton! . . . I said above, that I was forsaken by *my flirts.* The anecdote I am going to relate will prove the truth of it: but you will observe, that I have still *spirit* enough left to disregard such attempts.—

Some one proposed the other evening, that we should all go to B. where there is a subscription assembly once a fortnight, when the whole neighbourhood meet, in order to be *sociable*; the old women, to squabble over cards; the young ones, about partners: and when they have all fretted and fumed for four or five hours, they part, protesting they have had a most *agreeable* meeting. Without hoping for any very high entertainment, it was agreed that we should go, and accordingly we made our appearance in the ball-room about eight o'clock: four beaux were no unwelcome guests, and the ladies eyes told us as much. We took our rounds, bowing to some, and staring at others. After examining the features of each female, we got

up to the top of the room, where I soon espied Lady Caroline
Warren: she has long looked upon me as her captive, and as I had
not yet given her room to suppose me changed, I immediately
engaged her: Parker took her friend Miss Villars. . . . Our two lazy
companions pretended they were too nice to take partners, after we
had chosen the fairest among them: they sat by, equally despised by
the dowager and the spinsters.

You have seen Lady Caroline—she is not as pleasing as Miss
Egerton, but few women are so beautiful as her ladyship. As to her
understanding, I have always been so taken up in looking at her face,
that I have never been at leisure to take notice of that: but for *heart*,
George, that was totally forgotten in her composition; she knows not
sensation, but what arises from vanity: admire her beauty, and she
becomes charmed, not with you, but with your conversation: make
love to her like a hero in romance, she will listen to all you say—but
ask for a return, and she does not comprehend you.—The anxieties
of love might be detrimental to her bloom, and she would rather see
the world perish, than have that hurt.—I knew her perfectly well,
therefore was not surprised when I saw her quite out *of sorts* with her
partner, who, to speak sincerely, was drawing comparisons not much
to her advantage, and did not flatter her as usual. Digby, who was
idle, soon perceived the discontented looks she cast on me, and took
every opportunity of paying his court to her. When the second dance
was finished, she pretended to be fatigued, said she had promised her
mother not to dance more than two, and contrived to place herself
between him and me.—I was now become a mere cypher; not a
syllable did she address to me, and I heard her other neighbour run
on at a rate that would have satisfied the vainest of her kind. I
am not accustomed to be thus neglected—Vernon laughed—I found
myself piqued—knowing her dislike to Miss Gore, who has long
rivalled her with the men, and who has more cleverness, if she has
not quite so finished a form; when I saw her approach the bench we
were sitting on, I instantly got up, insisting on her taking my seat:
she had refused dancing that night, so that I encroached on no
man's property. Lady Caroline turned her head to see who I had
placed next to her: I stood leaning down, near Miss Gore, and
appeared to be entirely engaged by her conversation, without paying
the least regard to her: the lady was offended; I enjoyed my revenge,
and in less than ten minutes Digby was left to talk by himself; for
Lady Caroline attended only to the new-formed party.—She soon
after signified her inclination to go down the next dance; but I
begged she would not run the risque of *fatiguing* herself too much,
told her the weather was warm, and that Lady Surry would be
displeased with me, was she to exceed the *promise* she had made
her . . . It was her turn now to be piqued: she got up to go into the
card-room—I asked Miss Gore to go with me, observing that she

would find that a more pleasant place to sit in than the ballroom: she consented, and we got into a new scene of action; but it was not a more agreeable one to the haughty beauty, for I still continued to distinguish her rival. . . . The two ladies spoke now and then to each other: I was not obliged to take notice that it was with particular coldness; and I continued to mortify the fair one, who began hostilities, without pretending to resent her ill-usage.

We came home, and criticized on the behaviour of the female world: Vernon sneer'd at it like a man who had no tender connexions with it: poor Digby, humbled by his *fall from favor*, spoke highly of its charms, but sighed when he had done: the more fortunate Parker defended the ladies cause with good-humor: I should have been severe on the whole, had I not remembered the amiable Emma, who has merit enough to save the rest of her sex from my censure; and for her sake, I joined Parker in calling them the Best Work of the Creation. Adieu.

Yours, W. Walpole.

Miss EGERTON to Miss THORNTON.
Letter 17. Sunbury.

Let me, with returning health, resume my pen, and tell my Fanny, now, alas! The only friend I have, the sufferings I have endured.— Cruel Memory! Recall not those happy hours when joy sparkled in each line, and every sentence conveyed some new pleasure! But come, dark Oblivion of all past happiness, and, assisted by Despair, help me to paint the horrors that now surround me! O what a blow has my fond heart sustained!—Sidney, dear-loved name!—no more shall thy sound gladden my drooping spirits!—no more shall Emma have the blessing of having thee speak the words of wisdom and instruction to her! . . .

Why play thus with the suspence of my Fanny? Rather let me endeavour to calm my bewildered senses, and recollect the scattered fragment of my sad history. . . .

I could give no account of my Augustus, until a week ago, when I heard he had sailed for Russia—that was the only time he has been mentioned to me since the day after I had written my last—that dreadful day, which in my folly I had called lucky, brought with it the end of every joy. . . . My father (be witness, Heaven! I impeach not his tenderness) was sought by Sidney, who wanted to obtain his consent to our marriage: knowing his design, I retired into my dressing-room as soon as breakfast was over, and waited there some

hours in anxious expectation: every stir, during this time, caused a
flutter: and my heart bounded at an unusual rate when I heard his
steps in the passage: my eyes were cast down at his entrance: I felt
my face glow—but what became of me when on looking up, I
perceived my father tottering, and scarcely able to reach the chair
next to me!—I now foreboded the impending mischief, and without
waiting to hear what he was going to say, I threw myself on his neck,
crying, "O, Sir, you have already pronounced my doom; your looks
have forbidden me to hope:—you would have met me with your own
smiling countenance, was I to have been happy!"—Tears now supplied the place of words—he did not try to stop them, but looking
on me with compassion, his own eyes moistened.—"My child," said
he, embracing me, "do not disturb yourself thus with apprehension—
you have to deal with an indulgent parent, not with an insulting
tyrant who speaks his will, and will be obeyed without giving a
reason—your distress rends my heart—I am not equal to the task
which you and Sidney have imposed upon me.—Be more composed,
my Emma; let me beseech you to consider your father, whose peace
depends on yours, who lives for your happiness, and who, to pro-
mote that, would forget every thing else.—Attend to what I have to
urge; I will repeat what I said to Augustus: he is satisfied with me;
and will my daughter be more refractory?"—I promised by signs (for
speech was denied me) to hear, to be composed.—He then told me
all that had passed between him and Sidney; but my disordered head
does not retain one word of a conversation which from its effects
rendered me incapable of reflection: for, a short time after it was
ended, I was put to bed in a high fever, which brought on a delirium that lasted for several days; during which my father never
quitted me.—Wilson tells me, he would not suffer another attendant
to be about me whilst I continued to rave. On the fifth day I began
to regain my senses, and with them new aggravation to my misfortunes—I called incessantly on Death to come to my relief, but my
wishes were again thwarted; I was not to be so soon indebted to him
for his assistance; reserved doubtless, to be a monument of the rigor
of fate.—A whole fortnight, passed in a sick bed, reduced me to a
skeleton: I was not able to move when the fever left me. . . . It was in
this low state, that my father chose to acquaint me with Sidney's
having left England.—When we have once encountered the *worst* of
evils, we become insensible to smaller ones: I had lost all hope from
my father's refusal; the departure of my lover could not now kill me:
I heard it with such composure, that it astonished my informer:
dreading the effect of concealed grief, he tried to make me more
unreserved, by saying,

"Do you not regret his departure, my dear?—Indulge your
sorrow; your father will weep with you, Emma; he loves Augustus, he
mourns his loss. Do not be ashamed to shew your tears, they will

flow from a good cause; and I should esteem your heart less, was it not sensible of the worth of such a friend." The tears trickled down his cheek whilst he spoke; mine wanted but such an example to make them flow: we continued thus for more than an hour, and I found my heart lightened by this discharge. My father, at last regaining his voice, continued the conversation. "Sensibility, my dear child, which makes the disgrace of the weak and base, is the glory of the virtuous; it gives merit to every action; it leads them to the height of perfection: the insensible cannot find out a path, to which the heart alone can guide one; the practice of virtue with them is the effect of constitution; if they do right, it is because they feel no temptation to do wrong. You my sweet girl, are not of this set: in the midst of your sufferings, your father rejoices to find you are possessed of the treasure of sensibility.—It encourages him to hope, that she who has felt the force of love, will not be indifferent to the filial duties, and to the calls of friendship . . . Lament, my Emma, the lover you have lost; I consent to your bewailing him with all the violence of disappointed passion—but when you have paid sufficient tribute to his memory, I shall expect to share your tenderness—I claim it as your parent, I beg it as your friend: in those characters I will even now speak to you, not as to a weak woman who loves, but as to a rational being capable of feeling what I say. To mention my affection for you would be unnecessary, since every action of my life proves it: the return you have made has been full recompence for all I have done. If, in disposing of your heart without consulting me, you swerved, strictly speaking, from the obedience you owed me, I had no right to complain of you, since I exposed you to the danger, by placing in your way an object to be loved. I was not conscious of my error until it became too late to remedy it; but, grieved as I was upon discovering your attachment, I never once attempted to reproach you or Sidney with that as a crime, which, I confess, I could not help thinking reflected honor on you both. I only regretted, that fortune had been less partial to you than nature: but, as that could not be helped, it was my duty to interfere, and break off a connexion which threatened inevitable destruction.—Happily, the same principles which had caused the mischief, proved its antidote: the virtue of Augustus overcame his love; it gave me back my daughter when despair had hurried her to the brink of the grave. The same sentiment will now assist her in conquering an imprudent passion. I know her soul is able to triumph over every obstacle to its greatness; and whilst her lover is gathering laurels in the field, she will not be less heroic by her victory over love.

Shew me, my dear, that I am not mistaken; every effort you make will bear its proper value with me . . . I will not hurry you into dissipation, for I would have your cure the perfected work of reason, not the half-finished one of pleasure.—There was a time when the company of your father made you happy; that time, I am sure will come again, and I will wait its return with patience."

Was this kindness, my dearest Fanny, to be resisted? My heart told me it was not; and I obeyed its dictates in saying—Yes, my dear father, that time must come again: even at this hour, when plunged into the depth of melancholy, I feel its approaches.—Your daughter will atone for the indiscretion that has given you pain—she will henceforth be directed by you in every movement of her heart; it shall not beat but at your command. . . . After expressing all that parental tenderness could utter, he quitted the room in order to allow me leisure to recover my exhausted strength . . .

Ah! My Fanny no sooner had the agitation subsided, which this discourse had caused, than the idea of my Augustus destroyed again all the pious purposes I had made, and my soul owned no power but his.—Even at this time it rebels against the authority that would banish him from my remembrance, and threatens to take its flight with him—would it would do so! Then should your Emma die constant to her duty and her love. . . .

My father spends days in reading to me, in playing at cards with me, in a hundred unavailing endeavours to amuse me: he is not well himself; these shocking scenes have been too much for his shattered frame.—Heaven preserve this most precious of lives! A fear of its being in danger makes me more wretched than all my former calamities.———Join with me, my friend, in praying for its safety.

It has taken me three days to write this letter, which is so blotted by falling *drops*, that you will scarcely be able to read it; but it goes, to show you are still remembered by

Your
Emma Egerton

Miss THORNTON to Miss EGERTON.
LETTER 18. THE GROVE.

Were you less sensible of your father's kindness, my dearest Emma, I should not add my opinion to his, concluding your heart could not be susceptible of a just sentiment—but the impression his words made on you flatters me with hopes of being listened to, not because I can talk like him; but being actuated by the same motives, I depend on the same treatment for the sake of my intention. If I cannot quote my own experience to give weight to what I say, I have at least seen things by the dispassionate light of reason, and trust to your partiality for giving solidity to my arguments, where they are of themselves deficient.

On finding your fortune so much smaller than I imagined it, I spoke my apprehensions in a perplexed and confused manner; I had not got over my surprise at the intelligence Sidney had given me—I feared, but I could not tell what, or why—in that way, I could only caution you against hurrying into matrimony.—Your answer to that letter was filled with sophistry—you brought facts to disprove my assertions—you loved, and spoke as a person who did so—I found the absurdity of opposing reason to passion—I desisted, and waited the event with impatience.—The regard I had for you both made me anxious in the highest degree, to learn your destiny...I heard of it with the utmost concern; and giving way to my pity, I forgot every objection which discretion had raised to your union; and from my soul I wished it to take place.—Recovering a little from the first sensations, I began to reflect more deeply, and am now convinced that the present distress of my friends will conduce to their future prosperity.......I will leave Augustus to reap the fruits of his valour, and confine myself only to my Emma's share of the profits that may be derived from her misfortunes.

You cannot but suppose me, my dear girl, to be above every mean wish for superfluous riches; it is one of the last thoughts that would enter my mind: a thousand cares and vexations attend it, and swell the account we shall have to render hereafter of our past lives. "Great wealth is a great evil;" that's beyond a doubt—but what a distance is there between this state, and the small income you would have shared! Extremes are equally to be shunned; poverty is not less dangerous to our peace, than immense riches.—Granting that education creates most of our wants, that nature requires little for its support, and love still less, as they tell us; does not education become a second nature? And have you been brought up to live on a little?—And where shall we see an instance of this love which can stand the rude shocks of indigence, after having lived in affluence?—It may exist in a cottage, but it must have been bred there; for it will not, I promise you, condescend to go from the stately dome to the straw-built shed—it must breathe its native air; and even that will not without uncommon care, keep it long alive....This is a part of the miseries, and perhaps the smallest part too, that would have been your portion.—The indifference of an husband, shocking as the idea is, would be less so than to see him in agonies when he found it impossible to support his family; to meet him always repining, uneasy, wishing a period to his own existence.—Can there be in nature a more dreadful misfortune, than that of causing the misery of those we love? —Such, my friend, must have been yours....

Consider well what is said to you by two of the most disinterested people who could have spoken to you; your father, and your Fanny: strive against this unhappy attachment; if you are willing to vanquish, you must be successful. The greatest difficulties are to be overcome by resolution—it requires all yours to destroy this favorite passion; but your same will be proportioned to your conquest—that it may speedily arrive at its greatest height, is the first wish of

Your truly affectionate

F. Thornton.

Col. SUTTON to W. WALPOLE, Esq.
LETTER 19. BOND-STREET.

He who trusts in woman shall be deceived. . . . This observation is almost as old as the world, and will hold good unto the end of it.

You were mistaken, Walpole, in imagining I lived in Miss Courtney's smiles; that was an happiness not decreed for me: Sir Lionel Cowper has basked too long in the bright sunshine of her favor, to leave one warming beam for me. . . .

The first line of my letter tells you I have been deceived; the following ones will explain how.

I left Beresford's, as I mentioned I intended doing, and posted away to Waterlands, *on the wings of love*: I travelled at the rate of ten miles an hour, yet cursed the postilions during every stage for not driving faster. Night overtook me near Grantham, and obliged me to put up there. I had not been long in the inn when Murray came in. Seeing him alight from his carriage, as I stood at the window, I went out to him: we were both glad of the meeting, and agreed to spend the evening together.—I found he was just come from Percy's, having been with the rest of his friends to pay him a visit on his nuptials.— The common enquiry of What news? came of course—he had none, he said, unless it was a ridiculous incident that had occasioned a good deal of bustle at Waterlands.—I asked to hear it, little dreaming what it would disclose—"Was Harriet Courtney with Mrs. Percy when you were there?" demanded he.—*O yes*, replied I, as if I had been crier to a court of justice.—"Well, if you know her," continued he, "you know the arrantest coquette this day in England; and you will enjoy her mortification."—I had some doubts of this last; but those I kept to myself, so that I gave no interruption to his ha-rangue, *only* by cautioning him not to make too free with her, for she was my *particular* friend.—"Then I have done," said he bowing, "and beg you pardon for what has already escaped me." *It* had been sufficient to rouse my curiosity: he tried to turn the conversation, but I always came back to the same point: he in politeness still declined it, but finding at length that he had gone too far to come off—"I'll tell you what, Sutton," cried he, "all I say I will justify: you are well acquainted with my character, and may be able to guess that I would not advance a falsehood from malice. To attack the reputation of a woman, merely to indulge ill-humor, has always been in my opinion, the worst species of cowardice: as defenceless beings, they claim the protection of every man; and I would as soon stab an unarmed enemy, as hurt the good name of any female. What I was going to relate was the disappointment of a lady whose sanguine hopes had rendered her liable to deception: I took you to be an indifferent person in the affair, who would have laughed with the rest of the world at the story. Your warmth, on the mention of Miss Courtney's name, has shown me that you will not bear to hear her made a subject of ridicule: I should be loth to quarrel with you for a jest; therefore let the matter end here: you may hear of it from others, when it may come with more propriety than it can from me."—I felt no very pleasing motions whilst he continued speaking: to know there was *a story*, yet not to be able to learn what it was, was enough to make one suspect the worst. This was reducing me to the most deplorable situation; and I could not endure the thoughts of remaining in it a moment longer than was necessary to form the resolution of insisting on Murray's telling me the whole, and promising to hear him without resentment, as I knew him to be a man of strict honor and one who would not deviate from truth:—he still excused himself, until, tired out by my importunities, he gave me the succeeding narrative.

"Some little while ago, during my visit to the Percy's, Sir Lionel Cowper, who has not been long in England, from whence, I suppose, he might originally have departed with about ten ideas, not five of which now remain, though the whole of his possessions of that kind, came to pay his compliment to that family; and Miss Courtney, being the only disengaged woman there, was the only one, who, according to the custom of this country, could take as much notice of him as the puppy expected.—You remember, Sutton, you are not to be offended at what I say: but Harriet, who *is at all*, did not miss so favorable an opportunity of gaining an admirer: the whole artillery of her charms was played off upon him, and in less than two days there was so good an understanding between them, such familiar nods, such expressive looks, and such frequent whisperings, that one might have sworn they had been acquainted for years. I fancied the Baronet was fairly caught—I told her as much—she did not contradict it; for she thought so herself, and had, I dare say, already taken upon her, in her own imagination, the disposal of his fortune, and saw the *bloody hand* on her carriages and plate, and new pleasures breaking in upon her every day." —Pooh! muttered I peevishly, what's all this to the purpose?—It is hardly possible to guess at thoughts. "Not so very difficult," returned he, "when the head that forms them is not a very profound one—but you forget your promise—such another *pooh!* will strike me dumb."—You shall hear no more of them, answered I; but, go on.—"Then, as I was saying, the most violent intimacy subsisted between them; but no bliss is permanent in this life—Sir Lionel began to hint his design of leaving us: he was pressed to stay a few days more; but *urgent business*, the commonplace with all *fine gentlemen*, made it impossible for him to be *so happy*. The night before he was to depart, I overheard him tell Miss Courtney he should be exceedingly indebted to her, if she would favor him with half an hour's conversation before he went off: he had something of consequence to say to her.—It was agreed, that she should meet him at seven o'clock the next morning, as he was to go before the rest of the family was stirring.——Harriet now made sure of receiving this long-expected *tender*: punctual to her assignation, she got up, and found her swain waiting her coming, which was no sooner accomplished, than he in the plainest terms proposed to make her mistress of himself and his fortune, provided she would dispense with the *antiquated* ceremony of marriage and perpetual enslavement.—This was a stroke which she was not prepared for; and after rejecting with *indignation* (according to her own account) his insolence, she upbraided him with having deceived her with false appearances: but from this charge he exculpated himself, by vowing he loved her very sincerely, and renewed his offers to confirm what he said; but he could not help it, if they had misunderstood each other: his were what *he* called *honorable* proposals, and if she had affixed any other meaning to the expression, he was not to blame; matrimony was the last folly he should be guilty of. And making her a low bow, he decamped. . .

When we assembled about nine o'clock, no Harriet appeared. Mrs. Percy rang the bell, and ordered a servant to inform her that breakfast was ready: he came back soon after, and reported that Miss Courtney was very ill.—I own I took this to be only the common effect of parting with a lover; but Mrs. Percy having left the room on the intelligence of the footman, shortly after sent for her husband, who, when he had been some time absent, returned to me, execrating the foolish girl, and the impertinent blockhead who had made this *fracas*. She being a relation of his wife's, made him at first resolve on calling Cowper to an account for his behaviour: but I represented to him, as forcibly as I could, the absurdity of risking his life in defence of a coquette who had drawn on herself this insult, and whose levity of conduct must eternally produce such consequences; that, inexcusable as Sir Lionel was, there was at least as much to be urged in his defence, as in hers; that the more private this transaction was kept, the less her reputation would be injured; that, in short, the practice of dueling had ever seemed to me to be obliterating one folly by the commission of a greater. . . . Reflexion strengthened my remarks; and it was resolved that Harriet should be

sent home to her father, lest she should again fall into such errors, as
their house was generally full of company, and she would have more
frequent occasions of flirting there than at home.—The next day she
left Waterlands, and no more notice was taken of the affair: but our
secrecy was of no kind of use; the story was known all over the
country in a week, and has served for amusement to every creature,
as Harriet has not been equal in the distribution of her civilities, and
has consequently many enemies as she has ill-treated acquaintance.

I have now, Sutton, finished this history, which you were so
desirous of hearing; not have I 'aught extenuated, or set down aught
in malice.'—The girl is handsome enough to be admired by any one:
that, I presume, has been the reason of your wishing to know so
much about her; for I cannot persuade myself that, with *your sentiments*, you can be seriously attached to her."

This home thrust distressed me as much as any part of his
relation. I then discovered how much I had lessened myself, even in
my own eyes, by this new and unworthy attachment, and for a
considerable time could not bring myself to acknowledge to Murray
that I had loved such an object: I evaded his inquisitive look, but his
penetration was not to be so foiled; he found out how much interested I was about her, and compassionating the confusion he saw me
in, he added—"But it is not wonderful that you should have been
imposed upon by her; she is perfect in her art, and understands how
to adapt her manners to her company.—You must forgive me, my
friend, if I yet endeavour to open your eyes, and show her to you in
her real shape: it is a delicate point I have undertaken; but, to save
you from perdition, nothing should deter me. Did you ever see her
before you went to Waterlands?"—Never; and have not passed more
than five weeks with her, answered I; but during that time I saw
nothing in her behaviour but what was perfectly consonant to the
most rigid rules of decorum.—"*You saw!* You should rather have said
you could *not* see; for partiality had blinded you, (retorted he;) you
were acquainted with her for five weeks, and loved her very likely
from the first hour of that period. I have known her these four years,
and never having loved her, I think myself much better qualified to
draw her picture. Believe me when I tell you she is a composition of
vanity, affectation, and deceit; that under the appearance of giddiness
she hides the most refined stratagems; that she would sacrifice the
man who loves her, at any time, in order to attach one who is
indifferent to her. To my certain knowledge, she has served more
than once. Conquest is her ambition, and tyranny her delight. When
I first knew her, I was a younger brother, and not at all *the thing*
with her; she looked much higher. I was therefore, as an unconcerned spectator, at liberty to observe all her windings and turnings;
and in the course of my acquaintance I never met with a more

intricate character; for she has not sense enough to be fixed in her taste, or principle enough to be constant in her promises. She would have married the young fool who has just left her, because his rank in life would have suited her notions: but the man himself was as insignificant to her as any other.—These are ungrateful truths, my dear Sutton, to you; but it is better you should be apprised of them from me, than from your own experience."—I agreed with Murray in this and thanking him for his sincerity and friendship, I awaked as it were out of a dream, which had missed me for the last two months of my life; and having determined on making trial of the extent of her *art*, I told him I would go on to Percy's, and, when there, would see whether Miss Courtney would take notice of my keeping my appointment with her; and, if he she did, how she would act in consequence of it: if she did not keep to her engagement, by coming or sending to me, I should retire without showing the least symptoms of my disappointment or resentment . . . The next morning, we took our different routes. When I got to Waterlands, I found the house still crowded with visitors: no mention was made of Harriet; but the day after I got there, I received a letter from her, regretting the impossibility of her coming over, as her father had company, which she was forced to entertain; but giving me an invitation to their house. This I answered, by apologizing for not being able to attend her there; and this produced another epistle from her, in which, after reproaching me with the coldness of mine, she proceeds (on a supposition of my having heard *some absurd* reports concerning her) to assure me, that what had been called a flirtation between Sir Lionel Cowper and her, had been nothing more than what in her *gaïeté de coeur*, she should have done in my presence, and that he had only returned her *innocent* notice with the common attentions of a man of gallantry; that the country was always famous for scandalous stories; but that, as she perceived much circumspection was necessary to escape censure, she was now convinced of her former imprudence; and, as she saw her errors, she should avoid them henceforwards.———A few lines conveyed my *response*: they were these.—"Colonel Sutton presents his compliments to Miss Courtney: he too *sees* his errors; and as they are both so *clear-sighted*, they may possibly discover so many faults in each other, should they meet again: therefore he shall cautiously avoid appearing in her sight any more."

I waited some days after this, without hearing any thing more of her, and then set out for London. The dear Priscy Neville now engaging all my ideas, I soon forgot my little jilt, and, I assure you, never once meditated a *desperate action* on finding I had lost her. . . . I have been some time here, without having yet had courage enough to present myself at Miss Neville's door; nor dare I even send to her, for fear of receiving a prohibition to my visits.

But I have already swelled this to the size of a volume, and will not add more to it than the usual signature of

George Sutton.

MR. WALPOLE TO COL. SUTTON
LETTER 20. SPRING-PARK.

Upon my soul, George, you have shown yourself to be complete master of your passions. So you actually refused to see Miss Courtney, after going more than eighty miles with no other intent; and you assure me you are returned without the least design of committing a rash deed in your despair!—This is more than Roman virtue, and worthy of a *British Colonel*.—I love the man who can practise such heroism, and not, by cringing and fawning, gratify the wishes of a coquette. You know my aversion to that order of beings; I can hardly suppose them entitled to the common rights of human-ity, destructive as they are to the peace of mankind.—I have always looked upon the story of the Sphinx to have been the allegorical description of some Theban coquette, who by her charms first ensnared, and then betrayed to ruin, all who came near her.—The poetical monster represents the qualities of the human one in the figurative style of the ancients: thus the face of a virgin denotes the beauty of her; the wings of a bird, her volatile disposition; the body of a dog, her want of delicacy; the claws of a lion, her power of doing mischief; and lastly, her conduct is a riddle, more difficult to expound than any that has been yet invented.—You will certainly allow of his explanation, who have been so long under the dominion of that arch-flirt, Harriet Courtney, and have known each point to be just, excepting *her power of doing mischief*, which you escaped by a timely retreat. . . . . . .

Your example should be a warning to me, had I not chosen a mistress so opposite to yours in every thing but loveliness: mild, artless, and sensible; such as would make any man blessed, who shall have the happiness of being beloved by her. Whether this will be my fate or not, Heaven knows; but of this I am sure, that nothing shall be untried on my part, which can render me deserving of her fa-vor.—We break up to-morrow; my guests dispersing themselves various ways, and I bending *my way* towards Burton.

I am not quite in the secret about Miss Neville, but I *feel* as if you had acted wrong there: I remember you used to talk to me continually of her at one time; nay, you were constantly at her elbow when she appeared in public, and the charming Priscy was your first toast.—I was to have been introduced to her, but some accident or

other always prevented it.—This is a woman that, "with your sentiments," as Murray says, I should have set down for you to be "seriously attached to."—Not supposing you so great a philosopher in
disappointments, I dreaded your forming a connexion of the sort; but
after what has just happened, I shall never have any more fears about
you: so, if you can obtain forgiveness for having loved a less deserving
woman, (which, may I be shot if I would grant you, were I Miss
Neville) you have my consent to enter into new engagements as soon
as you please: we all love to be kept in countenance upon these
occasions; and your being of *the tribe* will be great consolation to

Yours,
William Walpole

MISS EGERTON TO MISS THORNTON.
LETTER 21. SUNBURY.

Diseases of the body are more easily cured, my dear Fanny, than
those of the mind. Returning strength declares my fever gone: that
has yielded to the skill of the physicians, whilst the healing balsam of
reason has been in vain applied to the malady which preys upon the
other. Nature has give me a strong constitution, with a weak heart:
the one has baffled all the attacks of sickness; but its feeble companion is sinking under the weight of its woes, and sighs hourly for its
deliverance from the cares of this gloomy state.—Youth is not always
a desirable thing, since it does not preserve us from misery, and may
keep us long in it, by its unwillingness to part with life.

   Do not, my friend, call me insensible for not having yet made
such good use of your counsels as might have been expected; time
alone can render me calm enough to taste the sweets of *prudential*
maxims: have patience yet a little longer with me, I know that I shall
at last be what you would have me; but there are many struggles to
be sustained before the happy aera of tranquillity can arrive to one
who has felt like me! . . . . . .

   We had a visit to-day from Lady Catharine and Miss Bishop: it is
the first time I had seen them for these six weeks; and I observed
evident marks of surprise in their faces when they entered, from the
alteration in my person.—Though Lady Catharine kindly endeavoured
to inspire me with all imaginable hopes of *recovery*, how unlikely
these to contribute to my felicity! But of that no more. . . .

   Kitty tells me Mr. Walpole is to be with them again in a few
days. After we had spoken of him very highly for some minutes, she
expressed hopes of his having got over some of his *refinements*, after

having so long conversed with *gay* men, who are but seldom troubled with such *niceness.*————"For example, (continued this vivacious talker) can it be believed, that any rake in the world would object to a woman for having loved another man before he knew himself? This would be expecting the purity of Vestals, which would but ill agree with their gross inclinations. From such associates then I flatter myself that Walpole will imbibe better notions than those he had: this will be of a piece with the rest of his *singularities,* for not a creature but himself could improve by bad company.—Have you ever heard him speak of what he calls *female delicacy?* He has thoughts on that subject more fine-spun than any thread in Arachne's web."—I told her I had heard him expatiate with great vehemence on the deficiency of some of the sex in that point.————"Deficiency!" returned she, my dear Emma, "she must be something more than woman, who is not deficient in his opinion.—He carries the joke so far, that if a girl in the simplicity of her heart, is struck with an handsome figure, and exclaims, O what a charming man! she is immediately degraded from her natural claim to *delicacy,* with him.—If a woman possessed of every grace and virtue were to inspire him with love, and he should discover that she had ever been attached to another, he declares he would rather fall a victim to his *tendresse,* than deign to accept a heart which had palpitated for another; pretending to advance that our affections, like our cloaths, wear out by use.—These are but few of his *curious* tenets in regard to us; but they are so characteristic of the man, that I need mention no more.—I have done all I could to teach him better things, but without any effect he has a great deal of his father's *oddities* in him."—At the conclusion of this, the coach coming to the door, our agreeable friends took their leave, after promising to give frequent calls at Sunbury, now they could be admitted.

My father's health does not mend—I have terrors when I reflect on this circumstance, which would drive me into madness, were I not to check the first approaches of them.—Should he!—but this would be the final blow—we should both fall together, and flying to the peaceful Asylum of the Unfortunate, forget all past sorrows—O for such a sleep! "It is a consummation devoutly to be wish'd." . . . .

But you will chide me, Fanny: I have none of that philosophic spirit which you supposed me once possessed of; but, with all my sex's softness, have a double portion of its frailty: will you not then give me up, as being composed of materials too slight to rise me to the height you spoke of?—Do not, I beseech you, low as I am, think me less sincerely

Yours,

Emma Egerton

FROM THE SAME TO THE SAME.
LETTER 22. SUNBURY.

Where will my afflictions end!—and when shall the wretched Emma again find ease? My prophetic fears have proved too true; my dear father will soon be torn from me—every day increases his danger.— Why does not fate accept my proffered life for his?—But this cruel complaint, which has so long hung upon him, will not quit its hold: he is pronounced, by the best of judges, to be in a decay. O my Fanny! until this hour, I have never known sorrow; all else appears trifling to this last and greatest stroke!—But let me hope this load of complicated mischief will at last crush this little frame, which has so long struggled with adversity, and that the hand of Death will have closed my eyes before he has deprived me of the best of parents. He still continues to walk about, but with such difficulty to support himself, that I am terrified whenever he moves.—He calls for me—I fly, my father, to obey thy welcome summons."

* * * * * * * * * * ** * *

New horrors, my dear Fanny, throng about me! I have not yet regained my senses sufficiently to relate the conversation we have had . . . . . . O my Augustus! Was it not enough to lose thee, without being obliged to accept of another lover?—Never will my heart yield to this infidelity—yet have I not said I would? Have I been able to withstand the intreaties. . . . . . "Have I then no tears for thee, my father? Can I forget thy cares from helpless years, thy tenderness for me? An eye still beamed with love! A brow that never knew a frown! Nor a harsh word thy tongue! Shall I for these repay thy stooping, venerable age with shame, disquiet, anguish, and dishonor?

It must not be!———Thou first of angels! come, sweet Filial Piety! And firm my breast. Yes, let one daughter to her fate submit; be nobly wretched—but her father happy." . . . This victim, Fanny, is thy friend.

Mr. Walpole, how little did I imagine his name would ever cost me a sigh! He is come to Burton, and come to me—I cannot support this idea. You shall hear by what arts I have been drawn in to give my consent; it was refining upon cruelty to use such means.—My father held the letter in his hand, when I went to him: it was from Mr. Bishop, who informed him, in the most friendly style, of Mr. Walpole's intention of coming to Sunbury to-morrow morning—Guess his errand!—I saw pleasure in my father's face, and without knowing the cause my own bore testimony of the same; I joyed in his.—Ah, to what purpose is my heart thus susceptible, but to be the sport of every passion!—"My Emma," cried my father, "I have news to tell you, which I trust will not be ungrateful to you:

the chearfulness I have observed in you lately, bids me to think you are arrived at the peaceful serenity I expected you to enjoy: my soul revives at it, and your happiness will add some days to my life. This letter informs me of Mr. Walpole's partiality to you."—I started back, as he reached out the paper to me, and begged not to hear its contents; that I had, in obedience to his orders, banished one lover from my heart, but that no other should ever occupy the place he had been forced from.—"Can you fancy, Emma, (said he, in a more stern accent than I had ever known him use before) that the fulfilling one part of your duty will suffice? Will Heaven be satisfied with half an offering?"—Oh! do not, Sir, drive me down the precipice of Despair, on the very edge of which I now stand shuddering!—Heaven requires no more than our imperfect natures can perform: be not you less indulgent to your child.—I must be unjust to Mr. Walpole were I to receive his vows; I must be unfaithful to *another* in returning them. Command me to die, I shall obey with pleasure; but I cannot consent to live in torment.—Will you, my dearest papa, will you see your Emma devoted to destruction; and shall thy hand give me up to wretchedness?—In saying this I seized that hand, and bedewed it with my tears.—My father was agitated; but he would not speak until he thought I had exhausted myself too much to persist in my refusal: then rising, he walked a few paces, and turning to me, "It is well, my dear—I am contented; my death will soon put an end to the power which bears so hard upon you.—You will not be without friends: these at Burton will receive you; they will be tender to you, and perhaps dependence may for once be less dreadful than it has ever yet been.—Yet," rejoined he, after a pause, "I did not think *you* could have submitted to such a situation. I even tremble to reflect on the hardships of the most eligible state of dependence; the many rubs thy heart must bear." My father's words chilled my blood; but when he added—"I do not mean, Emma, to force you into a marriage so repugnant to your inclination; you shall determine for yourself: Mr. Walpole's fortune would be no temptation to me; I would not wish to see him your husband, if I did not know him to be possessed of every valuable quality: besides, my heart was fixed on the match; its completion would have given pleasure to my last hours; I should have had no fears of death, could I have left you such a protector—but you refuse to gratify my wish; you will not let me be happy in this world, and your want of duty adds to my disorder, and hurries me into the grave before my time"—I heard no more, but falling back in my chair, remained senseless for some moments: when I opened my eyes, I found my father kneeling, and the first sounds that struck my ear were—"It is thy father kneels, my child, and begs to be indulged in his request. . . . . .

O my father (cried I, throwing myself on my knees by him) let us change postures; take my seat, and let me at your feet implore forgiveness—Now indeed you have been cruel to your daughter; any argument but this might have been withstood—but now I have nothing more to say; your will shall be mine—take my consent, whilst I have yet life left to give it.————Let Mr. Walpole come, he shall be heard—but I will tell him how I *have* loved! How obeyed!— "Your consent then," replied he, "will not avail—you have given me hope, only to make me more sensible of disappointment. No man of delicacy would accept of your hand on the conditions you have mentioned, and Mr. Walpole last of any: you are no stranger to his notions, they are *particular*; and the only chance you have to make me happy is by concealing all that has happened, from every living creature; let the remembrance die, even in your own breast."—Here I exclaimed, What then, Sir, becomes of that sincerity which you have always taught me to practise? Can I in honor hide from Mr. Walpole what has passed?

My father stopped me by saying, "General maxims, my dear Emma, will not always suit particular cases—your sincerity here would answer no end, but that of disappointing the man who loves you, and of making me wretched. . . . Mr. Walpole, I'll be found for it, would prefer being cheated into happiness to being made acquainted with your attachment. It is not likely, private as the affair has been, that any accident should discover it to him. You will not meet the object you have loved until you have long ceased to feel any extraordinary degree of tenderness for him: your husband will be dearer to you than any other being then; and you will wonder, perhaps, that he was not always so. At your age, child, the violence of the passions prevents their duration: I know that this very lover, now so passionately idolized, must in a short time become indifferent to you. Were I not convinced of this, believe me, I would not bestow a wife on Mr. Walpole so unworthy of him. The thought of your being left in a state of dependence would not be half so shocking to me, as that of having rendered an amiable man miserable, by giving you to him with a heart absolutely devoted to another. . . . But you assured me, you had banished Sidney from your thoughts; and I am convinced you have, by the difference there is now in your looks. Having gained this great point, can you, my dear, be so cowardly as to attempt no more?"

I protested to my father, that I durst do any thing, except impose upon Mr. Walpole; but that, to remove that difficulty, I would inform him of what had passed, in such a way as not to disgust him; and that, if he was really attached to me, his love would get the better of his prejudices, and I should secure my future peace by not having any thing to reproach myself with.—But this was not more persuasive than what I had first said; my father declaring, that I deceived myself in supposing I could depend so much upon my power over Mr. Walpole; that he had studied human nature, and had always found it more difficult to make a man renounce his prejudices than his faith, being more wedded to ideas of his own forming than to any others; that the more unreasonable the thing was, the more unlikely it was it should be removed by rational arguments; that after a course of years, spent in a strict adherence to all the duties of a good wife, I might hope to have such a sway over him, as to reform his judgement in these matters. "Be it your care, my child, to act so as to give consequence to all you say, and your influence will be powerful; but your behaviour, and not your beauty, will secure it. I shall not look upon your consent to see Mr. Walpole as any thing, unless you also promise solemnly not to acquaint him with Augustus's love." To enforce this, he again employed all the resistless eloquence of paternal tenderness. I promised, my dear Fanny; I could not refuse any thing that would make *my father happy*: I left *him* quite easy—and will not this content my restless soul?—Ah! no, degenerate as it is, it dreads being "nobly wretched."———But its fears cannot recall the dire sentence: that being passed, death, or resignation to its fate, must be the consequence.

To-morrow!—how swift the hours fly which are to determine my lot!—O come, filial obedience, to strengthen my failing courage!—it demands all thy wonderous power to enable me to perform the task of duty.

My father silenced, but he has not convinced me: *concealment* still appears to be contrary to justice.—I dare not reflect more on this point, lest, following the dictates of sincerity, I should blast all the hope I have raised. . . . If it be possible, my friend, say something to reconcile me to myself, for at present all is anarchy and confusion in the bosom of

Thy
Emma Egerton.

MR. WALPOLE TO COL. SUTTON.
LETTER 23. BURTON.

Having had no rival to apprehend, no capricious parent or guardian to deal with, on my coming here last week I made known to this family my design of applying for Miss Egerton, and had the pleasure of having it received with every testimony of approbation; every one joining in pronouncing her to be the most unexceptionable of all womankind. I did not require this to fix my resolution; yet there is something very pleasing in having one's choice approved of. You, who are fond of investigating causes, will, I make no doubt, place this to the account of self-love, as it is a flattering proof of the goodness of one's taste: but do you seek for *causes;* I am satisfied with feeling the *effects.* The next day I spoke to my divine Emma and with her leave, to Mr. Egerton: my proposals were accepted, and things are in a train for my becoming a Benedict in a hurry. Is liberty to be regretted, when we sacrifice it to such a goddess? But how can you answer that, who have never seen my Emma?

I found great alterations on my return to Sunbury: Sidney is gone to Russia, to seek "the bubble Reputation even in a cannon's mouth:" Mr. Egerton is far gone in a decline, and my charming girl has been extremely ill since I went from hence: Lady Catharine apprised me of this; and lucky was it that I had been so prepared, for she is changed beyond imagination, and is now only the shadow of that beauteous form which used to be so much admired.—But it was not "a set of features, or complexion," that enchanted me; I loved the soul which animated her fine countenance, that yet appears, and bids defiance to care and sickness. Her anxiety on her father's illness is never lessened; she watches his looks; her whole attention is engrossed by him, and she can hardly find time to thank me when I join in her attendance on him, and by my assiduities seem to partake in her concern. The departure of Sidney has been severely felt by both the father and daughter; Emma wept for the friend of her infancy; Mr. Egerton mourned the child of his adoption, the son of his Sidney.—Lady Catharine tells me he is grown visibly worse since this event took place: I do not approve of the young hero's leaving England at this time; though he certainly had no idea of Mr. Egerton's danger then, and the calls of honor must be obeyed. Thus much for his excuse; and may victory attend his steps!—

The gentle Emma, so formed for love, is not yet brought to return mine as she should do: a prey to grief, she does not attend to any other sentiment—but as her coldness is not the effect of prepossession in another's favor, or aversion to me, but the consequence of a sorrow respectable in itself; as it proves the greatness and justness of her sensibility, it adds value to the heart I would gain. The death of her father will leave her leisure for love: her manner assures me that my fondness will be repaid, as soon as she can forget her loss: it may be a work of time to accomplish that; but when the hour does arrive, I shall be amply rewarded for my patience: that it will come, cannot be a dubious matter, since her heart cannot be insensible, or my passion abate. I am importunate to have an early day named for her becoming mine, as I shall then never leave her to sustain alone the melancholy office of watching over her dieing parent. Mr. Egerton joins his prayers to mine, as he finds himself going fast, and would fain leave her in safety before that. . . . .

The sad scene makes an impression on me, which even my approaching happiness cannot efface. I came back to Burton, after visiting my beloved, so low and dejected, that a stranger to my real circumstances would conclude me to be a discarded lover on the point of dangling from a willow-bough. Kitty applauds what she calls my *humanity* (much of that, to be sure, in sympathizing with a mistress in distress), but wishes I would forget a little of it when I leave Sunbury, for she cannot bear the *dismals*: no one feels more for their friends than she does; but as her sensations are violent, they are not lasting. She would not make a wife for me, with this disposition; give me one who is not easily caught, but, being once attached, will be so for ever. This makes me satisfied with my Emma's slow progress in love: her heart, less *inflammable*, will be more entirely warmed: she is not versed in the common knowledge of girls of her age, who generally made more lovers than years to count; I shall be the first who teaches her *la lingua d'amore*.—What joy will it be to hear my lovely scholar utter sentiments which only I have inspired! I do not believe, George, that I shall be a jealous husband; but I know I shall be exceedingly delicate in my notions of a wife's behaviour: she who pretends to charm me as such, must have all the amiability of Miss Egerton: she consents to be mine, and secures the bliss of

Yours,

William Walpole.

Miss EGERTON to Miss THORNTON.
LETTER 24. SUNBURY.

They are in such a hurry to finish this marriage, that I am scarcely permitted to think on what I am going to undertake. Perhaps, my dearest Fanny, it is best policy not to give me time for reflexion. O what an horrible thought is that! Have I then reason to fear reflexion?—does not this imply guilt? The upright mind can bear to search into the hidden corners; it can stand the test of self-examination—what then is mine, which shuns itself, and turns with horror from the view?—I dare not, my friend, desire you to answer this question for me—my conscious soul already does it.—But a few weeks since Augustus left me; and here am I on the eve of vowing to another that constancy which only he can claim.—Can I do it?—Fond fool as I am, my heart misleads me—I had no right to promise him; and he who has the disposal of me, has ordained me to quit this chosen object.———Just Heaven, assist me! Since it is in obedience to thy great command, I yield up the mortal dearest to me! Bless *him* with every good!—may his soul never feel the pangs of mine!—may he live to enjoy that happiness, which the lost Emma can never find on earth! . . . . .

Is it thus I prepare myself to become a bride? Does not Mr. Walpole merit an undivided heart?—He does, and mine henceforwards must be wholly his.—Generous, tender, and deserving as he is, he demands all the love I can bestow—that, alas! How small a portion for worth like his!—Still does this rash passion mingle itself in every thought. I meant, my friend, never more to have mentioned the name of Augustus; but no sooner did I take up my pen, than it became marked on the paper, and the weak Emma had not resolution enough to erase it.—I could almost believe we have two souls in each body, else whence come these opposite desires, these different wishes?—But do they not rather belong to one and the same? So many sure proofs of its frailty.

My father grows worse every hour—I cannot support the thought of his dieing, and therefore indulge any that delivers me from this terrible one.———He fainted this morning whilst I was sitting by him: frightened, nearly distracted, I ran into the hall, where I met Mr. Walpole just coming to enquire about him. Never did he appear so pleasing to me; my terror affected him—I could not speak; but catching hold of his arm, I led him to the next room, where we found my father recovered from his fit: joy at seeing him alive, made me more than commonly attentive to my lover: I thanked him for his well-timed visit, told him his was the most welcome face I could have seen, and in short gave him many assurances of my preference. He looked happy; my father rejoiced in seeing it; and the idea of having done right made me for some hours fancy I was so too.

There is no higher pleasure than that of contributing to the felicity of others—it is a consolation, which yet is left for me: I will then forget *self*, and be satisfied with the sublimer power of bestowing happiness on others. There is a grandeur in that thought, which raises me above all meaner considerations, and carries me at once to the height of my ambition.

Before this reaches you, I shall no longer bear the name of Egerton.—There can be no parade at such a time as this—you will believe that I am not concerned at this circumstance: I could not, I am afraid, support the loud mirth so usual on such occasions and all my boasted *greatness* would forsake me in the midst of noisy rejoicings.

The late Mr. Walpole left his estate so tied down, that it would take up too much time to have proper settlements drawn up; these are to be made hereafter, it seems: this prevents the delay of lawyers, and favors the impatience of my friends. It is immaterial to me what provision is made for me, hoping that I shall not long stand in need of the goods of this world . . . But beware, Emma, of falling again into the state thou hast just quitted! Remember, but three days are allowed, before thou art summoned to the altar with the man whom thou wilt swear to love.—Let his image then reign in thy heart, and, excepting thy Fanny, give him no rival there.—Let tenderness justify the deceit which duty has commanded, and teach Walpole, that she who has loved one worthy being, may be equally attached to another.

Ask of Heaven, my Fanny, to strengthen me, and make me able to perform the noblest of efforts; that of conquering our passions, in submission to its laws.

Adieu! I will no longer venture to dwell on this theme, for fear of trespassing a third time against the virtue I have embraced: I never can against the friendship I owe you, my dear, but must ever remain

Your affectionate

Emma Egerton.

MISS BISHOP TO MISS THORNTON
LETTER 25.

Our friend, my dear Miss Thornton, is too much taken up with her various employments, to write to you now; and as I judge of *your impatience* by my own, I resolved that you should not be long uniformed of the new name which she took upon her three days ago; and making all proper allowances for the shortness of the time, she already answers very readily to it. I assuredly have helped to make her so well used to it, as I am every moment calling out *Mrs. Walpole,* as much from my passion for novelty, as from my not being able to stir without her in this *dull* place. Have you ever been at a wedding, Miss Thornton? I never was before; nor do I ever wish to be again, unless it agrees better with my notions of one, than this did.—Poor Mr. Egerton's illness rendered it improper to have any company but our family invited to it: I knew this; but still my head was so stuffed with the descriptions which my old nurse used to give of the festivity of such a day, that I could not bring myself to imagine this would be one of the most woeful I had ever seen. The first disappointment I met with was in seeing Emma pale, trembling, and ready to faint more than once during the ceremony: having always heard a vast deal of her excessive timidity, I was convinced this had occasioned all these tremors, &c. and still hoped that when we got home, there would be an end of all these uncomfortable ways. In this I was much deceived; for we had not been a great while in the house, before Emma retired with my mother: we waited in expectation of their re-appearance; but finding they did not make it, Walpole proposed, that he and I should seek his bride and my mother. We set out accordingly, and after some search, discovered they were in the dressing-room: in we bounced; but I quickly wished myself out again; for Emma was in a flood of tears, and Lady Catharine in deep discourse. Walpole was alarmed, and eagerly enquired into the subject of her grief. My mother, the common friend of both, told him, that Mrs. Walpole had been talking of her father's situation until she had wrought herself into an agony about it. He went up to her, intreating her to be comforted; and added, that he flattered himself she would not on *that day* indulge more sorrow than she had been used to do. She gave him her hand, in token of her not doing so; he carried the precious gift to his lips, and wiped from her cheeks the trickling drops.—After much persuasion and many struggles, she put on a more placid aspect; but her face, the whole day, reminded me of the old simile of "an April-day," one moment a gleam of smiles, the next a shower of tears. This was not likely to produce mirth, and has cured me of any inclination to see a wedding.—At Emma's request, I was left with her; but things are growing now much *too serious* for me, so I shall move for going home in a day or two: as I can be of no real service, I must be rather an incumbrance; for, to be sincere, a sick room is my aversion, and sighs and wailings my dread. I leave to those, whom the Fates have been pleased to "deck most amiably 'in tears,'" to pursue their weeping: for my share, I am contented to exercise the less becoming faculty of risibility—which that I may do, it will be needful for me to quit this mansion, where every visage speaks misfortune near.—I am exceedingly sorry for Mr. Egerton, and pity Mrs. Walpole most heartily; but there is a prevailing principle in my temper, which bids me fly from melancholy as the worst of pests.——That you may never be in the way of it, is the best wish which can be formed for you by

Your affectionate
Humble servant,
Catharine Bishop.

MR. WALPOLE TO COL. SUTTON.
LETTER 26. BURTON.

The last solemn scene is closed, and Mr. Egerton is no longer sensible of the infirmities of nature: the livid and emaciated body no more shrinks with pain.—He is happy: the virtuous must be so; if religion had not told us, reason would have informed us of that truth. He lived but ten days after he gave his daughter to me: our whole time has been since spent in smoothing his passage from this, to the other world.

Emma bore with amazing fortitude his approaches to the last moment; her apparent resignation surprised me: but her grief had been restrained, to burst forth with greater violence; for as soon as she knew her father could not be hurt by it, she gave vent to her oppressed heart: I never beheld such a picture of distress!—It was with difficulty I forced her from his bed; and when that was accomplished, all my rhetoric could not prevail on her to go to Bishop's.— She would not leave the dear remains, but would watch by them, until she had paid the last tribute, by attending them to the grave.

After fruitless endeavours to convince her of the absurdity of increasing her affliction, I affected to be angry at her obstinacy, and putting on an air of reproach, I asked—if she had forgotten that she had a husband? Never did question bring about so sudden a change—she looked at me an instant; then, as if she had recollected herself, she dried her eyes, and told me she had no more to say; I might carry her where I pleased: glad of having her in this mood, I took her passive hand, and conducted her to the coach, which had been waiting some time at the door.—But we had not arrived at our journey's end, when I began to repent of the stratagem I had made use of. The smothered sorrow, not having been allowed to take its natural course, put on the terrifying appearance of frenzy: she had not spoke a word after we quitted the house, until we got within a mile of Burton, though I had tried by every endearment to make her forget the harshness I had been obliged to exercise; but starting on a sudden, she demanded, in the wildest manner, "who I was, and by what authority I had dragged her from her father?"—When I had told her who she was with, and soothed her for some time, I asked her, if she did not know me?—"Yes, Sir," replied she with great quickness, "I know you—you are *my husband*." The emphasis with which she uttered the last word, proved the effect it had had on her—I could have killed myself for having made so bad an use of it— but without attempting to excuse what I had done, I immediately called out to the postilions, and ordered them to drive back to Sunbury. She took my meaning, and reclining her head on my bosom, she wept plentifully.—When we arrived, I was determined not to controul her in any of her fancies; but to follow her through all the mazes which her sorrow should invent. She did not go into the room where the body lay; but hurrying into her dressing-room, I went in with her: here we sat until late in the evening. She had not eaten the whole day: when the supper was served up, she still refused to taste any thing: I told her then, that as my eating depended on hers, and she had declared she would not have any supper, the things might be removed, for I would not sit down to table without her. This had the desired effect; her complaisance got the better of her first resolution: she sat down, saying she would eat a bit of chicken, rather than that I should fast longer. About ten o'clock she begged I would let her see her father once more, for that she had never passed a night without paying her duty to him: I accompanied her into the chamber where the corpse lay. She was not now outrageous in her expressions; but, as if struck with awe on entering the place where the most solemn silence reigned, she moved softly up to the coffin, and looked for some time on it; then throwing herself on her knees at a little distance from it, her sweet eyes cast up to Heaven, she seemed to be lost in meditation.—After she had thus indulged in all "the luxury of grief" for near half an hour, she arose, and beckoned me to follow her. Going back to the room we had been in before, as soon as we re-entered it—"My dear Mr. Walpole (said the lovely mourner) I am infinitely indebted to you for the part you have taken in my affliction: never can I forget your tenderness; it has preserved me from despair.—I have had time for reflection, and will go to Burton to-morrow morning as early as you please.—You are very right in what you say—I increased my distress unnecessarily; but the first attacks of sorrow are hard to be resisted: let this be my apology with you: I will for the future remember I am a Christian, and as such, under an absolute obligation to submit to the decrees of Providence."

Charmed with her words and manner, I never once interrupted her during this speech; though at the conclusion of it I was vehement in expressing my admiration of her. She rewarded my praise, by smiling through her tears . . . She passed a sleepless night, and was up very early the next morning. When we had breakfasted, she enquired if the coach was ready: I had ordered it before, and handing her into it, we drove to Burton, where the whole family expressed the most friendly concern for her.

This dear girl has been a spoiled child, who never knew what contradiction was: meek as her disposition is, she resents the least degree of asperity, not indeed by returning it, but by—the more infallible method of disarming it—her tears.

Lady Catharine spends all her hours in my Emma's apartment; and Miss Bishop, who boasted so much of her vivacity, has sacrificed a great deal of it to partake of her friend's melancholy: she never appears before her whilst Mr. Bishop is with her, lest *his* fondness should remind her of the loss she has sustained in *her father*; nor does she use that word in speaking of him when my wife is present. These are delicacies, Sutton, that show Kitty's heart to be capable of very refined sentiments; she rises in my opinion every day: one must be in the situation I am in now, to be fully sensible of the merit of such actions.—Grief then, I find, improves the heart; it humanises, it renders us more fit for society, by making us dependent on others for relief; and, in consequence of the ease we procure from our friends, more partial to the human species in general. But I forget that one must be at Burton to experience fully the charms of sympathy; such souls are not to be met with every where; ours are such *friends* as few are blessed with. Yet will I not be so great a misanthrope as to suppose *the sort* confined to this family alone: you, my dear George, would prove me unjust; for you have upon every occasion been the *real* friend of

Yours,

William Walpole.

FROM THE SAME TO THE SAME.
LETTER 27. SPRING-PARK.

As soon as the funeral was over, Emma desired to come to Spring-Park. I thought the season too far advanced to carry her further into the country, and represented this to her, after informing her that a house in Portman-Square had been fitted up for her reception, if she chose to pass the remainder of the winter in town: but finding her much against that scheme, I at length consented to her coming here. We have no company here at present; a pestilence would not depopulate our neighbourhood, more than the coming of Christmas does. But luckily I have not been married long enough, Colonel, to have any objection to a *tête à tête* party; and time passes very agreeably, though we have none of your gaieties here—Emma's voice and harpsichord afford me more harmony than any of your operas: her sentiments improve my heart more than any which your players repeat: nor do your meetings at Almack's and Cornelys's give any entertainment so elegant as her conversation. From this sketch you may perceive how little I can wish for any amusement more than what my own house produces. The dear girl is now in that pleasing state when the heart is just recovering from a deep wound: all is calm and tender, and her melancholy seems now to be the effect rather of gentleness than of sorrow. . . . Could I suppose you as unfashionable as myself, I would ask you to join us—yet, upon second thoughts, you shall not see my Emma until she has regained her native charms: good air, regular hours, and my care, will make her a complete beauty again in a very short time. You may allow me to be vain of my wife's person, since I never was so of my own.—Not much merit, you'll say perhaps, in this last circumstance: but, let me tell you, George, I have had some *civil* things said to me; and the coxcomb never takes the trouble of examining into the judgment of his admirers—it is sufficient for him that he is admired. Then it is plain that I am not one; and, as times go, this is *high merit*, and I have a right to some share of commendation for it.

I could not get Kitty Bishop to come down with us; she had no idea of being thrown into the vapours with leafless trees, hollow winds, and all the horrors of being seventy or eighty miles from

London before May. When she is tired of that delightful place, she promises to visit us in Dorsetshire: by that time you may make the *quartetto*, or sooner if you will please

Your affectionate,

William Walpole.

COL. SUTTON TO W. WALPOLE, ESQ.
LETTER 28. BOND-STREET.

Take back, my dear Walpole, the epithet of *happy* which you *once* bestowed on me; it is yours now, by every claim—may you enjoy it until the charming Emma robs you of it, or your friend wishes you to lose it! Your kind stars have doomed you to the pleasing employment of weeping with, or of drying the tears of, your beloved; and you may join in her sorrows without the cutting reproach of having caused them. How is your fate to be envied, when compared to mine! I should not complain, if a knowledge of my crime could reconcile me to the punishment inflicted on it—I plead guilty; but, far from finding this any alleviation to my torments, the stings of conscience only serve to give new sharpness to them.—You have told me you *felt* as if *I* had not behaved quite well to Miss Neville: I honored you for the propriety of your feelings; but yours were only the forebodings of an heart interested for the conduct of a man, with whom you are connected by the ties of friendship: your sensations were only just what they should have been, and not attended with the pangs of remorse, the sure consequence of deviating from the paths of rectitude.———O for those lucky moments to return, when I talked to you incessantly of my Priscy! It was then I knew all the joys of an attachment founded on the firm basis of virtue. If I had not absolutely given a solemn promise of marriage to this admirable girl, I had at least convinced her by every action, that I meant to have no other wife; and I never yet could make those absurd distinctions, which many of us do, between speaking what we mean, and implying it by looks and deeds. Miss Neville gave me a preference, that left me no room to doubt, from the tenor of her behavior, which was guided by an unerring prudence, that she looked upon me in the light I wished her to do. When a man singles out a young woman, upon a footing with himself in point of birth, there is but one view which he can be supposed to have. She had certainly then a right to consider me as her own, and I wished for no greater happiness than to be so.—I had *dangled* about her for more than three years, when her sister's imprudent marriage and subsequent misfor-

tunes called for her all tenderness; and she in some measure seemed
to have withdrawn her affections from every other object, in order to
lavish them on the inconsolable Mrs. Wentworth. I had called on her
several times, when she had either been engaged in attending her
sister, and refused to see me; or she had come into the room where I
was, so absorbed in melancholy as hardly to seem sensible of my
being there. Amiable as her motives for her slighting me were, and
thoroughly acquainted as I was with them, I could not help being
wounded by her indifference. I fancied myself entitled to as much of
her attention as ever; and finding I no longer enjoyed it, I falsely
concluded that she had no more of that regard for me which I had
hoped for.—I informed her of my intention of going into the country for a few months, and begged to hear from her when she could
spare time to write. She wished me a good journey, and promised
that I should have letters from her: prepossessed as I was with mean
suspicions, I imagined her coldness more visible in this visit, than ever
it had been before; and I set out for Priscy's, convinced of her never
having loved me. When I got there, the sprightly Miss Courtney
attracted my notice by her bloom, her *enjouëment*, and a thousand
nameless graces which played about the laughter-loving damsel: these
however would have caused no more than admiration, had she not,
by a peculiarity in her manner when she spoke to me, and the very
glaring difference she made between me and every other man who
pretended to distinguish her, shown a partiality which at once raised
me in my own esteem, and called upon *my gratitude* to return it. My
connexion with Miss Neville had given me no opportunity of knowing the wiles of coquettry; superior to all the little arts of low minds,
she had always treated me with the genuine effusions of an heart
tender, delicate, and noble: from this pattern I drew all my ideas of
virtuous women.—Harriet, with the same mind, (as I conjectured)
had the additional merit with me of *loving*: my imagination, fired at
the portrait of such united charms, idolised it—I no longer felt the
calm refinements of the sentiments Priscy used to inspire: all was
tumult, and unremitted ardor—the joyous hours flew with rapidity in
the company of this enlivening prattler.—In a few weeks I had gone
farther in declaring my passion for her, than I had done in as many
years to my former flame. I was astonished when, on sober reflexion,
I perceived the lengths I had gone; for, angry as I was at the amiable
Priscy, I had no fixed plan of giving her up when I first flirted with
Miss Courtney: the pain her indifference gave me spoke plainly how
dear she was to my soul; but drawn in, by innumerable snares, to
converse frequently with this artful girl, and blinded by my own folly,
I discovered, when it was too late, that I had said more than I could
honorably recede from, unless I pleaded a prior engagement, which
now scarcely held good in my opinion. Thus divided in my sentiments, I hesitated for a while how to proceed: post after post arrived,

without bringing me a line from Miss Neville; and Harriet was hourly proving her tenderness for me by some new instance of it: these preponderated, and in an evil moment I wrote to the first, told her my suspicions of her coldness had been confirmed by her silence since I had left town; that *my esteem* for her was unalterable; but that, as I could expect nothing more from *her*, I had been tempted to offer my heart to one who returned my love with equal warmth; yet I did not presume to dispose of it without obtaining her leave for so doing. Her answer to this impertinence was such as, by my soul, forced me in my highest raptures to lament her loss!—

After this, we dropped all correspondence: my head ran only upon the ecstatic bliss of Harriet's being mine; and if a disagreeable recollection now and then obtruded itself upon me, I flew to my Siren, and it disappeared. I did not acquaint Priscy with my attachment to Miss Courtney, as she and I had agreed that to be unnecessary until her father had been consulted; but I framed an excuse for my returning to him after I had been at Milfield. You know the success of my visionary scheme; therefore I'll say not another syllable of it.

Mortifying as it was to be abandoned by her, I did not permit myself to think of it after the first surprise was over; nay, I even persuaded myself that I was callous, and could not be affected by any attacks *she* could make upon my peace. The disdain I felt for a Sphynx, as you properly define a coquette to be, seemed an assurance of my not being hurt by her fickleness: whether it was so or not, I did not take leisure to consider, being then sensible only of the wrongs I had done to a more deserving woman. Occupied with this reflection solely, I hurried up to London, meaning to deprecate Miss Neville's wrath, by the most open avowal of my errors, and, if she would accept of it, to expiate them by an unshaken fidelity for the rest of my life. I had been several days in Bond-street, before I could bring myself to attempt so arduous a task, as that of obtaining forgiveness from a person so justly incensed. The more I thought over my transgressions, the more difficult it appeared. Grown quite desperate at last, I resolved to delay no more, but either to be relieved by her pity, or to be destroyed by her inflexibility. I immediately directed my steps towards Park-street, summoning up all my courage as I passed along Grosvenor-square and the two Brook-streets. When I came to the door, I had not effrontery enough to look up as I was wont to do, in hopes of catching a glance, from the windows of that face whose benign influence had so long ruled my fate.—After repeatedly rapping, a man who belonged to an adjacent shop came out of it, and informed me, that Mrs. Wentworth and Miss Neville had been gone above six weeks from that house, but where they had removed to he could not tell. I was planet-struck at this intelligence; it seemed to portend the most disagreeable events:

my Priscy had never before taken a step of this sort without acquainting me with it; she had done it now, evidently, to avoid my visits:
but of what could I complain: I had deserted her first, and this was
but a small part of what I merited from her. I stood motionless on
the spot where I had heard of her departure for some time, not well
knowing whether to go in pursuit of her.—After naming over a
catalogue of her acquaintance, to find out a proper one to make
enquiries of about the sisters, I set out, and called at a dozen doors,
without gaining admittance at any. On going home again, I recollected that it was concert-night, and probably I should meet some
one there, who could direct me to their habitation. I dressed, dined
at Boodle's, and went there afterwards. On my going in, the first
person I saw was Miss Bertie, whom I had seen oftener with her than
any of her other visitors: this riveted me to her side, and I soon
found an opportunity of introducing a conversation about *her friend*.
"Were you not amazed," asked my companion, "at the suddenness of
her quitting town?" Without waiting to hear my reply, she went on
informing me of the remarks that had been made on a retreat which
was totally unexpected; as, whatever inclination Mrs. Wentworth,
might have had for solitude, it was generally supposed that Miss
Neville had *reasons* for continuing in the world—"but you and she
have settled that matter, I dare say," added Miss Bertie, with a very
significant look. It required some dexterity to come off here with a
tolerable grace: mine failed me, and I was going to change my seat,
when this provoking *enquirer* obliged me to keep it, by running on
in the same strain, "Come, come, Colonel, since you don't care to
give me a direct answer to that, I must insist, at least, upon your
telling me how to address my letters to her; for I happened to be
out of town when she took her flight, and have not since been able
to learn where she is gone to." This quite disconcerted me: I began
to make some excuse for my ignorance, but stammered, and was so
confused, that, not knowing what to make of me, she called to Lord
Carleton, who was standing near her, to know whether there was any
thing improper in what she had said. My Lord protested he could
not see any impropriety in it, but, shrugging up his shoulders,
observed, that lovers could not be too cautious in these days. I left
her to the *sagacious* peer, and slunk away from that part of the room,
but without gaining any great advantage from my change, as I could
have no satisfactory account of my fugitives. Fatigued with the idle
prate of those who mentioned them, I would trust no longer to their
surmises, but determined on visiting every place where I thought it
likely they should have concealed themselves. I did so, and after the
most unwearied diligence employed in the search, I am come back to
London dispirited, and out of all hopes of ever finding them.

Such, my dear Walpole, is my state at present: without any relish
for amusements, I live in public; hear and see all that passes, without

finding myself dissipated enough to forget Miss Neville, or entertained enough not to regret her. If infidelity was always thus severely
punished, how seldom should we hear of distresses occasioned by the
caprice or perfidy of lovers! . . .

But I will not detain you from the enjoyment of Mrs. Walpole's
company, so much more calculated to make you happy, than the
lamentations of a correspondent who has not now a comfort left,
saving that of being

Your friend,
George Sutton.

[End. of Vol. I.]

Miss THORNTON to Mrs. WALPOLE.
Letter 29. The Grove.

When we act properly, my dearest Emma, we do not require the
applause of others to make us happy; a more certain voice than that
of shouting multitudes speaks to us: we feel the satisfaction of having
performed our duty, and that compensates for all the pain we have
endured in bringing ourselves to do it.—You will agree to this, and I
make no doubt are ready to confess to me, that your present felicity
exceeds in greatness all your past woes.—Who would desire to
purchase by a crime the gratification of any passion, when there is
such happiness in subduing it?

The death of Mr. Egerton has been a dreadful trial to you; but
Heaven, in sending us calamities, is always so bountiful as to send
consolations with them. Your father's long illness must, in some
degree, have reconciled you to his release; whilst his virtue would
make you rejoice in his future prospects. . . .

I would not, in the first hours of affliction, offer to console you;
that friend has very little sensibility, who pretends to oppose the
dictates of nature in such a case.—It is rather by showing that we can
be as violently affected, that we should endeavour to render the
unfortunate sensible of the unseemliness of immoderate grief; we are
more struck with the actions of others, than with our own: the tears
of a friend divert our attention from the object which had before
engrossed it; and the division once effected, sorrow is soon weakened:
we find our tenderness redoubled for the being who has wept with
us, and forgetting the dead, we are entirely taken up with him who
yet remains to lighten our care by his sympathy. Let the first transports of any wretchedness once abate, and resignation each minute
gains new strength. You, Emma, have causes for it, which few have
known————you can reflect on having, by your obedience, added
joys to your father's last hours, and robbed Death of his horrors—
you have repaid your obligations to the kindest of parents—and your
pious care softened the last struggles of expiring nature.—Will you,
after this, permit a sigh to escape you?

You owe to Mr. Walpole, as to an affectionate partner, the
sacrifice of this unavailing sorrow: you are entrusted with his peace,
as well as your own; and he may demand an account of it at your
hands. Be careful of it then, my dear————

It is incumbent on you to remove his *prejudices* by a conduct
which shall show him, beyond a possibility of doubt, that he is dearer
to you than any thing else in this world. Every thing which makes
you careless about him, call it Grief, or dignify it by what name you
will, is an offence against the duty you owe him; and he may with
reason suspect your love. Whether the memory of your father, or of
any one besides, interferes with his right, he will be injured. Many

III

people ridiculously confine the practice of virtue to some particular act. Thus, for example, the woman, who would not for the universe be unfaithful to her husband's bed, fancies herself perfectly chaste, though she tries to attract the admiration of every pretty fellow who comes in her way, listens to the flattery he bestows on her; goes home, compares his behaviour with her lord and master's, whose notice she has not been ambitious of attracting for some time probably: she sighs at the difference, then grows out of humour, repents of the choice she has made, calls herself unhappy; but still plumes herself upon her *unsullied virtue*. Say, my friend has she much cause for this self-approbation; and is chastity confined to barely refraining from absolute adultery! Is not the wife obliged to be equally pure in thought as well as action; and can she be called so who permits every other to usurp her husband's place in her wandering imagination? You will not hesitate about this: remember then, Emma, that he who has so extensive a claim in one point, has the same in all others. The chearless melancholy companion cannot expect to meet with the treatment which a more pleasing one would do. Men naturally inconstant are soon wearied with the dull office of hearing complaints, and of vainly trying to remove them.—Depend upon it, that, if you do not make home agreeable to him, Mr. Walpole will never hold himself obliged to be there.—I would not alarm you, but give you warning of a danger which you may yet shun. I never apologise for speaking thus to you; friendship is my inspirer, and you are too well convinced of the sincerity of mine, to suspect I am less than ever

Your affectionate

F. Thornton.

MRS. WALPOLE TO MISS THORNTON.
LETTER 30. SPRING-PARK.

If I have, my Fanny, derogated from that high character which you might have expected in *your friend*, attribute my failure to the frailty of a woman, who, though willing to be great, cannot all at once arrive at it; but trust to my *willingness*, and your rudiments, for my proving in time equal to your expectations: convinced by what you have taught me, Mr. Walpole shall see no more of my tears, nor shall you hear another murmur from me. I should indeed bless the Fates which gave me such an husband: he is all my father prophesied that I should find him, indulgent to my follies, and partial to the smallest appearances of merit. He does not wish for me to express a wish;

but, watchful of every look, he prevents my request; and before I have got words to speak my wants, they are supplied.

We have been left wholly to ourselves since we came here: this affords us an opportunity of studying each other's dispositions. I am not very *clair-voyante*, but I hope to be enough so to find out how to please him: wishing to do it will not always succeed, unless one understands how to set about it.

Spring-Park is a fine place; elegance breathes around it.—Mr. Walpole's mother, who was daughter to Lord Rivers, and aunt to Lady Catharine Bishop, was a woman of taste; and not being quite happy, from having married an humorist, she used to find her chief amusement in ornamenting her house and grounds with every embellishment which art could invent, and money purchase. This, and the forming of her children, who were a son and two daughters, made time hang less heavy on her than could have been supposed; as she was not allowed to go much abroad, or to entertain a great deal of company at home. The loss of her girls, who died within a year of each other, and the absence of her son, who had been sent to school, shortened the life of this valuable woman. Mr. Walpole commemorates her with the truest affection, and gives her so great a preference to his father, that there is no danger of his ever treading in his steps, for all what the giddy Kitty said: his mother's early precepts have made a lasting impression on him.

On my arrival here, he carried me to the apartment which she used to occupy; and giving me a bunch of keys, begged me to accept of all I found in the cabinets which those would open. I have not so much curiosity as is in general ascribed to our sex; but, after keeping the keys a week without trying any of them, I began to fear that it would seem like a disregard to the present, if I did not look at it. I then opened the cabinets, and was dazzled by the lustre, and surprised at the quantity, of jewels and trinkets which they contained: diamonds, rubies, sapphires, and pearls, were so thickly laid in every drawer, that I could have fancied some benevolent *Fairy* had paid me a visit. Extravagantly gaudy as female dress is at present, I have more finery than it would be possible for me to wear at once.

Some days after, this liberal donor brought me bank-notes to the amount of an hundred pounds; telling me, he should pay me that sum quarterly, that my ward-robe might be proportioned to my caskets. Of what consequence do the most insignificant gifts appear, when presented by the hand of an amiable giver! The glare of jewels, the tinsel of cloaths, never until now had attractions for me; but, bestowed by my husband, they are precious to me. What a bad heart should I have, if it remained insensible to such kindness! My dear Fanny, your Emma feels all that gratitude and esteem require: and are not those the very *best* sentiments of the heart? . . . . .

I found several of the domestics here, who have lived with the late owners. The house-keeper, an elderly sedate person, for whom Lady Bel. had an uncommon regard, was recommended to my notice by Mr. Walpole as such: she has lived above twenty years at the park, and seems very proper for the place which she fills.

The steward too has been long in the family, and received a very high encomium from his master on being introduced to me. But of all the *ancients*, none pleased me more than a venerable, grey-headed gardener, who remembers three generations since he came to live here; but told me he hoped he should not survive the fourth, as *we* looked better disposed to be happy than most of those he had known. There is a simplicity and heartiness in him, that charms me prodigiously; and to preserve the partiality which his first address created in me, he constantly culls the choicest productions of his hot-house and green-house, to adorn my room at this time, when the garden does not yield one fragrant sprig.

My own Wilson still serves me in her former capacity.—And thus you have a full account of my household, which is settled much to the satisfaction of

Your very affectionate,

Emma Walpole.

MISS BISHOP TO MRS. WALPOLE.
LETTER 31. BURTON STREET.

Pray tell me, my dear Mrs. Walpole, how you contrive to pass your time, at this dreary season, secluded from all that's gay? I can form no guess at your amusements. You and Walpole may support conversation as well as any two in the universe: but the most ingenious will sometimes be at a loss for new subjects, when there is no change of scene. I can fancy you making the justest remarks, and discussing the most knotty points with great fluency; in fine, never at a stand for words, when objects present themselves—but there's the rub! Those objects are so few, and never diversified: so that, unless you repeat the same thing over and over, you cannot talk! Even in this constant succession of new faces, new anecdotes, and new entertainments, I now and then complain of a want of variety: what then should I do if confined to one house, one companion?—I should place myself in the chimney-corner, count the dull hours as they slowly rolled, imagine I saw the figures of men and beasts in the fire, then nod over the drowsy thoughts which such an existence would inspire. . . .

Your friends hear with astonishment of your remaining the whole winter in the country; nobody can account for so strange a whim! The ladies pester me with enquiries about Walpole: "When may we expect to see him? What is the reason of his not being already in town?" I tell them that he follows your inclination in this, as he is *in duty* bound to do in every thing: and I thought, as they knew he was married, this would have satisfied them; but I find it does not: in this *polite age*, wedlock does not lay any restraint on the parties engaged in it. Let your husband then come and speak for himself. I can inform him that, though he has committed such a *faux-pas* in gallantry, as that of making a love-match, his good-natured admirers will not discard him, unless he should be hardy enough to justify his fault, by persevering in it to the neglect of all his *quondam* favorites.—Let him look to that: such a *sottise* might be productive of the worst consequences, as it would indubitably hinder *you* from shining in the *beau monde* as you ought to do. Half a score of the best-bred flirts in town wait your coming, to inlist you in the roll of Fame. You married dames are the only ones who can pretend to be distinguished by men of *ton*: they never intrigue with any other, under forfeiture of the character it costs them so much to accomplish. The man of *highest* fashion chuses the wife of *his friend*: but, should he be so destitute as not to find one creature who can be called so, he then attaches himself to some woman noted for her prudence, or one whose help-mate will be most apt to feel the loss of her affection; and when he has tarnished her reputation, the affair makes an *eclat*: allegations are brought against her in Doctor's Commons; witnesses appear, counsellors plead; and, if recrimination does not stop it, a divorce ensues; when the lady's family bribes the gallant to make her an *honest woman* again, as the vulgar *judiciously* term it, by taking her, covered as she is with ignominy and vice, to be his wife, and thereby allowing a plurality of husbands in spite of our Legislators original designs.

We girls, who have not been admitted into the *honorable order*, are looked upon as mere blanks in society, and are left to the *insipids*, who chuse to perpetuate their names in a lawful way, and to increase the pleasures of the elegant part of mankind by enlarging the number of wives.

If after knowing this you are not desirous of appearing on the grand theatre of life, I give you up as a woman of no taste, and must disown all intimacy with you—you must be contented with being my father's friend; for I cannot entirely abandon all pretensions to being a *modern*: you, who are *provided* for, may follow the Antediluvian system; but the bare suspicion of such a crime would ruin my fortune in the world.

Thus in a concise manner I have disclosed to you both, the chief mysteries of genteel life: if you slight them, the fault lies at your door, and your punishment will be, to be totally forgotten by the *gay*, though the *good* may idolise you.

Is there no great virtue in thus devoting so much time to *country cousins*, when every minute may be so charmingly employed? Gratitude though, I recollect, is amongst the old-fashioned qualities; and as you will be sensible of the favor, I will not dwell upon it, retaining *still* a few nursery-notions; among others, that of not exacting from those who are so willing to give all due praise to

Catharine Bishop

MRS. WALPOLE TO MISS BISHOP.
LETTER 32. SPRING-PARK.

Say what you will, my dear Miss Bishop, I shall not believe you incapable of enjoying the same content I do, in my situation: it does mighty well to describe the pleasures of a town life; but tell me, whether, amidst the most enlivening of them, your heart is so satisfied, as not to wander sometimes from the place of entertainment, in search of some new joy not to be found there? You own, that you complain of a want of variety now and then: the happy never *complain*, Kitty. I wish for no change, for the present gives me all I desire. I am willing to be stupid, if by stupidity I obtain happiness: the means are harmless; the end, what every one pursues, though not always with such success.

The friendship of Lady Catharine would be all I should covet, did I think you the creature you would pass for; but I am acquainted with you, and therefore claim your esteem also. You are too wise, my dear girl, to be amused by folly; and too virtuous not to abhor vice however exalted by rank, or disguised by mode. Pleasure enchants you for awhile, but it never makes you less amiable: your vivacity diffuses an innocent joy, which does not deprave you heart. I have seen you entering a public place in the highest spirits, yet stop, and show evident signs of sensibility for the beggar who has craved your charity, and imparted his piteous story to you; and had it not been in your power to have relieved him, you would have felt no raptures from the amusement you were going to. Do not then, my good Cousin, imagine you can impose upon me by your instructions: you would despise the admiration of the *gay*, if you were not sure of having the approbation of the *good* with it.

How unmercifully do you deal your satire on the loose wives of our age, and on the contemptible wretches you make them such! They merit all your severity, and much more; for to discountenance vice is the first step towards a reformation: but let us not confound the innocent with the guilty, and brand the whole state of matrimony with infamy, because some have defiled it by their licentiousness. The great world contains many couples who do honor to it; and wives are still to be seen, who would have shone in the purest times. The First Female in the kingdom is a bright pattern of every domestic excellence, and her example is followed by numbers of the fairest and noblest: among these we count a Portland, a Manchester, a Buccleugh, a Thanet, an Abingdon, more than one Spencer, a Delaware, a Torrington, a Wenman, and innumerable others, whose beauty adds the highest lustre to their prudence, and who might save this age from the censures cast upon it by those morose moralists, who are for ever exclaiming against it.———Generous minds are led to excell by emulation; and I should think it more to the purpose, to set before a pupil of mine a finished character in real life, for her to copy, than to persuade her no such existed. Vice will be more abominated if it is not supposed to be so common: therefore those satirists, who are so fond of exposing it to the light, seldom gain any benefit by it, except that of gratifying their own spleen. . . . . . But I fatigue you, my lively friend, by precepts which you have no need of, since you may be classed amongst the virtuous and the charming, whenever a youth as deserving as my Walpole shall persuade you to enter into that set which you have affected to condemn: when you have done that, he will teach you how to pass the gloomiest season in the country, or any where, without once regretting those "vanities that tire," and do not leave one pleasing trace in the soul. The dull *chimney corner* will be the most agreeable place in the world to you, when you have a companion who can make you as happy as is

Your

Emma Walpole.

MISS THORNTON TO MRS. WALPOLE.
LETTER 33.

Do not, my dearest Emma, restrain the sentiments which Mr. Walpole's behaviour must necessarily produce in a soul so grateful as yours is. I shall not dispute with you on the signification of *words*; we may differ only in our interpretation of them: your *esteem* is, I dare believe, all that it should be, and means as much as my warmer expression would do. Let it increase then hourly, and be as blest as his worth and your own can make you.

Could I have predicted, my friend, when first I came home, that I should have been so reconciled to my situation here, I should never have lamented to you our not having a *Walpole* in our neighbourhood.—Do you conclude that use alone has wrought this alteration, and that I am one of those weeds that take root and flourish in every soil, without requiring any more culture, only time to vegetate? Be undeceived, nor think me of so easy a disposition; I should have withered in the Grove, had it not been changed, by the power of a young *magician*, into the terrestrial paradise.

Sir Charles Noel has been the potent agent who has thus unexpectedly improved the place; or rather *my eyes* have been the spell, which having drawn him here, the rest followed of course—but it is not very interesting to know how, unless you know what has been the change.———After he had been several times in company with me, he was pleased to say, he could not *live* without me; and though I did not take this declaration in its literal sense, few men having died for love; yet, to avoid all *danger* of such an accident, I graciously consented to his making proposals in a more *common-sense style* to my uncle; those were too advantageous not to gain him over to his interest. Matters being thus readily adjusted, I am in a fair way of ranking soon among the *chaperonnes*.

In the interim, the presence of a swain, agreeable in his person, polite in his behaviour, and chearful in his temper, gives a new appearance to every object about me; and the days glide away in an enchanting manner.

I am not the only person who experiences the joys of this state; my aunt is enraptured, and actually *admires* Sir Charles more than I do: I might be *jealous* of her raptures, did they not arise from the thought of seeing me so well settled. I am exceedingly sensible of her goodness to me; but I cannot help being now and then a little petulant with her; for she is in one constant fidget from morn to even. Such a *bustler* I never met with before: every article must be finished as soon as it is mentioned. Her *friend* Noel encourages her in this; and I should be hurried out of my wits between them, did not my cautious uncle interfere. He will have every point secured, before we are married; and this gives some check to the haste of the others.

I was not a little pleased with one *trait* in Sir Charles' character, which came to my knowledge without his: when the settlements came on the tapis, Mr. Bridges, though only connected with me by marrying my mother's sister, offered to make a large addition to my fortune, which my disinterested lover would not hear of; but wishing to serve the young gentleman who is to succeed to the estate, he begged that he might be the better for his refusal.—He is a very distant relation of my uncle's, and has never been noticed by him; owing, I am afraid, to his having been the next in the entail. Men never cordially love their heirs; the very worthiest of them do not look kindly on those who are to supply their places. If it be *natural* not to do so, it is a terrible blot on humanity, since it must proceed from their knowing they were themselves impatient to supplant their predecessors; and suspicion is the certain conse- quence, and which must make their heir displeasing to them. I am loth to believe this dislike then to be so natural. I hate every idea which lessens my own species in my esteem. To increase philan- thropy, is to increase our happiness; wherefore then degrade the beings who are to administer our pleasures, by supposing human nature capable of such horrible crimes, and fix a cause for this, which may be a casual circumstance?

My uncle, unable to resist such a pleader, immediately consented to it, and he already sent four thousand pounds to young Mr. Bridges—a benefaction that does him more credit than fifty times that sum at his death to keep up the splendor of the family: he has also written to invite him to the Grove, and is charmed with the friend who put him in mind of doing such good actions. We have often agreed, my dear Emma, that the pleasures of generosity are more sensibly felt than any others. I add too, that its rewards are more liberally bestowed than any others; for every body joins in doing justice to Sir Charles's merit on this occasion: Mr. Bridges declares that he shall not lose by this donation: my aunt, with tears in her eyes from excess of joy, calls him the best of his sex; then congratu- lates me on my conquest. . . .

You can have no notion of any creature half so fidgetting as she is; she has been at least half a dozen times in my room since I began this letter, to ask what silks, what laces, what ornaments, I would chuse to have?—Just what you please, my dear Madam, has been my usual reply: but this does not do; I have had whole cargoes of different patterns brought me, and have been forced to fix on a hundred things, whether I would or not.—I hear her coming again: what's now to be done, I wonder? . . . It was only to inform me, that Sir Charles was below: finding I did not lay down my pen, she expressed her surprise at my being so composed; observing, that, if I was left to myself, the match would not be brought to a conclusion these seven years: so saying, away she trudged, and was down stairs in a few minutes, that my lover might not be alone until I made my appearance.—I go, my Emma, to prevent the good souls from growing quite impatient—but I must make *him* learn some of my composure (as my aunt tells it) in time, that I may not be worried all my life long with a *bustle*.

Adieu! Continue to love me, even after I am no longer

Frances Thornton.

MRS. WALPOLE TO MISS THORNTON.
LETTER 34. SPRING-PARK.

No one, my sweet Fanny, more truly rejoices in your flattering prospects, than your Emma, who more than any other knows your deserts.

Mr. Walpole is acquainted with your Sir Charles, and speaks of him as you do: he remembers him at the University, and afterwards met with him at Turin. Every body must approve of the partiality you feel for him.—I am not less earnest than Mrs. Bridges to have you, Lady Noel, though not quite so violent in my manner of expressing myself about it. You need not, I think, desire to know more of his character than the instance you mention shows: he must have an excellent one who can act such a part; and do not you, by unnecessary delays, give him room to accuse you of not setting a proper value on it.

We have had a visitor with us for some days, a Mrs. Bromley, who was a ward of the late Mr. Walpole's: she wrote to my husband a few weeks ago, and intimated her wish of being acquainted with me, as her long residence in the family gave her a sort of claim to all those who belong to it.—He gave me the letter to answer: I begged to see her at Spring-Park, whenever it should be convenient to her to honor us with her company. I told him what I had done: he did not seem displeased, but received her with great civility when she arrived.—She is a fine looking woman, and affects to have a vast deal of *hauteur*: I say *affects*; for when she is off her guard, there is more of levity than haughtiness in her manner. Mr. Walpole is frequently put out of humor by the familiarity of her address to him; yet this may be only the effect of her intimacy with him in his earliest years: but this is no excuse with him, who is so very nice in regard to the conduct of women.

She is a widow, has two sons, and is not likely to break her heart about the loss of her spouse, who, she informs me, was a strange unpolished wretch, that knew nothing of the world, yet fancied himself better versed in the ways of it than any one: she lived eight years with him, and had reason to repent of her haste in taking him, during every hour of that time————but he is gone; and the next who enslaves her, must have rare perfections indeed.—These are her own expressions: but I am mistaken, Fanny, if she really has such an objection to the state she rails at: for she is not a little desirous of drawing the attention of the men on her. She declares "Walpole is grown the stupidest animal on earth, since he married! She remembers when his gallantry was as universal, as it was pleasing—but matrimony is the bane of all that's agreeable." He hears this with an half-smile which shows more of contempt than applause. He told me this morning, that he hoped she meant to leave us soon, for he was heartily tired of her.

I am the most charming of creatures with her: my looks are consulted on every occasion; my dress is commended, my person extolled, and my wit (this is a new discovery!) surpasses all that ever was heard: I have but *one failing*, and that is being too gentle. I should laugh more than I do, when she is running on thus, if I did not perceive Mr. Walpole grow grave as soon as I begin to attend to what she says. I have found out, my dear friend, that he is passionate to a great degree, though he is always so tender of me, as to become calm the moment I appear; but I should be loth to be the person who put his patience to the trial, and am therefor very careful of not doing any thing to displease him. I wish with him, that Mrs. Bromley had left us, lest her being here should make home disagreeable to him: he has lately been more silent, and much graver, than he used to be: he is continually on horse-back, or strolling about the grounds, under pretence of enjoying the newly-returned sun. But I am not to be imposed upon by this; I know that he quits the house, because he does not like the company in it. As I dare not tell him what I think, I pretend not to take any notice of his frequent absence; he might perhaps suppose I intended to reproach him for it, and I am sure he will not bear that. This chattering widow was yesterday, after dinner, speaking as usual of her husband in a very disrespectful style.—"Why the devil did you marry him?" cried he. Because, said the other, I was disappointed in the man I had loved, looking steadfastly at him.—"You loved!" answered he with a sneer, "that word is oftener misapplied than any other: every one talks of *loving*, few know what it is. A woman feels a preference for a man's fortune, because it is considerable; for his title, because it would satisfy her ambition: he offers them to her, and they are accepted, for *she is in love with him*." She would have continued the subject, but he arose, and taking up a book, walked out. When he was gone, "Good heavens!" exclaimed she, "what a vile opinion has he got of us! Certainly he has met with some very mercenary woman, who has given him reason to speak thus of us."

I did not care to enter into any particular conversation with her, and proposed going to my harpsichord, at which I sat till tea was ready, and Mr. Walpole had joined us. Mrs. Bromley, softened by music, or intimidated by the seriousness of his countenance, was more reserved, and better behaved, than usual.

Adieu! My dearest.
Yours ever,
Emma Walpole.

Mr. Walpole to Col. Sutton.
Letter 35.

Who do you think, George, has been to visit us? No other than that
impertinent Mrs. Bromley, who, when she could not *ensnare me*,
made such furious attacks upon my father, and was actually on the
eve of becoming my mother-in-law, when death snatched her from
her *intended.* Upon the strength of this (which she fancies I never
knew) and her having been a ward of his, she imagines herself
connected with the family, and wrote to desire I would introduce her
to Mrs. Walpole. I had no design of taking any notice of this request;
but happening to give Emma the letter, she, in her great politeness,
sent her a pressing invitation. When I found the deed was done, I
would not prejudice my wife against her, by relating all the pranks
she had played to get possession of my estate; but charitably hoped,
that eight or nine years had made some improvement in her principles—She came, to prove my error.—Her incessant clack broke the
heart of that poor dolt her husband, who fell in love with her at the
play, and married her ten days after their first meeting, without
knowing any thing more of her than that she had a pretty face, and a
tolerable fortune. She soon taught him, to his cost, that a termagant
spirit might be concealed in smiles and dimples: he sunk under her
violence after a few years, and left her guardian to his children (he
durst not refuse to do it): she has the sole management of the
fortune, until her eldest son comes of age. This may induce some
indigent fellow to tie himself for life to her, and make him regret his
poverty and peace in the midst of riches: thus may every man be
punished, who, in marrying, is guided by such sordid motives!—
Emma knew not what to make of her: at first she was the high-flown
dame, hardly condescending to look down on any smaller mortal: all
was awful and sublime. I was pleased at the change: but finding that
did not succeed, she relaxed her rigor; and such languishments, such
advances followed, that it required all *my nicety* to defend me. Did I
not always say, Sutton, she was—what I will not write, though you
have often heard me speak it, when your good-natured soul has been
inclined to pity her, and to call me censorious: you will never do so
again, when I have related a scene to you which passed some days
after she came. My innocent Emma, who is as unsuspicious as she is
ignorant of art, would frequently leave me tête à tête with Mrs.
Bromley. In this situation, there are some women who expect to
be *particularly* noticed: she was one; but I should not have been
aware of it, if she had not, in a very different tone of voice from
what I had ever heard from her, said, "Mrs. Walpole is a very
lucky woman,"—I am glad you think so—fixing my eyes on hers,
to find out what she alluded to. I was not *vain* enough to detect
her immediately; but she determined not to let me escape in

ignorance.————"Without fortune, without knowledge of the world, to conquer a heart like yours—but she does not appear very sensible of her happiness."—O, replied I, when a woman once endeavours to lessen a wife in her husband's opinion, she fairly confesses herself jealous.—"I should never have thought of that," said she, putting up her lip in disdain, "I did not mean to depreciate Mrs. Walpole by mentioning her insensibility: it is the fault of nature, not her's: she is extremely amiable; but there is a coldness in her, which I never yet found in any person of her age."—I began to grow angry—she took such pains to pacify me, that I soon lost my ill-humor; but her words made a deep impression on me, and I resolved to watch Emma's looks more narrowly than ever I had done. When she came back to us, I seated myself by her, and taking up her work, I began to ask a number of questions about it: she, not imagining that I really asked to gain information, made me some vague answers, and turned to Mrs. Bromley, with whom she continued to talk on some very trifling subject. I changed my place, and she seemed totally inattentive to me: I repeated to myself—There is more coldness in her than ever I found in any person of her age.—A second repetition of it confirmed the observation, and my sullenness rose in proportion. Mrs. Bromley left us, to go to dress: I still remained silent: Emma looked at me, as if she wondered I did not speak; she arose, and coming towards me, said, in the most melting accents, "Are you not well, Sir?" laying her white hand on my forehead as I leaned back in my chair. The *sir* prejudiced me strongly against her enquiry, and I muttered out, Yes, *Madam;* what should ail me?

"Nay then you are angry, my dear Mr. Walpole," said she in a tremulous voice.—"Have you done any thing to make me so?"

"Not that I know of," answered she, withdrawing her hand, as if afraid.

Then you must think me exceedingly capricious to take offence without cause. "Indeed I don't," cried the dear girl eagerly: "it is very possible for me to have acted wrong, without being sensible of it; but if you will tell me what I have done, I shall be much obliged to you;" seating herself on my knee, and reclining on me.—There was no withstanding such a gentle apologist: I encircled her with my arms, and bid her continue to act as she had done always, and it would be impossible to find fault with her. She was still in this situation, when Mrs. Bromley returned from her toilet: she drew back, as if amazed at seeing her thus, and screamed in an affected manner, "What an unfashionable pair!"—Emma would have disen-gaged herself from me; but, as I chose to prove how unjustly she had been accused, I held her in my lap: she told me she wanted to dress—dinner would soon be served, looking at her watch. I was not desirous of having another conversation with the widow, therefore desired my wife would not change her cloaths that day, as I thought an *undress* most becoming to some women.—"Mrs. Bromley then," said she, "will forgive me, I hope, since I have so good a reason for not being finer than I am."—"O Ma'am," replied the astonished lady, "I should be very sorry if I was the cause of your not consulting your husband's taste—he must be the best judge of what is most becoming."

The flattery contained in this speech did not reconcile me to her: I felt myself stiff and formal, whenever I was to speak to her; and prone to contradict her, let her advance what she would. She quickly guessed that her *insinuation* had been displeasing to me, and in the course of the day she hinted, in very plain terms, that the source of her unhappiness in marriage had been a *disappointment* in love, endeavouring that her eyes should speak still plainer than her tongue, when she said this.—I spent as little of my time as possible with her after this; for the woman who forgets the delicacy belonging to her sex, is of all beings the grossest. But she has left us, and we are again completely happy.

Three or four months have made a great change in our scene: spring has renewed our verdure, and repeopled our neighbourhood. Variety has *some* charms; yet, faith, I think we were full as comfortable when left to ourselves, as we are now.—You will doubt this, Colonel—I can't help that—your incredulity be your punishment— you are not blest with an Emma, or you would not refuse to credit me.——But come and see how we go on: *mia sposina* longs to be acquainted with you; and I am always sincerely

Yours,

William Walpole.

COL. SUTTON TO W. WALPOLE, ESQ.
LETTER 36. BOND-STREET.

Commend me to the man who vaunts his *nicety*, with so little opportunity of having it proved!—Do you fancy, my dear Walpole, that I shall be greatly edified by your resisting the attacks of Mrs. Bromley? So far from it, I am rather surprised to find you paying so much regard to her, as to be affected by an observation of hers: but this is the way; we listen to the opinions of others 'till we insensibly imbibe them, and without knowing it we adopt sentiments contrary to our own, and are not always amended by the change. I have seen the bold *hit-or-miss* remarks of a fool, from a certain manner in delivering them, stagger the wisdom of a philosopher, who, not being prepared to confute them, has been obliged to yield to impudence.

Here truth has been sacrificed to violence; but when the words suit any particular foible, an idiot may lead the wisest man who ever lived. Your natural temper, being inclined to *disquietude,* readily caught at Mrs. Bromley's hint: I question even whether you were not *obliged* to her for furnishing you with an excuse for being dissatisfied.—I talk of *you* as of mankind in general: every one has some ruling weakness; and those who flatter it, become agreeable to us, without any other recommendation. You confess yourself out of humor when she first spoke of the coldness of Mrs. Walpole; yet a few *civil* words from her, seasoned to the palate of your self-love, soon appeased you: though, not a long time after, it required all imaginable condescension in your Emma to make you tolerably patient when she addressed herself to you, yet there is not the least doubt of your *loving* her.— Strange inconsistency! But so it continually happens, that those we are most attached to are made most unhappy by our whims.—Do not call this the consequence of the passion: Nature never gave birth to so monstrous a production; her dictates are mistaken by her vitiated sons. Love was intended to bless us, and not to be a source of endless mischief: when we abuse the means of happiness, we are justly cursed by feeling the effects of our imprudence. Do not you, my friend, like me, repent, when too late, of not knowing your own interest.—I am concerned to hear your account of *that scene*; it was drawing yourself into an unpleasant dilemma for no end.—What if Mrs. Walpole, unconscious as she was, had chosen to have gone up to dress before Mrs. Bromley did it, from thence had come down to dinner without giving you an opportunity of playing off *your airs,* or of coming to any explanation about your *sulkiness;* how many pangs would you have suffered without the least necessity!— You trusted to the gentleness of your wife's temper: beware, Walpole, of being so ungenerous, as to impose on an amiable woman, because you think she won't resent it, or of souring your own disposition by imaginary affronts—the real evils are just as many as a Job could bear in this life. . . .

I am in a testy mood, you'll think, when I find fault with more of your last letter; but there is a paragraph which I cannot pass over without criticism—You say "there are *some* women who expect *particular* notice." When chance throws them into a tête à tête with a man, it is, I am sorry to say, a maxim with too many of us, to make the most of such opportunities; nor have we always sagacity enough to find out whether or no it will be pleasing to our companions. You pretend that Mrs. Bromley *expected* your notice: I deny that you could be sure of that at first, though the event proved her to be one of those who did; but in this case, as we all do in most others, you judged from consequences, and could not have been authorised to have taken any liberties with her until she had given you encouragement: but upon bare presumption you proceeded. Conjectures of this kind are too apt to be erroneous; and I would rather disappoint an hundred *wantons*, than raise a blush in the cheek of one modest woman.

I believe I shall soon be with you, for I am tired of every thing here, and shall be glad to find a region where the inhabitants are happy enough not to be envious, and wise enough not to be ambitious.—Adieu! Yours ever,

George Sutton.

MISS THORNTON TO MRS. WALPOLE.
LETTER 37. THE GROVE.

I should have little faith indeed, my dear friend, if I did not believe you sympathised very sincerely in all my concerns: I have never yet known the feeling heart of my Emma indifferent to the agitations of any being, much less of one who has been always blessed with her friendship, and who in return has never formed a wish for happiness in which she has not been included.—This knowledge of your sentiments makes me, in writing to you, dwell on many circumstances trifling but to so partial a correspondent.

My aunt's *haste* has been such a spur, that even lawyers have been forced to travel with unusual speed in drawing up the writings: this accomplished, a few days now will put a period to *my reign.* Sir Charles' house is not above eighteen miles from this: he proposed our going there, that I might give directions for any alteration I chose to have made in furniture, &c. We agreed to go, and last Saturday, the day we fixed on, we got there to dinner. We found Lady Noel, Lord and Lady Wilmington, and Mr. Noel, ready to receive us. Sir Charles' mother has great remains of beauty, and a certain dignity in her whole deportment, which obliges one to keep a very respectful distance. Her children treat her with a kind of reverence, which confirmed me in the notion, I had at first sight, conceived, of her being extremely imperious: they observe every turn of her eyes; they are, by the bye, the most sparkling and brilliant that ever I saw. I thought I could perceive an air of anxiety in my lover when he presented me to her, but it was quickly dispelled by the very gracious reception she gave me; yet this, and the frequent repetition of *civil things*, which during the time we staid she said to me, did not prevent my feeling myself exceedingly *humbled* in her presence.

Lady Wilmington, her daughter, is handsome, but not so much so as her mother must have been at her age; but her ease, and particular kindness to me, rendered her much more agreeable, though there is something whimsical in her humor.—Her Lord is smart and genteel enough in his person, but not remarkably striking for this, or any other quality: yet the match was brought about entirely by love; for at the time they were first acquainted, my Lord had a father and an elder brother living; and Lady Noel meant her girl for the Marquis of Kent, who was passionately enamoured with her. She was forbid to harbour any thoughts of young Wilmington; but opposition only served to fix her his: she peremptorily refused to hear the Marquis, to accept of his proposals, or, in fine, to marry any one but the man objected to. She told me herself, that, until this, *a look* from her mother had been equal to a positive command with her; but that, finding she was not so absolute when she came to oppose her, she had gained courage from hence, and carried her point by dint of obstinacy. Lady Noel, tired out by her complaints and her constancy, bid her at last to dispose of herself without ever troubling her again: she took her at her word, and in a short time married. She was in disgrace at first; but her brother's intreaties, and the plea of her not having engaged without a *kind* of permission to do so, brought about a reconciliation. The death of his brother, and that of his father, which followed in a few months, made him at once an equal, and a desirable match for her.—She promised to be a great deal with me when I am settled at Noel-Castle, as she hates my Lord's mansion-house, and every part of the country about it.—I could see him pained by this declaration; but she claims the privilege of saying what she pleases.

The next in the group was Mr. Noel, a very fine, elegant young man: I really don't know whether he is not handsomer than my Sir Charles; but as I have never reckoned beauty of a consequence in a man, this is no disparagement to my *elected*. But this Edward is a mighty agreeable creature, and the brothers are uncommonly attached to each other.

After having spoken of the family, I must now say something of the dwelling, which is a grand pile of building, and situated most agreeably on a rising ground: it was built on the ruins of a castle destroyed in the Barons wars, and retains the same pompous appellation; but being a *modernised* one, it has no muddled moats about it, no draw-bridges to defend its entrance, nor do you find within it winding stair-cases leading to dark towers.—We staid there until Thursday, and had but just got home when Sir Charles was obliged to go to London for a short time. He comes down next week, and is then to be *made happy*, as he says.

Whilst this promising aspect of Fate is turned towards me, my heart still sighs, my dearest Emma, for one unhappy object, whose looks reproach me with cruelty, and whose merit deserves a better lot.—You have often heard me mention Mr. Howe as one of my *real* lovers, and I have as often regretted to you the indifference I felt for this poor man: with the highest esteem, (this word conveys a colder meaning with me than it does with you, witness your *last letter but one*) I never could prevail on myself to own another sentiment for him.—It was not in my nature—I could not blame myself for it—our hearts had not been made to pair and fit each other: there is some mistake in his; mine is not its counterpart.—I was sorry for him; I said so, and refused him in the softest terms; expressing, at the time, the greatest sense of the honor he did me, and wishing to preserve his good opinion without accepting of his love. Disappointment did not render him unjust; he saw through the coldness of my words, the true feelings of my soul, and promised to be satisfied with my friendship.—He intended, I make no doubt, to be as he spoke: but, though we may restrain our passions, we cannot annihilate them; and Mr. Howe has languished ever since, without permitting a murmur to fall from his lips. When he found that his countenance would betray his sufferings, he refrained from coming any more to the Grove.—It was many months since I had seen him; for he carefully avoided every place where we were likely to meet: I heard, from several people, of his being in a very bad state of health, and of his being advised to go abroad. I wished him to be out of the neighbourhood before I gave myself to another. As I was amusing myself with drawing two days ago, the door of the library where I sat was thrown open, and Mr. Howe announced. Guilt never looked more aghast than did your Fanny. The unfortunate invalid, too deeply engaged with his own embarrassment, did not seem to observe mine, but immediately began a conversation which still increased my uneasiness: he informed me, that he was come to take a last leave of his friends at this place; that he should set out, in a few days, for some warmer climate; but he could not refuse his heart the small indulgence of once more seeing—he hesitated an instant; but finding me affected even to tears, he immediately added—the *family* at the Grove. I quitted him under the pretext of going to let my aunt know of his visit: she joined him directly, and in her good-natured, hospitable way, would not hear of his leaving us for the rest of the day. I had walked out in hopes of his going away without seeing me again. I was shocked, when I went down to dinner at finding him among our guests. Compassion made me more attentive to him than to any other person at table: I was even pleased that Sir Charles's not being there gave him a right to all my notice. He was very sensible of my kind intentions, and thanked me more than once for being so good to him: but at going away he whispered to me, that "it was doubly cruel to be thus amiable, and thus 'insensible.'" After reflecting a little he observed, that the last epithet could only be applied to me by such a wretch as himself; for he had been told there was a man happy enough to be *loved* by me: he wished him, in *that light*, every blessing, and hoped he would prove worthy of the treasure designed for him. He then hurried out of the room, as if to hide emotions he was afraid of showing. What a reflection was this for the creature who knew herself to be the cause of his sufferings! I declare to you, my Emma, I scarcely ever felt more keen anguish: I retired early to my chamber, and was obliged to read over Sir Charles's letters, and to contemplate his picture for some time, in order to calm my troubled spirit. Are there, my dearest Mrs. Walpole, any women inhuman enough to enjoy the pain they give? I have heard there are such in the world; but I cannot credit it, imagining we are all formed with pretty much the same sentiments, though perhaps with different degrees of sensibility: every one would not, very possibly, sit like you or me, and weep over the victim to their charms; but surely no one would *wish* to reduce a worthy man to this state!

My aunt, who was a true *marplot* on the occasion, must advise Mr. Howe strongly against leaving his own country, and quoted fifty examples to him of people who had left their native air to perish on a foreign shore. I winked at her, trod upon her foot, and did all I could to silence her, but to no purpose, so earnest was she in her advice: he did not, I hope, pay more regard to her, than she did to me.

My uncle cautioned him against the impositions he would meet with from his being an Englishman, and recommended to him to go to Lisbon rather than to France, as his money would be more likely to return from thence into England, thro' the channel of trade, than from our natural enemies, who never part with any of their ill-gotten gains. Do you not admire the spirit of patriotism which appears in such various shapes in different beings? One set meets at the London Tavern to raise subscriptions, and wrangle for the good of the nation—another, at Standard Tavern, *priding* themselves on greater *refinement* of principles, talk loudly, without doing more than their neighbours. The Squire drinks, the Merchant trades, the Soldier fights—all for this end, if you believe what they say. My uncle's counsels will match any of the glorious efforts that are made in the good old cause.

When will Miss Bishop be with you? She must certainly have gotten a surfeit of London by this: the pleasures of Ranelagh do not make amends for dusty streets and sultry air. I will add no more to this pacquet, which has already passed the bounds of an ordinary epistle. Adieu then, my dear; believe me always

Your affectionate

F. Thornton.

Mrs. Walpole to Miss Thornton.
Letter 38. Spring-Park.

Poor Mr. Howe, what a situation is his! Well might you, my
Fanny, fret for him: it is a dreadful pain to know one has caused
the misery of a fellow creature, and it may still be aggravated by
the superior worth of the sufferer. I pity you, my sensible friend,
almost as much as I do your despairing lover. . . . This is a fine
lesson to you on the mixture of good and evil in this life: at the
moment when your joy rises highest, and you are on the point of
saying your happiness is complete, this discontented shadow is
drawn forth to your view; he comes to prove that no human bliss
can be perfect, and to teach you that the greatest pleasures will
have allays. Were we to be thoroughly satisfied here, we should no
longer think of hereafter: let us bless the merciful hand which has
thus mixed the draught of life, and without repining swallow the
potion as it comes.

You ask, my dear girl, if there are women inhuman enough to
enjoy the pain they inflict? When we judge from our own hearts,
questions of this kind are easily answered; but in this case I think
that rather too narrow a compass to move in, and I would quit
myself to enter into a wider field—that of the world; but there my
inexperience would soon lead me into a labyrinth, from whence
nought but vice would furnish me with a clue to get out. At our
ages, women can hardly gain knowledge of the world, without
risquing the loss of every valuable quality: after many years of life,
experience is purchased at a lesser price; but even then can we be
reckoned gainers, when innocence is exchanged for wisdom? I own I
shall part from ignorance with regret: it is the best security for our
most pleasing sensations; it insures that unsuspecting confidence, that
general good-will, which we feel for all the human race; it knows
nothing of ill, it can suspect none. Happy state of the unknowing!
Long may I taste its pure joys! For our peace's sake then let us
imagine, that every woman, like Fanny and her Emma, would mourn
the wreck of hapless love. . . . .

Kitty is come to us, and *a l'ordinaire* all life and spirits: she is a
most entertaining companion, and not a less desirable friend: in your
absence she seems to be the only one who can in any measure supply
your place to me.

Yesterday Lord Surry's family dined with us: it consisted of
himself, his lady, and two daughters old enough to be brought out (a
number of younger ones are kept up in the nursery until these are
provided for).—To pay proper deference to the *head* of the house, I
shall begin by speaking of his Lordship, who is the fine gentleman of
the last age, gallant and ceremonious; an indifferent husband, a very
tender father, an uncertain friend, a kind master; made up of contra-

dictions, yet never treated with contempt—so much more respect does the world pay to *quality* than to *qualities.*

Mr. Walpole, from whom I learnt the characters of my visitors, says Lady Surry is a prudent woman, has been the best of wives and mothers; but from living so much at home she is deficient in many of those *agremens* which make an agreeable companion. I could not perceive she wanted more than a few fashionable phrases to make her conversation just as unexceptionable as her behaviour: he is doubtless, though, a better judge of the *agreeable* than I am; therefore Lady Surry must not be placed among them.

Lady Caroline Warren, the eldest daughter, is a perfect beauty; but it is not of the winning kind: she is thoroughly convinced of her own charms, and looks with disdain on the less lovely: her manner is of that sort which mortifies and disgusts all those who are not so well assured of theirs.

Lady Georgina, not so completely beautiful, is infinitely more charming: the laughing Graces sport in her countenance, and every glance of hers shows an heart innocent and gay as playful childhood can make it. I am very fond of this little girl, who in her artless way told me she was quite delighted with this visit to Spring-Park; that her mamma had promised she should come to see me as soon as they came down, and she had never suffered her to forget it.

Mr. Walpole, who is always ambitious of having me appear to advantage, was more than commonly so on this occasion: he was in my dressing-room twice or thrice during the time allotted to the toilet: he did not like this colour—that ornament would best suit my face—I must put on my *petit-gris.* —After all these directions I was left to my own taste: I was glad he had told me *his*, as I resolved to follow it. I did so, and found him in the drawing-room when I went into it: he advanced to meet me, repeating with the most flattering look, as he led me to a seat, "then most beauteous, when least adorned." Encouraged by the approbation of my husband, the plain and simple dress I had on seemed to me the most pleasing of any I had ever worn, and I was entirely satisfied with it when our brilliant guests were ushered in. Finery did not excite a desire, but for my Walpole's sake I wished to have been as handsome as Lady Caroline. She was hardly seated when she whispered to Miss Bishop, loud enough for me to hear—"What a pity it is, that Mrs. Walpole has not more bloom! She only wants that to make her a very pretty woman."—Her remark quickly repaired the faults she complained of, for in a moment I felt my cheeks glow. Kitty saw my blushes, and replied with great tartness—"When beauty is the *smallest* perfection a woman has to boast of, she may lose some or all of it, without being less amiable.—Mrs. Walpole's paleness is no blemish, as it only renders her more exquisitely delicate; but your Ladyship may see her *now* as you wished her to be, for her complexion is greatly improved since *you* spoke."

She did not deign to speak again on the subject; yet my good friend took several opportunities of praising pale beauties; in which the sweet Georgina joined, though her own face bore all the marks of ruddy health.

I was not sorry when they left us: there is a formality in *the first visit*, which makes the end much more agreeable than the rest of it. I have frequently thought, during the time when people are thus stiff and shy, that it has been calculated rather to destroy than to encourage society, the establishing such a mode of proceeding: and if, instead of the *prescribed* form, every one was left to pursue their own inclination in regard to visiting, we should never meet with unwelcome guests, or ungracious receptions. . . . Sir Charles, I hope, is with you again; and the stirring Mrs. Bridges hastening the wedding preparations. Kitty dictates a thousand things for me to tell you; but as it is impossible I should write so fast as she talks, and as she has taken her stand just at my elbow, I believe the best plan I can execute, is that of resigning my pen to her. . . . She will not accept it, declares she has abundance of letters to write, but begs I will for once give up to her humor, (which cannot endure so dull an employment just now) and accompany her in a walk. I must comply. Adieu, my dear Fanny.

Yours ever,

Emma Walpole.

MRS. THORNTON TO MRS. WALPOLE.
LETTER **39**. THE GROVE.

Hold, my dear friend, and do not be so desirous of hurrying me into matrimony.—I find it is not so easy to manage our *captives*; and what must it be when they become our *tyrants?* —For my share, I don't care to venture my peace on such weak foundations as the professions of a lover. I require better security, and am not likely to find it, it seems, as I differ from most folks in my notions, I am told—but you shall judge how justly.—Sir Charles came from London last Wednesday, loaded with gew-gaws of every sort, in order to gratify *female vanity*, no doubt; not to say a word of the *pride* the men take in having their wives as fine as their neighbours. I received his *presents* with infinite condescension, and was praised highly for so doing. He was engaged today to dine with some gentlemen at a club held weekly a few miles from hence. We parted in great good-humor with each other, and he promised to be back by eight o'clock: this made me decline going to Mr. Glanville's with my uncle and aunt in the afternoon. I sat whiling away the hours with reading and working; when, just as the clock struck eight, I saw Sir Charles come driving into the court, his horses in a foam from his expedition in travelling. I had no objection, I allow, to this *seeming* impatience: it made me conclude he had been as anxious to return to me, as I wished him to be.

The same speed attended his steps, and I found him in the room with me in an instant. I testified my joy at his appearance; but observing a something extraordinary in him, I thought it necessary to assume a more distant air. This did not hinder him from approaching me with a freedom which he had never before attempted. I now suspected that *his friends* had obliged him to drink more wine than he is accustomed to do. He very soon saw the change in my behaviour, and immediately changed his own. Shortly after, he proposed our taking an airing in his phaeton, which was still at the door, saying it was a fine evening, and should not be lost. As I did not imagine him very fit to be trusted with the reins, and his horses not being very quiet ones, I peremptorily refused going. Whether he guessed my *suspicions,* or was heated with drink, it's hard to tell; but without any more provocation than this, the gentleman flew into a passion, and demanded in an authoritative tone, "What were my reasons for not going with him: was I afraid of trusting myself with him?—He knew not how I could pretend to love a man I did not chuse to confide in."—Amazement had struck me dumb for an instant; but when I had somewhat recovered myself, I answered with great firmness, "That, whatever my reasons were, it would be of no importance to give them to a person who was too *angry* to be convinced by them: besides, I did not suppose myself bound to account for my conduct, when I was certain of its being proper."

He affected to be more calm upon this, and begged I would let him know why I showed such distrust in him, that he might remove it if possible.

"When you set me so good an example," said I, moderating my resentment, "I shall doubtless follow it; and as you have *begged* to hear my reasons for not agreeing to your proposal, I shall no longer refuse to give them.—You are to understand then, Sir Charles, that there would be a glaring impropriety in my being seen driving about the country in your phaeton, with no companion but yourself: you would not have made such a request at another time; and *at this* I should be more to blame than ever for consenting to it."

"You fancy I am drunk, Madam; but you are deceived—I am perfectly in my senses, and know what I have said."

"I am sorry for it, Sir, since, bad as the excuse is, it would have been better to have pleaded intoxication, than to have owned you committed a fault in your *sober* senses."

"What fault have I committed, Miss Thornton?" interrupted he. "Is it a crime to have expected you would have been above *vulgar prejudices*, to have given me pleasure? I confess I cannot reconcile your behaviour now with the foregoing part of it. A woman who *loves* will give up a trifle to make her lover happy."

"Stop, Sir," said I, "and learn from me, that the woman who was *above* what you call *vulgar prejudices*, would be *beneath* your regard. She who shows an indifference to the opinion of the world, deserves the censures of it. This is not such a *trifle* as you may think: appearances are all that people can judge from; and when those are *improper*, it is very reasonable to conclude they will be condemned.—I shall always be happy in making you so; but I will never purchase happiness by an imprudence—It would be no compliment to you to do so, as I should prove by it that *your esteem* was of no great consequence to me. To act contrary to the conviction of my judgement, would be departing from my principles; and would as assuredly draw on me your contempt, as it would the reproaches of my own heart."

Saying this, I took up my needle, and was going on with a piece of embroidery which I had been about when he came in. This was a new affront. As he grew more *quarrelsome*, I became less disposed to indulge him, and went on with my work a little longer.—These creatures can't bear the least contradiction: fawning and kind as you please when nothing happens to ruffle them; but throw the smallest obstacle in their way, and adieu to their good-humour. Sir Charles is certainly as *mild and patient* as any of them: but even he could not endure opposition; for finding I did not instantly quit my work, he snatched up his hat, and with a profound bow wished me a good night. This was unexpected; but as it was not my business to make the first advances towards a reconciliation, I returned his *wish*. Altercation had kept up my spirits; but when I saw him drive off, all the woman's softness took possession of me, and I burst into a flood of tears. After passing some time in this way, I began to cast about how to evade all my aunt's enquiries about Sir Charles, whom she was to have found here at her return. I determined at length to retire to my own apartment before she came, and to order my maid to tell her I had got the head-ache, and had gone to bed, desiring no one would disturb me: this was done; and about nine o'clock I overheard the good old lady in the next room, catechising Walker about me.—"So your mistress is indisposed, I hear—How long did Sir Charles stay?"

"I really can't tell, Ma'am; but I fancy, when he came, my mistress was so bad with the head-ache that she could not talk to him, which made him go away."

I laughed at Walker's officious zeal, which prompted her to give so *curious* a reason for his sudden departure: it was not a satisfactory one to my aunt, who, notwithstanding *my prohibition*, would come in to see* me. I shut my eyes, and shammed a sound sleep when she approached the bed: this made her easy as to *me*; but the absence of my lover still troubled her. I envied the state which made her feel no inquietude, but what arose from curiosity, which, as it was of no very material consequence, I did not think myself obliged to gratify. I could not do it without accusing Sir Charles of having in some sort misbehaved; and, whatever honor I might have gained from publishing my part in the conversation, I should find no consolation, since his *faults* appear to be a reflexion upon me.

After passing many hours without once forgetting myself, I got up, to try what conversing with my dearest Emma would do towards composing my mind.

I weep, I am miserable; yet what cause have I to be afflicted? Have I not done right? And if Sir Charles Noel is unreasonable, should I be unhappy?—He is not worthy of my tears if he requires me to do wrong; and I should rather rejoice that I have offended him by the strictness of my notions, since in acting thus I must have secured his respect. In this strain have I passed the night, in arguing myself into peace, but without effect: yet hard as it is to suffer this, were I again in the same situation, I would again do as I did then, convinced as I am of the rectitude of my conduct. Why then mourn?—Because the man I loved, he whom I thought more than mortal, has proved himself unworthy: he has lost himself in my esteem, and yet he is dear to me...But I will wait until to-morrow before I quite condemn him: a night's repose will restore him to himself, and he perhaps will come back to me, ashamed of his proceedings. With what joy, my dear friend, shall I behold my penitent! Adieu! I shall fatigue you, without benefitting myself, by writing.

MRS. THORNTON IN CONTINUATION.
SUNDAY MORNING.

How unjust was I, my dear Mrs. Walpole, in doubting for a moment of my Noel's return! Not a soul was up in the house, excepting myself, when he arrived here. I had just put away my letter, and was looking out in admiration at the glories of the rising sun, when I saw a carriage coming to the gate: I quickly discerned whose it was. After much knocking and ringing, he at last gained admittance. I went to my watch, and found it a little after six. My next thought was, to go to *my glass*: this told me no very agreeable truths; my eyes swelled, cheeks wan, and lips parched. I had half a mind not to have been seen until I had slept: I threw myself down, and hoped to have taken a nap; but pleasure was as great an enemy to me now, as anxiety had

been before, I would not go out of my room until I heard my aunt's
bell ring; for I now *again* considered myself as the *offended*, and
therefore did not design to make any concessions. When the family
was stirring, I went, as usual, the first into the parlour, where I found
my dear conscience-stricken Sir Charles waiting my coming. As soon
as he saw me he immediately accosted me with these words.

"I am come, my dearest Fanny, not to justify my last night's
behaviour, but to intreat your forgiveness of it.—I really was not so
intoxicated as not to know all that passed, though I had drank too
much to be quite rational: your health had been too often toasted,
for me to have been sober.—In this situation, men are more void of
sense than brutes: it is a vice which has always been detestable to me;
it will for the future be more so than ever, from its having made me
offend you."

"I am not angry now," said I, "since you no longer persist in
your error———to know that you have committed one, is sufficient
punishment to a sensible soul; and I ask no other atonement than
your acknowledgement of it. I have some apologies to make, as well
as you: you were not master of yourself at the time; but I, who had
my cool reason to direct me, should have been more considerate than
to have provoked you, by continuing to work when I found you
objected to it."

"No, no," replied he; "You were right, undoubtedly, not to
oblige me in any thing, after the ill use I had made of the liberty
you allowed me of being with you."

When two people are thus willing to confess they have done
wrong, there is no fear of their being long at variance: our difference
was quite made up before Mr. and Mrs. Bridges came to us.—Sir
Charles had left me with a resolution of going to Noel-Castle, but
had not gone ten miles when, repenting of his rashness, he stopped
and waited at an inn until morning, when he could come back to the
Grove, and repair his folly. He gave *business* as an excuse to my aunt
for his having gone away before she came home: and as I had
prepared him to hear of my *head-ach*, every circumstance passed off
without suspicion.

The first hour of a reconciliation was the very time for making
me fix a day for our marriage: he did not neglect it, and Thursday
next is named . . . . . .

I cannot abide your Lady Caroline Warren, and am glad Miss
Bishop has more *tartness* in her manner than you have: she is fit to
deal with such a conceited girl.—I should guess that Nature lost so
much time in forming her features thus nicely, that she could spare
none for the embellishment of her intellects: or is it that education
having taught her nothing but how to manage her charms, she has
never been able to find out any other subject to employ her thoughts?
I believe there are more fools made after, than before their births.

It is lucky for you, Emma, that I do not wrangle often; for *this dispute* of ours has swelled my letter to an enormous size. After Thursday I must no more presume to *contradict*. Alack! How hard upon us, to be obliged to resign our favorite *right*, and to mortals, too, full as fallible as ourselves! But that which I vow to do shall be performed, though it may now and then revolt against the inclination of

Your

Frances Thornton.

MISS BISHOP TO LADY NOEL.
LETTER 40. SPRING-PARK.

This day's post having brought us a *flourishing* paragraph, concerning the marriage of "Sir Charles Noel, Baronet, of Noel-Castle, to Miss Thornton, of the Grove in Warwickshire;" every body was eager to pen a something upon the occasion, expressive of their feelings.— Walpole was for an epithalamium; but when he came to invoke the assistance of the Deities, a multitude of objections occurred. Matrimony never was upon a very respectable footing on Olympus; he considered, therefore, he could have no hopes of much *assistance* from that quarter: and what's a poem without an invocation, you know? Then there was not a simile which suited his Fanny; not a Goddess in whom he did not find out some blemish, nor a celestial husband whom he could propose as a pattern to yours. These difficulties discouraged him so much, that he protested against writing at all.

Mrs. Walpole then undertook to felicitate you; but sick and puling as she is, she was better disposed to make a funeral oration than an epistle upon this subject: yet she continued for some time to struggle against her natural bent, until Mrs. Sayer (the house-keeper) a matronly body, finding her at her desk, strongly remonstrated against her writing; saying it was not proper, in her *situation*, to sit *poring over* any thing; that confinement was the worst thing in the world for her; and, in short, gave her so many *wise* documents, that she was forced to rise, and leave the task for me. Since, then, it is decreed, that I should speak for myself and the others also, you may guess that I shall say a vast deal, being commonly very *verbose*: but I hate repetitions; and as there have been an infinity of weddings since the original institution of the ceremony, there is not a new idea left for me to utter on this occasion: in this distress I can only tell you, that all here wish you every happiness which can be found in an union of hearts. As you could have no doubt of this from those you call *friends*, it would be unnecessary to employ more words about it, especially as *wishes* avail but little in such cases, unless the parties are well inclined to be happy in themselves. That both you and Sir Charles are so, must be allowed, and would have been equally so without this airy help. Having now shown how significant such complimentary expressions are in general, I must claim an exemption for our *sentiments*, which derive the highest value from the warmth and sincerity of the hearts which dictate them. You are to esteem then this letter very differently from those you will be pestered with from the votaries to form.

As I have addressed you as a bride, my dear Lady Noel, I shall now talk to you as a wife. Are you impatient to hear *my sage* instructions?—I begin then by caviling at the conclusion of your last letter to Emma, in which you *piously* purpose never to contradict *your spouse*, merely because he is such. I never thought such doctrine would have been broached by you; it was worthy only of the non-resisting gentleness of our meek friend, who, born "to be controuled," does not find any hardship in obeying. For my part, the *jus divinum* of husbands seems to me full as oppressive as that of kings; and, had our parliament been properly *mixed*, both would have been abolished together; but, *excluding us* from taking any part in the formation of the laws, like all usurpers they tyrannise, to ensure by tenure what they do not hold by justice. Our men are not only the sons, but *heirs* of liberty, and, like the eldest-born, run away with all the inheritance from us defenceless beings.—"Wherefore are we born with high souls, but to assert ourselves, shake off this vile obedience they exact, and claim an equal empire o'er the world?" —Wherefore indeed! I'll answer for it, there never was an Hampden, a Selden, or a Russel, who had a greater aversion to *passive-obedience* than myself: and why should I be more obliged to it by the laws of my country than they were? You will tell me I have never been *in love*. No, thanks to Heaven! I have not, and hope I never shall, if those two syllables are so powerful as to tame my aspiring spirit. I would not lose the *glory* of being the *patroness* of my sex's freedom for all the joys of a romantic passion. . . . But unless I find I am likely to make a convert of you, I shall not explain myself more fully. I shall judge, from your next, what progress I have made.

After passing some weeks here, *en trio*, our party was increased last night by the arrival of Colonel Sutton: an acquisition, let me inform you, to any set; for he is agreeable and handsome. If I could depend upon Walpole, he is *non-pareil*: but I would never take the character of an Orestes from a Pylades: I chuse to make use of my own unbiased judgement for finding out the merits of an object. I have already given this a deal, methinks, in calling him what I did; for I am not very easily pleased in my companions.

We are plagued eternally with *intruders*: if I did not entertain myself with tracing the singularities in each, I should be stupefied with their visits, which are as long as they are dull. Mrs. Walpole, I perceive, *takes* mightily with her country neighbours; so civil, so affable, so ready to pardon all their awkwardnesses, and so provided with good-natured pleasure to save them from my raillery—it's very edifying, I protest; but it does not hinder me from taking *them off* as soon as their backs are turned: and I always extort a smile from her, thought she endeavours to screw up her mouth, for fear of encouraging my *wickedness*.

If Mrs. Sayer does not change her *prescriptions*, you may hear often from

Catharine Bishop.

LADY NOEL TO MISS BISHOP.
LETTER 41. NOEL-CASTLE.

On reading your letter, my dear Miss Bishop, I felt my happiness increased by the wishes it contained: no bliss on earth is so great as not to receive addition from knowing such hearts are interested in it: mine, I acknowledge, vast as it was before, has extended since I have been assured that I am so tenderly remembered by my friends at Spring-Park.

I would not have my Emma put herself to the smallest inconvenience to write to me: I am convinced of her good disposition to do it, and that shall content me until Mrs. Sayer, and the rest of the adepts in the art of nursing, shall think fit to take off the interdiction. You, my sprightly correspondent, must, whenever you can find leisure, indemnify me for her silence: all *libertine* as you are in your ideas, I shall not be afraid to engage with you; nay more, I promise myself an entire victory over you some time or other: the day will come, I foretell, when you will renounce your own will, and prove more true pleasure in complying, than ever you found in commanding. It is easy to practise obedience when we are ruled by the master of our choice: his power is the *prop* of our weakness, not the destruction of our liberty. The husband who is divested of his authority, is incapable of affording protection; and therefore, unless we could *fight* for ourselves, it is safest and best to let him enjoy his prerogative, that we may reap the advantages of it. I have only mentioned yet the meanest incentive to this submissive conduct: when we come to speak of the others, I am sure of bringing you over to my way of thinking. Were we kept in subjection only by fear or interest, we should really deserve slavery; but when love, the great interpreter, guides our steps, the harsh word *obey* no longer fears us: when desires are mutual, it is puzzling to determine who exacts, or who complies.—

"He rules, because she *will* obey:

She, in obeying, rules as much as he."

You, who are so very obliging to all your acquaintance, would make no difficulty in being so to the person you love: cease then to suppose that you would deviate from an established law, rendered sacred by divine and human ordinances.

Rebellion has often produced tyranny, as well as sprung from it: the husband who is fretted by constant opposition, grows more severe: for instance, she who refuses to stay at home when she is desired, cannot expect to find it an agreeable place at her return; nor can she hope to be more attended to when she makes a request. To be happy, we must consider mothers as well as ourselves. By the rules of politeness we learn to yield up our opinion to another, rather than by persevering in it to appear *rude*: we sacrifice our most precious hours to a thousand impertinents, who from rank, or some such fortuitous circumstances, claim our notice for the same end: we endure daily mortifications for the sake of being reckoned well-bred: and shall we, when conformity becomes our first duty, relinquish it? But you are already convinced; to accuse you of being *obstinate* would be an injury: though you should not make an absolute recantation, I shall not fail to set you down amongst the *tractable* females, who make a much more advantageous figure than those unnatural Amazons, who grasp at power, and throw off the beauty of the fair, without attaining the wisdom of the men; becoming thereby loathsome to both sexes.

Would one imagine that *une nouvelle epouse* could give lectures on such a theme?—But your wit inspired me; and although I have not written on this side of the question with as much success as you did on the other, yet, as I have taken the *best* part, what has been defective in the stile may be hid by the justness of my sentiments, and you will not have carried the debate against me.

I left the Grove a few days after I married: my aunt, uncle, and two or three more of my friends, came here with us. We have lived ever since in a state of racket and dissipation, every moment bringing some new face to the castle. I shall be glad when this gives place to a more peaceable life.

I have the cleverest *flirt* imaginable for you, when you please to show yourself here. Edward Noel would exactly suit your taste; so gallant, and so lively! He charms all the *belles* here; but as I reserve him for you only, I have insisted on his being my *cicisbeo* until I have provided him with a proper mistress. He declares that he cannot have one that he likes better than me; but as he has never seen you, and I am rather too nearly connected with him, he may, without any breach of gallantry, forsake me as soon as I can get an opportunity of introducing him to you. I have already so sisterly an affection for him, that I am anxious for his welfare, and would place him in your hands as the best he can be in. I began to apprehend that he would have slipt through my fingers soon after he came to us. Sally Glanville, who is a sweet, blushing little girl, a near neighbour and intimate acquaintance of mine at the Grove, and who, as my bride-maid, attended me when I came home, struck the youth with great admiration on his arrival: for two days, he never moved out of the sphere of her attractions; but she not shining kindly upon him, he was quickly detached from her. She would be a dangerous rival, I can tell you; for few women are endowed with so many native graces. She has been brought up by her grandmother, who never travelled fifty miles from an obscure village in Devonshire; but good-sense does not require the knowledge of what is termed High-life, to make its possessors, polite and graceful in every action. Sally's rural breeding might reproach above one third of our very *fashionable* acquaintances: natural civility, not being cramped by absurd maxims, is always consistent, always easy, and unaffected.

Mr. Glanville, her father, is also with us: he is a sensible, unprejudiced man; knows human nature, and makes large allowances for its frailties; pities the unfortunate, but never despises them; enjoys good company as much as any one, yet can live in solitude without repining; for this understanding supplies him with thoughts, and his heart makes him always pleasing to him. The loss of a very notable wife affected him sensibly, and made him recall his daughter from her retreat, to inspect his household. A small estate, and five children, demand great economy. This amiable girl makes the prettiest figure in the world in her new employment: her little brothers and sisters pay her great deference, yet love her just as they should do.—If I have any knack at divination, young Bridges, who has been some time with my uncle, does not regard her with indifference; and his *partiality* prevented Edward from being favorably received. I wish it may be brought to a match; for the young man seems well disposed, and she will comfort my poor aunt for my absence.

Do you not wonder that I have written thus much, without mentioning Sir Charles! Considering how much he fills my thoughts, it is wonderful, I own; but he is a subject I mean to treat with the *highest respect*, and shall not expose myself to the ridicule of one who professes to disdain the weakness of the heart. I keep my *tendernesses* for the indulgent Emma, who will understand them. I adapt my discourse to my company; I would not talk to a prelate of a masquerade, nor to a gambler of honesty; neither would I make *you* yawn by dwelling on the charms of love, though I have as much friendship for you, as for most of those who are dear to

Your

Frances Noel.

Mrs. Walpole to Lady Noel.
Letter 42. Spring-Park.

I must have imitated that unhappy Queen of Spain, my dear Fanny, who used to feign that she *longed* to do a thousand things, which were forbidden by the formal customs of that country, if my *camerora major* had not been less rigid than hers; but as she does not pretend to *manage* me, I take the liberty of following just as much of her advice as pleases me, and would not defer writing to you any longer. . . .

Kitty mentioned Colonel Sutton's being with us: prepossessed in his favor, from Mr. Walpole's regard for him, I was not surprised to find him extremely agreeable, on our first acquaintance; but I cannot explain to you the sort of esteem I now feel for him. He behaves to me with an attention more minute than that of a lover; yet his affection is like that of a brother. He is always near me, always anxious to give me pleasure, is my constant companion whether I stay at home, or go out in the chaise, when the rest are riding. Kitty calls him *my shade,* and not without reason.

His humor, I should guess, was originally lively; but he seems to be oppressed at present by some misfortune, for he sighs frequently, and is so often absent, as not to know what passes, especially in a large company: our free-spoken friend told him yesterday, that he looked as if he had lost his heart, and wanted to find it again. Mr. Walpole laughed exceedingly at the speech; but I thought the Colonel would have been more obliged to him, if he had let it pass unnoticed.

This morning, as he and I were sitting together, after he had ruminated for some minutes, he asked me if I knew where Sidney was ? I started at the name.————"I mean," continued he, "whether you can inform me how to direct a letter to him, for I know he is gone to Russia; but a gentleman has written to me, to beg I would gain that piece of intelligence for him, as he is desirous of acquainting him with the alteration in his uncle's sentiments towards him."

This uncle was his father's elder brother, and never would see him when he lived at Sunbury.—It would not be possible for me to repeat what I said; for my whole frame was so agitated , that memory could not record a syllable of it. I made some answer, which was sufficient to let him know my ignorance of his abode. He saw me distressed, and instantly dropped the conversation, without one prying question.

I was impatient until I could retire, and pass a strict examination upon myself about the cause of this strange emotion on hearing a name which is so familiar to me. I found my heart, my dearest Lady Noel, ready to justify itself, or I should not have looked up with confidence in my husband's face when we met.—It did not bound with rapture at the sound of Sidney: it would not have been moved by it, had not that name recalled to its recollection those happy days, when, blest with a father's tenderness, it knew no wish beyond what it enjoyed, nor dreaded the evils that were wrapt up in futurity.— Believe me, when I solemnly assert, that my Walpole holds an undivided empire in my breast, and that every other man is now indifferent to me. But why do I make this protestation? Could it be a dubious matter? Impossible! Virtue shudders at the supposition: I would not for the creation suspect that you, my beloved friend, should have ever thought so vilely of me.—No, Fanny, I would not have sacrilegiously prophaned the altar at which my faith was plighted, by offering my hand without the consent of my heart. You, who heard every sentiment of my soul, now that I should have been inexorable to a parent's prayers; that force or pity could not have dragged me to the church, had I not found myself sensible of the merits of the object destined for me by my father: and I call heaven to witness, that, since the day I became his wife, I have never had a thought which could disgrace that tie. This is the only time I have ever suffered myself to remember there was such a being left in the world as Sidney; but in doing it, I forget he ever was dearer to me than friendship could make him. . . .

MRS. WALPOLE IN CONTINUATION.
WEDNESDAY.

I was not very well when I began to write on Monday, and have not been able since to finish this. My mind had been cruelly racked with apprehensions of committing a crime, in being so much affected by the calling over past events; and I had but just pacified it, by the assurances I had of its innocence, when Wilson came up to me, with all the marks of concern in her looks, to inform me, that she had for some months led a very uncomfortable life with Mrs. Sayer, who, having been entire mistress of the place for some years, assumes uncommon power over the other servants, and has taken a particular dislike to her.—At another time I might not, perhaps, have shown any regard to this complaint; but being low, and my spirits in a flurry, every trifle appeared of consequence then.—This poor creature, I knew, was attached to me from my infancy; she had been my mother's attendant, and had never in her life offended me; yet I should be forced to part with her: it was necessary I should do so, for Mr. Walpole had full as many reasons for being partial to his house-keeper, as I had for being so to my maid: I could not bear the idea of putting his love for me to such a trial, as that of asking him to discharge an old servant, for whom he had more than once expressed a preference. I told Wilson, that since they could not live together, she must prepare to leave the house: her tears redoubled at the sentence, but I could not repeal it. Her distress did not help to reconcile me to the expedient, yet no other offered: I felt my heart wounded to the quick, but I resolved not to open it to any one. In this temper I returned to the company: the moment I appeared, Mr. Walpole observed my dejection, and said to me in a low voice, "You have been crying, my love! Has any thing vexed you?" I answered in the negative: he pressed me no farther about it, but watched my countenance so narrowly, that I feared he would detect the falsehood I had been guilty of. I then tried to be chearful; but I am so wretched a counterfeit, that I could not carry on the deception, and relapsed again into my first state. The next day, my melancholy still remaining, I perceived that Mr. Walpole was gloomy, and out of humor with every one; that he seldom spoke, or took the least notice of any thing: when he and Miss Bishop were riding out, as usual, in the morning, I meant to have shut myself up in my own apartment, that I might have brooded over my cares without interruption: I was going as they went out of the room, but found myself withheld by the train of my sack; I turned to see whether my chair had not caught hold of it, but discovered it was Colonel Sutton who detained me, until the door was shut after the others.

"Forgive me, my dear Mrs. Walpole," said he, "for my presumption: I saw you rise with an intention of retiring; but, as I wished to speak a few words to you, I prevented your doing it.—I may be an impudent fellow in your opinion; but I promise you I am an honest one, and mean merely to serve you, by what I am going to say. You are a very young woman, and at your time of life every body requires an adviser: I am not capable of being so good a one as many would be; yet, as no other person undertakes to be yours, you must permit me to have that honor."

I assented to it, and he thus went on:—"Walpole has the best heart on earth; it is devoted to you: but he is extremely nice, nay, sometimes, even captious in his disposition; and it is not an easy matter always to please him: but I can give you one unerring rule to go by, which will never fail to keep him in good humor; that is, placing an entire confidence in him: conceal nothing from him, and he will never be dissatisfied. Generosity is his *forte*: he will pardon every thing you own to him; but reserve is so odious to him, he would renounce his dearest friend, if he suspected him of it. You married before you could well discern his character; so that, in thus drawing it to you, I hope you will not think I mean any imputation on your penetration, since nothing but time can develop such mysterious windings, as the heart of man is formed with. Our Walpole has as many intricacies in his as any of us; but I will be bound for his improving upon you from a thorough knowledge. His father was an humorist, and he was a petted child; he has therefore some hereditary, and some acquired flaws in his temper: he is sensible of them himself; but he is offended, if those he loves are *afraid* of him. Your timidity may sometimes be misconstrued by him: I counsel you then to have less of it when you address yourself to him: be assured he cannot thwart you, and when he finds you confide so absolutely in him, he would sooner die than disappoint you. I speak as one well versed in all his ways: we have been intimate from our juvenile days, and I have never found him unreasonable, when he is properly treated."

I thanked this kind *adviser* for his trouble; but the more I reflected, the less able I was to prevail on myself to disclose this disagreeable affair to my husband: I could neither bring myself to tell it, nor could I hide how much I endured from it: I then experienced the truth of your observation, "that when people once give way to causeless apprehensions, the imagination never fails to dress up a new bugbear in every thought." Fears multiplied every moment, and when Mr. Walpole came back, I was so harassed by them, that I could scarcely keep myself from fainting when I heard him: my disorder made him forget his displeasure, and he hung over me with all his usual fondness. As I did not go down stairs for the rest of the day, he was most part of it with me; and during this, I told him all that had happened amongst our servants; but I told him likewise, that no entreaties should make me keep Wilson. He desired me to do as I would as to her, but swore that Sayer should go, for having cost me so many tears: after great intercession, however, I procured her pardon, on condition that she and my maid both remained, but without ever interfering with each other.

When this trifle was adjusted, my dear Walpole, without the least acrimony, reproached me for having concealed any thing from him, and asked me, "whether I was afraid of him? He knew himself to be of a fiery temper, but he did not think he had ever been ill-natured to me." Ashamed of my childish terror, I engaged that this should be the last complaint he should ever have against me; and I felt my confidence in him to be so great, that I was going to acquaint him with every incident of my past life—but oh! My friend, there was one

1787 illustration to vol. 2, by permission of
Michigan State University, East Lansing.

fatal secret, which I durst not avow, and that secret imbitters all my hours!—I tremble, lest accident or design should betray it, and my silence be interpreted as guilt: yet, I have not lived long enough with him to venture at convincing him, that, though I *have* loved another, I have still a heart left, worthy of all his tenderness. He talks so oddly on this subject, and adheres so firmly to his own conceits about it, that I have not fortitude enough to bear up against his arguments. Kitty and he quarrel incessantly on this point: she assures him that *our* affections are full as renewable as *theirs*; then asks how often he had been in love before he married?

To this he pretends, that difference of education makes the cases not parallel; that women are confined, and taught from their cradles to preserve a purity of sentiment, which constitutes their highest merit, and fits them for the narrow circle of domestic joys; and that, when once a female transgresses the bounds assigned her, be it by coquettry, or a greater breach of chastity, she forfeits her primitive virtue: the first amounts to a prostitution of the heart, as the other is of the person; and he should be sorry to make any great distinction between them: that the rover man, whose province it is to govern, is early initiated into all the scenes of life, that he may acquire the necessary knowledge; and from *habit* can form connexions with a number of the fairer sex, without *really* loving more than one. To controvert this, would not be to remove his prejudices; they are fixed, and nothing less than an age of unremitting constancy in my love for him will effect an alteration in his opinion. When years have given weight to my asseverations, he may be brought to believe me when I refute his system. I shall be more attended to when the endearing name of Mother is added to that of wife. I must leave it then to some distant period to prove me what he imagines me to be. Unhappy attachment, which, without being criminal, has been the cause of such lasting uneasiness to me! If imprudence is thus severely felt, what must guilt be? Save me, gracious Heaven, from the knowledge! And let me ever remain entitled to the glory of being Lady Noel's friend,

Emma Walpole.

LADY NOEL TO MRS. WALPOLE.
LETTER 43. NOEL-CASTLE.

Profit, my dear Emma, from the new friend you have gained. Colonel Sutton seems to be calculated for the task he has engaged in; and though I am no advocate for the *Platonic scheme*, yet I fancy you may cultivate this friendship without danger, as he does not aim at

any more than instructing you how to render your husband and
yourself happy. He, as being intimate with Mr.Walpole, will be better
able to direct you as to his particular turns of humor: but there are
other points in which I shall still continue to advise. With a disposition more amiable than most, permit me, my Emma, to caution you
against that over anxious manner of feeling about every circumstance
that happens. The parting with a good servant would be a loss, and I
do not wonder that you viewed it in an unpleasant light; but to fret
yourself sick about it, was descending greatly from the character of a
sensible woman. If you give way thus to every little trial that comes
upon you, you will find the burthen of life much too heavy to bear,
for the most fortunate among us meet with crosses every day. We call
sensibility a dangerous gift: we make it so by our misapplication of it,
for Heaven designed it for the sweetest of our possessions; but if we
play the unthrifty prodigal, and lavish it on every call, we change to
the bitterest pangs our best comforter. The child who cries for a
rattle, may be quieted with it; but it is not thus with the grown-up
person: the toy is wished for, and, if refused, is of consequence
enough to be a matter of grief; but let it be obtained, the enjoyment
does not compensate for the trouble of *wishing*. Strangely compounded as we are, we hate pain, yet court it; we covet pleasure, yet
abandon it when it invites us. You forgot all your happiness, and lost
two or three days of it in *brooding over* (to borrow your own expression) a trifle magnified by the vapors of melancholy.—Fye! Mrs.
Walpole, I did not expect this! You, who should have learnt philosophy from disappointment!—But let me ponder a while before I
upbraid you again: you were not well; and our machinery is so
contrived, that the mind, though ever so noble, is subject to the
body, and disease preys upon it: the brightest understanding is
obscured by a fever; the most intrepid courage quakes under the
attacks of an ague; and the activity which immortalised the name of a
general in our father's days was at last conquered by a lethargy. It
was sickness then which damped your spirits; I am ready to suppose
it, that I may not blame you for murthering your peace by a voluntary surrender of it. Stoicism vainly cries that pain is no evil; a more
powerful voice contradicts it, and the stoutest yields on the pressure
of it. Patience, and not want of feeling, is the only remedy we can
rely upon: that informs us how to make a proper use of it, to
consider it as a friendly visitation sent us from above to wean us from
ourselves, an expiation for our sins, and a purifier of the soul. Fretful-
ness and impatience are not more unchristianlike than impolite: it is
adding thorns to our pillow, and uniting crimes to misfortunes when
we give way to them.

But whilst I am *sermonizing*, my own business is neglected, and I
hear Sir Charles running into every room to seek me; for the card-
tables are set, and the company waiting for me: there is no harm in

making it wait a little; for whether folks are counting their fingers, or their fish, it makes no great odds: the abuse of time is much the same; nay, it is probable less mischief may be done by the one than the other; so I shall not hurry myself.

I retract—Sir Charles does not agree in that opinion, and I must go down immediately. Adieu, my dearest.

Yours ever,

Frances Noel.

Miss Bishop to Lady Noel.
Letter 44. Spring-Park.

Not fit to be entrusted with the soft overflowings of your bosom!— be it so; I consent to be excluded from this part of your confidence: you would not be sooner tired with talking to a distracted auditor, than I should be in hearing what I cannot relish.—I am not of the dove kind. As far as gallantry can go towards putting us into good-humor with ourselves and others, I am its humble servant, but not one step beyond. I am not inclined to languishings and *crazing cares,* nor will I place my bliss on the *constancy* of man: the very sound is become a jest. When I change my state, it must be for some surer emolument than that of being *loved for ever.* Nothing is permanent on this side the tomb; and, of all blessings, those of love are least durable: how then should I trust to it!

As for Edward, I am persuaded he is a very pretty fellow, and will make an excellent *flirt*—though there is rather too much kinder in the composition of his heart: but Sally's charms have, I hope, spent most of it; for nothing is more troublesome than to have an agreeable creature, after having amused one for some time with mere flirtation, turn to a downright *whimperer.* Forewarn him against this; for, assure him, I shall never attach myself to a younger brother.— They may be the best gentlemen, but they are the worst husbands women like me can chuse.—I have not the most distant idea of starving on *la belle passion,* nor of living worse after I marry than before . . . I *venerate* the heroines who have so thorough a contempt for money, as to throw themselves into the arms of beggars. They are very sublime mortals; but not being formed for this venal world, they should be placed in some region where they could live upon the slenderest diet. Now, as geographers have never mentioned a proper climate for them, no place that I know of would do so well as Bedlam, where bread and water would be their food: its insipidity and lightness would suit their *gout* as well as their pockets.

But to return to my *delectable flirt*; you can form no notion how
welcome the offer was to me, forlorn as I have been since I came
here: nothing have I met with in the shape of that useful animal; the
men are all *Arcadians* or *Savages*, equally remote from that
character . . . I will give you a specimen of one of each sort. Soon
after I arrived, we were blest with the sight of a very civil, inoffensive
youth, whom I set down in "my mind's eye" as a good improveable
subject. Frederick Forrest has no despicable person, if he understood
how to make the most of it: he is docile, obliging, and would do like
other people if he could tell how to set about it. I thought it incumbent on *me* to take him under my patronage, seeing him so well
disposed; and I endeavoured to teach him several *bon ton* tricks: for
some time he played very shy, either growing afraid of me, from
hearing me ridicule his companions, or from taking my kindness
towards him to be ironical; but at last my redoubled civilities dispelled his fears, and the pleasure I expressed on his appearance
brought him frequently to the Park. If he came in a morning, I made
him escort me on horseback, and kept him to dinner: if he paid an
evening *vis*, I called upon him to assist me at the tea-table: his
assurance never rose above the limits I chose; and he made the
greatest progress in the science of talking *nonsense agreeably*, making
up *les yeux doux* if a lady did but move her lips to speak: he would
whisper the veriest trifle with an air of meaning, pick up a fan or a
glove with grace, and in returning it squeeze the fingers gently. I was
proud of my *elêve*, and made sure of having him to myself for the
season: but how changeable is the mind of man! Frederick, in the
high road to preferment, has been stopped by the allurements of a
little rustic, in whom simplicity has been more powerful than all my
learning: and this promise in genius is on the verge of ruin, by
marrying a girl without a shilling. Such an accident might have
disgusted a less sociable disposition than mine: but I waited to repair
the loss with Colonel Sutton, whose acquaintance with the world
would prevent the fatigue of instructing, and the dread of being
deserted by such an ignoble disaster. He came, but not for me; *my
wit* has no effect, unless it is now and then in extorting a laugh from
him: I partake in his general compliments, but nothing else: he is
Emma's *sylph*, and cannot afford time to attend to me. When I saw
her in such good hands, I thought Walpole might have been spared
for me. Here was a new disappointment, but no very grievous one;
for cousins and married men are not such mighty desirable flirts! Had
it been otherwise, this *pastor fido* would have been quite negligent of
every fair one but his own—Reduced to this desperate condition, I
had no resource left but in *plaguing*, as I could not *please*.—I fixed
on a *snappish* old codger for my butt, who has numbered a full half
century, and has never yet found out a mate. Of all beings, an old
batchelor is my aversion....There is much to be said in defence of old

maids—women have but *chance* for being pleased in a lover—they must stay until they are asked, and it's a million to one if the offers are such as can or will be accepted; in which case celibacy is obligatory.—Now, the man allowed by custom to range from nymph to nymph, authorised to fix on which he likes, and who, if rejected by her, is not discouraged from pursuit by the cruelty of one, but flies to some kinder she, and is full as well pleased with her—he, I say, has no excuse for remaining single; and must be a Cynic indeed, not to be warmed by merit, or dazzled by beauty, some time or other. My Diogenes shows his contempt only to the ladies, and on those he has no mercy: it would put a diffident woman out of conceit with herself to hear him talk of us; but, as I don't care a pin for the opinion of one who can be no judge, I *battle* it out with him. He advanced the other day, that *we* were vain, fantastic, and froward; insolent in power, abject without it.

I turned to Sutton, and observed, that those who had been *slighted* by us, were always most abusive: the reason was obvious enough; but they only doubled on themselves the disdain they found so insupportable.

Mrs. Walpole coloured, and the men wondered that I should enter the lists with such a savage: but I bid defiance to his brutality. He imagined he should silence me by saying, "More men had been cloyed by kindness, then destroyed by disdain."

I replied, that "one who had conversed so little with the sex, could know nothing of it."

He *thanked* God for his ignorance, and I *chaunted* Amen. He asked, "Why that?"

"Because you would have been like the rest of the world, and I should not have had an *oddity* to have entertained myself with."

He did not comprehend what I meant by an *oddity*.

"Why such a creature as you are; for I know not what else to call you. Had you been husband, or father, you might have had a more honorable denomination: but, according to the Roman edict, you can have none as you are—not a citizen; for you do not contribute to the benefit of any place, by adding to the number of its inhabitants—not a man; for you have no social principle in your nature.—*An oddity* then you must be; and my award is ratified by the authority I quote. . . .

My antagonist having nothing to say for himself, but the common cant of such contemptible censors, marched off upon finding no body heeded what he mumbled over, about chattering magpies—having the last word—female obstinacy,"&c. &c. &c. and I had the pleasure of having fairly routed him. He has been here two or three times since, but has not offered to make any comments on us in my hearing; though he pays us off in thinking, I make no doubt. But as long as his *pericranium* contains all his malice, he may enjoy it unmolested by me. When he gets a *migraine*, or *vertigo*, he may have recourse to medicine; and I shall recommend spleen-wort to him, as properest for the constitution of his mind at least. . . .

After this ditty, you need not be half so sharp as you are, to guess how acceptable *Edward* will be to me. I should have striked across the country, to have reached to Noel-Castle ere this, had I not engaged to pass the summer with the Walpoles: but as my beau is kept in practice by you, I am easy about him.—I beseech you to let me know, before we meet, lest he should be shocked when he sees me, that I am not blooming as Sally Glanville; nor near so beautiful as *la bella Ceutrina*—that I am more *agreeable* than *handsome*: but as he must be willing to discover that until we are well acquainted, he must not be too hasty in giving his sentiments of me. . . . . This may serve him to dream on, until he can have the felicity of hearing me. This may likewise suffice for your Ladyship at present.

Adieu!

Catharine Bishop.

MRS. WALPOLE TO LADY NOEL.
LETTER 45.

Such a preacher as my Fanny would make proselytes amongst the most reprobate. What effect then may you not hope to produce in one so ambitious of doing right as I am? But *patience* may be as necessary for you as it is for me; and, with a soul which soars far beyond the narrow bounds of negative merit, I have a feebleness of resolution which does not permit me to rise to any height. But, though the more striking virtues may not be in my power, that of resignation (not the least meritorious) may be practised by all; it is that which seems to be particularly designed for me from the disposition I am of. "The smoothest course of nature has its pains;" and it is essential to me to be armed against the hourly calls I have for the exercise of this patient and submissive conduct, since I feel everything that happens: the glance of an eye has pained me to the heart; the addition and omission of a word has hurt me. I am not singular in this, for there is no exemption from suffering: the only difference is, that "the Feeling of another's woe, the Unfeeling for his own," sheds tears.—Pity forces them from those on whom Heaven has smiled, and makes them borrow affliction rather than there should be an exception to the general curse, which involves the posterity of our disobedient parents in misery. . . . .

I have said that Colonel Sutton appeared to labour under a gloom that did not agree with his natural temper, which still broke

through it at times, rather hiding for an instant, than dispelling the
cloud that returned again immediately, as if recollection checked his
rising gaiety. I have wished more than once to learn the cause of
this; but it never transpired in the smallest degree until two days
ago, when, having heard that Lady Caroline Warren had accepted of
Lord Clarendon's hand, a man to whom no objection could be
made, if disparity of years is not one, we were all making our
remarks on the news, and each spoke what they thought of it. Miss
Bishop, who has no opinion of the lady's sense, admired at her
making so *prudent* a choice. Mr. Walpole execrated the expression,
and the woman who consulted *that* only in marrying. I defended
her, by saying it was not impossible but that she might, exclusive of
his title and fortune, have seen many perfections in him; that tastes
varied as much as person; that he who charmed one, might disgust
another. Colonel Sutton agreed with me in this; but added, that the
taste of a coquette was as changeable as her dress, and hardly
merited to be called by one fixed name. He said this as if he felt it:
but I should not have minded it, if he had not, when left along
with me, renewed the discourse.

"So you think it possible that Lady Caroline Warren could prefer
a man, some years older than her father, to the young and pleasing
D'Arcy, who offered himself to her, and was rejected?"

"I can only urge variety of taste," answered I: "it is capricious,
and does not adhere to the precise rules of judgement. I can conceive no other motive for Lady Caroline's taking Lord Clarendon,
but her preferring him: but her liking him better than Mr. D'Arcy,
though it may amaze, should not make us blame her."

"Far be it from me to blame her, if she really had a preference
for him: but I have experienced, Mrs. Walpole, that women are
oftener biassed by ambition, than by love in chusing."

"You have been unlucky," said I, "in your connexions; for that
does not seem to be the reigning passion of our souls, since more of
us are made wretched by the last."

"I have some grounds for disbelieving that; for of two, whom I
attached myself to, and of whose affections I made sure, one neglected me for her friend—the other jilted me for a wealthier lover.
The causes differed, but neither could have loved . . . . . ."

"I can't determine that," replied I: "the jilt could not, I should
imagine, have had any attachment to you; but she whom you accuse
of neglecting you for her friend, was not destitute of sentiment, you
must acknowledge. If her friendship made her seem more negligent
of you, from the kindness she showed to another, who perhaps
demanded her particular tenderness for a time, it does not follow,
that she was positively indifferent to you. A virtuous woman will
restrain her love, as soon as it becomes inconsistent with her duty. I
cannot help thinking, that she who is capable of acting up to the

friendship she professes, must be a valuable woman; and it is cruel to blame her for that as a fault, which is certainly meritorious."

"Such sentiments, Madam, do honor to you. I have long been convinced, that in forsaking Miss Neville I gave up all right to happiness; and, like every wrong-headed man, I repent of my error when it is too late.—Mine is a long, and not an entertaining story; therefore I will not relate it to you: if you care to hear it, Walpole will tell it you. Two letters which I will show you, will give you some insight into it: they are not very much to my credit; but when I know myself to be guilty, I submit to the humiliation of being condemned."

I took the letters from him, and quickly after retired to peruse them: you shall have copies. There are some things in Miss Neville's worth reading; whether it is that one is naturally interested for the injured person. . . . That a lover should change his mind, does not carry any of the *extraordinary* with it; but I did not think *Colonel Sutton* could have been unjust to the merits of such a mistress!——

I leave you to finish the inferences that may be drawn from the two letters, and am your ever affectionate,

Emma Walpole

To Miss Neville, Park-Street.

"AFTER having known and loved you, for three years, with a tenderness which I fancied was reciprocal, I did not suppose that in asking to hear from you, when I left town for some months, I had laid too heavy a tax on your complaisance. The *sang froid* with which you parted from me; the indifference, which had been manifest for some time in your whole deportment, whenever I *intruded* upon you by my unwelcome visits, should have prepared me for this, had I not strove against conviction: but the suspicions, which were lulled by my wilful blindness for a while, are now too well confirmed, by my not having received a line from you since I came to Waterlands. This has succeeded to your intention: your coldness has destroyed the remains of a passion, which, from being distasteful to you, can no more satisfy me. . . .

With the highest esteem for your character, I resign all pretensions to *your heart*, which, from a principle of *justice*, you might have called mine, after all the pains it cost me to gain it: and I ask from you the liberty of bestowing my own on one who does not leave me doubtful of her being sensible of its worth. Had I found Miss Neville thus, I had never desired more to have made me ever hers.

G. Sutton.

To Col. Sutton, at Waterlands.

WHY ask me for what is no longer mine?—She, who is so much more sensible of your worth, Sir, has already deprived me of the power of retaining, or of resigning, your heart. As I am ejected, I need not pretend to abdicate; but I do not even dispute her right to you: we reign by election, and she who is chosen by *you* must have the best title. May she make you as blest as I wish you to be!

Had your *suspicions* been brought as accusations against me, I could have cleared myself; but as you are satisfied that I should be guilty, I consent to appear so, being desirous of saving you the regret of having wronged me. To justify my silence, I should be obliged to enter into a detail of distressful circumstances, which would but ill suit with the situation of an happy lover. You have not leisure to weep with the friends you would wish to forget: yet I will not quit you for ever, without telling you, that, however *indifferent* you have found me in those visits you have termed *unwelcome*, I have never had a thought, in which you have not been concerned; nor did I feel a sentiment, to which you did not give rise.—My sister required the most diligent attendance from me: I gave it, assured in my own mind, that *you* would approve of every action which contributed to raise my merit. I deceived myself: even *you* were too selfish to find that a virtue, which did not add to your pleasure; and I expected a refinement not known to the heart of any, which seeks for gratification at the expence of every humane and generous consideration. . . .

Be happy, Sir, with a mistress who has no unfortunate friend to deplore: wailings and lamentations are not the chains by which you will be bound. I find it now; but that friendship, to which you have been immolated, yet remains to comfort me for one who could feel its value: to that I devote myself, whilst you are triumphing in the joys of your new connection.—

Begone, all degrading softness: I will not descend to breathe one repentant sigh, nor one wish to recall the fugitive.—Enjoy, undisturbed, the pleasures of *mutual* love, and forget

Pris. Neville."

Miss Bishop to Lady Noel.
Letter 46. Spring-Park.

I am off—Edward must not hope to have *me* for a flirt. My aims are much higher now: it did well enough when I was down o' the mouth, and could see no brighter gleam, to catch at such an offer: but times are altered, and we change with them commonly.

Hear what my mother tells me in her last, then no longer marvel at my variability.———

"The Duke of Kendal, just come from Italy, and the very quintessence of a Maccaroni, has been to see us, and intends visiting at Spring-Park very soon. He wants money, and would marry a woman of fortune, whose alliance would not *disgrace* his dignity. You may have him, if you will; for he does not desire more than thirty thousand pounds. Mr. Bishop, who is as well acquainted, as I am, with your *penchant* for *coxcombs*, bids me salute you Duchess of Kendal."—

After this, how should I think of a Plebeian dangler?—As I live, here comes a cavalcade bespeaking the approach of the *great man*: let me reckon; one, two, three, four. Mercy on me, a whole troop of horse! This is as it should be: but I must leave you, to adorn myself for *captivating*. I shall be an hour and half at least; it is already past two.

IN CONTINUATION.

Ah, woe is me! Better had I staid and finished my letter; for I have *seen*, I have *looked*, without success: but for the whole rise and progress of this *malheur*...After a train of six horsemen, up whisked a *vis-à-vis*, finer than the finest, lighter than the ear of Phoebus; four long-tailed bays, and postilions covered with lace—a ducal coronet has a beautiful effect upon a carriage!—I waited to see no more, but gave orders for my most becoming suit to be brought out: some time was lost in deciding which *that* was; but a sage green, striped with silver, carried the day from its elegance. Caps, hoods, lappets, all underwent the same scrutiny....Equipped at last, down I ran, and swam into the drawing-room, with all the *confidence* of good-breeding.———

"Your Grace will give me leave to present Miss Bishop to you.— Miss Bishop, this is the Duke of Kendal."—Walpole, *master* of the *ceremonies.*

The head sunk in between the shoulders, like a turtle's, served the Duke for a *bow* upon this introduction. My supple knees bent *more gracefully*, I thought. This over, he threw himself again on the sopha, tossed himself back in it, and cast one leg over the other, and in this indolent attitude surveyed the furniture of the room, or his own Brussels ruffles. This man is of a contemplative turn, or, perhaps, has a remarkable fine *gusto*, which will not let him observe *common objects.*—Whilst I was thus cogitating, in came Mrs. Walpole, attired with the simplicity of a nymph, and more lovely than ever. This animated Venus, concluded I, will certainly rival the statue of the Medicis, and give some scope for his admiration. She went through the same forms I had on my entrance, and his Grace maintained all his vacancy of countenance, until, turning from her to go back to his seat, he caught the prospect from the windows: "This view is quite *pittoresque!*" Over joyed to find he did not mean to entertain us with a *pantomime,* I would have continued the dialogue: "Yes, it is generally reckoned a very fine one."

Here ended the first *conference.* Next to a mute, I fancied a Maccaroni must be the least *compagnonable* of all mortals. I was not much out about this. We sat down to table: I tried again for some conversation, and was again baffled. Walpole began to talk of France and Italy; I was all ears. . . .

"Pray, did the *Principessa* . . . return to Rome soon after I left it?"

"O *Delfino crudele!*—She never appeared there after Arlington quitted us.—*Come se grande, amoré!* This accomplished woman renounced all commerce with the rest of mankind, after she lost him. *Misera Principessa! Doglienze inutili, disperazioné infruttuósa.—But you may remember the affair."*

"I do," replied the other; " a very nonsensical one it was—I did not believe it would have been *remembered* by her after they parted."

Very instructive this! thought I.

"Did you see Smythe at Florence as you came through?"

"O the Bore! I was dieing with *ennui* whenever he spoke! So talkative, there was no possibility of escaping the head-ache with him. Then his sister, too, affected to be a *bel-esprit,* which I mortally hate."

That's not wonderful, for *contraries* cannot agree: but this I kept within my teeth.

Walpole dropped the ungrateful subject, and mentioned next some of the beauties of the French court; *Mademoiselle d'Orleans,* and *Madame de Guemenée, he singled out, as being unusually attractive.*

"Cosi, cosi," said the insensible: "my heart was not touched by either."

How should it? said I aside, for it has never been found yet.

He went on with, "And there's *Madame de* . . . . who is an absolute Hyena."

I borrowed a pencil, and marked down *two new words;* the only instruction I had any chance of gaining from this rhapsody.—*Bore* and *Hyena,* I made no doubt, would, by their meaning when I could get at it, unriddle all the cleverness of the Duke's discourse to me. I searched the dictionaries: I found *Boor;* but, besides the difference of pronunciation, which I might have got over from his speech being corrupted by speaking several tongues, I could not reconcile its signification with what followed. The other was still more unintelligible; and I was compelled, after all, to note them down as words that "had much of sound, with a plentiful lack of sense." . . .

In the evening, cards were proposed, our guests being considerably increased by the arrival of several new ones. I had not been in the room when the parties were made; but, as I crossed the saloon in returning, I saw a most superb figure, to whom I dropped my *best* curts'y as he stepped back to make way for me. When I got in, I heard his Grace of Kendal say, "I wonder *Villars* does not come!" My fancy directly drew some French nobleman, with whom we were to be made acquainted. Recollecting the foreign appearance of the *fine gentleman* I had paid my obeisance to in passing, I did not scruple to entitle him *Duc, Marquis,* or *Comte de Villars*: but represent to yourself the doleful catastrophe of my ideal hero, when I saw him walk up, and with a servile demeanour carry a purse to his master, who waited for that to begin the game.

Is this the fate of great names? cried I to myself.—Why, at this way of going on, our English travellers are more to be dreaded by the nobility of France, than our warriors are—these being *only* death, the others disgrace, upon their posterity. The dust of Alexander stops a bunghole—the name of Villars swells the *suite* of a new-created patrician of England, not made so by his merit. So fades all human grandeur!

My conjectures had so often misled me, that I would form no more about this *sport of nature*; but, without forerunning in thought any of *its* designs, I staid until the action expressed what was to be understood: but even here I was continually at a stand; for, as it was moved by different springs from any thing I had ever seen, I could not always tell what it would have meant. Had the *Sieur Perico* not better constructed his puppets, the *Fantoccini* would not have been so much in vogue. He might make a proper preceptor, I should think, to these creatures, who, having neither heart nor brains, would be moved by mechanism: he would at least make tolerable actors of them.————

I am very sorry to find Lady Catharine has confounded the Maccaroni with the coxcomb.—If there is any comparison, the distance between them is the positive to the superlative degree, in regard to their foibles; but their merits will not stand together in any point.—The *common* coxcomb has taste enough to *like* one person better than another, to have his cloaths cut fashionably, to frequent the company of the ladies; good-humor enough to be easy, and is vivacious enough to amuse: not a melancholy, woe-begone, self-important prig, puffed up with affectation of pre-eminence in knowledge; too proud for content, too high for ease......

I have had such a surfeit of *setting my cap*, that from this period I abjure all premeditated strokes, and will remain until my *twin soul* is brought to join me by *the destiny* that framed us for each other. Kind powers, preserve me from having lost him on *Ganges shore!* as some author hints....

Our *man of quality* left us, after lounging away three days here, without being one whit more conversable from first to last. The queerness of my old *misanthropos* is even more bearable than the dullness of a Maccaroni.————

Sutton bade us adieu at the same time; which gave something of
a solemnity to their departure. We all miss the agreeable companion
in him.

The itch of writing possesses me, I think, since I have been
stinted in talking: how are you to be compassionated for having at
this time engaged in a correspondence with me! But fare you well;
I'll curb my pen now.

Yours,

C. Bishop.

LADY NOEL TO MRS. WALPOLE.
LETTER 47. DOVER.

I have but a moment's leisure to inform my dearest Emma, that a
sudden freak having seized Lord Wilmington and Sir Charles, a party
was formed for a trip to Spa; and the morning after, we set out for
this place, to embark for Calais. I received your letters the post
before, but cannot now answer them, as the racket of an inn, the
impatience of my fellow travellers, and the fatigue of coming post for
so many miles, are great impediments to scribbling. Kitty may depend
upon hearing of *beaux* and *petits maîtres* from every quarter. All joys
await my friend, and shorten the days which are to divide her from

Her affectionate

Frances Noel.

LADY NOEL TO MISS BISHOP.
LETTER 48. LISLE.

Prosperous gales wafted us in a few hours across the narrow seas that
part our happy island from the continent, and brought us to the first
stage of our journey on this side of the water. No place abounds
with such convenience as England, to make travelling pleasant: bad
horses, insolent post-boys, and rough roads, make me often repent of
my haste in setting out on this expedition. Yet, not too national to
be just, I must confess, that there are *agrémens* to be found every
where. The town we are in at present has many beauties, and is
worth the pains we have been at to see it. A garrison, and a vast deal
of good company, make it a very agreeable residence. We have *des*

Comédies, des Bals Paré, des Assembleés, and other diversions; and *les charmantes Angloises* do not appear without a large detachment of officers to attend them, whose regimentals, though not of the *true martial* color, nevertheless make no bad show. Lady Wilmington is *au comble de ses desirs,* when surrounded by them, as to forget my dear Noel, who is satisfied that I should be *admired,* so I do not *admire*: he is safe; for as long as I have him with me, I shall never see perfections in any one else.

We shall not be many days longer here. Direct to me at Aix la Chapelle. I am already impatient to hear of my English friends, and shall be more so, if at my arrival there I do not find letters from you. We shall visit Brussels and Antwerp, and make some stay at Paris. I shall ruin myself in laces, silks, and knick-knacks; though my good aunt fancied she had supplied me with sufficient for my whole life. One *travels*, you know, to get rid of *narrow* notions; therefore mine will be more enlarged of course than hers upon this score. . . . I am constrained to divert my thoughts with these *bagatelles*; for there is a weight about my heart, on being in a strange land, where language, air, people, all differ so widely from my own, that will not let me indulge reflexion too deeply. Use may do much; but I should not believe it, were it affirmed ever so strongly to me, that a native of one country could in six weeks, or two months at most, be so charmed with another, as to relinquish all thoughts of his own: yet how many of the *petits voyageurs* come back so truly *Parisian,* after these tours, that one would conjecture they had never been out of its *faux-bourgs!* I have often been stunned by their complaints of the difference between Paris and London, and as often mortified by the contempt they have shown for their own metropolis. When I have seen both, you may rely on the most impartial account.—Adieu! If you do not write, dread to meet

Your

Frances Noel.

MISS BISHOP TO LADY NOEL, AT AIX LA CHAPELLE.
LETTER 48. SPRING-PARK.

Wherefore should I write, my dearest Lady Noel, to give you pain! Yet to retard the discovery is not to remove the misfortune; and you will too shortly hear of your wretched friend's fate: from my hand the blow may be softened by the part I take with you in it. The dear, unfortunate Mrs. Walpole is in the utmost danger; her days curtailed by the shock—of what? For here my information ceases. I will be as satisfactory as I can, and for that will go to where this alarming alteration began. We had been invited to dine at Lord Surry's to-day. Emma was not able to go, but insisted that Walpole and I should keep our engagement. We pressed hard to be excused; but, on her saying she should be obliged to go if we would not leave her alone, she in a manner forced us from her. We, eager to get back, ordered the carriage earlier than common, and sat upon thorns until we could get into it to return. The moment it stopped, "How does your Lady do?" cried Walpole, not waiting to hear the answer, but skipping up the steps to have ocular satisfaction as to his enquiry. He had almost reached her room, when he met her woman, who stopped him by these words: "My Lady, Sir, is so ill that we are terrified out of our senses!"—"Where is she?" asked he with a voice choaked with agitation, "and whom have you sent for to her? Why did they not dispatch a messenger to let me know it?"—This brought us to her; but no terms can describe the state we saw her in; panting for breath, convulsed, and struggling in agonies, whilst terror and grief sat on her face, and seemed to redouble at seeing us. The afflicted husband, not able to support himself, would have sustained her in his arms; but her averted eyes, and the efforts she made to disengage herself from him, made him desist; though he will not lose sight of her, but sits behind her enveloped in the profoundest dejection. . . .

When I could get any one that would speak to me, I questioned them about what had passed, and have picked out, that about four o'clock an express arrived, who said he brought dispatches for Mrs. Walpole: the servants, not suspecting any consequence from the delivery of them, carried them up to her: Wilson, who was in the room, says she turned pale on breaking open the seal, and seeing a packet inclosed, directed to Mr. Egerton; that she read all the papers contained in it, excepting one, and put them into her desk, but all of a sudden sunk down on the floor in a swoon; that Wilson called for help, and they immediately applied salts and other volatiles to her nose, which brought her to herself in some sort; a surgeon was sent for, who opened a vein, but no blood came; and that they had sent to Lord Surry's immediately, but the man, having taken the horse-road, missed of the coach, or we should have been prepared for this scene. It is now five hours since she was first taken, and she is yet speechless. The messenger who came with the express, told them it came from Sunbury, but could tell nothing more of it. In this uncertainty, all conjectures are fruitless: I am filled with apprehensions of I know not what. I will not send this, until some light is thrown on this darkness. . . . .

About midnight the suffering Emma first articulated the name of Sidney; then raising her head, looked wildly round the room, and seeing Walpole, cried, "Shield me from him!" I had gone up to her in great hopes of prevailing on him to retire, as I thought it increased the woes of each, their being together. My entreaties had no effect, but I remained there with him. On hearing her speak, he sprang from his seat to her, and, half-distracted with joy, seized her hand, on which he imprinted a thousand kisses, calling her his angel, his best life, and every thing that could express his tenderness—She listened to him awhile, then bursting into tears, "Go," said she, "leave me, I am not what you call me. But poor Sidney would not have hurt *you*! Heaven pardon us both—he would have died without your sword."

"My beloved Emma," cried the despairing Walpole, "do you not know me?———Have I done any thing to offend you?"———

"I am very ill," replied she in a faint voice; "I know not what passes about me, but I believe it is all a hideous dream—you seemed to me to be covered with the blood of Sidney, and going to stab me with the same sword with which you had killed him."

"You are very ill, my sweet love—but it is only your fever which gives you such ideas: you cannot be hurt by any one, whilst I am near you." . . . .

"O!" said she, laying one hand upon her heart, the other being still in his; "and is it a fever, which lies so heavy here?—I am almost suffocated with it.". . . .

He assured her it was nothing more, and begged her to keep herself quiet: but that was not to be done; for as her pulse quickened, she grew more delirious, and was so earnest for his going, that he at length left the room, after having passed the whole night in it. His removal leaving her more at liberty, her wanderings were less violent, but more pathetic.

"Venerable shade of my father," exclaimed she at one time, "and thou hovering spirit of the murdered Augustus, hear me, when I call upon you to assert my innocence!—And you guardian powers, save me from my husband's suspicions!—Where is he, Miss Bishop?—He has not abandoned me to my wretchedness? Oh, tell him," continued she, "that my heart will bear searching—but his prejudices have ruined my peace of mind. . . ."

I pacified her by saying he was only gone to bed for a few hours, after having sat up all night.

Her fever, and her anxiety, hastened on other pangs; and proper assistance being sent for, she was brought-to-bed of a daughter about seven o'clock that evening. As it was necessary she should be kept quite still, even I was not permitted to pass the night in her chamber. I went to the disconsolate husband, expecting to be welcome as the bearer of glad tidings to him, when I told him that his Emma was better, and had presented him with a girl; for, though his estate is intailed, I had often heard him declare, that, so his wife was well, he should not mind which the child was. I was impatient to utter my felicitations; but the sight of him prevented me: I found him with a packet of papers lying before him, on which his eyes were fixed, without reading; his arms crossed, and his whole appearance expressive of horror and surprise. He did not move on my entrance: after a little pause, I accosted him with congratulating him on the news I brought him.

"Joy cannot reach me, Kitty, for I am beyond its power! These fatal papers have explained a secret to me, which will never let me feel it more.". . . . .

"What secret, and whence came these papers? You terrify me by your manner."—"Alas, my dear Miss Bishop!" cried he, clasping his hands together, and casting up his eyes to Heaven in frantic grief; "you cannot guess at my misery, nor can I speak it—but you shall hear how I came by these papers.—On quitting *Mrs. Walpole*—blasted be the wretch who forced that name upon her!—I enquired of the servants what had happened during my absence from home, and whether any accident had occasioned the dreadful change in her.—I was told she had received this parcel by express.—Roused by this, and recollecting all the incoherences she had been talking, I wanted a key to the whole: her maid showed me where she had laid the letters; and opening the desk at my command, she gave them to me.— Unsuspecting of treachery or deceit in such a form, I did not hesitate to read the cursed lines.—Swift destruction seize on all who wrote them, and hurl them with me into despair!"

Emma's ravings had been moderate to his, on the conclusion of this speech. Torn by conflicting passions, I apprehended some desperate end to this scene, and was more than once on the brink of running away from his fury.—We went on for many hours in this way; but, as he had not slept the night before, nor had lain down for a moment in the day, about one o'clock I proposed retiring: he agreed to it, and I was glad to find myself in my own apartment, for I had been greatly fatigued by the past. I had not cause long to rejoice, for Walpole was in the adjoining room, and walked up and down with hasty strides the entire night, unless when stopping to give vent to his swollen heart in mangled sentences, such as, "Ill-fated lover!—Unjust, yet dear Emma!—I will not bear it!—This, this is too much, good Heaven!"—Such were the moans of this poor dissatisfied man; which could not be *soporifics* to me, you will know. . . .

The next day Mrs. Walpole, being very calm, asked to see her husband: I was in the utmost trepidation, lest he should refuse to go to her, fearing the most shocking consequences might ensue from his unkindness at this time: I would not let any body make the request but myself, that I might represent to him the necessity of his complying. He had shut himself into his study, and had not been with me the whole morning: I went to the door, and knocking at it, "Who is there?" quickly sounded—naming myself, he let me in.— "You are not inhuman, Walpole," said I to him, "or I should not risque your displeasure, by desiring you to do what would be contrary to your nature.—Mrs. Walpole wishes to see you."

"Impossible!—I am not to be fooled again, Kitty; nor will I be called the murderer of Sidney a second time—she has seen the last of me—it must be so, for both our sakes—I disgust her; and she wounds my soul by her treatment.". . .

"Prithee, my good friend," replied I, "have you caught her fever? For nothing else can account for the disorder of your intellects.—Did ever mortal quarrel with a person in the paroxysm of a delirium, for mistaking them?—Last night, I supposed you might have had reasons for your complaints; but since you have now discovered them, I am more tempted to laugh at, than to pity you.—You would, doubtless, dispute the point of honor with a lunatic, if he chanced to dare you to it.". . . . .

"What may be play to you," interrupted he, almost in a rage, "is death to me—but you have heard my refusal, and perdition catch" . . .

"Hush, hush," cried I eagerly, "you shall not swear until I have said all I have to say to you upon this topic"—I put my finger upon his lips, that he might not break in upon my harangue, which I began thus————"If it is your pride which has been hurt by poor Emma's ravings, you have an enormous portion of it: but I would not affront your understanding so much as to imagine it. Your sensibility then let it be, which has received the shock: but will you advance that as an excuse for not going to her?—No, that cannot be; for the feeling heart must be sensible of such distress as hers; and, instead of retaining anger, you would melt into tenderness for her, when you heard of her languishing, nay, perhaps struggling in the very agonies of death, and wishing to behold you once more before her eyes are closed for ever."

"Spare me, my dearest Miss Bishop (said he, sobbing audibly) the horrible representation, and do as you list with me—I am ready to follow you . . . but that you may not think I am devoid of reasons for my unwillingness to see her, take these abhorred writings, and know how I have been undeceived.". . . .

"I will read them another time, (taking them from him) but we must hurry up now to Mrs. Walpole, who may be uneasy at your delay."

I did not conduct him to her without some dread; for the disposition he was in did not promise much in her favor, and her state would not bear rough usage: but the sight of her reduced to the last gasp, and the poor little infant who was laid on the bed by her, softened him into a forgetfulness of all his wrongs. He bedewed both with his tears, but tried not once to speak: this dumb eloquence, more affecting than reproaches would have been, quite overcame the unhappy wife, who made a sign for him to withdraw in a very few minutes . . . He obeyed with alacrity . . . . . This visit has been attended with the return of many frightfull symptoms; and the doctors have forbidden any one being admitted to her, until she is out of danger. These orders come very opportunely; for Walpole could not have gone through the hardship of concealing his senti-ments, nor could she have survived many such meetings.

How it will end, Heaven only knows; but at present every thing threatens the worst. I am harrassed by continual alarms about her life, and terrified by apprehensions about him; for sorrow, indignation, love, and disappointment, govern him by turns, and either make him outrageous, or desponding.—This is but the fifth day since she was taken ill, and her disorder is not yet come to a crisis: but it may be some preparation, in case you are to lose her, to hear of her illness; therefore I shall send this off, and with it the chief contents of the letters which have given us all so much uneasiness. Read, my dear Lady Noel, and lament the misfortune which has involved so many amiable persons in wretchedness.

* * * * * * * * *

In the outward cover were a few lines, signifying to Mrs. Walpole, that the inclosed having been sent to Sunbury, they had from thence forwarded it to her by a special messenger.

The letter addressed to Mr. Egerton contained two others, and a sealed paper, which has not been opened yet. The first epistle came from a Scotch officer in Russia, who acquaints Mr. Egerton, "that on the eve of the 15th of June, Mr. Sidney, who had been some time in the same regiment with him, gave him the papers he had now sent him, and begged that, if he out-lived the next day, he would forward them to England; that the armies came to an engagement early the next morning, which was long and bloody, but victory had declared for the Russians, after the loss of some of their bravest men; that among those fell Sidney, regretted by all, having shown an intrepidity and valor in the action, which would consecrate his name to fame in the annals of that country, and might any where raise him to a level with the most renowned heroes; that, after the battle, his body had been found covered with wounds, and had been interred with the highest honors that could be paid to the memory of a soldier, who died in so glorious a manner."

This panegyrist then goes on with telling Mr. Egerton how exactly he had observed his worthy friend's charge, in getting this packet conveyed to him by the safest and most expeditious way which his situation would admit of; condoles with him on the death of so deserving a young man, but in the veteran style observes, that he who has fought well, has done all that his well-wishers need desire of him; and that he himself is prouder of having been intimate with such a brave fellow, than he should be of calling the first man in the world his friend.

I had almost wept myself blind in going over this; but when I opened the next, and saw the name of the now slaughtered Sidney at the end of it, I was obliged to lay it down, and summon all my resolution before I could attempt to read it.———This also is to Mr. Egerton, and had been written the night preceding the engagement . . . . .

CAPT. SIDNEY TO R. EGERTON, ESQ.

"To quiet your fears, I became a voluntary exile from my country; and to lose my poignant reflections, I sought out the din of war on a new theatre. But I find that I have lost sight of you, and of all that England holds dear to me, without having been able to get rid of these cutting *reflections*, which still pursue me in the midst of camps and warlike sounds.———But no more of whining: my prophetic soul tells me, that ere sunset to-morrow I shall be released from every pain which flesh is heir to. Suffer me to dwell upon the cheering thought, for it's a long while since the wretched Augustus has felt joy. O my generous benefactor (for your *refusal* has not robbed you of that title) can you not imagine with what exultation I view the face of death, after having parted with more than life? And will not the loss of Emma give you some idea of my feelings? You, who prize that treasure as you ought, may guess how I suffered in yielding her up to the duty she owed you! . . . .

"Here let me cease; for on this theme magnanimity itself would turn coward: *my* heroism is subdued. Stern duty, what art thou that demandest such a sacrifice! My rebellious will disowns thy power. If the vows of love are binding, *your daughter* was *my wife*, and from thence my claim to her exceeded yours—base villain as I was for giving her up! Pardon me, thou dear injured angel!. . . . But whither am I running? Shall I, by repenting, forfeit the merit of the brightest action of my life! No, my adored Emma, I am not sorry for having, by flight, preserved you from sullying that piety, which makes the brightest charm in your character. Your father was the person to be considered first: his will was absolute; and I should have violated the most sacred right, in having prompted you to disobedience.—It is my boast, that I did not in any way try my influence over you on this head: I resigned *my love* to *your duty*; had I refused to have done so, the sincerity of it might have been doubted; I should have preferred myself to you. . . . .

Still I am straying from the point on which I meant to write; I am wasting time in vainly recapitulating facts, whilst the hour draws near which will make all the past horrors appear as nothing. At such a time, mindful only of your lovely daughter, I have done all I could towards making her days less irksome than mine have been. The paper which you will receive with this, entitles her to my small fortune, which, though too scanty a provision for two to live on, (according to the calculation of prudence) will enable her to make such an appearance in the world, as a single woman, as will satisfy her unambitious wishes, will save her from the vile necessity of being forced into marriage to keep her from poverty; a procedure which her nature would disdain, but which you, my dear Sir, from the precarious state of your own health, and from your apprehensions about her future safety, might have greatly urged her to. This little bequest, then, may defend her from want, and calm your fears; leave her without controul in her actions, and preserve you from abusing your authority and her from making vows which she cannot keep; for I know too well each movement of that heart which I helped to form, to suspect it of inconstancy: if I am not permitted to live with, it will nevertheless continue to live for me only, and my memory will be the only object of its tenderness. You might have made her the victim of your prerogative, and have joined her hand to one more gifted with wealth; but her affections are out of your reach, and too securely lodged ever to be removed: then let my legacy, if I am doomed to return no more from the field, be the surety of her freedom.

I beseech you not to look upon me as one predetermined on destruction: death or victory is my aim; but I will not rush upon the enemy's weapon, and finish by suicide, the meanest proof of cowardice, an existence, which, though painful hitherto, may from the exploits of to-morrow gain such happiness, as will compensate for all I have felt.—Suffer me, my dearest Mr. Egerton, to enjoy the hope of yet calling Emma mine, when my services shall have lifted me above *myself*. Transporting idea, which endears life to me, and will make me, when called to battle, march assured of conquest! With such a reward in view I number the tardy minutes which are yet to pass before the charge sounds.

Thus I am doubly armed against the uncertain events of to-morrow's dawn. If I conquer, my Emma crowns me—if I fall, she is provided for; in either, all propitious Heaven! be thou praised; but stop not here in blessing the sweet angelic girl; shower on her all those graces which virtue and innocence deserve! Nor be thou, my worthy friend, forgotten; thou best guardian of my youth, and kindest director of my riper years; but may you share with my beloved in all the favors which the most smiling fate bestows. So prays, so has *always* wished,

Your,

Augustus Sidney."

MISS BISHOP IN CONTINUATION.

I HAVE had little else to do but write, since I have not been allowed to converse with our dear Mrs. Walpole; which has enabled me to copy over every syllable of the poor Sidney's letters. I heard with wonder of his attachment; for, fond as he always appeared of Emma, I could not perceive more than the fraternal affection in his behaviour. But when one is told of any thing, many trifling circumstances, which had passed unobserved before, recur to one's remembrance. The melancholy, which was visible for some time in Augustus, when he was at Sunbury last; his sudden departure, Miss Egerton's subsequent illness, and the gloom which remained many months after, all serve now to corroborate this affecting story. But this half-distracted lover has advanced assertions which do not hold good, yet which are the bitterest lines to Walpole, who works himself into a frenzy when he repeats—"preserve you from abusing *your* authority, and *her* from making vows she cannot keep; for I know too well each movement of that heart which *I* helped to form, &c. &c."

When I quote his own experience to invalidate this, and appeal to himself whether Emma has ever shown herself insensible to his kindness, he either answers Yes at once, or cries, "If she has not, her sensibility has been all art, d–mn'd art, to impose upon the dotard of a husband."—The next instant, shocked at his own injustice, he will say, "Art was not made for Emma, she wants no such mask: to hide any of her natural sentiments, would be depriving herself of a charm." Thus does this ill-starred mortal pass from one extreme to another, when he gives expression to his thoughts, which does not often happen......

I should have told you, that Mrs. Walpole begged, the day the child was born, that it might be called Annabella, after my aunt.—I mentioned this to the father, who told me, he did not care what name they gave it, for a girl was of no sort of consequence to him. Piqued at his disregard to the sex, I twitted him with the great Sully's answer to Henry the Fourth on a similar occasion. I have no patience with such murmurers, as if *we* were not as beneficial to the universe, as the strutting boobies who would be the supreme rulers of it in everything. But let me not involve Walpole in the crime of those, who would not have daughters in their families; his vexation had just then made him ungracious, or he would not have shown the least dislike to his girl, whom, since that, he has gazed at with parental regard.

In my next I hope, my dear friend, I shall have some better tidings to spread, for believe me truly yours

Cath. Bishop.

From the Same to the Same
Letter 49.

Catch it, ye winds, and bear it on your roseate wings to Aix.—Emma lives, and will continue longer with us, though belonging to a better world. I am too extatic, my dear Fanny, to be very succinct in my account: but when I have informed you of so happy a turn, you may overlook all my inaccuracies.—On the sixth day after I wrote last to you, her fever subsided, and the physicians gave hopes of her doing well. She began to be sensible of every thing; caressed her little Bel; asked to speak with me, that she might enquire about Mr. Walpole, whom I advised her not to see until she had regained more health, as he would *affect* her spirits by his *solicitude* about her. Though she did not appear convinced of the truth of this, she acquiesced: pressing my hand, she called me "kind flatterer," and charged me with assurances of love to her husband. The day after, she said she was impatient to enter on her vindication, and would see him; but I again over-ruled this, and agreed that in two days more, if she would compose her mind, by not supposing he was offended with her, he should pay her a visit: in that space I employed myself in framing his mind for the meeting, all my anxiety being left he should fly out when she came to recount past events. It demanded all my skill to compass this: partly by soothing, and partly by threats of her *relapsing* if he should terrify her, I at last brought him to engage that he would not be violent with her. No plenipotentiary ever had a more difficult treaty to negotiate than mine was, between two people who wished to make each other happy, yet did not know how to do it as they were then circumstanced.

The appointed hour came, and we were summoned to attend her: my heart palpitated: Walpole seemed wavering, but I carried him off before he had time to escape from me.

He found the trembling Mrs. Walpole supported by pillows in her chair, an ashy paleness on her skin, her sweet eyes from her thinness grown to twice their size, and her charming hands and arms emaciated and sallow. Never did sickness more tyrannically exert its malevolence; but not all its depredations had destroyed the beauty of her countenance, or the gentility of her form. On the sight of us a languid blush overspread her cheeks, and the pearly drops moistened them. The husband, not dreaming that she could have been so reduced, retreated some paces with surprise; but recovering himself again, went up to her with an affectionate look, and embraced her: neither was able to say what they felt for a short interval; but Emma, after having wept abundantly, grew more easy, and after several attempts to begin a speech, which she judged to be necessary on the present occasion, at length delivered herself in the following terms.

"I owe my life, my dearest Mr. Walpole, to your goodness, and the only use I can make of it will be in dedicating each moment of it to you: no other care has indeed employed me since I married, but that of pleasing you: the success I have met with made the happiness of my days; but there was an *obstacle* which I have long tried to get over, and have never been capable of removing it until now. I have but an imperfect recollection of what passed during my illness, but I well know that I was uncommonly affected whenever you appeared: I uttered reproaches when I felt the tenderest sensations for you; it was the effect of a bewildered imagination: yet I thought I perceived an air of chagrin in you; and the last time you came to me, I was sensible of a coolness in your behaviour. This made me enquire of Wilson, whether you had read the letters which I had received from abroad. She told me you had: the sentiments I knew you professed, made me conclude myself lost to you; it was this apprehension which brought on the most dangerous attack that the fever made upon me. I called incessantly upon you; I asked for you, and was always assured that you had been assiduous in coming to my room, but that the fear of infection had made the doctors forbid any one's being let in. The concern I fancied you felt for me made life desirable: I begged of heaven to spare me, and it was pleased to grant my petition: I am restored to your generous tenderness, and know no other want.—Enfeebled as I am by disease, I cannot now expatiate on the *cause* of my suspicions: they are all removed; and I shall soon be re-instated in my health, when I will disclose every circumstance that has befallen me." ...

"You must not talk too long, Emma," said I, glad of an excuse to interrupt her; "nor will we tire you with our company: we will come up again some other time; and now you had better take some repose while we go down." She is never wilful, and here gave way to my importunities; and we made our exit, to the great relief of Walpole, who is not used to bridle his passions, and who, during this, was twenty times on the verge of violence.—"I have religiously observed my word to you," said he, as we came out; but I will no more pass it to do the same. I cannot endure that Mrs. Walpole should imagine she can blind me by her professions—how can she love two? Mr. Sidney was certainly dear to her, or his death would not have been so bewailed. *His memory*, now, will be the object; and I shall still be the dupe of her artifices—That will not do, Kitty; *ou rien*, is my motto; and if I cannot possess her heart, I resign all right to her."

"You will not separate yourself from her? Reflect a little, my dear Walpole, on the ridiculous figure you are going to make: you part with your wife, because you are jealous of—a dead man."

"Psha!" returned he, "those who are buffoons, may make any act appear ridiculous, by their representation of it; but I am superior to the sneers of witlings, and shall only consult the *delicacy* of my own feelings.—That will not let me live with the most lovely of your sex, unless I am equally beloved by her."

"Tut!" cried I, "in retort for your Psha; "Whoever made such an uproar about that vague word, *delicacy*, as you do? There are not a dozen people in the world who agree in their meaning about it."

"That may be; but I shall always square my conduct upon *my* notion of it."

"And he that's too nice," replied I, "cannot be much *wiser* than the *witlings* you think yourself so superior to." (I owed this for his coarseness to me just before.) "But I waste my breath in arguing upon a matter which will not bear debate. *Prejudices* are a thick cloud upon the face of reason; but I hope you will have *humanity* enough to break this gently to Mrs. Walpole."

Had he not been *highly polished*, his irascible temper would have shown itself in revilings, or invectives, against me; but his *deference* to *the fair* made him take all I spoke as the *whistling* of the *wind*. He kept moving backwards and forwards in the room all the time, rubbing his forehead, or biting his lips, to hinder himself from answering me: when I held my peace, he *responded*.

"If you think I would hurt my wife, Miss Bishop, you injure me exceedingly—I will guard her from every evil which can be feared: but I will not, I cannot, tamely submit to live on indifferent terms with her. I have no intention of coming to an open rupture with her: she claims my compassion more than my resentment; and I absent myself, to rid her of an odious restraint, and to wean myself from her too.—When I am less enthusiastic in my affection for her, we shall be more upon a par; and I shall not feel distraction whenever she draws a sigh. She shall dispose of my fortune, of every possession belonging to me—but I will not be with her . . ."

"Now," says I, "you have been severer on your *delicacy* than I could have been; for you have burlesqued it, by letting me see that you think Mrs. Walpole *may be* satisfied with the disposal of your fortune, without sharing your love. If you judge of others from yourself, riches would compensate for every thing else—if not, you have forgot the resolution you made, of not *hurting* your wife; and cruelty is very incompatible with *delicacy*: therefore you must no longer assume this disguise for your vagaries, but either conform to general manners, or own yourself an humorist." . . . .

Away he bounded like a parched pea, and would not deign to hold converse any more with me. When I had lost my disputant, I had nothing left for it, but to consider how to prepare poor dear Emma for this new affliction . . . In this emergency, my active invention began to play about, and presently furnished me with a well-connected story to tell her. When I went to call upon her, I prefaced my imposture by saying, that I had advised Mr. Walpole to ride out that afternoon, as he had been so much confined lately. This saved her from regretting his absence. I then hinted, that besides his concern about *her*, he had been a good deal perplexed about his friend Sutton, who had been likewise very ill; and that, as she was growing well, I had been urgent with him to go to London for a few days, to have the satisfaction of seeing how he was. She immediately swallowed the bait, and even went so far as to impute some of the gloominess of his looks to this last; pitied Colonel Sutton, but did not show any inclination to her Walpole's going from her. As this did not take entirely, the next morning I went with an addition to my fiction. This man, said I, is much worse: our letters are just brought us, and your husband is so affected at his, that he dares not come to you, for fear of making you low. He has ordered the chaise, and is going to set out.—"Will he not take leave of me?" asked she, in alarm.—"I do not think he should; for every disagreeable incident retards your recovery, and taking leave is not a pleasant one."

I could not get her to assent to the propriety of his not bidding her adieu; therefore I once more essayed to work upon him, and having related all the lies I had been forced to invent, I intreated him to go up and reconcile her to his journey. He was *adamant* for awhile; nothing was to persuade him to it; he could not carry on female deceptions; he would not stoop to a falsehood to ransom his dearest friend from destruction. But when he had fatigued himself with fine-drawn objections, and I still persisted in my intreaties, to get rid of me he was led to her.

I withdrew, and left them together, having suffered too much already from their interviews. . . . He made some stay with her, and returned, holding his handkerchief to his face, hastily bid me farewell, and got into the chaise.

I ran up to Mrs. Walpole, and found her attendants busied in applications to keep her from fainting. If a temporary parting caused so great an effect on her, what will his neglect do? I began to write this in great spirits; but they have slagged since this has happened, for I augur much mischief from this obdurate man's absence. Haste, my dear Lady Noel, and come to your unfortunate Emma, for she needs such a friend as you are, to shelter her from her miseries.—I do all in my power to comfort her, but I have not such an ascendency over her as you have.

It was but yesterday that Walpole went: she had a wretched night, her nurse says, and has not taken any nourishment to-day. I must go, and by showing her child to her, make her wish to live. I am

Yours very affectionately,

Catherine Bishop.

MR. WALPOLE TO COL. SUTTON.
LETTER 50.

Meet me in Portman-Square next Thursday evening, my dear George: I am going there to forget myself, if I can...... *My wife* has given me a daughter, and is recovering, after having been in the jaws of Death...... But O Sutton! wherefore do I talk of her? for she has never known one sentiment for me, but those of disgust, or fear.— Mrs. Bromley marked her *coldness* from her first coming to us: I too might have seen it, had not my senses been bewitched by her, and left me without any knowledge but of her loveliness. The veil which concealed her deformities from me, has ben too suddenly rent; and though I still doat, I can no longer be cheated. Happiness and I have shaken hands—we shall meet no more, for Emma has decreed it.

I could have forgiven reserve, had it been general; but to *conceal one* secret only, was making a distinction that hurries me into madness.—It was tacitly owning that she felt herself culpable, and could not tell me a fault, which she would not amend.—I have been deceived by her in whom my whole trust was placed; been robbed by her of my soul's treasure. Faithless Emma, to make such a return to all my fondness!—I will tear myself from her, and seek in dissipation to banish all thoughts of wife and child, since they are too intimately connected to be disjoined!

I will meet you, and declare to you the whole of this dark transaction, if my jarring sentiments will let me be master of myself enough to do it. It will be no easy task to say how I have loved, how I have been wronged!—how divided by grief, revenge, and pity, is the soul of

William Walpole.

LADY NOEL TO MISS BISHOP.
LETTER 51. ALBEMARLE-STREET.

Attentive to the calls of friendship, your second letter, my dear Miss Bishop, put a stop to my rambling; and I insisted on coming back to England, that I might tender all assistance to my undone Emma, on whom misfortunes crowd so fast, that comfort cannot find place near her: yet I hoped my voice would have been heard through them, and that my sympathy would have been acceptable. Sir Charles agreed to come home; Lady Wilmington pouted; her lord grumbled at our parting: but my Noel would not gainsay any project of mine, and paid no regard to their objections. We set out, and arrived in a short time in London. When I had planned the visit to my dear Mrs. Walpole, in a hapless hour I complained of a slight indisposition, the mere fatigue of travelling; but if the plague had raged, and there had been a probability of my having caught it, Sir Charles could not have been more uneasy about me. Before I could turn myself round, the College in Warwick-Lane, I thought, had assembled at my house: such grave faces, and such inquisitive creatures, put me out of all patience: I should not have answered a word, had not the Dowager Lady Noel (who came to assist at the *consultation*) awed me into good manners. When I had betrayed myself to them, I was obliged to depend upon them, and was ordered (for this, it seems, is the despotic language they speak) not to stir for some weeks, as I had hurried myself already more than I should have done.—I blubbered, and vowed that I would go to Spring-Park, let who would oppose it. If I had been only to have managed *the son*, I should have been with you by this; but when *the mother* interfered, and desired me not to make the hopes of the family prove abortive, I had nothing to do but submit to this intolerable confinement, which I bear so ill, that, if Sir Charles had not more temper, he would never support it as he does; staying with me, and making it the employment of his days to render mine less tedious. Lady Noel also pays me close attendance, but rather watches than amuses me. . . .

Not thus does Emma behave under disappointment; she would not have misinterpreted kindness, from seeing it through the mist of discontent: and shall not I, her friend, acquire some of her virtue, and bend to the yoke without murmuring?

How light are my adversities! Scarcely can I give that name to any incident of my life: and how has her small span been chequered by variety of woes!

This last the weightiest of them! What heart can remain unbroken under the stroke of such barbarity? I picture to myself all the pangs which she must suffer, who loved and honored the husband that abandons her; and I quake for the life of my amiable and too sensible girl under this severe trial.

Mr. Egerton carried not his view beyond the advantageous offers that were made for his daughter; but her presentiment made her often be disturbed with fears of what has since come to pass. She would have entrusted Mr. Walpole with her unlucky attachment; she begged to be permitted to do so: but her too politic father would not consent, and charged her, as she valued his peace, not to mention Sidney.

Silenced by this, she has been the martyr to her duty. Misguided husband, not to accept the blessings which heaven sent him with such a woman! But he may regret too late his abuse, and wish to make reparation when it will not be in his power.

I shall be curious to hear how he conducts himself without her, and whether satiety has not had more hand in this separation than his mock delicacy.—

Yet in that case he would not have felt so much in quitting her: but there are such contrarieties in men's hearts, that he who lifts the dagger to your throat, may turn aside his head to avoid seeing the blood; and he who has condemned his wife to pain, might perhaps have wept over her.—

I shall again fall into my unjust censures, if I do not go to my dear Noel, and in him find that mankind may be perfect. Take a proper opportunity of letting my sweet friend hear that I am in the same kingdom with her, and hope very speedily to see her.—

As to you, my dear Kitty, I cannot testify the grateful sense I have of your extreme kindness to this deserted sufferer, whom I love as a second self; but your own sensations will reward you better than the highest encomiums from

Your ever affectionate

F. Noel.

MRS. WALPOLE TO LADY NOEL.
LETTER 52.

Just emerging from the shades of death, I perceived nothing that could recall me to joy, until my Fanny's arrival showed me there was yet some one left to reconcile me to life. Yes, thou dearest to my soul from friendship's ties, (which have never yet wrung me with remorse) I hail your return to England as my prime, nay, my sole joy. How narrow is the hoard which is bounded by *one!* Such is mine, niggard as my after is! Yet, Lady Noel, has it given me a husband and a child. Oh! The soft emotions raised by those names! Why are they not as favorable to me as to the rest of the world? Because my wayward fortune prevails, and dashes all my draughts with its poison. It has divorced me from my husband, and makes my daughter fatherless; turns my pleasure into torments, and punishes my obedience as a crime. I am worn down by calamity: "rare are solitary woes, they love a train; they tread each others heels—and make distress, distraction."—When you left this country, I could have challenged it to have produced one more happy than myself: but how treacherous is prosperity! In the full enjoyment of woman's best happiness, the love of her husband, I had consigned to oblivion all the tears which former misfortunes had drawn from me, and I looked fearless on to the day that should give me the power of refuting my

Walpole's prejudices: it was that which armed me against all dread of
the painful hour, and made me more chearful than most in that
condition are, I found myself far from being well that day on which I
was destined to ruin: I staid at home by myself, having prevailed on
the others to go to Lord Surry's: in the afternoon I had lain down,
quite overcome with lassitude: I had not been long thus, when I was
disturbed by their coming in with a large packet, which they told me
had just arrived by express. Startled at the circumstance, I was in a
tremor when I took it, and breaking the seal, found it had been
transmitted to me from Sunbury. The direction was written in an
unknown hand; but the dear name of Robert Egerton made my heart
overflow. This envelope contained all that shocking tale which Miss
Bishop has sent you. I read it all but *the will*, and had only strength
left to carry the whole collection of papers and put them into my
desk, uncertain how I should disentangle myself from the perplexity
which this affair had thrown me in. A prey to all the warring passions
of the mind, my weak body sunk under the conflict; I felt my breath
shortened, my nerves convulsed, my brain on fire, and my heart
contracted. A thick vapor arose before my sight, and in coming back
from depositing this dire story, I fell down in a fit. The last thing I
remember, was the dread I felt of Mr. Walpole's discovering what had
passed. Many hours elapsed before my speech returned. Happy had I
been, had it been denied me until my senses also had been restored!
It is not in fancy to paint the horrors of my imagination during that
time, in which reason now and then, by faint glimmerings, made me
know my wanderings, without enlightening me sufficiently to prevent
them. In this state I may truly say, that the sense of misery was the
only one I retained entire; and that was keen enough to make me
feel the whole extent of my wretchedness.————
   As my husband had been the last object I remembered before
this delirium came on, so was he the first I recollected when it went
off. I begged to see him: he appeared; but oh, my friend, how
different from what I had known him! No raptures, no
acknowledgements for the little cherub who was by my side when he
came in. A sullen sorrow seemed to have deadened all other sensation. It was not *by tears* that a husband and a father should have
shown himself. This too well informed me of what I had most
apprehended: the evidence of my servant afterwards left me no room
to doubt it. A second attack of fever followed, and for several days
my soul hesitated between life and death. I was not unmindful of
the principal cause of my disorder, and the name of Mr. Walpole was
the only one I spoke. The friendly Kitty furnished my women with a
story of his tender solicitude about me, in case I should ask to see
him again: under pretence of my fever's being malignant, they made
me satisfied with his absence, whilst the concern *they gave him* about

me rendered my recovery wishful, and hushed the tumults of apprehension. I grew better by degree, and we met again: he silent and
pensive still; I oppressed and conscious. I began to apologise: my
voice failed, and it was not possible for some time to understand me.
As I gathered courage from his meekness, I thanked him for his
goodness, in such a way as at once expressed my gratitude for it, and
the warmth of my love. He attended without making any reply to
me. The conversation was ended by Miss Bishop's taking him away, that
I might not exhaust myself by talking too much. This ever kind girl
would again have deluded me into peace, by her well-concerted scheme
of telling me that he was obliged to go to London to see a sick friend.
Ready as I was to take hold of any straw that would keep me from
sinking under his displeasure, I caught at this fable, and pitied others
when I myself was the only person in distress. He saw me once more at
my earnest entreaty: when he would coldly have turned from me after
bidding me adieu, I grasped his arm, and in the posture of a supplicant I
besought him to hear and judge of me as I deserved; for I now perceived
that his going away was not to see Colonel Sutton, but to avoid me (He
either did not chuse, or could not carry on the deceit which had until then
made me bear with his leaving me.) He was touched with my action, and
raising me up, conjured me not to attempt dissuading him from a purpose,
which had cost him dear in making, but which he was convinced was the
only way to make us both easy in a course of years; that he at that instant
underwent all the anguish which a heart, distracted as his was with many
sorrows, could feel. The agitation with which these words were pronounced,
made them more dreadful. I still held him, when, finishing this, he seemed
to be going; but my feeble hands were not able to contend long, and he
burst from me when I thought him secured by my hold. I heard the chaise
drive off a few minutes after. . . . . . .

He has never written, or taken the least notice of me since: yet,
Lady Noel, I live! This small fabric sustains shocks which would
destroy the strongest! I survey the wreck of all my hopes, then
wonder how I have escaped. Forgive me, Heaven, if in wondering I
repine too at it: the tomb promises me a quiet, which here I shall
never know!———

Take care of yourself, my dear Fanny, and do not venture to set
out for Spring-Park until you have the consent of every body. I am at
present so incapable of pleasure, that a visit from you even would not
rouse me from my stupidity.

Kitty, formed to enliven, exerts all her talents to make me more
like herself; but, indebted to her intention for this, I have not yet
improved from her efforts. She dandles Bel; sings and dances to her
throughout the day; but the little wretch seems to be as insensible to
her vivacity as her mother. Age may increase her spirits; mine will not
be assisted by that, alas! for years will not habituate me to sufferings.

Should you accidentally hear of, or see Mr. Walpole in London, acquaint me with what he does, and how he looks. I may perhaps add to my sighs by this; but my anxiety to learn every thing that relates to him, makes me willingly compound for this. Then do not conceal a syllable from me; there is some degree of ease in knowing the worst. . . .

Miss Bishop will be taken from me soon: her brother comes over from his travels next month, and she must go up to see him: reluctantly she mentioned it, for her good-nature is hurt at leaving me thus lonely. But solitude has no terrors for me: I shall be properest company for myself; for no one else is so forsaken, so destitute of joy, as

Your affectionate
Emma Walpole.

[End of Vol II.]

Despondence, my dearest Emma, is an addition to the misfortunes which Heaven has sent you; such an one as makes the others heavier, and calls down fresh ones on you, from incurring more wrath. You may tell me, I talk of comfort, who have never lost an husband; but if I did not know that submission was required of the afflicted sinner, I would by my lamentations drown yours; so deeply am I interested in my friend. But despair is repugnant to every dictate: we were created, and sent into the world, to struggle through many hardships; some to serve for examples to deter others from vice, some to prove that Virtue enables her votaries to rise above all terrene objects. The vicious receive adversity as a punishment; and, according to the use they make of it, it heals, or corrodes. The virtuous welcome it as a fiery ordeal from which they come purified and cleared from the taint of the world.—Thus will you, by the practice of patience, soften the asperity of afflictions, and lay up endless happiness.

Miss Bishop called upon me the day after she got to town, and spoke better of your health than I durst have hoped: it is an inestimable gift, my dear Mrs. Walpole, and should be highly prized: I am at this time suffering for my imprudent disregard to it. When I am once more released from the medical crew, I shall be the most exact observer of regularity in my hours, that ever you saw.

I had been for some days quite *robust*, and scorned all the wisdom of those who talked to me against making too free with myself, when we received a card from Lady Rivers to invite us to a ball at her house last Monday. A private ball is my delight, and I accepted of the invitation. Sir Charles was ready to escort me, since I had resolved on going: Lady Noel *advised*, in a distant way; but I turned a deaf ear to her ladyship, and issued forth after my long imprisonment. We met a *genteel* crowd when we got to Berkeley Square, amidst which I quicky distinguished the beautiful Lady Clarendon, and your Walpole, for the superiority of their elegance. I had laid my injunctions on Noel to seize the first moment to introduce me to your *truant*; and upon hearing him named, I reminded *mio caro* of his engagement. When the formality of the circle was removed by the getting up of the dancers, Sir Charles brought up Mr. Walpole to me. He was civil, and regretted his having already chosen a partner, or he should have requested the *honor* of being mine: I said that I did not mean to dance; then asked whether he had heard lately from the Park? "No, Madam," answered he going up to Lady Clarendon, whose hand he had engaged before.

They began, and I went into another room where there was less racket. Shortly after, Mr. Walpole, Lord and Lady Clarendon, came to us: they would have made a *Loo* party, and I was offered a seat with them, but declined it when I found they intended to have *unlimited* Loo.

There was plenty of less *prudent* people there, and the table was surrounded in a trice. Several were lookers-on: I leaned over Mr. Musgrave's chair, who sat opposite to your husband, my *constant* Sir Charles standing by me. Walpole observing us, cried, with a very particular meaning in his countenance, "Faith, Noel, one would suppose you an old man married to a young wife, you are so afraid of losing sight of her."—"Is there nothing but *fear*," returned my husband, "Which can make a man desirous of being always with an amiable woman?"

"At your age there may," replied the other.—Lord Clarendon heard this with visible discontent and his *silly* lady took pains to let us see she applied it as it was meant. Yet, I am persuaded, neither she nor Mr. Walpole design to do any thing that can injure him: but disproportionate matches seldom are happy ones; and it demands an extraordinary quantity of prudence, with so much beauty, to escape censure. . . . I should not, my dear friend, have noticed this foolish passage, if you had not commissioned me to be exact in my account of what regards this man, who has promised to visit us often if we will admit him when he comes: I have given my porter directions accordingly.

Kitty was at this ball, with her brother, who is of a more *saturnine* complexion than she is; but he is nevertheless a pretty-looking youth.

A violent fit of sneezing, when I got back, bespoke the bad consequences of my jaunt: a hoarseness and cough succeeded, and have spoiled the finest plan in the world; for I was to have been to-morrow night at the masquerade, and the week after at Spring-Park . . . But this luckless cold has frustrated all; and the badness of the roads, with an infinity of *impassable barriers*, have been raised against my going into the country.

I hear your Bel. is extremely handsome: it would be wonderful if she was not; for, *sans compliment*, both you and Walpole are perfectly so.

Remember my advice to you, formerly, of not letting your meditations roll on the same point always: it is not worth our while to grieve or rejoice to excess for any thing in this globe. Adieu, my dear: reckon on my being always

Your affectionate

Frances Noel.

Mrs. Bromley to Mrs. Walpole.
Letter 54.

My friendship for you, my dear Mrs. Walpole, enjoins me to give you information of an anecdote, which at present engrosses the conversation of the town, and which in reality you have the greatest concern in, as it may render the absence of Walpole less grating to you, by showing how unworthy he is of your regard.

No body was at a loss to tell his motives for coming up so early to London, though some malicious whispers were circulated about *your* having given some cause of disgust: all who knew you, knew how improbable this was, and did not see him for ever with Lady Clarendon, without ascribing his indifference to you to his attachment for this idiot, whose scandalous indiscretions have long been the tea-table talk.

The old Lord was called jealous-pated and suspicious by the *best-natured*; but the more penetrating exculpated him, and blamed the guilty. They have not been on the most peaceable footing for many months: but last night, Lady Clarendon having taken it into her head to go to the masquerade in opposition to all he could say, he would not accompany her. It is imagined that she did not go immediately to Soho, as it has been proved that she did not get there for some hours after she left her own house. Had her folly ended here, she might have escaped detection; but, emboldened by her guilt, she did not boggle at coming home at three o'clock in the morning with Mr. Walpole . . . Her lord's abused love could not brook this insolence: he sent her to her father's as soon as the day-light appeared, and has agreed to allow her a maintenance suitable to her rank. He has left town and retired to his seat in the country, where he possibly mourns the misbehaviour of this ungrateful woman. . . . .

The noise this had made is not to be written; but you may guess in some sort at it. There are parties formed on each side, and the three have each their advocates: I am one of the *poor husband's*, who certainly has been the injured person. As to yours, I shall only admonish you not to bestow any thought on him, unless it is to show how much you despise him. There are many methods of doing this, which would be practised, in the like case, by

Your sincere friend,
And humble servant,

J. Bromley.

Madam,

The misapplication of a word cannot impose upon me. I judge of *my friends* not by their protestations as much as by their deeds, and must inform you, that *the friendship* which induced you to repeat that infamous *anecdote* to me is not of the kind I chuse to entertain.... You have offered an insult to me, in abusing my husband (whose *failings*, if he has any, I am much happier in being unacquainted with, than in the knowledge you are pleased to fancy it so much of my interest to have); and you have still farther offended me by the conclusion of your letter. Had I no regard to the respect I owe to Mr. Walpole, *yet my pride* would keep me from treating with contempt the man whose name I bear.—But setting this aside, there are so many better arguments against your *advice*, that I must be as great an *idiot* as any you know, were I to be prevailed on by it to give up my own opinion, which convinces me, that to retaliate an injury, even when we are certain of its having been done to us, is not the way to take satisfaction.—But who can presume to vouch, that either Lady Clarendon or he have been criminal? Is it from the tongue of Calumny that we are to condemn the accused, or from appearances?

The first would blacken the spotless innocence of a saint, and forge guilt for the most irreproachable, merely to gratify itself. The other, too subject to the malice of this not to falsify, cannot, in equity, be admitted as positive proof. Where then shall we find it since neither report nor equivocal circumstances are to be taken? Shall I answer this question, by telling you how I endeavour to conform myself to the precepts of that charity, which bids us to love our neighbours as ourselves? I do not set up as an *example* of any singular perfection: but I make it a point never to censure those who can be excused; for I am not to learn that *misrepresentation, accidental meetings,* and abundance of other *helps* to a story, are employed to prove facts which never happened; and though a woman cannot be called *innocent*, who by her indiscretion incurs the suspicion of the world, she may not yet have sinned beyond forgiveness: there are many degrees between imprudence and unchastity. It is a laudable maxim, in general cases, to suppose they are not far removed from each other; for to bid defiance to the public voice, is most avowedly showing a want of that *pudeur*, without which the virtue of women is insecure. "The wife of Caesar should not be suspected;" nor should any female, who really values herself: but the fumes of flattery, the intoxicating pleasure of general admiration, and sometimes the artifices of the admirers, have decoyed many to the destruction of

their reputations, who would not have parted with their virtue for
all the joys of life. With a weak understanding, and a great deal of
youth, this unfortunate Lady Clarendon has probably been drawn
into the predicament she is now in; and, far from seeing her in
the light of a *rival*, I do not balance to grant her all my commis-
eration, as an unhappy woman, more vain than frail, more aspersed
than guilty.

Mr. Walpole may have neglected me; but who for that shall say
he has seduced the wife of another? May he not have discovered
faults in me, which, though he is too generous to publish, may have
forced him to leave me? I do not complain of him: and does not this
confirm his being right? Cease then ever in future to teaze me with
tea-table chat, when it makes him appear less amiable than he is: the
attestations of the whole town should not make me condemn him,
unless I could be convinced that a few months have wrought such a
change in his principles, as to have metamorphosed him into that
monster called Seducer.

Lord Clarendon has been doubtless instigated by jealousy, or
misguided by appearances, to conclude his wife has been criminal:
under the dominion of either, he is to be pitied, as a worthy man,
who is trepanned into misery by the delusions of his own temper, or
the carelessness of her conduct. . . . . I am, Madam,

Your very humble servant,

E. Walpole.

MR. WALPOLE TO COL. SUTTON.
LETTER 56. PORTMAN-SQUARE.

Always out of the way, Sutton, when I am most in need of you. Why
the devil did you not stay in town a few weeks longer? You might
have kept me out of an ugly scrape by your wary proceedings: but
the past cannot be brought back; so I must make the best of it. I
aimed at nothing more than *common gallantry*; but when jealousy
blindfolds a man, he stumbles at every step: so Lord Clarendon has
fallen into a fury, because I took care of his wife, and brought her
home safe from the masquerade. This has thrown me plaguily out of
my schemes; for I thought to have passed my time, until Newmarket
meeting, in playing the fool with this lovely simpleton: but this
mistake of his Lordship's has made me too serious for that, aye, has
even made me sick of flirtation . . .

You remember my resolution on coming to town: O to forget
the fatal source of it! But that will not be; for the ghost of my

departed joys haunt me incessantly. I have sought for pleasure in vain
since I quitted. . . . I shall play the schoolboy, as poor Jaffier says, if I
dwell more on this *
* *

London offered me an ample range, and I entered into its
dissipations with all the spirit of a young beginner, having never
before partaken much of its pleasures, from my father's severity, and
from my own indifference to them. I did not find myself the easier
after having dined at taverns, sauntered into public places, and seen
all the ingenious devices of the age, *pour passer le tems [sic]*: the
painful void remained. I sought the company of the fashionable: there
I found amusement for my ill-humor, by deriding the men, and
flattering the follies of the women. In conformity to the reigning
taste, I selected one fairer than the rest, to whom I attached myself
as far as an English *cicisbeo* can do. I had always admired Lady
Caroline Warren for her beauty; I saw her full as charming when
Lady Clarendon, and without any reluctance styled myself her slave.
Our long acquaintance, and the rout I had always made about her,
gave her a sort of preference to me; and I have known her, upon my
coming into her box, make whoever sat next to her change places
with me. A pretty woman needs not make many advances before we
take the hint. I formed no plots against her, but I was always near
her; and in her notice I felt myself better pleased than I had been for
many weeks. Upon the arrival of the young Bishop in England, Lord
Rivers, to introduce his nephew to the greatest advantage, invited all
the first people in London to a ball at his house. There I saw Lady
Noel, who is a fine creature too. I danced with Lady Clarendon: I
had engaged her some days before, or my *loyalty* would have been
subdued by this charming stranger. Soon after we stood up, "See
where my Lord has placed himself!" said my partner, "he stays there
to watch me." "Rather say he has fixed on that spot, as the properest
to admire you from; for, though an husband, he must be an admirer," answered I. She laughed out at my speech, and shaking her
head, told me I did not know him. This was an opening for me to
think him jealous, and it was likewise an incentive to me to make
him more so. I observed he followed us down, and, when we came
to the bottom, seated himself at her elbow: this provoked me, and I
was as particular to her as I could be. To get rid of his frowns,
which almost distorted his face, she proposed going to cards; I did
not oppose it: we sat down to Loo, she between us; still she played
boldly, and lost a considerable sum. My Lord cautioned her against
her extravagances: she replied, that he brought her *ill luck*: this drew
from him a sarcasm on her, and they absolutely quarrelled at the
table. I was nettled at his surliness, and calling to Noel, who stood
by his wife, I made some remarks on his assiduous attendance on
her. . . . . . . When the card-table broke up, Lord Clarendon insisted

on their not staying supper: she as absolutely persisted in staying. After much resistance, she was compelled however to go. I offered to conduct her to her carriage, but he had undertaken to do that. I confess I pitied the poor young woman for being so treated; but I soon forgot her when out of my sight.

The next evening there was to be a masquerade. I had a ticket; but having sat down to play, I did not recollect it, until some one coming in reminded me of it. It was then past twelve o'clock: went home, and slipping on a domino, I was soon of the motley throng. Every room was filled. I accosted a German peasant, but was not encouraged by her: I then joined a party of Indians with their squaws, but found they were not of the *amicable* tribes. A French nosegay girl patted me upon the shoulder, and I expected would have given me some diversion; but, upon talking to her, I perceived the satyrical Miss Bishop had put on that dress; and as I do not like to be always baited by her, I left her for a demure Quaker, in whom the spirit was so quiet, that I, loth to disturb it, turned about to a hoydening Columbine, in whom I saw Mrs. Bromley. When I had tried so many to no purpose, I gave over all hopes. It was rumoured, that an Allemande was dancing below by a gentleman in a cook's dress, and a pilgrim. I hurried with the rest to see it, and when it finished staid there, as that was cooler than the rooms up stairs. When I had grown weary of myself, to vary I was again going up; but as I stood at the bottom of the steps leading to the Cotillon gallery, I beheld a divine form, in the habit of a Diana, who, staring giddily about, missed her step, and spraining her ancle by it, fell into my arm, which I had extended to receive her. I carried her in them to a more commodious place, and tearing off her mask to give her air, I found Lady Clarendon had been the person I had succoured, and that even *a Diana* was liable to make a *faux pas* in such an assembly. I got water and drops for her, which soon recovered her. She was in great pain from her hurt, and wished to go home: as it was only two o'clock, and she had not ordered her chair until four, she grew extremely uneasy: I offered her my chariot, which waited in the square, not having designed making a very long stay where I then was: she immediately agreed to take it, and sent me to let her company know that she had met with an accident, and could not remain there any longer. This executed, and the chariot being come up, she leant on me and got into it, I stepping in with her: we drove to Grosvenor-square, where, when we arrived, I would again have been her supporter; but she intreated me not to go into the house, as my Lord would be displeased at her being with me . . . . . .

This did not hinder me from sending the next day to enquire about her: I was thunderstruck at hearing that Lord Clarendon had gone out of town early that morning, and that his lady was gone to Lord Surry's. When I went abroad, I was told by every body of this separation, but was myself the only one who wondered at it; but from the shrugs and winks of the speakers, I was informed, that *I* should have been the least surprised at it. Enraged at the injustice which had been done to an innocent, and shocked at the suspicion of having debauched the wife of any man, I did all I could to clear her: I called in Harley-street, and was refused; but begging that, if Lord or Lady Surry was within, they would permit me to speak with them on important business, I was ushered into a parlour, where, after waiting some time, the Countess came to me. Will you believe me, George? I never was so abashed in all my days, as I was in seeing the mother, whose looks upbraided me with having tarnished the reputation of her daughter, from the disregard I had paid to the opinion of the world. Methought I was one of the skipping race, who feel no raptures but in spoiling the good name of a woman. I did not give Lady Surry leisure to reproach me; but going up to her, I began with unfeigned contrition to blame my imprudence, in having offered *my* chariot, when other equipages might have been procured, which would have been more proper for conveying Lady Clarendon home. She palliated my fault, by deeming it rather an oversight committed through good-nature, than an intentional breach of decorum; but when she came to relate the consequences of it, not all her mollifications could prevent me from cursing the act.—Lord Clarendon had been averse to her going out that evening; but she had promised to go, and protested that nothing should keep her from the masquerade: after many words had passed between them about it, he ordered his chariot, and drove to Arthur's, and she betook herself to her dressing-room; and when she had come forth a finished goddess, she went to several houses where they admitted masks; at last came to Soho, where she did not get until it was very late. Every object there, it being quite a new scene to her, was delightful. I had never seen her until she slipped down the stairs, though she was a very distinguishable figure.—My Lord did not return for hours after they had parted; but when he came home, and heard she had been carried to Carlisle House, he was exceedingly angry. When we stopped at her door, he had peeped through the shutter, and observed my liveries and carriage: this was no softener to him; but when she came up lame, and took very little notice of him, complaining constantly of her ancle, he in ire demanded how she came to be hurt, and insinuated, that if she had staid quietly within, she would have escaped all the impertinent familiarity of puppies, who took liberties with every one who invited them to it, as she did, and one of whom, he supposed, in whisking her about in a Cotillon, or some such improper action, had sprained her ancle. She scornfully sneered at his mistake, and said, if he was always so much out in his judgement of things, it was no wonder he wished to make her behave so differently from the rest of the world; but this should be a lesson to her not to depend on his notions of any thing. This did not mend matters; and when she had thrown him into a passion, she was too much frightened to own, when he asked, who had come home with her. After prevaricating for some time, he confounded her at once, by saying he had seen me. He took her blushes for so many witnesses of her crime, and, flouncing out of the room, imprecated the vengeance of heaven to fall upon him, if ever he lived longer under the same roof with her, than the remainder of that night. By break of day he wrote a letter to her father, in which he loads her with accusations, and returns her to him with an allowance of twelve hundred a year—then set out for his seat.

So concludes the whole of this affair, which will furnish scandal for the next month to come, and which has cured me of fluttering about any woman; for I am not able to tell you the pangs I have felt on having parted, though without reason, a couple of people who might, but for me, have been blest. It is only Beelzebub who would destroy the happiness he cannot enjoy: I protest to you, that such malignity is not in the heart of

Your

William Walpole.

COL. SUTTON TO W. WALPOLE, ESQ.
LETTER 57.

I believe you, Walpole, when you assure me of your remorse; but I am concerned that you have plunged yourself into such a state, by a species of vanity which justly deserves the reproaches you meet with. Had you been directed by me, you would, instead of entering into the pleasures of the town, have returned to Spring-Park, where, by making use of your sense, you would have found the happiness you will fruitlessly search for elsewhere. I frankly told you what I thought of your leaving Mrs. Walpole, under a pretext of *delicacy*, which, from being *outreé,* degenerates into folly: you might at least have heard what she would have said for herself, and have tried how far sincere she was in her professions, by her behaviour. I'll pawn my honor for her having redoubled her tenderness to you, had you conducted yourself towards her with gentleness; but he who squanders away the means that are given him, must not hope to recall them when he wishes. This capital error produced all your others: had you not abandoned your own wife, you would not have forced Lord Clarendon from his. Call you it an *innocent* recreation, to increase the jealousy of an husband? You would be mortified if any one compared you to the barbarous Nero or Domitian; yet what rack could the cruelty of tyrants invent, more terrible than the pain you wantonly gave this poor man? Was it by your particularizing Lady Clarendon, that you would have removed his suspicions? You, who could not stand the bare apprehension of your Emma's thinking of *the shade* of a former lover, might, I should have supposed, have made large allowances for the uncanniness of another, who perceived himself neglected for a *smarter* beau. I cannot make out your right to *select* a favorite; but, if you would, could you not have fixed on one less critically situated? Your heart was not touched; you was not dragged towards her even by this *weak plea*; what then can you advance for your having defaced the fair image of virtue in her, and ruined her fame beyond retrieval? The not having possessed her person does not make you free from guilt: you estranged her affection from her Lord; you exposed her to the ignominy of being accused by him, and slandered by the public; and I will be judged by you, as *an husband*, whether this is not offending against virtue in every sense? Your carrying her home in your chariot at that late hour, though contrary to decorum, was much less criminal than your behaviour at Lord Rivers's, which was the groundwork of their separation, if I have any guess. We never stop at the first lapse, but go on from little to greater, until we are swallowed up in vice: the pilferer who takes pins, ends in the highwayman or housebreaker at Tyburn: the *flirt* becomes an intriguer, and sticks at nothing to accomplish his desires; ruins the woman he professes to *love*, (a contradiction in terms) and after a youth of gaiety, grows nauseous to others, and insupportable to himself, ending in disease and despair the existence he has misused . . .

Lady Clarendon will, I hope, be improved by the chastisement she has had; but, if every woman would consider that she who tempts danger shall perish, we should not hear daily of the thoughtless creatures, who are lashed by us for their ease; and by their own sex for losing the *garb* of decency, which, when all is said, is very essential to their keeping that of chastity. A bold woman is a bad one; an unthinking one will come to be so too. Is not reserve the shield of modesty? And how can she defend hers, who parts with its guard? Enquire of the wretched victims who people the stews, and you will find that more have fallen from their own imprudence, than from the wiles of men. He who would not betray an innocent girl, does not respect a forward one: the diffidence of virtue is as remote from the levity of coquetry, as from the squeamishness of prudery: it neither runs into danger, nor flies into violence on the slightest provocation: it shuns all extremes, as derogatory to its dignity; awes the libertine into reverence, and charms by its meekness the worthy.—

Examine this, and if you feel it, quit the shameful track you are in, go back to your wife, and repent of the injuries you have done her: so be restored to your peace, and to the esteem of

George Sutton.

MRS. WALPOLE TO LADY NOEL.
LETTER 58. SPRING-PARK.

I do not write often to you my dearest Fanny, because I would not disturb your happiness: the voice of grief is clamorous, and would interrupt more dulcet sounds. I therefore suppress mine, and should not take up a pen but to prevent you from suspecting my friendship is abated by absence or misery. . . . .

Miss Bishop sends me long and lively letters; but I cannot bring myself to keep up any correspondence, excepting now and then with you.—The fortunate are easily amused; a light heart lends joy to every object that comes near it: those who are otherwise, as a completion to their misfortunes, are more nice, and demand something more than common incidents to excite their laughter. It is long since any thing has provoked mine, though the smiles of my dear babe make me sometimes less solemn; but the sentiments they raise in me are not of the kind which noise makes known. They bid me live, to make her happier than myself; and I am not yet so fond of life, as to find the necessity for it a matter for rejoicing: this damps me when the mother's heart dances at sight of her, and would make me glad as herself when she stretches out her little arms to come to me.

Without partiality, I see her beautiful enough to make me anxious about her in future: should she continue thus, that beauty will attract, and like the honey be defiled by the flies that blow upon it. Envy may defame, love may more fatally blast it. . . . . .

Had I had a boy, it would have been dearer to the father, and less alarming to me. The circumstance of his disliking this is a link added to my affection for her: she is to me as an helpless being, orphaned in her birth by my *folly*, and looking up to me as the only parent she can find. This retards my soul when it longs to wing its flight to Heaven. I should live, my Fanny, I should buffet through the waves of adversity, to save my Annabella from the evils that environ her—but my strength will be exhausted shortly, and the billows will overwhelm me. I have long struggled, but sorrow must at last finish the work it has begun; it does not, like the fever, suddenly kill; but it as surely ends the patient.—Could the same shroud wrap us together, how gladly would I be in it with my precious infant!—But be resignation my endeavour, and let me bury in silence all impious wishes, which cannot be conformable to the will of the Supreme Disposer.

I know Mr. Walpole could *mean* no wrong to Lord Clarendon; but, my friend, how inexcusable was the lady in applying his joking with Sir Charles to her own lord! Their *story* has reached me here, through the unthankful officiousness of one who miscalled her tattling Friendship.—It has sown new seeds of sorrow in my heart; though I will not suspect my husband of being so lost to honor and religion, as to have entirely occasioned the separation: but to have done it in any degree, is bitterness to me.—You do not, Lady Noel, write to me as you used to do: you are too sincere to deceive, too kind to wound me, and therefore would not animadvert on this piece of intelligence. It was well meant; but to know *all* would be best for me.—

My father, peace be with thy spirit! My complaints do not, I hope, pierce to thy abode but, if they do, thou wilt not hear me arraign thy conduct.—I am not wretched from aversion to the husband thou gavest me, but from his indifference, which could not be foreseen by thee.—Hear, Heaven, that Sidney's death does not pain me like Walpole's absence! The ties of childish passion, how slender to those of marriage, strengthened by the dear pledge I have now with me! In whose features the father looks and speaks to me every moment. She is a fine miniature picture of him—may she never resemble in her fortunes her mother, and

Your friend,
Emma Walpole!

LADY NOEL TO MRS. WALPOLE.
LETTER 59. ALBEMARLE-STREET.

Blistered be the tongue, or hand, that gave my Emma the distressing news of Lady Clarendon's disgrace! May all its purpose be marred, as your joys have been!—It is marvellous to me, that these ill-omened blabbers are suffered to prowl about the world, picking up all the dismal reports that are abroad; and those who so addicted to *croaking*, that, rather than not do it, they will wound the ears of their best friends with the most direful relation, unfeeling as they are of the grief they give.

This eagerness to relate the *surprising* has made me break off all acquaintance with several, as perilous companions; for the *love* of gossiping, and the *love* of truth, rarely meet together in one.

Those who are so taken up with other folks concerns, cannot attend to their own: but, so far from being valuable for this *public-spiritedness*, they are to be shunned as nuisances.—I do not desire to know who was your informer: Kitty and I have abused *her or him* most vehemently, on finding you had been told of this scandal, which might have been hid from you without the least detriment: but since it has been broached, I shall tell you all that can be known from *surmise*, which is all we have to go by.—Some jealousy, and some indiscretion, make this, as most other matrimonial dissensions, pretty equally the fault of both parties. Mr. Walpole, as having been the lady's usual attendant at all public places, was naturally enough pointed out as the disturber of their quiet.

He has since absented himself from every assembly where it was likely they should meet; compensating now for the contempt he had before shown to appearances.

He has called on us sometimes since I met him at Lord Rivers's; but not having done so lately, Sir Charles, on enquiry, heard he was gone down to ——— where the election for a representative in parliament comes on in a few days, and for which he stands candidate . . . . .

Lord and Lady Wilmington are come over, after having been most of the winter in Paris, from whence she is returned *toute à la Francoise. Milord* says this jaunt has been so expensive, that she must stay in the country all the next year, to recruit their fortune. She does not like Wilmington-house; but if he speaks her fair, and will remain there with her, I am certain she will not oppose it. She has a heart susceptible of the most passionate fondness, which she would entirely bestow on him: but she is humorsome, and expects too much from him to be happy; for with a large share of *good-nature*, and many other estimable qualities, he has a tepidity of soul, that ill assorts with the temperature of hers. She reminds him of the long *persecution* she endured for him, when she is stung by his negligence about her; but he who could *forget* it ever, is not to be amended by her reproaches. She knows this, but cannot be calm when he shows it by his *sans-souci* air and behaviour. They make but a discordant pair, though they did go through great trials for each other: but I have seldom or never seen the constancy, which sprung from such motives as theirs, which could bear the rubs that must be encountered in the state, where those who are most united will sometimes differ.

Hers was the effect of stubbornness; his, of avarice. Her friends repugnance to the match made her his: sixteen thousand pounds, which was her fortune, was a prize for a younger brother, and one too who has a *good idea* of the value of money; which is the only vice in him, between you and me. There is some original flaw in the choice, that accounts for so many *love-matches*, as they are named, being so unhappy; yet *that* seems to be the only conductor, one would think, in chusing a wife, or a husband. But Dan Cupid is continually impeached for crimes which he has never had any part in: thousands, who never invoked him, accuse him of having been cruel to them: they have made themselves miserable, and blame him for it. The temple of Plutus swarms; his altars blaze, but the flame warms not; and those who have rekindled it, would buy love with the polluted offerings, and are enraged when it flies from them.—Others, wishing to be more acceptable, bring to him, as God of love, victims tricked out in his mother's garments, but who, not having her *cestus* with the rest, are left without one grace, when those of youth and beauty are gone. He grants their prayer in part; but he cannot stop *fickleness*, when brought on by *failings*; and deluded mortals are unhappy, without his participation.

We are all ready enough to justify ourselves, though we bespatter our best friends by doing it. This makes Lady Wilmington rail at my Lord for his indifference, when she has sent him from her by her *humors*, though her heart pants after him. This makes him insensible to her love, when he complains of her caprice. Sir Charles chides his sister; his mother gives it always against *her* when they have disagreed, and speaks of my Lord's *good-nature* and forbearance, when she has said the most vexatious things to him. She comes to me, and finds me more complaisant to her; for I could not bear apathy in my Noel, and pity her for having met with it in her husband.———

My dearest Emma, why talk to me in the dismal style you have lately adopted? You paint the frightful *charms* of Death with such colourings, that I shall begin to suspect you are going to prefer them to the lively friendship of your affectionate

F. Noel.

Mr. Walpole to Colonel Sutton.
Letter 60.

The daemon of ill-luck pursues me still: I am brow-beat and frustrated by it in every attempt! Hear how I have been served lately. On Mandeville's death, I offered myself to represent the borough of ———. I had every inducement to make me secure of carrying it; but who can trust to the promises of electors! I had been invited down by the principal freemen—confound their insolence for doing it, until they had been sure of success!—I found numbers were still to be gained over when I got there. I undertook to do it: there is but one way of doing it, we all know; cringing to the richer, and corrupting the poorer more openly by the distribution of money: both may be comprised in the word Bribery. We purchase votes from

some by flattery, from others by gold: each has his *price*. It is harder
upon me to play the courtier than the spendthrift; I did one and the
other to obtain a seat in the house. I had often heard it said, that
ambition takes us through many dirtier ways, than any we go
through in the humbler paths of life. I can confirm this; for no man
ever waded in such filth as I had to do with: such a pack of scoun-
drels as I had to deal with, such treachery, such knavery of every
kind! I was eager for the coming on of the election, to deliver me
from such company.———Two days before it an opponent came
down, who threatened me with a stout contest. He was an East-
Indian loaded with *lacs of rupees*; but I did not fear him, having
expended as much cash as would have bought half the land in the
county. I opened half a dozen houses; beer and ale flowed from all
the conduits in the town; I gave magnificent treats to every comer,
took every method of keeping up my popularity, even that of *pledging* the greasy rogues in drinking, making myself as sick as a horse
before I went to bed of a night.

The day came which was to declare me a senator. I went to the
Town-hall, saw there my brother candidate, and held him in derision
for attempting to *oppose me*. Two or three of my *staunchest* adherents
had sent me word that morning, that they were called out of the
town by business: this did not raise a fear in me, who could not be
defeated, from the great majority I had *secured* in my own conceit.
The voters polled; I found it going against me, and saw several of my
men go over to my antagonist, who in brief, was declared duly
elected, notwithstanding all my certitude. I quitted them, with many
anathemas on their corruption and my own absurdity. Upon diving
deeper into the affair, I found that *the Nabob* had spent two thousand more than I had, and had jostled me by that. From beginning
to end, it had cost me near seven thousand pounds. I came back to
Portman-Square with hollow pockets and unquiet mind. I foreswore
elections, as I had done flirtations. The turf and cards were now my
only solace: ill fortune was as much annexed to these; but I was not
so openly bubbled by those I met there, as I had been at—. I lost at
the club in London, in four nights, twice the sum I had thrown away
in *douceurs* to the freemen. At Newmarket I did not van a single
bett: the horse I chose was always distanced; my unlucky voice was as
ominous as Lady Wronghead's fist: Arion would have been beaten,
Bucephalus would have lost his spirit, Eclipse himself would have
been *eclipsed*, had I betted upon them. I was not in the secret, and
there are mysteries in all trades: I have paid for engaging in this; but
since I am in for it, I shall not stop now, though, pinioned down as
I am, it is a difficult job to raise money: but I must mortgage my
estate for my life at an exorbitant interest, when there is no other
way left to procure it; for my pleasures are too few to be lessened
any more. . . . .

Have I not already sworn to you, Sutton, that I cannot return to Spring-Park? I dare say Mrs. Walpole would be all benignity and forgiveness; but it must be her inclination as much as her duty, which can make her tenderness of any avail. I would as soon fawn upon a mistress who should spurn me from her, as upon a wife who does not love me as I do her. How can she, who regrets a *lost* lover, find herself disposed to another! Could you, George, but get me to believe she did, I would not wait until fortune had repaid my loan at the gaming-gable, but fly to my Emma's arms with more extasy than the day on which I took her trembling from her father's hand—

"So dear a bliss my bosom could not know,
When to my raptured breast I clasp'd the maid,
As now her wedded fondness *could* bestow."

But that cannot be—I came excluded from it by a . . . . prior engagement; and your oratory will not remove the prepossession from her, or

Your friend
William Walpole.

COL. SUTTON TO W. WALPOLE, ESQ.
LETTER 61.

Perverse man, thus to draw yourself into troubles which were never designed for you to know! I am discouraged by your persevering in your wilful follies: yet once more will I reason with you on your manner of running on from one mischief into another. Walpole, you will rue the hour in which you threw yourself into sharpers hands. You are a novice in the arts they practise: when you have been plucked by them, you will join to the horrors of being pennyless those of self-condemnation. You, who could never bear the least misery, how will you endure these, the worst complication that can fall to one lot! You are now assassinating the peace you lament. Of all characters the gamester's is of the blackest dye: it annihilates morality, stifles every sentiment which the heart of man can feel *honest* pride in possessing: it levels all ranks in life, confounding the degrees betwixt the gentleman and the blackguard; they become upon an equality from living together. Many a nobleman sits down with his groom, or any other menial servant, who, by some turn of the wheel, is able to stake as high, and pays his *debts of honor* with as ready a hand, as his lordship. Do we not see some of our haughtiest men (in other respects) stooping to familiarity with the vilest *scum of the earth*—the dregs of the people, who, from having had more luck than honesty, can thrust themselves into the clubs where high and low meet upon the same line? Of what wretches is yours composed? Of the very refuse of mankind, whose crimes have made them improper for any thing but gamblers, whom you would be ashamed to own acquaintance with out of your club, yet who are there cheek by jowl with you. If evil communication is so contagious (that it is, will not be denied) what but roguery can be learnt from rogues? And those of the worst sort too, who are more dangerous from coming within the letter of the law, and therefore are not to be punished by it for the devastations they commit upon our property. They have but one end in view, that is *gain*; and for that nothing is untried, which *finesse* and knavery can practise. I would sooner put my head into the mouth of an hungry lion, than my fortune within the reach of such: the beast would be less ferocious in the pursuit of his prey; he would be more pitiful to it.

The four *honors* are the deities which gamesters worship; and being of the infernal kind, they are the scourges of the world: ravaging and destroying are their pastimes; every connexion is broken at their command; childless parents, widowed wives, mourn their tyranny. Look around, and you will find that the generality of the most famous frequenters of the turn are the least happy in their domestic lives; and for a plain reason—they neglect the means, and often meet with a retaliation for the indifference they show.

The vice of drunkenness transformed men into brutes, changed their outward form, and brought disgust with it. Gaming, without causing so sudden an alteration, makes even more execrable monsters of them: it changes the heart, and its effects are still more deplorable; faces distorted by the anxiety attending on the employment, minds warped by avarice, bodies decayed from late hours, and the two forementioned foes to *Hygeia*.

The chances being the only thoughts belonging to the sharper's trade, when he has spent most of his life in calculating those, he fancies the universe governed only by them: and the first time they are unfavorable to him, he who has never found any occasion for *soul* in his commerce with mankind does not remember that he has one, but, to rid himself of *mischances*, puts the pistol to his head, and rushes into a place where *kings* and *knaves* have no interest, where *shuffling* will not pass, and plain *dealing* makes him intolerable to himself.

And these, my dear Walpole, are the associates you have chosen! Some of them, you will say, are persons of rank; but are they the men you would have fixed on, had they not infected you with their pernicious follies? You, who never sought amusements, but from the judicious and the elegant, can you now find it in such a herd, whose cheating they think refinement, whose low cunning sits in the place of wisdom?

Recollect yourself whilst you may yet recede, and do not, by seeking to recover your losses, tumble into the gulph which is not farther than a step from you. If the twelve thousand pounds which I have in the stocks can be serviceable to you, I will draw it out; but it is on condition that you make use of it to release yourself from the harpies who have surrounded you: it cannot else be of utility; for, at the modern rate of playing, it would be but as a drop of water thrown into the sea; it would not give you a quarter of an hour's *diversion*.

You are abusive to the freemen of ———; but you seem to have no reproaches to make yourself, forgetting that the *tempter* partici- pates largely in the guilt. Besides, as you would have sold your vote in the House, you should have expected to have bought your seat. An extravagant man will be a needy one. Your freemen of ——— knew the *general* interest would be betrayed as soon as you got into parliament: they therefore, as *individuals*, were for making as much as they could of you. I do not mean to justify bribery; but I would still less excuse the giver, than the taker of it. You will be ready enough to *excuse* me, I dare say, for putting an end to this.

George Sutton.

MRS. WALPOLE TO LADY NOEL.
LETTER 62. SPRING-PARK.

Ah! My dear Fanny, shall I never have done with complaints, and must the most amiable of men contribute only to my unhappiness!—You told me of Mr. Walpole's going to the election at ———; but you could not have told me of the ruinous consequences of it: those are now too plain to me. Last week the steward came to me, and, with tears streaming down his honest face, apologized for the freedom he took in acquainting me, that the expences of the family ran very high; that he had supplied Mr. Walpole with immense sums since he went up to London, and that his frequent demands had left very little money in his hands. He knew his late employer had put it out of his son's power to ruin his estate; but he had, at his death, found a considerable stock of cash, which would have answered all his wants, had he not engaged in gaming and electioneering, at which he had expended above forty thousand pounds in a few months.—When I begged he would put me in a way of retrenching, he observed, that this was a very expensive place to keep up; that a large house required a number of servants, &c. &c. and that it was impossible there should be less spent here than there was; but that there was an antique mansion-house in Yorkshire, which old Mr. Walpole had now and then visited, and which, from its remote situation, would suit the purpose of retrieving

our fortune in a few years, if I could prevail on Mr. Walpole to retire
there with me. . . . This I knew I could not do; but I reflected, that, if
by saving some small share of his income, I could prevent him from
being distressed, I should not demur about it; and this determined me
on writing for permission to go down to Yorkshire, where retirement
and solitude would hinder any appearance of grandeur from being seen
about me.—His answer was short—I might please myself in every thing;
he never meant to controul me.—Is this, Fanny, the husband who six or
eight months ago would not have been seen to frown before me? Cruel
man, now to treat me with an indifference bordering on contempt!...Thus
licensed, I am preparing to take myself and my daughter from this
beautiful place: but of what consequence is the circumstance of *place*? Can
I any where suffer more than I have done here? Did the high-raised roof,
the gilded cornices, the painted panels, or inlaid floors, give me the
smallest consolation, when I found myself deserted here? If not, why feel
sorrow at leaving it? Ah! Lady Noel, pride causes more pangs, than real
misfortunes often; it makes us blush at *seeming* poor, more than at *feeling*
so: if we can appear like our neighbours, we care not how much we are
pinched within doors. How many flaming equipages are filled with empty
purses, and heavy hearts! And is it only this imaginary good which I am
sorry to part with?—Something more too; for, in being obliged to quit
the family-seat, I foresee the want of many of the conveniences, as well as
luxuries of life: my little Bel. will be degraded from the rank she was born
in; she will be nurtured in penury—but, if her father dooms her to it, I
have no right to object.

   On Monday we depart: Gracious Heaven, fortify my mind against
the weakness of being affected at so trivial a sacrifice! I do not
mention it but my heart sinks, as if, in leaving Spring-Park, I left the
whole world.—What an absurdity! Do I not remain in the same
kingdom with my friend? Shall I not find the same opportunities of
corresponding with her? Yet this frigid North chills me whenever I
think of it. Every body in the house looks as if they felt the same
sensation, when I speak of making preparation for our journey. When
the flurry of moving is over, I shall be enabled to weigh more justly
the real advantages of this step: I know I shall be fond of my seques-
tered habitation as soon as I am settled in it, though I am so unwilling to abandon this.

   I have empowered the steward (under an injunction of secrecy)
to receive Sidney's fatal legacy, and to employ it for Mr. Walpole's
use. It is the only way it can compensate for the trouble it caused
him: it is too insignificant to assist him much; but, if it purchases an
hour's pleasure for him, it will be well spent.

   You shall be informed of my arrival in Yorkshire as soon as I get
there. Adieu until then.

Emma Walpole.

FROM THE SAME TO THE SAME.
LETTER 63. ROSE-COURT.

My prophetic heart spoke truly when it bad me grieve for Spring-Park. Oh, my dear Lady Noel, what a falling-off is here! But before I describe this, let me say how I left that place.—Four days after my last, when I had worried myself and every one else with packing and regretting, I began to make the intended reform in my household. Sixteen servants were discharged, and there remained no more than those I had found in the house on my becoming mistress of it: those who remained, were the faithful few, whose long services had entitled them to a fixed residence there. They gathered about me when the time of my going from them drew near, and, by the concern they showed, made me more loth than ever to go: my reverend favorite the gardener, as I was getting into the coach, snatching the child from its nurse, and taking it into his arms, dropped on one knee, addressing himself to Heaven, whilst, dissolved in sorrow, he uttered the most fervent prayers for the infant and its unhappy parents. The action, his manner, and the ejaculation, moved me more violently than any part of this scene had done; and I was hardly sensible when we drove from the door. I was roused from this, by finding myself environed by perils and dangers from the badness of cross-roads, and the trouble of having so young a companion in my travels: short stages, late hours, and all the other impediments to expedition, detained me ten or twelve days on the road.—After traversing barren moors, and unfrequented paths, we at length stopped at a little gate, which closed up the entrance to a house encompassed by an high wall, which did not admit the least view of it: when we had waited at the outside for some time, an old man, stooping under years and infirmity, hobbled to the gate. Shall I, my Fanny, avow my folly to you, and tell you that this sight redoubled my horrors? Which became still more insupportable, when on going in I saw the mouldering ruins of an once superb dwelling, lying in neglected heaps about it—here windows, which gaped for the glazier's assis-tance; there doors, whose rusted hinges echoed through the passages when moved: worm-eaten tables and chairs; and chasms in the walls, through which the hooting of the owl, and the cry of the bat, entered every moment. I turned back, not knowing how to advance where every object presented me with such views: but whither could I fly?—When we had scrambled through several dark rooms, we came to one wing, where time had not made quite so much devastation; a large room, wainscoted with oak, and lighted by one huge window, which the painted glass served to dim, and render gloomy at midday: the lowness of the ceiling, and the brownness of the floor, completed the emblem of a dungeon. Out of this I went into a smaller, which I call my parlour, and from whence I can see nothing but an immense grove of firs, whose darksome shade seems for contemplation made. The bed-chambers are not much more numerous or agreeable. This house and estate came into the family by the marriage of an heiress, sixty or seventy years ago, and was for many years kept up in great splendor; but taste altering, this was abandoned for another, and has been left to decay in the possession of an old farmer, who, satisfied with occupying the kitchen and offices, has left the better apartments to birds and mice to inhabit. Such, my dearest friend, is the company, and such the accommodations, I have here. Poor Bel. The first day we got here, unused to such sights, she screamed incessantly, and could not bear the darkness of the rooms; but "degrees make all things easy," and she, as well as myself, has grown less fretful.—I have done more; for resolved on being pleased, I have undertaken to have the garden cleaned and new planted: the sweet shrub, from which the place takes its name, grows in abundance about it, and makes the chief pride of my garden . . . .

As I shall only spend the four hundred a year, which in happier days was allotted to adorn my person—when I had a husband to please in dress!—it was necessary for me, on coming here, to lay down my carriage, and to reduce my attendants to Wilson, one man, and another maid servant. It is much more difficult, my dear Fanny, to conform to poverty after affluence, than for those to abide its rigors who have never tasted plenty. The farmer and his daughter, who have never been in another place, enjoy the quiet of this, and are not affrighted, as I am, at its dullness: they do not compare it to Spring-Park, and sicken at the difference.—I walk about, and hope in time to find charms of some sort or other hereabouts: but not an human visage have I beheld out of my own precincts. I am not fond of strangers; therefore this should be no misfortune: yet, when the mind is disturbed, every thing is complained of. I am unjust in not telling you, that the lanes, though untrodden by any feet but mine, are really pleasant; the fields are clad with as lively a verdure as in Dorsetshire; the woods are full as beautiful; and the birds, without the help of the nightingale, give me most melodious concerts. The house, even from its resemblance to the *colour of my fate*, has some charms for me; it gives me subject "for meditation even to madness," and I indulge myself in it to the full. Whatever dislike I felt to it at first, I find now that it is wisest and best to parley with my woes, and by frequent converse become intimate with them: it is the way to lose the dread of them, and to harden my heart against new ones.

Yours ever,
Emma Walpole.

LADY NOEL TO MRS. WALPOLE.
LETTER 64. ALBEMARLE-STREET.

Amidst the dreary regions of the north one pleasure will be felt by Emma, I am convinced, that of hearing *her* friend is mother to a lovely boy; whose birth would have finished the height of my happiness, had I not had *my* unfortunate friend's destiny to have deplored.——

And is it Mrs. Walpole who is condemned to inhabit the solitary Rose-Court, where owls and bats have, by long possession, reigned sole proprietors! Forbid it, friendship.—No, Emma, never shall you whilst I have an house, live in that miserable den. We are going to Noel-Castle to-morrow, where I shall prepare apartments more suitable for you. You shall not be buried in Yorkshire; and to what end!—But, without *lessening* Mr. Walpole, I will endeavour to dissuade you from thus renouncing all the harmless joys of the world. You are wrong in supposing, that continually meditating on your woes will make them less painful to you; you would sooner lose your reason by this than your feeling: every recollection is a new pang; and to think of them always, is to keep open the wounds which bleed afresh at each thought. Believe me, your heart cannot be *hardened*, but it may be broken, by the load you lay on it; for, "far as distress the soul can wound, 'tis pain in each degree;" and you will ineffectually attempt to deaden your sensibility by the method you propose. Fly from your darksome abode to your Fanny, and a more chearful dwelling. I shuddered for you in reading of your first entrance into the moss-grown ruins. Mr. Walpole, I presume, has never been there himself, or he would not have consented to your going.

Sir Charles is looking over me, and charges me to insist on your coming to us; he even promises you shall be as much of a recluse with us as you are now, if you should still hold it necessary to be so; do but let me have the satisfaction of some-times talking with you, and of seeing that you are well taken care of. Our bantlings will make the charmingest couple in England; your Bel. shall teach my Charles all her antics, and he shall repay her, as soon as he has sense enough to admire her beauty. We shall find employment enough in the nursery to keep off all disagreeable thoughts.—Come then, my sweet Emma, and leave at Rose-Court all your sorrows, or bury them in the sympathetic bosom of

Your

F. Noel.

MRS. WALPOLE TO LADY NOEL.
LETTER 65. ROSE-COURT.

My ever kind Fanny, why will you make requests which I cannot comply with, since I must not leave the habitation I have chosen? Would it not be improper, after having left Spring-Park at my own desire, now to change again? I must not, by my fickleness, encourage Mr. Walpole in thinking I have no *opinion* of my own. He shall know that I *can chuse* for myself in this as well as in every thing else, and that I am steady in pursuing the resolutions I am capable of making.

You say true, my beloved friend; I should have joyed in your felicity, had I heard of the birth of your son in the *most dreary of regions*: in this I felt it in the liveliest manner. May you ever find increasing happiness, without any damp from the miseries of your friends! You must not, shall not sigh for me at such a time; for I am happy, Fanny; happy in the testimony which my own heart gives of my not having swerved from the dictates of my duty. Need there be more to make me contented? There does not; and my *darksome abode* is brightened every hour by the serenity of my mind. Solitude, my dear Lady Noel, has nothing terrible, but what we give it from our erroneous judgement of it: correct that, and the stillness of the desert ceases to be shocking. I wander alone for a whole day; and when night comes, I feel myself considerably improved in the art of thinking. When the sun puts on his best robes, my girl is carried out, and accompanies me in my walks: yesterday we had rambled farther than our usual boundaries, when a black cloud suddenly gathered over our heads, and threatened us with a shower: I looked about for some shed to protect us from it, but could perceive nothing near which would serve for that: we turned down a narrow lane, whose hedges almost met together, and after putting aside the branches which obstructed our passage, and walking some length in it, a small building appeared at the end of it, and terminated our prospect. Taking it for some farm-house we made up to it, and knocking at it, begged to be sheltered there from the rain, which now poured down in torrents.

We were conducted into a small room, where, from the collection of books, the tambours, musical instruments, and gentility of the furniture, I concluded it could not belong to the sort of people I had at first imagined. A moment after, I found I had been more successful in this last conjecture, by the appearance of a lady, who acquitted herself of the ceremonial due to her guests with infinite politeness. Her figure was *prevenante* without being fine, her countenance was placid, her voice plaintive and soft, and the whole air of her person such as inspired good will from the beholder. She insisted on bringing dry cloaths for us to put on, and interested herself so much about us, that I lost my wonder at the adventure in admiring the humane stranger, who regarded only the distress we were in from the accident, without seeming to recollect she had never seen us before. We feel for ourselves in feeling for a friend; but the kindness we show to the unknown can only spring from urbanity. I revered the disinterestedness of our hospitable entertainer, and the universal benevolence of her nature. Bel. appeared to understand my sentiments; for she returned her caresses as if she had been sensible of her goodness to her, and, when we got up to go, cried at being taken from her. The child's partiality pleased her extremely, and she requested that I would suffer her to cultivate a better acquaintance with me and her young friend. I was overjoyed at having it in my power to gratify her and myself. We parted with equal acknowledgements on both sides, and I am constantly on the watch for her approach, which I expect will be very shortly—John tells me a lady is at the door: it must be her.—

In Continuation

It was her; I went out to meet her: she apologized for the earliness of her visit, but said she was obliged to be at home again in a few hours; and as her time was not quite at her own disposal, she took the first she could get to wait upon me. From this I supposed her confined by some sick husband or decrepit parent; but she soon rectified my error by saying, "I have the advantage of you, Madam, in knowing to whom I address myself: retired as we live, my sister and I heard that Mrs. Walpole was come to reside at Rose-Court; and though we had not the pleasure of being personally acquainted with you, the name was perfectly familiar to us. We have often mentioned, with concern, the very dull life you would lead after coming from a gayer place. There was an awkwardness in visiting without some kind of introduction, which has hindered me from doing it before."———

I renewed my thanks to her for her civilities to us yesterday, and for crowning them by her coming today, and begged to know from whom I had received such favors.—

"My name, Madam, is Neville; my sister's Wentworth: we came here about a year ago to seek for retirement, which we have happily found."———

A confused idea arose in my head upon hearing of Neville, which I could not make out for some time; but I have discovered since, that it proceeded from the letters I had read from and to Colonel Sutton. As I never found an opportunity of hearing the story of them from Mr. Walpole, I cannot decide whether my neighbour is the same as the lady those treat of, or not. When we are better known to each other, I shall judge of this.—

We discoursed, during her stay, with the ease which always bespeaks an inclination to be as pleasing to, as we are pleased with, our company. She told me, that when they came to Rye-Farm, they found it overgrown with weeds, and in the utmost disorder; but that, after they had agreed to take it, they never desisted until they had brought it to its present pleasant appearance. She engages, by her aid and directions, to enable me to beautify Rose-Court as they have done their farm. When she went from hence, it was with reluctance; but Mrs. Wentworth, she said, was not in a situation to be left long alone; that she had met with misfortunes, which had weakened her spirits to a degree that almost amounted to despondency; therefore she would take her leave, and hoped soon to see me at their house.—This I engaged she should do.

I felt my heart exhilarated by the agreeable conversation I had had with this new acquaintance, from whom I expect much benefit, as she let drop some expressions, that indicated her having surmounted many difficulties by her fortitude. This *practical preacher*, my dear Fanny, will indubitably effect my reformation, and save you the fatigue of listening to my murmurs: she will, however, never displace you in the affections of

Your

Emma Walpole.

LADY NOEL TO MRS. WALPOLE.
LETTER 67. NOEL-CASTLE.

Must one travel to the extremity of Yorkshire, my dear Emma, to find agreeable companions? Well, long as the journey is, behold me ready to set out, was it not for the two Charleses, who will not let me stir without them: and really, when I go to seek *adventures*, I do not care to take such incumbrances with me; though, give them their due, I have no doubts of their both contributing to my pleasures every where. But, admitting that to be indisputable, there are a multitude of other bars to my peregrinating now. First and foremost, Lord and Lady Wilmington came down with us, and do not mean to move off in a hurry: she *hates* Cornwall, he *loves* money, and both are agreed in remaining here: I would I could add they were as well *agreed* in other matters; but indeed they are perpetually *shouting* at each other. I will give you a specimen of their behaviour: about three weeks since, he and Sir Charles called upon Mr. Manners, who does not live far from us: he proposed their making a party to pass a few

ways in seeing the curiosities of the neighbouring country: Lord
Wilmington closed with it; Sir Charles would not go, unless the
Ladies were to be with them: this was to be settled when they came
home, and accordingly he asked Lady Wilmington and me whether
we chose to go: she is very big with child, and not disposed to
racket much about; therefore we declined it. This put a stop to my
Noel's going, but not to Lord Wilmington's. I perceived the poor
Julia to be horribly hurt at the difference in our husbands; but she
was above taking any notice of it to hers, who went off early the
next morning to join Manners and half a dozen other young men,
without being sensible that his wife could suspect him of unkindness.
Lady Wilmington suppressed her sentiments before her brother, but
vented her sighs in my ear when we were left together. I knew how I
should have suffered in such a case, and could not wonder at her
complaining. After a week's absence, during which she had never
heard from him, he came back, and was offended at the cold reception he met with from her. Not long after he went, Sir Charles
received a visit from a French gentleman, who had shown us particular civilities at Lisle. The Marquis de Sabran, with all the *politesse* of
his nation, is sedulous in his attention to women, which, from an
Englishman, we should suppose proceeded from something more than
common gallantry; but from him it is only an habitual softness of
manner, which he has acquired from education. Lady Wilmington
took very little notice of the Marquis, whilst her thoughts were full
of her Lord's indifference and his absence; but the instant he returned her resentment made her affect to attend only to this stut-
terer. It was visible that my Lord observed her, and did not relish her
procedure. I advised her against employing such mistaken means of
reclaiming her husband's heart; told her, that in lessening her own
consequence by coquettry, she vindicated his inattention; that no
unlawful arts should be employed in aiming at happiness: but she
silenced me by replying, that, as she was convinced she could not
wound his *tenderness* by coquetting, she was resolved to mortify his
vanity, which could not bear to see her prefer another to him; that in
managing her brother, who had much sensibility, there was no
occasion for my making use of art, as he would never deviate from
the rules I prescribed him.—There was some show of justness in
these arguments; but, my dear Emma, who ever found the man who
could be amended by correction, which he cannot properly feel? I
own I tremble for a pretty woman, who endeavours to pique her
husband into fondness by encouraging other men: she engages in a
scheme which may blast her own character, but which has never yet
been of any use. Poor Lady Wilmington will be hurt continually,
whilst her Lord may be provoked by her to anger, but will never be
sensible of her intention, unless, like Pygmalion, she could animate
the statue by her love. Of all misfortunes, that of being connected

with a person of his disposition would be least endurable to me: what
is generally called ill-usage would awaken all one's pride, and, that
offended, one could easily detach one self from the love object; but
one of these frigid hearts, who have by prepossession on our side, or
by assiduity on theirs, rendered themselves dear to us, destroys our
peace by the slowest tortures, and it takes whole years to subdue the
ill-placed attachment. You may discover from this, my friend, that I
should more readily submit to be insulted by Sir Charles, than to be
neglected by him. But to continue my narrative—Lord Wilmington,
finding she still went on in giving a preference to the marquis, and
even appeared to make a ridicule of him, by sarcastic laughs and half
sentences, which she stopped at when he drew near, lost all his *good-
nature*, and, to revenge himself, went with his jovial friends, Manners,
&c. to the music-meeting at Worcester, without consulting her, or
even mentioning his design until the evening before he set out. No
sooner was he out of sight, than Sabran was totally disregarded, and
she shut herself up to weep the ingrate whom she had absolutely sent
off. He has been gone two days, and she keeps her room, to avoid
showing her *weakness*, as she calls it herself, and her brother's re-
bukes, who is out of all patience with her, for thus *girlishly* playing
with her happiness.—Lord Wilmington, he says, cannot stop his
tepidity, but she might her whimsicalness; that, if she expected more
tenderness from him, she should set him the example, and not by
pouting frighten him from her.—Much, my dearest Sir Charles, may
be said on both sides: I could be as good an advocate for Julia, as
you are for his Lordship, but that I will not contradict you: nor will
I longer detain you, Emma, to hear that few wives are as blest as

Your

F. Noel.

MRS. WALPOLE TO LADY NOEL.
LETTER 68. ROSE-COURT.

Was it only the *indifference* or *insults* of husbands, my dearest Lady
Noel, which were to be apprehended, it would be easy to shun the
evils of life, by not entering into matrimony; but Miss Neville's health
is consumed by grief, without having any such tie. I kept my purpose
in writing upon her shortly after she had been with me: she ran out
to me as if she had impatiently wished my arrival. There are some
souls so near a-kin to our own, that they are quite congenial, and
become a part of ourselves. Such is this of Miss Neville's to mine: I
find my heart expand itself the moment we meet, and ready to

confide all its cares to her, and to receive hers. Our liking is mutual;
she banishes all reserve when we are together. The first afternoon I
went, I was presented to Mrs. Wentworth, who retired immediately
after, as if the sight of a stranger was disagreeable to her: I was
uneasy at the supposition, and signified to her sister that I was afraid
I had discomposed her. "No, my dear Mrs. Walpole," answered she,
(her eyes twinkling as she spoke) "my unfortunate Matilda has no
objection to seeing *you*; but she cannot stand the first appearance of
any person: she has secluded herself so long from society, that she
will never again be reconciled to it. Very lively tempers cannot
struggle against misfortunes, as more pensive ones can: my sister's
spirits sunk under hers, but I will go and prevail upon her to come
to us again." She went, and Mrs. Wentworth accompanied her back,
and sat with us all the time I staid, but did not join us often in
talking, saving now and then when any subject was started, which
alluded in any sort to her own case. I spoke of Bell's partiality to
Miss Neville: to this she replied, that, had Heaven favoured her, her
sister would have had a nephew, who would have been as *partial* to
her; but, (sighing deeply) "I was not destined to be happy, and that
last chance was wrested from me by the same inexorable fate which
has persecuted me in every hope." "My dearest Matilda," said Miss
Neville, "always repining at the dispensations of providence! What is
the fate you accuse, but the will of your Creator, whose *fiat* gave you
being, and whose power preserves you still, though you oppose his
will? He has afflicted you, my sister—as a dependent on him, you are
obliged to submission; as a christian, you should chearfully accept of
his decrees, since he sends them as harbingers of his favor. Resignation is the lenient balsam which should heal our anguish; it is the
sweet comforter which gives us an earnest of that bliss, which will
hereafter reward the practice of it . . . We cannot command happiness,
we should be often at a loss how to chuse it; but in being resigned
we merit it, and no virtue is overlooked by the eye of Heaven.—My
mother, who entombed every joy in my father's hearse, used frequently to tell me, that the atheist, who affected to deny the existence of a God, was not more absurd than those who acknowledged,
yet refused to fulfill, his orders; that murmuring against his ordinances was blasphemy against his justice, and defying the wrath of
omnipotence. We have all, my Matilda, met with trials; and those are
to be envied who have supported them best." Mrs. Wentworth
nodded assent to these pertinent remarks; and Miss Neville began to
discourse on some other matter, in which she contrived to draw out
her sister's talents, which were designed to figure in the highest
sphere of life, but which grief has destroyed in great measure.————
    This disconsolate widow (for such I found she was) had been
uncommonly pretty and genteel: her features, though altered by her
tears, yet retain many traces of their beauty, and her smile is not to

be withstood.—As we are to be very good neighbours, few days pass without our calling upon one another. In one of these calls, Miss Neville gave me the following account of herself and Mrs. Wentworth.———

"We are the daughters of the worthiest and happiest couple who ever entered into Hymen's bands; but my mother's happiness was not of long duration, for my father died when she was hardly five and twenty: my brother, who was the eldest child, was about seven years old, my sister a year younger, and I not entered into my third year. We were left under the guardianship of my mother and Lord Newport, both of whom acquitted themselves of the trust in the most exemplary manner. The first thing I can remember is the tears of my remaining parent; and the impression they made on me gave a seriousness to my mind, which I have never since lost: this perhaps taught me to reason before other girls knew how to think; and this recommended me to my mother for a constant companion: equally fond of us all, she nevertheless preferred my conversation to my brother's and Matilda's, whose sprightliness did not tally with her solid gravity. James was put to school, and from thence to the university, and then went to make the tour; so that he was not much at home with us. When he came over, he soon married; and my mother's jointure being a very large one for the estate, he was glad to accept of an American government to enlarge his income, and embarked for that country, where he still resides, having a numerous offspring to provide for.

Lord Newport, who is a distant relation of ours, and whose lady was a prudent woman, would often press for our going into public with her as we grew up; and our mother still shunned all gaiety. My sister eagerly seconded their requests, and was carried about to every amusement: the lively descriptions she gave of the sights she had seen, the fine speeches she had been made to hear, and the charms of her admirers, did not once tempt me to enter into such dissipations; my choice led me to listen more willingly to my dear mother's maxims than to all the rhetoric of beaux; and I fancied her face more lovely than any sight I could behold in the great world. Observing the contrast in our tempers, it was her chief care, from our childhood, to inculcate in the strongest terms to us to love one another, and to make us of consequence to each other: she would frequently pardon one any fault which the other wept for, saying the concern of the innocent should expiate the guilt of the offender. This made us always ready to excuse; nay, we would rather have been chastised than have sent our brother or sister in disgrace: often, when Matilda in romping had torn her frock or tumbled her cap, have I changed with her, and taken the chiding which was given for it; and when, in learning to write, I have not followed by copy, or made blots and mis-shapen letters, she has signed her name at the bottom of the leaf, and submitted to reproof for being so bad a scribe. James was as generous, in suffering for us whilst he was with us: but the sisters, who had never been parted, were *the friends* who were to abide by each other throughout life. Never did stricter amity subsist between two: this brought Matilda back to me with pleasure, though she quitted the most agreeable entertainments; and it made me happy in parting with her, when it was to enjoy any of those diversions she was so fond of. My excellent mother, when I have been sitting by her side after declining some joyous party, would say to me, —"My dear, you are too thoughtful for your age; you will stupify yourself by it; and what is more to be dreaded, you will hurt your health by this sedentary life: but, above all, I fear you will acquire from your mother an habit of disliking chearfulness: but you must not do it; your sister, whom you love so passionately, will cease to please you if you grow gloomy and morose; and if you once are disunited, either by interest or inclination, you will find nothing in the world that is worth cherishing. Friendship is the only sentiment which can be depended upon; never love, unless this is the foundation of it; for believe me, that the attachment which does not begin from this, will never satisfy an heart like yours. Matilda may be caught by outward form, and will not ponder over every action as you do: she may love with violence, and she may be made unhappy by it; but she will contribute herself to it. You, Priscy, may be rendered miserable by the carelessness, by the almost unavoidable failings of men: beware then how you chuse, for your first preference makes your destiny. I am well acquainted with the dispositions of my children, and I praise Heaven for their being such as a parent may boast of; but they are as opposite as they are amiable. Preserve always the same regard for each other; it is the best advice I can give you; and when I am taken from you, I shall resign my breath with satisfaction, in knowing that my Matilda will enliven you, and that my Priscy will check her vivacity when it is too great." . . .

Were I, Madam, to repeat all the instructions which I received from this inestimable directress, I should be months in talking of her; it is my darling theme: but I will forbear, for my emotions, I see, affect you; and I cannot speak of her to this day without feeling all the pangs which the loss of her occasioned us.—At twenty I became motherless: at that age the understanding knows all the value of such a friend, and the heart has not by repeated blows been inured to suffering: judge then how I mourned for my mother. My sister, full as sensible of the misfortune, joined me very sincerely in affliction, and it was some weeks before she recollected there was one joy to be found in the world, excepting that of intermingled sobs and tears.— Lord and Lady Newport visited us every day, and showed themselves deeply interested about us. We remained in Sackville-Street, where we had always lived, until the summer came, when our guardian, not forgetting the kindness he had ever expressed for us, gave us an invitation to go down with him and his lady to the New-Forest, where they had a house. We accepted of it, and were treated as part of their own family: no people could be more friendly. We were new faces in that country, and it was a sort of fashion to admire us. We could never quarrel about our lovers, for day and night were not more different than the sisters: Lord Newport usually styled us his Tragic and his Comic Muse. Mirth and rejoicing certainly appeared in Matilda's train; no amusement succeeded without her: she drew around her every soul who wished to be gay; the men were idolaters of her charms; the women allowed her to be agreeable. Few are so fortunate as to be universally approved of; she was one of the few, for she robbed no one of their due by aiming at conquest, or by under-rating their merits: her wit was innocent, her beauty unassuming; she laughed from lightness of heart, not from ill-nature and exultation.

Boothby Lodge was resorted to by all the good company which could be collected from the different parts of the kingdom; we never spent a day without making a large circle, even when no unexpected strollers have come in. Amongst the persons whom I saw there, many pleased my taste, but none touched my heart for a long time. My sister held out against all the flattery of her followers; but she was not proof against the good-humored jocularity of Mr. Wentworth, a young naval officer, who, with all the ingenuousness found in most of his profession, had every quality which could make him pleasing in Matilda's eyes: he was the very counterpart of herself, and the house resounded with their "gibes and jokes."—He was nephew to Lord Newport, and second son to a gentleman of large possessions; his elder brother had been married several years, and had no child, so that he was considered as the hope of the family. His passion was not suspected for some time, as the deference he paid to my sister was looked upon only as the effect of their similarity of humor.—Miss Otway, a lady of large fortune, had gone down with us to Boothby Lodge, and I imagined I saw her treated as if designed for the younger Wentworth; but as this was only surmise, I never ventured to disclose it to any one. She was one of those women whose characters are made up of indefinitive terms, *almost* pretty, *almost* sensible, *almost* agreeable; one could not properly say what she really was: she never gave offence; but the same cause which made her inoffensive, made her incapable of charming.—Fond of being in public, yet not easy when there; convinced of her own consequence from her riches, without despising others; she never tried to improve herself, but came out into life just as Nature had formed her: luckily it had not given her any vices, but no one could love her. The admirer of Matilda was not likely to be one of hers. I remember, upon my saying one day, that Miss Otway was a very good kind of young woman, he congratulated me on my penetration, for he had never been able to find out half so much in her.—We came up to London after Christmas: Mr. Wentworth had made great progress in my sister's heart: she loved well enough to grow thoughtful. We have often smiled at our changing characters, for my calm seemed vivacity when compared to her dejection. When they had bound themselves to each other by the most solemn promises, Mr. Wentworth came one day in violent agitation, and intreated her, by all their tenderness, to consent to marry him without his friends being consulted, as he had hinted his attachment to his uncle, who had in return expressed *an objection* to it, which he knew his father would never get over —He used all the power of a lover to prevail upon her, and had gained his suit before I knew of it; when my sister told me she had engaged to meet him the next morning at St. James's Church. I cannot determine whether surprise or vexation most possessed me. I represented to her all the mischiefs she would draw on herself and him by precipitating themselves into a state which demanded the utmost circumspection to guard against the troubles of it, even when the most auspicious circumstances concurred to make it easiest: I reminded her of the respect due to his friends, and of her own obligations to Lord Newport. He had furnished her with what she thought strong pleas against these, by telling her, that his father would be less incensed at their marrying without asking his leave, than if they did it after he had refused it; that his uncle had no objection to *her*, and that no other woman should ever be his wife. She did not require half so much to make her consent. He had meant to have informed his family of his intentions, months before; but he found new obstacles raised by it and could not do so. My sister indeed, afraid of having it broke to his father, had begged of him to wait some time longer; his sudden haste now had conquered all her difficulties at once; and a licence being had, she was punctual to her appointment the next morning. They were married—we went to Richmond, where we staid until the letters, which Mr. Wentworth had written to make known his marriage had been answered.—They were answered, but in such a manner, as cut off all hopes of a reconciliation. Mrs. Wentworth and I were wailing in the garden, when he brought us a letter which he had just got: it was from his father, and to this purpose.

You have joined perfidy to disrespect; you have betrayed your own honor and your family's expectations; ruined the wife you have chosen, and can never be forgiven by

Your offended father,

Marmaduke Wentworth

We were petrified on reading this: the wrath of a parent seemed to me to call down the vengeance of Heaven on us, and I already

felt all the miseries which must attend us from it: my sister's countenance showed the same apprehensions; but they vanished, when he
embracing her, cried,—"You are mine, Matilda, and the powers of
hell cannot rob me of bliss; nor can my father's reproaches make me
repent the step I have taken: the uniform I wear will give us bread,
and love will indemnify us for the want of the superfluities of life:
will you not, my angel, share my little pittance without repining?"

"Yes," replied she, smiling upon him, "and with my Henry bid
defiance to poverty. You have not ruined your wife, for she is richer
in being yours than empires would have made her. But how have you
betrayed *your honor* in marrying me? Is there another female who
should call you hers? By all that's handsome, not another who has
ever heard me say I loved; but there was one for whom they would
have had me sigh. My uncle, in his great concern for my welfare,
took Miss Otway last summer down to Boothby Lodge; and sent for
me to meet her there, thinking that eighty thousand pounds was not
to be resisted. I was not to know the snare that was to be laid for
me, lest I should except against going. I went, I saw Miss Neville,
and no other could charm me. When I had been there some weeks,
Lord Newport asked my opinion of the great heiress: I told him I
had never formed any about her. He then disclosed to me the wishes
of my friends: I made no reply to this; but never let it transpire, for
fear that your generosity should make you offer to give me up. The
morning I came to Sackville-street in such distraction, I had learnt
from my Lord, that my father was coming up to town to be present
at my nuptials; that he and every one of them expected I should
immediately make proposals to Miss Otway; that, unless I did it, I
should be entirely discarded by them. I told him I had engaged
myself to you; but he swore nothing but the marriage ceremony
would hold good as an engagement with them; and, to prevent all
further connection with you, he would instantly go and state the case
to you, relying on the greatness of your soul for freeing me from this
imprudent attachment. I protest to you, my love, that the anger I
was menaced with did not move me; but this last threat harrowed up
my soul: to be deprived of you was more than I could bear. This
made me play the hypocrite for the first time: pretending to be
cooler by degrees, I promised at length that I would go from him,
and speak to Miss Otway, who had been kind enough to encourage
the hopes of *my relations* by her favorable opinion of me. Instead of
going near her, I flew to you, and obtained your promise to meet me
at church the next morning: I then went to Marlborough-street, and
waited at one end of it until I saw Miss Otway go abroad; then
called and left my name at her door, that she might conjecture from
thence, that, had she been at home, I should have declared myself to
her; as it was probable she would meet Lord or Lady Newport some
time in the day, who would tell her of my intended visit to her. I am

not used to employ stratagem to compass my designs: I felt myself embarrassed by this, that I deliberated whether I should not go to my uncle, and reveal to him at least all the deceit I had practised; he had spoken in the highest strain of you; but when I reflected on the stern manner in which he had talked of *my imprudent attachment,* my resolution wavered; I kept out of his sight for the rest of the day. You are my bride, and I should have forgotten there was any thing else to be minded, had not these reproachful lines, and your enquiry, made me recollect what I have been telling you. And will you, Matilda, not pardon a deception, which was to secure my best prize! If you think I have *betrayed my honor,* I will be branded for a villain, not else. . . . .

He appealed to the tribunal, which he was assured could not condemn him.—We went back to Sackville–street, but no submission could mollify the Wentworth family: this did not, however, disturb the happiness of the new married couple; they were all in all to each other. In disobliging Lord Newport, we had lost our steadiest conductor. My sister and her husband were but bad economists; they never thought of retrenching, but made the same figure they had always done: like a true sailor, he squandered gold like dross, and thought nothing too expensive, which was to adorn or please his wife. His pay, and the interest of her fortune, which was no more than five thousand pounds, not being sufficient to defray the charges of their living, they broke in upon the principal. In a little time their finances were disordered, and this at long-run made him more considerate. When they had been married above two years, he was appointed to a ship, which was to be sent to carry stores to the coast of Africa. This was the only cloud which had overcast their days since they had come together. Matilda presaged the destruction of all her happiness from the burning sands of Africa, and hung about him as if she would not be divided from him: she besought him to take her with him; she had no fears of any kind, but those of parting. His eyes would fill whilst gazing on her, and force him to turn away to hide his struggles: he spoke of his voyage as a short passage, which would not detain him many months from her; charged her to preserve herself for his sake, and for the sake of the unborn infant, who, he did not doubt, would be the peacemaker of the family; and that would enable him to remain always with her, after this trip. . . .

Their separation was such as I had dreaded. My poor sister, destitute of comfort or joy without her Henry, for days was insensible to all my solicitude about her; but remembering his last charge to her, she began once more to hearken to the voice of friendship, and to wish to live. We removed from the house in Sackville-street to a smaller one in Park-street, where we lived with great privacy, seldom stirring out, or admitting any but select friends.—She heard of his safe arrival at Goree, and we were told from the Admiralty, that the ship would soon be in England again. We had buoyed up ourselves with the highest hopes of seeing him in a short time: we read one morning in the papers, that a vessel had come from that place, and waited to hear the post-man's rap with all the eagerness of expectation, not suspecting but that he had letters for us as replete with good news as we could wish. He came; I hurried to take the packet from the servant; the stamp informed me from whence it came, but the black wax made it drop out of my hand. Matilda, unable to bear my delay, came herself for it, and, more heedless than me, without looking at the seal or writing, opened it. She shrieked out, and threw it from her, as if it had contained some venomous reptile. My tremor subsided, or rather was drowned, in my cares for this dear afflicted. I picked up the letter, and saw it came to let her know that Mr. Wentworth, a few days after he got to Goree, had been seized with a violent disorder frequent in that climate, and had died the third day of it. I would not, if I could, paint to you, Mrs. Walpole, the situation of this fond wife, thus reduced: the recollection even now freezes my blood, and I shun it when it would obtrude itself upon me.—

Lord Newport very humanely came to call upon us, as soon as he supposed the first transports had been over; but the sound of his name, as if it had revived every misfortune, threw my sister into such agonies, that she was as bad again as ever. He then wrote, and expressed great tenderness for her, telling her that Mr. Wentworth's father waited only for her being brought to bed, to make a competent provision for her and the child. She was deaf to all their offers, declaring she would never be obliged to the destroyers of her Henry; it would be an injury to his *manes* to court the favor of those who had refused to help him when alive. I expostulated with her on the cruelty of depriving her child of its inheritance, and told her, to avert the horrible consequences of a father's malediction, which had already reached her dearest half, she should do all she could to wash away the stain of disobedience from his memory. She became more reasonable, but she could never see any of the family: this made some of it suspect her of harbouring resentment for the obduracy they had shown; and upon her being shortly after delivered of a son, who lived but a few days, they dropped all correspondence with her.

It is incredible what an alteration these accidents made in her; her spirits, her beauty, all left her, never to return again. She may be said now to drag out the remnant of her life with unwilling sloth, for her whole desire is to rejoin her Henry. She is sensible, at present, of the guilt of marrying without consulting his parents; she deplores it as the executioner of her husband, and the scourge of herself: it is the only crime she has to lament, but it is such an one as rends her heart with contrition; and she often declares, that resignation would be easy to her, if it was not for the remorse she feels for having been the means of his sin."—

Miss Neville concluded here this narration, as it was time that we should part; but she is to give me the rest of their story when we meet again. Though she has been so silent about herself, I am sure she must be the person Col. Sutton wrote to.—Priscilla is not a very common name, and her living in Park-street puts it out of doubt: but, my dear Lady Noel, what could detach him from such a woman? Is inconstancy so inherent to the heart of man, that, rather than not change, they will quit the most amiable for the vilest?—It cannot be, for such a suspicion would exclude the whole sex from mercy. But I should be instructed, by Miss Neville's going away, that it is full time to bid you adieu.

Yours always,

Emma Walpole.

Mrs. Walpole's to Lady Noel.
Letter 69. Rose-Court.

Whence comes it that my Fanny writes not to me? Does absence disunite friends, whom so many years have seen together? Impossible; for you are not one of the *fickle kind*; you will not vary because you have loved me *long enough*. Be that depravity the vice of man alone! It is six weeks since I have had any accounts from Noel-Castle. I have so few pleasures, that I cannot afford to lose one; without your correspondence, I am a bankrupt in joy: be more exact then, my dear, in answering my letters, and relieve me from the inquietude which your silence creates in me.———

Every unaccustomed appearance alarms me; a note folded in a new shape, a strange hand-writing, the mention of an unknown name, every trifle, in fine, calls up my fears; and I live, if the expression may be allowed, in a continual anticipation of complicated misery. My nerves are shattered, and my mind is depressed, by the misfortunes I have known; yet, my friend, I have learnt some fortitude from the pious sisters, and do not groan under the weight, as I was wont to do: but there is no contending with sickness. . . . it is that which makes me shrink with causeless terrors.

Not long ago a letter was brought me from Colonel Sutton, filled with the most liberal sentiments, and tendering me all the assistance which his fortune or friendship could procure me. There was nothing so out of the common track in his benevolence; the bosom friend of my husband, the free-heartedness of the soldier, might have prevented my being surprised at such a letter: yet involuntary tears stole down my cheeks, and I shivered as if the cold hand of Want had already pressed upon me.—Why this offer *now*? Said I to myself: am I more likely to need *charity* at this time, than I was some months ago? Yet he did not write then!—"The already plunder'd need no robber fear;" and Fortune has not one arrow left in her quiver to wound me, was I not ingenious in contriving my own disturbance.—Whilst I was thus apostrophisizing on Col. Sutton's writing, Miss Neville came in, and found me still weeping: she would have retired, but that I desired her not to leave me: "Mine are not the tears of grief, my dear Madam," said I to her, "but the suffusions of an heart overcharged with gratitude and wonder. My benefactor is not unacquainted with you; he told me, long before I saw you, of your extraordinary qualities." A modest flush rose on my speech; she could not guess who had been her trumpeter: "One who loves as well as knows you," answered I, "but whom, I am afraid, you no longer esteem." "There was but one man, Mrs. Walpole, who ever was permitted to profess himself my lover; and he left me for a more deserving mistress." This I assured her could not be, and repeated all he had said to me about his *attachments.*—"Little souls," replied she, "may rejoice in hearing a rival has revenged their cause: I feel no more in knowing that Colonel Sutton has been jilted than I did before.—To wish his return to me would be a meanness which I would never forgive in myself. At the time he abandoned me, I did not imagine him liable to the frailties of mortality—He was the anchor of my hopes—he failed once, and never more can be relied on. . . . but I am glad he can be serviceable to you—he always was ready to serve his friends."———

I would have interceded in behalf of this worthy man, but she declared to me that such an attempt would drive her from me, without shaking her resolution. "I promised you," proceeded she, "to tell you how we came to give up the world: I have seen you often since, without having had courage to begin a topic which has cost me so much anxiety; but now that you have given me an opening, by talking of Colonel Sutton, I will fulfill my word.

It was at Boothby Lodge that our acquaintance was made: my sister's vivacity left me but a small chance of being much noticed by any one who was likely to engage a young woman's heart: the grave and the plodding attached themselves to me; and all those who were driven to despair by her, came to complain to me: I soothed the last, and I patiently listened to the others; but I wished to be freed from them all:—Colonel Sutton came to spend a few days there: he had all the graces that woman could admire: he had particular regards for me; I was sensible of it, but I did not surrender my heart, until he had proved himself far above the troop of those who had buzzed about me. He did not flatter me with vain praises; he hardly paid any attention to the beauties of my person; but he would place himself the live-long day by me, and enter into every sentiment I felt. We were upon that sort of footing which banishes all apprehension of treachery: he consulted me upon every action of consequence which he was going to perform; he reposed his whole soul on my care; my counsel directed him: and in return I confided to him all my doubts and fears; made him acquainted with all the secrets of the family, and found him so grateful for my confidence, that I thought it out of possibility he should ever be less so. Thus assured, I gave way to all the partiality I felt for him, and my enthusiasm almost deified the man who thought and spoke as he did. I had lived in this delusion for near three years, when my sister's affliction called for all my attention. I sent for this friend when we heard of Mr. Wentworth's death, and his tears streamed with mine: he came or sent to ask about us daily. But in the midst of distress, one does not always act consistently: I could find no pleasure whilst Matilda was in such danger; and my lover was neglected for my sister. Some days before she lay-in, he let me know he was going into the country, and begged I would write sometimes to him: he went, and I had two or three letters from Waterlands; but my attendance on the sick room never gave me a moment's leisure, and they remained unanswered for three weeks. I now and then looked at, and was shocked at the difference I saw in myself. Sitting up and constant fatigue had worn me to a shadow—sorrow had furrowed my face—no lillies and roses were now to be seen there; but haggardness and paleness were their successors.—I should have been mortified at the change, had I not been persuaded that it was my mind he had been attached to; and this I knew could not be hurt by my sympathizing with Matilda.— She had not left her chamber when I received another epistle from Mr. Sutton: it was the last, and you have read it, therefore I will not dwell upon it.—But, oh! Mrs. Walpole, how cruelly was I undeceived in this paragon of perfection, as I had always called him! Let those who have been in such a situation, think for a moment how the heart suffered from such intelligence. Can there be a severer stroke than that of being torn from all we love? If there can, it is in being obliged to despise the object you have most esteemed.—Both were combined in this renunciation of mine!—And I was to smother all my grief, lest Mrs. Wentworth should be affected by it: she could not well have borne more than her own. This made it prey on me unmercifully—it even contracted my soul, and made me for a while think there did not exist such a thing as *honor*; that its laws were mutable, and might be varied at will: this made me suspect men to be capable of the most atrocious crimes, and in destroying my dependence on them it made me desirous of shunning their society.

My philanthropy drooped with my confidence. I took aversions to all who spoke of Colonel Sutton to me. An old friend of my mother's, who came to see me one morning, hinted to me something of the report of his going to be married in Lincolnshire; from that hour I avoided her, as baleful to my nature.————What has he not to answer for, who made me guilty of such injustice?

When Matilda began to recover, "Let us go my sister," said I, "to some place where no sight can recall the past.—If it can be done, let us inclose ourselves in some retirement where man cannot come."

"Let me do that; but for my Priscy better things are in store.— Love will be propitious to your virtuous desires; and Colonel Sutton will not disappoint your well-founded hopes of happiness"........ I could no longer withhold from her the secret I had hitherto kept. —My loved sister behaved as I had expected: she even ceased to weep, that she might rail at the perfidious creature who had forsaken me. I had never ventured to say to myself that he had acted ill: I could not suffer her to do it, but she would not be argued out of it. As soon as she could bear the motion of a carriage, we quitted London, and after some pains found out this snug house, where if we could *forget*, we should be happy. I did not acquaint one of our visitors of our intention, because I meant to have our retreat as private as could be. It has been so; you are the only person who has been under our roof since we came to Rye-Farm. . . . The sound of Walpole was well known to me, from Colonel Sutton's intimacy with the family: this drew me to wish we could meet with you accidentally, when I was told of your coming down to this country: and the acquisition of such a neighbour is the only obligation I shall be indebted to him for." . . . .

My reason applauded Miss Neville for this declaration, though I was sorry too for the Colonel: but is she not right to abjure all commerce with mankind, after having found such baseness in the best of them?—I had settled this point, when she went on, "I said that *my soul was contracted* by the disappointment I had met with; but let me explain to you, that it was not a lasting impression. When I had ruminated for a time, I found that this dislike to the world was a savageness not justifiable; that it was the effect of a narrowness of mind, which would make me deserving of the cruelty I had met with. I now view inconstancy in the light of a foible, brought on by the gratification of those passions which men think themselves at liberty to indulge. The palled appetite loathes the food, though ever so palatable, which has been often served: the licentious heart can no more bear to be confined to one object.—Yet are not all men false, for all do not by criminal indulgences vitiate their sentiments: we have a Sovereign who gives greatness to the regal dignity, by an exact observance of all the duties of a private man————a Camden, not more renowned for his abilities, than for his probity. . . . .

But I will be even so merciful to the whole race, I will suppose that those who *deceive* us do not do it from malice pretense: a man means, most likely, at the time he swears, to keep his oaths to us; but he is thrown into the midst of temptations, and he is perjured before he has had time to reflect. Novelty attracts, arts are employed, and he must have extraordinary virtue who escapes. This palliates the falsehood which would not else be pardonable . . . I can forgive my bitterest foe; but I can hardly ever renew the confidence which has been abused: let this then, Mrs. Walpole, hinder you from pleading again for Colonel Sutton."

I must obey an injunction so enforced; will not speak for him again.————I have tried to make out the difference in the characters of these two sisters; there is a wide one, though each is amiable and agreeable in her way.—By the flashes of wit which now and then break out in Mrs. Wentworth, even at this time, I can fancy that she has been the liveliest of companions, and the very sort of young woman which her sister described her to be. Miss Neville never perhaps said a *bon mot*, but she never spoke a word of nonsense, I dare say *

IN CONTINUATION.

My apprehensions are verified, and the hour is arrived when patience is vanquished.—O, Lady Noel, was it for this that I have been so long without hearing from you! But it could not be concealed from me; my remittances have been slow in coming for the two last quarters: the horrible truth is now out, and Mr. Walpole cannot longer support me. Write to me, Fanny; tell me where this wretched man is: what will become of him now that ruin has seized on him?—

Yes, Col. Sutton's letter is now expounded; my suspicions told me truly. He wrote from knowing that I should be reduced to the necessity of begging soon . . . But I will not be a burthen to my friends, their kindness shall not be repaid by robbery; far preferable would it be to me, to earn the bread my child and I are to eat, than to be fed by the charity they offer.————

Tell me all, and I will promise you to bear it better than this dreadful uncertainty will let me. Where is Mr. Walpole? It is his distress that terrifies me: he is violent, and may be driven to despair; but this is too much to be thought on.

Yours,

Emma Walpole.

Lady Noel to Mrs. Walpole.
Letter 70.

Arm yourself, my dearest Emma, with all *your fortitude*, and do not now sink under calamities which you have so long sustained.—Mr. Walpole is well; he has been unlucky at play; but he may, with care, save himself from the state you are so apprehensive about: hope should not be parted with until nothing remains.

To give you some ease, by keeping off the suspicions which haunt the unhappy, half instructed in their misfortunes, and ready to suppose the worst from innuendoes only, I will give you the whole account which I have had of his losses.—

He has attended Newmarket and York races, has been constantly engaged in some game of hazard, and in a few months has, by these means, dissipated more than the revenue of many a petty prince. I have heard frequently of his losing thousands of a night; but you had sufficient knowledge of this from your removing from Spring-Park, and it was neither necessary nor pleasurable to dwell on the subject; so that I have hardly ever mentioned it to you. Lately it has been whispered, that he could lose no more, having already lavished all that he could raise. I thought your allowance had been small enough to have been overlooked in the general havock; and as I could not write any pleasing thing to you, I have been silent of late, but I have not been unmindful of you: I made Sir Charles write to Edward, to desire he would call upon Mr. Walpole; I waited for his answer, which came last night, and which I will give you verbatim.

"I went to Portman-Square: on knocking at Walpole's door, a man came into the area, and looking up at me with a curious eye, as if he would be *sure* of me before he opened the door, I repeated my rap: his own man opened it half-way, and put his head out to examine whether any *worse-looking* fellow than myself was near.—I asked for his master. Sir, if you will walk into the hall, I'll let him know you are here."—So saying, he disappeared for a short time, and returned to usher me into his room.—He got up at my entrance; but his greetings were of the coldest; seeming rather to look upon my visit as an intrusion than as a friendly call. He had a table near him, on which lay a heap of tradesmen's accompts: by them stood a bottle of Champagne and a large glass.—Our conversation was broken, and long pauses intervened between each question and answer. I was decamping after a decent stay, when Sutton came in and stopped me a little. . . .

He went towards the table: "What have we here?" cried he, "Wine in a morning! This is a new sight.—Noel, do you usually take it?"—I said, "No.—I had it for my own drinking," replied Walpole with petulance, "when a man has nothing else to do, he may try to find out a *new* amusement, I hope."—

And would you try to drown *real pain* in *Champagne*, my dear Walpole? Said his friend: is that the utmost stretch of your invention?—Be advised by me, and do not vainly attempt to forget your discontents by calling up false spirits: they will leave you more depressed, after a few hours, than they found you.—Come, let me ring for Turner to take away this unseemly appearance."

As Walpole made no answer, Sutton did as he proposed. When the servant had retired with the bottle and glass—"How did you rest last night?" asked he: "As well as a person could do," said the other, "who never went to bed: those who can enjoy peaceful slumbers may take the pains of courting them: I cannot pursue the blessing that flies me—I fled that which was *designed* me, but it cannot now be helped. I shall abide by all the consequences of my own obstinacy, and welcome destruction, let it come in any shape.—I know, Sutton, you are going again to talk to me of *reason* and *philosophy*—empty names, which cannot serve my turn. Save yourself the trouble of argueing—I am not afraid of *confinement*; my own house has been so long my prison, that I can have no objection to any other, was it but for change.—One purpose I will never break, which is that of not hurting my friends by my extravagance.—My poor Emma, and her daughter, may be indebted to their humanity; but for myself—

He faulted so much in speaking this, that I could not stand it longer; but quitted *the friends*, extremely affected at the distress of this thoughtless man, who has hampered himself by his reliance on the *integrity* of sharpers, and his ignorance of their legerdemain tricks. He had no chance with the set he engaged in.

This, my dearest Mrs. Walpole, is all that Edward says of your husband; and this, I should think, must be less terrible than your apprehensions have been. Lowness and exaggeration are inseparable; the one forms the first bodings, and the other swells them to an *hydra-woe*, as a conceited author calls it.—

You shall refuse all Col. Sutton's friendship; I consent to your not accepting of the smallest help from him: but, Emma, you will forfeit all my esteem, if I am not to be the banker you make use of. Where have you been taught to call that *robbery*, which is the lawful property of any friend? Are not our hearts cemented by the strongest bonds, and shall our fortunes be divided? It is shameful to talk of being under *obligations*: you thought my friendship repaid by yours, and was satisfied with the return you made to it; and can you imagine *money* can add an obligation to what I have already given you? It is the littleness of pride only that can make self, the vile dust of Guinea, appear of any estimation: it has no value but from the use we make of it; and, if *my friend* is not served by it, it must be because she disdains the giver. The gift, I knew, could not be worthy of her acceptance: see then, my Emma, how I shall resent the refusal; and let me be an exception to the resolution you have made! Sir

Charles himself shall not hear of what I send. Make as free with my purse as I should do with yours in the same circumstances, for I am most sincerely

Yours,

F. Noel.

MRS. WALPOLE TO LADY NOEL.
LETTER 71. ROSE-COURT.

I am all conformity, my dear Fanny, to the decrees of fate. Things are not so bad as I supposed them: a moiety of my income is more than I want; that I have by me, and therefore have returned your bank-bill. Pride and poverty are sworn allies; the well-born beggar feels no pang so sharp as that of receiving *a dole*. Should I become a dependent upon you, my friendship would no longer counterpoise yours; your generosity could not save me from the humiliating idea of being *obliged*; I should lose my friend in my benefactress; the superiority of that title would force into *reserve* and *respect* your late equal; I should strive to renounce the recollection of *intimacy*, that the abject servility of the *hanger-on* might not be neglected; I should dwindle into something *lower* than the mendicant who plies the streets, when you reached out your hand to serve me; I should be *poor* in my own opinion. Let indigence come; I do not fear its approach; but defend me, Heavens, from disgrace! You tell me, Lady Noel, that in *my circumstances* you would make free with your friend's purse. Ah! Fanny, you must be situated as I am, to know how you would act. I can say, for I once was as you are now, how I should have behaved, had I heard of misfortunes which wealth could remove; but never until this have I been blessed to guess how the heart would feel, when offered to be relieved by a *friend*. . . . . . .

Pride it may be, but it is not *littleness*. Could I bring myself to accept, I should not wish to conceal your alms; it is not what the world would think, it is only what I should feel, that I consider. There are beggars enough to hinder its being surprised at your *giving*, and distress is too common to let it be wondered at that I should *take*; but it has nothing to do with my sensations, and it is those that I am to mind: they are such that will not let me, even from Lady Noel, accept of gifts which I cannot return. But have I not already said, that a small matter will furnish subsistence for us? And why should I mention want? That is yet afar off, and a thousand incidents may avert it from ever coming nearer: *one* I have every reason to expect; but it will be time, when my *expectations* are on the eve of being fulfilled, to acquaint you of it.—Fanny, do not be angry with me for refusing your favors; my soul could not endure an additional misery: could it have done so, I would have been your pensioner; but *your pity* itself would be too much; the *full cup* cannot hold another drop; it is humbled already sufficiently, and *pity* would not raise it. Love me always, and for my sake love my daughter; but do not wish to *oblige* me by pecuniary offerings: those must always be rejected by

Your affectionate

Emma Walpole.

MISS NEVILLE TO LADY NOEL.
LETTER 72.

A stranger, Madam, addresses herself to you, in behalf of Mrs. Walpole, who has been for some weeks in a very declining state of health, and who is now so reduced, that she must be near her dissolution. . . . She talks for ever of *her Fanny*, and expresses such eager wishes to see you, that I have got permission from her to write to your Ladyship, and to beg, if you have not quite given her up, that you will come to her immediately.————

  She has supported, without complaint, all her ills; but the fragile body was not a fit shrine for her heroic soul: it has sunk under the resistance that made to the attacks of grief.————An hectic, which is oftener brought on by disease of the *heart* than of the *lungs*, has not left her strength to walk across her room, and every portentous sign is to be seen in her: if then you wish to find her alive, do not delay your journey.

I am, Madam,
Your very humble servant,

P. Neville.

MRS. WALPOLE TO W. WALPOLE, ESQ.
LETTER 73.

The hour is approaching, which will free you from an unfortunate engagement, and restore you to yourself, and to the world, which I rendered odious to you—that hour, which I should dread as a final separation from all that's dearest to me, did I not hope, that it would be happier for those I love.—In my death I see your release from an insupportable bondage; and my child, in losing her mother, will find a father, whose fondness will be more for her good than the weak efforts of maternal affection could have been.—I conjure you, my dear Mr. Walpole, to let your indifference descend into the monument with me, and to cherish the sweet puppet I leave behind, as you would do the daughter of a wife more beloved than I have been.—Her tender age, her engaging ways, would ensure your love to her, did not your prejudices against me raise obstacles to it.———— But once more, a departing mother begs, and begs of a father too, to be kind to her helpless infant.........

Forget the wife you would not pardon.—I will dispense with your not grieving for me; but I cannot die with such a slur upon me as your anger would leave, did I not vindicate the conduct which caused it. You will be more patient now than when I would have talked of it before. Whether I ever did *love* another, is not very material; my heart had sensibility enough to feel the sentiments I inspired: it would have been constant to Mr. Sidney, had not my father forbidden it; but I knew my duty too well to devote myself to a man who was not approved of by him. I detached myself at his command; and at the time I married you, I loved you as sincerely as woman could do. Had I been indifferent, you, from your extreme tenderness, might have taxed me with ingratitude; a vice not to be found in such a disposition as mine. You did not love as insensibly; I returned (perhaps with less apparent fervor) the passion you felt for me: *violence* is not natural to me, but I have all the warmth of heart which a lover could wish for. You had no suspicions of the contrary until that letter, which informed you I had been attached to another.—Without staying to hear what I could say—without wishing to be dispossessed of the errors you had imbibed from a false delicacy, you left me, Mr. Walpole—gave me up a prey to all the wretchedness of a neglected wife. My conscience acquitted me to myself of intentional guilt. I had always held it as a sacred rule, that, what it was criminal to act, it was criminal to think of: and Mr. Sidney never for a moment usurped that place in my thoughts, which you alone were entitled to. So far I can call upon the purest spirits to witness for me.—They also will witness, that not all your indifference, nay your very contempt, has been able to make me forget the love you once had for me. That I *was* happy once, made me feel more keenly the wretched change. This has hastened the period of my life; it has made me wish for death, at an age when the hopes of living are strongest, and the promises of lasting pleasure most commonly are greedily swallowed. I could not expect to find any after I had lost you. Was it but granted me to behold you again—to hear you utter a *requiem* to my parting soul, I should not reproach my fate with having laid one hardship on me, as my last moment would be so blest.—If there was a name more binding than that of a husband, I would implore you by it to hasten to the expiring

Emma Walpole.

MR. WALPOLE TO COLONEL SUTTON.
LETTER 74. ROSE-COURT, TUESDAY.

The summons I received from my dying saint did not allow me time, my dearest George, to wait for your coming back from Windsor. I left London at one o'clock on Sunday morning, and never stopped at any place, longer than the horses were putting to, until I got here. Sir Charles Noel was waiting at the gate when I alighted, and by his countenance forbid me to hope much from my enquiries about my Emma. "She *yet* lives," was his best reply; "but you must not see her without her being apprised of your arrival."—"Go then," said I, "my dear Noel, and let her be told that I am come—that I am come to prevail on her to live, or to die with her."———"Walpole, you must be more composed before you can be admitted: she is too weak to be disturbed by any rashness: it would quickly extinguish the almost-wasted lamp of life. But," continued he, "Lady Noel, who has been some days with her, shall by degrees let her know that you are in the house. She has asked several times, whether we thought you would come."

Inhuman wretch as I have been to give her such a doubt! O George, how should she suppose me, after my barbarous desertion of her, yet capable of being touched by her distress! What a reflexion does this raise!

I gave Sir Charles my word that I would wait quietly in any corner until I could see her, and that Lady Noel should have the management of our meeting. When he had brought me to this, we entered the house. Gods! exclaimed I, forgetting the promise I had made, what a dwelling is this for *my wife*!—"Peace!" cried he, "your voice may be heard by her, for the walls have been thinned by the falling out of bricks; and the solitude of the place makes every sound be noticed."— Sutton, this is the habitation to which my once idolised Emma has been confined: she who never entered any but the stately dome, who never saw walls which were not decorated by the artist's nicest labour, she has been driven to seek a covering for her head in the time-beaten ruins of a building where I would not lodge a favorite dog; and driven by *me* to this! That the earth did not open under my feet, and ingulph the monster who thus violated all its laws!

I was sauntering over the frightful waste, when Noel came towards me with my daughter in his arms. "Here's a young stranger, Walpole," said he, "who has been asking for Pappa." The angel repeated *Pappa* after him, and held out her sweet mouth to kiss me. The voice of nature is more strong in this babe than it has been in me! Instinct has made her fonder of her father than he has been of her. Sink down with confusion, thou reprobate, nor dare to think that heaven can ever pardon crimes of so black a kind!—Yet, George, if repentance—but it comes too late, for I have killed my wife!

When I had taken my child, and wetted its pretty face with my tears, which the poor innocent did not comprehend the meaning of, but patted me with its little hands to make me take more notice of her, I gave her to her maid, and went into a parlour which led into the room where they had told me Mrs. Walpole was. Here I have sat for some hours listening to every stir, starting up at every step I hear, and placing my ear at the keyhole in hopes of catching the music of her voice—But she speaks not—perhaps she cannot speak, or that her spent lungs do not afford her strength enough to make herself be heard at this distance—I must be nearer to her for I cannot, my friend, bear these excruciating doubts.

I went to beg of Noel to let me go to her—that could not be; but he went in, and let me slip into the room behind a large screen which was put up to keep off the wind of the door, and from whence I could overhear all that passed. I had but just got there when the beloved of my soul, on seeing Sir Charles come in—she lying on a couch, and her head laid in Lady Noel's lap—in a low and interrupted tone, said, "Fanny, he will not come—he will not hear my last sigh—but I charge you to tell him that Sidney's death—that the dread of poverty—that nothing which regarded myself, could have hurt me—but that his distress has killed me. He *will not* come, did I say?—Alas! My friend, he *cannot* come perhaps—Oh, that I could be carried to him! —that I could be with him! And by my tender participation soften the rigors of imprisonment—he would then know how I love him!"

Lady Noel made a sign to Sir Charles to speak, for she could not. "There is no cause, my dear Mrs. Walpole," answered he, "for any of your apprehensions—I have had a letter from Walpole—he is on the road, but dares not appear before you, after the injuries he has done you, until you send him your orders."

"Is he then coming? But does he know so little of me as to suspect me of being angry! Do, Sir Charles, write instantly to him— Say that it is I who should crave his forgiveness—that my quivering breath waits for his coming to receive its last respiration. But write this speedily, lest it be too late. My Fanny," proceeded she, looking up at her, "you have undertaken a task too hard for you—you cannot support the sight of your Emma's dying—but reason should teach you, that I shall be happy after I have thrown off this incumbering flesh which has so long subjected me to misery—and let that reconcile you to our parting. The decree is irreversible which has ordered that we should do it; and whether now, or a few years hence, it does not much signify."

I became so loud in my grief, that Noel, fearing she should be sensible of it, hastened to open the door, and forced me out with him. I would have rushed in again, have presented myself before her, and have poured forth my remorse; but he intreated me, as I valued her safety, not to go as yet.

I enquired what medical assistance she had had: he told me that he had sent for all that could be had in this and the bordering counties; that they had declared, with one consent, that the disorder lay beyond their art; a declaration which does as much honor to their skill as to their honesty: for they might have tampered, and clogged her with prescriptions for a long time, and then, without any risque of reputation, have given her up, when they had found her incurable.

She has been informed, that I may be expected to-morrow; and she observed to her Fanny, that this was the best opiate she could have had tonight.

Thou, "tired Nature's sweet restorer, balmy sleep," visit her wearied eyelids, and gently strengthen her languid frame! Give her back that sweet calm which my detested villainy has robbed her of, and check the fell power of sickness.

To-morrow, Sutton, I shall see her. O heaven! If yet I may pray, grant me to see her such as my doating heart would have her! But, if she must be taken hence, then graciously call me with her!

There is not a sound to be heard in the house—a sepulchral gloominess reigns, and a stillness that makes me think myself already in the vault of my deceased ancestors—But could I carry this load of grief there, it would no longer be a peaceful dwelling—I should disturb their houses with my cries—I should be the troubled ghost to haunt them in their deep sleep! But in heaven there is mercy, and in the grave my toils will cease; or, George, dreary as the idea of annihilation is, I should wish for it rather than suffer as I do.

Adieu! be happiness your portion. Your crime, when likened unto mine, shows as the venial trespass against morality, to the foul sin of murder. "The bad, when compared to worse, appear as good.". . . .

Yours,

William Walpole.

MR. WALPOLE TO COL. SUTTON.
LETTER 75.

These eyes have beheld her, and have not yet burst their strings.—
Base organs, that cannot describe the feelings of my heart, and weep
as many drops of blood as I have given pains to the most perfect of
creatures!—But she is even more than that: she that I have offended
is some benignant Celestial Spirit, who designed to leave her native
heaven to conduct me to it, and whose company I have disdained—
fit inmate as I am for fiends!—They encompass me, and will draw me
into their hell, if my Emma is taken away. . . . . . .

After lingering out the long hours which Lady Noel had prescribed for me to remain without seeing her, I was at last allowed to
show myself.—But, Sutton, the slight glimpse I had had, the day
before, did not apprise me of the alteration I should find in her. Her
friend was chaffing her temples with vinegar, as the angelic sufferer
leaned against her, and seemed fainting with weakness.—They informed her that I was come: she raised her eyes; but the light was
too much for her, and she closed them, not having perceived me. I
stood immoveable, and durst not approach, lest the phantom should
vanish into air at my touch.—"My dear Emma," said Lady Noel,
"you wished to see your husband; he is by you—Will you not look at
him?"—"I did not understand," replied she, when you spoke first,
that he was in the room.—"Where is he? The light dazzles my eye-
sight so that I cannot find him out."

"Here, my love," cried I, throwing myself upon my knees by her;
"here is that wretched husband who has murdered you!":

"You must not say so," answered she, laying her icy hand upon
me, and feebly pressing mine with it, "I die a natural death.—The
badness of my constitution only has reduced me to this point: and
you cannot be stigmatised with my murder.". . . . . . .

"O Heavens! If you die, my Emma, hanging would be too small
a punishment for my share in your death.—It is the cruelest of
homicides to kill by inches: it would have been lenity to have cut
your throat at once, and not by the slow poison of sorrow have
brought you to the grave.—Then racks and tortures be my execution-
ers, and all the horrors which my mind now feels!". . . . . .

"Come," said Lady Noel, "do not talk of dieing now: Mrs. Walpole
will not be so much in love with death, if she has you with her."

This well-timed turn took off from the solemnity which was
taking place at this interview; and Emma was glad to be diverted
from the recollection of her misfortunes, which these self-upbraidings
would have brought on.

She has had better rest the three last nights than she has, from
what Wilson, had these three or four months. She has been fed from
my hands, and tells me she will try to live if she can make me happy

by it. I have assured her that will be the test of her loving me.—
"Then," answered she, with an heavenly smile, "I shall certainly
recover."

Be it so, my dear Sutton, and I ask no other boon of Destiny—
My adorable Emma will be the ultimate end of every wish.—Like
Romeo, I shall revive, and be an emperor, when she shall breathe
new life into me by her kisses.

The Noels are to go in a few days. Her Ladyship complains that
I have usurped her office, and leave her nothing to do for her
Emma, whom she had nursed so well, though with less success than I
have done, it seems.—This charming woman has, blended in her, all
the vivacity of Kitty Bishop, with all the softness of my wife.

I am really *nurse in chief*, for Bel. has taken such a fancy to me,
that she will hardly be from me a moment. Pleasing employment, to
tend on the two most beloved objects on earth!—But do not envy
me, my friend, until my *best-beloved* is restored to health, and has
dispelled all the anxiety of

Your

William Walpole.

Mrs. Walpole to Lady Noel.
Letter 76. Rose-Court.

Shall I not, the first day I am able to write, employ myself in thinking that dear friend, to whom I have such obligations; whose soothing cares kept me from falling under the weight of my
afflictions? . . . I am recovering apace, my Fanny, and my dear Walpole
regains his peace in proportion to the progress I make towards being
well. He, as well as I, praises the true friendship which brought you
and Sir Charles through so many difficult passages to our obscure
retreat.—"Paradise has opened in the wild," since this messenger of
peace, this dear husband, has come back to us.—Bel. will not be
taught to speak by any one but her pappa, and quits me at any time
to waddle to him when he comes into her sight.

I have sometimes observed him lost in thought, and pensively
meditating, when she has been playing about him. Two days ago he
caught her up, and sighing, called her his poor girl, whilst his eyes
proved the sense he had of the word *poor*.

"Why so much compassion, my dear Mr. Walpole," said I, "for
one who does not think herself unfortunate?"

"May she never feel it, my Emma! But her father must regret the
prodigality which has brought her to beggary.—He must grieve for

his crimes—they have extended farther than himself—they have reached you and yours."

I begged him not to trouble our present repose with unnecessary regrets: that we would breed up our children to be as unambitious as ourselves; that if they did not covet riches, they could never want them. As to myself, I asked whether the chintz gown I had on did not become me as well as the finest silk would do; whether it did not fit me as well, nay, even better than a more clumsy garment would do: and this may always be purchased with our income. The want of a carriage could not be felt by me, for I was always fond of walking; and I had a variety of pretty walks to show him about this place, as soon as I was better able to go about.—He called me his admirable monitress, and wondered he had not improved more from hearing me.......

Miss Neville, who would not come to me as long as she thought I had so much company, sent to me to-day; and on my desiring to see her in the afternoon, she promised to be here.—I prepared Mr. Walpole for it; told him her story, and her opinion concerning Colonel Sutton; and engaged him not to mention his friend to her. He did not; but he will write to him to come down and appease her himself. He is delighted with the scheme, and enjoys beforehand the happiness that awaits this faithful sharer of his heart.—Adieu, my dearest Fanny; he will not let me write longer, lest I should tire myself.

Your ever affectionate
Emma Walpole.

MR. WALPOLE TO COL. SUTTON.
LETTER 77. ROSE-COURT.

If friendship cannot bring you here, let love do it. Your *divine* Priscy is near us: only two fields and a short lane divide her house from ours. Emma and she have been acquainted ever since the latter came into Yorkshire. They have *talked of you:* your *angry dear* has stopped the gentle pleadings of *my love,* and has prohibited the mention of your name again. But do not be disheartened by this. You would not have much to boast from her kindness, if you were indebted to the intercession of your friends for her acceptance of you: they will never be able to speak as you will do for yourself; nor could she so *properly* pardon a lover who does not himself sue to her. Ladies you know are punctilious, and often consult *forms* more than *feelings.*—But need I repeat more to prevail upon you? If I *need,* you had much better stay away, for you are not attached as you should be to Miss Neville. And by my soul, Sutton, I think her worthy of your whole heart: this is no small present; yet I cannot grudge it, for my Emma speaks with amazement of her virtues; and she is my oracle......

She is coming to herself again: the love-darting eyes beam with all their mild effulgence; the faded cheeks are regaining their glowing tints; the whole person returns to its loveliness: such a certain restorative is content: and this, George, she enjoys in much greater abundance than ever she has done since I called her mine. She has lost all that fearful diffidence, which that accursed Mrs. Bromley took for coldness, and which ever after I fancied I perceived in her: she speaks to me with that assured certainty of pleasing, which gives new charms to those we love, as it seems to declare they judge of our hearts by their own, and, from knowing themselves to be pleased with us, conclude us to be equally so with them. The timorous speaker, from doubting of my approbation, has often missed it. I cannot avoid thinking she is reproaching me, all the time, with the harshness of my temper, when the down-cast look and half-pronounced words show her to be dubious of my applause.—You would have cured me of this, and have persuaded me, that timidity was the characteristic of my Emma's meekness, and could not be got over: but I find she has conquered it for my sake, and the victory is flattering.—Had I listened to you, I had not, it is true, required this of her; nor had I, my friend, played the spendthrift, and left myself the gnawing remembrance of having misbehaved to such a wife: but, filled with notions of my own wisdom, I scorned to follow counsels which did not coincide with my whims.—The earliest rule I laid down to myself, was to shun imitation: this has often made me singular in supporting opinions which nobody else had advanced: it made me form a system for myself, which I adhered to with all the obstinacy of a *schismatic*: hence came my maxim, "that women could not, without determining their original tenderness, express the least regard for more than one man in their lives."—Thus, *straight-laced*, as I may say, I carried my delicacies to an extravagant length: I had never met with any obstacle to my career in life: I spoke with boldness, and few took the pains to contradict me. In this uncontrouled sway I married, and uttered my sentiments freely before my wife, who heard them with fear, from the knowledge of her having concealed from me, that an amiable man had been dear to her in some degree. I was wrapped up in *this wife*, and the smallest suspicion of her not returning my love was enough to make me frantic. I found her ill—saw her dieing, and discovered that Sidney had been slain: what could I think of this? Passionate, and hurried along by the conflict in my mind, I staid not to hear her explain herself upon the subject, but plunged into every folly that could contribute to distract my thoughts. I never reflected, that Mrs.

Walpole could have been terrified by my violence into dissimulation, but held her concealment to be an incontestible proof of her criminality. I might probably have persisted in this mistake until her death had satisfied my vengeance: but those ruinous pleasures, which I had pursued with such avidity, forced me at last to think: in the dull hours of confinement I took a retrospective view of my conduct: I considered your advice, and I could have flown to my Emma's feet for pardon: but shame first with-held me, and then the reflexion of going back a beggar to her. This fixed my despair to its farthest bounds, as I imagined: the shafts of it rankled in my bosom, and I wanted to try whether wine would not be kinder to me in its effects than the other means I had used to gain ease. I should have become an arrant sot, had you not by your vigilance prevented me.—distress had made me see myself in the right light; and from this knowledge I grew more rational. I abhorred the *system* which I had adopted: I hated myself for my arrogance in presuming to introduce such rigid maxims, to the disturbance of society; and I found all the husband and the father awakened in my soul. When I was sorrowing in the thought of the unsurmountable bar that parted me from the wife and child, whom I had but just been taught how to love as I should do, Mrs. Walpole's letter arrived. Figure to yourself, how agonising the representation of her death must have been to me, who, besides my attachment, which interested me so much in her life, was subject to all the rage of Tisiphone's fury, as the murderer of her........All my other misfortunes were expunged by this, and nothing else was remembered by me. I ordered Turner to have four horses put to the chaise, and to get ready for setting out immediately for Yorkshire.— He stared at me—I repeated the orders.—He then reminded me, that my house was beset by bailiffs, who would never suffer me to escape their clutches if I passed the threshold of my own door. I was like a person hastily roused out of a dream, and could not for some minutes believe my senses. My valet acquainted me, that on Sunday I should be freed from these spies, and could then go off.—Sunday! What, cried I, must I wait so long for the absence of these hell-hounds?—Pray, what day of the week is this? For I would rather fight my way through them than stay eight and forty hours more. "Sir," replied he, quaking at my impetuosity, "this is Friday night, and I will bespeak post-horses for one o'clock on Sunday morning, when you may go off very privately."—There was too much plausibility in this, to have it disregarded. But, my friend, the intermediate space between the getting of the letter and my journey, was passed in a state that may be better guessed than described.—Impatient, and restless at all times to execute every project I form; only suppose what I must have been then!—When I had once left Portman-Square, the swiftness with which I travelled, gave some respite to my troubles. I have already told you how they increased on coming to this place, and will not repeat the heart-rending tale.. . . . . Once more am I happy.

Always thine,
William Walpole.

COL. SUTTON TO MISS NEVILLE.
LETTER 78. ROSE-COURT.

Had I ever heard that the unhappy had asked in vain of Miss Neville for compassion, I should not have ventured to have applied to her now: but as I come under that denomination, I hope I may, without too great presumption, expect to gain admittance. If I have offended heinously, I have also repented greatly: not, I own, sufficiently to atone for my failing; but, in leaving scope for your clemency to exert itself, I confer new pleasure on you, and heighten my own gratitude by enhancing the favor. Could I merit your forgiveness, I might demand it; but, as it is, I shall receive it from you as a free gift; for which my heart will be more beholden to you, than for any tribute which could be paid it.

I have long sought you, my injured Priscy; and the not finding you has been the canker-worm to my peace: it could not survive your loss. The siren that deluded me from you, had not the power of preserving it from the storm, no more than the inclination to attempt it. She retaliated upon me the wrongs I had done you: but, had she been as constant as she was alluring, she could not have satisfied the man who had been *your* lover: in my most impassioned hours, I felt the difference between the two, and the flimsy heart of the coquette could not conceive or nourish the flame which her charms had inspired. I looked at Miss Courtney, and sighed for Miss Neville.—But I would speak, not write my defence. I would obtain your leave to come to Rye-Farm: the respect I pay to you will not let me do it without, because I have heard from our friends, that you have declared you would not see me . . . Repeal, Madam that inhuman sentence, and do not by inflexibility sully your fame, which has been hitherto spotless. Do not bring down to a level with tyranny the virtue which, when moderately exercised, makes the most respectable *trait* in a charac-ter. But that firmness, which may be your glory in many actions, would not be a diminution of your goodness. Godlike souls cannot desire revenge: leave that to the vulgar wretches, who are too pusillanimous to defend themselves from injuries, but who

triumph in the opportunity of returning them upon their enemies.—"to err, is human; to forgive, divine." And it is this my
Priscy will chuse to do, and thereby bless

Her sincere and affectionate

George Sutton.

MISS NEVILLE TO COL. SUTTON.
LETTER 79. RYE-FARM.

Nothing, Sir, could have been more unexpected than your letter,
brought by one of Mr. Walpole's domestics: I supposed it was a billet
from my friend at Rose-Court; and in that delusion opened it: had I
been suspicious of its coming from you, I had not done it. But when
I had begun it, a curiosity, *perfectly womanish* I confess, made me
wish to know what could be said in extenuation of perfidy. It was a
subject which I was totally uninformed in. I read your *defence*, as you
style it; but whether I am not capable of judging in the cause, or
whether you have, from disuse, lost the art of imposing upon me, I
know not; but I have not been able to find one reason why I should
admit you as a visitor at Rye-Farm. You once thought you loved me;
I had then more youth and beauty to fix your love than I have now:
grief has blighted every charm, and left me plainer than years could
have made me. How should I then risk again the tranquillity which I
have gained from having no lover to disturb me by fears of his
mutability? Shall I throw away my dear-bought experience, and barter
for a few months, perhaps *days* of constancy, the calm of indifference,
and, when I have been disappointed a second time, have my credulity
to add to other weaknesses?—Can you pretend to be *sincere*, or
affectionate, when you ask me to do this? The crocodile is sincere
when it decoys the traveller to devour him; the bear is affectionate
when it embraces to destroy: man is not less treacherous or cruel in
his aims.

Should I not court deception, if I again trusted to professions I
have already found to be fallacious?

Inflexibility is turpitude in your account, when it exceeds the
limits you have set it; that is, when you are prevented by it from
enjoying the pleasure of betraying. You do well, Sir, to disapprove of
it: firmness does not belong to your inconstant heart; it would
confine you in your rovings, and condemn you to insipid sameness.
But I am not to be told by you, what I owe to myself: my purpose
is the result of the conviction of my judgement. I will not see you;
not from being vindictive in my temper, but from being resolved not

to be again deceived. The clemency you call upon me to show, you would not fail often to make me exert, were I fool enough to do it now.—I can be inflexible without being tyrannical: I can be inexorable to an improper request, without losing any of my compassion for the *unhappy*: if you are one of that sort, I pity you; but I cannot relieve you without endangering myself, and you cannot wish me to do it without forfeiting your right to it.

The friendship which gave you such umbrage yet remains: my sister is as much the object of my regard now, as she was when you left me: she will always be so; for there is a solidity in *our attachment,* which does not yield to undeserved suspicion. We are united by principle, not by fickle taste; from a thorough knowledge of each other's hearts, not from a vain desire of being admired, or a still more detestable motive, that of being dear to each other, until difference of place or time should make infidelity the *choice* of the one, and the punishment of the other.

Will not Colonel Sutton now wave all his pretensions to visiting us?—and shall I not be acquitted by him for not granting the leave he would have had from me, before I had given him such reasons for not complying?

I have never blazoned abroad my injuries: I brought into solitude the wrongs that might have been divulged by my stay in the world. I have not, in my own mind, condemned you for being guilty of more than custom may have entitled you to do.—Whether I am haughty, and do not care to allow I have been affronted, or generous, and will not reproach you for it, is not of consequence enough to be discussed: I only tell the fact, and you may decide as you please upon it.

The coquette, who could be shook off without an distress to either party, would be a properer object for your love, than the grave and steady

Priscilla Neville.

COLONEL SUTTON TO MISS NEVILLE.
LETTER **80.** ROSE-COURT.

Your anger, Madam, would not have wounded me as your contempt has done—I knew myself to be the aggressor, and I acknowledged my crime—I did not pretend that would be reparation for it; but I submitted to your mercy, and could not doubt it. You have overcome your own nature to punish me; you have borrowed the language of an unfeeling woman to make me sensible of an error, which I have incessantly deplored—you have brought us more on a par, and, by the pain you have given me now, can no longer say you have been the person most aggrieved. I have now some cause to complain of you; and by the title of *injured*, which was once all your own, I intreat you to hear me: you may be more kind to that, as being yours, than you were to that of *unhappy*, which you knew nothing of from *your own experience*. The stubborn heart, which is not to be moved by supplication, is not compatible with the amiability of my Priscy: she was gentle as descending dews, mild as the eye of pity, and would rather have lessened the malice of sin, than, by aggravating the frailty of an offender, have rendered him more obnoxious to himself. But it is no longer the same Miss Neville; retirement and contemplation have made her crabbed and unjust; she has forsaken society to indulge her dislike to mankind, and from her prejudices judges of my sentiments.

Be your *obdurate purpose* meritorious, and let me not be cheared with the least hope of forgiveness; but do not refuse me the small comfort of hearing you speak my doom: it is not much to allow to the man who once was high in your esteem. You cannot be so cruel as to deny this, surely!—The exact observance of the distance you have kept me at, since I came here, warrants me to ask for so trifling a gratification.—If ever you loved me, if ever you expect to be credited when you speak to some more fortunate man, who shall be hereafter beloved by you, permit me, Madam, to see you. I do not threaten to break through the restraint you have laid upon me; I have not temerity enough to obtrude myself upon you, unbidden; but I will not desist from my intreaties, until I have prevailed: my whole happiness is at stake, and I will be indefatigable until I have gained it.

Mrs. Wentworth would employ her friendship, I am convinced; she would, in the milkiness of her nature, intercede for me: there was a time, when I would not have been indebted to the mediation of any one for my Priscy's smiles; but, degraded as I am, I should now accept of her kindness on any terms, and treat the condescension of seeing me, as the summit of my hopes.

View me, Madam, as a delinquent, ready to expiate, by any sufferings, the offence which he committed from levity, not from sober reflexion. We are not ourselves when jealousy assails with all its fangs: the confused brain does not discern with precision; it swells into substantial injuries the shadows that are presented to it. It was from an excess of love that I was disturbed; a more luke-warm heart would have been easy under the appearances which I could not endure; it would have admitted a rival in your affections: but would it, my dearest Priscy, have been worthy of yours, without that genial warmth which made its chief merit with you?—Age and security would have corrected the exuberances of mine: had you been my wife, your sister would have been equally dear to you; but I could not have feared a change in my regard—Consent to be that, and be assured of my invariable constancy.—The *mutability* you might apprehend in a lover, could not then be suspected; I should never lose sight of your excellencies, and should infallibly be as exact a copy of them, as the wishes of my soul, and the docility of my temper, could make me. *Principle* would make my *attachment* as certain as your friendship is. To be implacable, cannot be right: it proves more of rancor, than of justice, to pursue with unremitting rigor the fault that is confessed. How shall I be convinced that you are *not vindictive*, when I see you exercising all the cruelty of the most vengeful? Resent my infidelity, show your abhorrence of it, I will join you in blackening the crime; but show some consideration for the sorrow of the culprit, and encourage his return to righteousness.—Is there a greater bliss than that of gladdening the sad heart, or a more exalted attribute than that of mercy, which never yet rejected the penitent? . . . . . .

The diminution of your beauty cannot affect my passion: I shall love you better for every hunger which I have caused: the pallid countenance, as it shows *my power* over your heart, will be to me more charming than all the vermilion which the prime of youth lends to those untutored in the cares of life. Let me have the joy of admiring those trophies of my love, those endearing marks of your regard.—I am not the base *betrayer* you take me for; I yielded to my jealousy of you, not to my partiality for another: I was imposed upon by your behaviour, and did not believe that I could have been regretted when I wrote that collection of absurdity which made you resign me to Miss Courtney and humiliation. Your answer staggered my suspicions, but you did not desire to remove them; and I had then entangled myself in new nets. No sooner was I disengaged, than my unalienated heart smote me for having forced it from its allegiance: it burns with all the fire of its first fondness to return to your confidence; to be re-instated in your favor, and to enjoy again the happiness of hearing from your lips that pardon, on which depend the hopes of

Your

George Sutton.

Miss Neville to Col. Sutton
Letter 81. Rye-Farm.

Your perseverance, Sir, would have been more glorious in a better cause; but, as it carries the point in view, you will not be ashamed of it. Satisfaction, not honor, is your *ambition*; and the pleasure of being successful will outweigh, in your calculation, the reproach of having meanly begged for a favor, which you should have commanded, had you not, by a breach of faith, lost your authority. You have tired me out by your importunity; and I grant you the leave you ask, though I do not find myself disposed to think you less punishable than I did at first: but to rid myself of a correspondence, which is become very troublesome to me, you shall be heard; I will see you—but it must be the last time you expect such an indulgence from me. My reason condemns the softness of my heart, which still argues for you, and which has given the verdict for your admission, against the wiser dictates of its counsellor: this you owe to the unaccountable weakness of its still retaining for you some of that tenderness, which it had too sincerely felt ever to divest itself of.

But do not infer from hence, Sir, that it shall ever govern me again. I can more easily subdue my passions than submit to be dishonored by them: I can stifle the love which would be disgraceful to me; can renounce the man, who is not such as my understanding would make me esteem.—He cannot be such, who is to be caught by the shallow bait of coquetry; or who, from his excessive vanity, will not permit me to show any attention to my friends. The imbecility which renders him liable to be duped, or the insolence which makes him expect such entire subservience to his will, would make me reject his proffered hand, though my heart were to consume from my love for him. I will not be ruled, in the most important choice to be made, by the blundering infatuation which can give what grace it pleases to the chosen; can give veracity to the oaths of men, generosity to their sentiments, integrity to their manners—make me deceive myself with false lights, and, when accident has discovered it to me, subject me to the abject necessity of weeping for the contemptible wanderer. I have done that, Colonel Sutton; and I will never pass through again the contention caused between the pride which disdains the insulter, and the softness which forgives and regrets him.—The jar of elements does not raise more violent commotion than the soul suffers, in being robbed of its favorite idol—whom it has decked with all the ornaments which mistaken virtues can give it, and in whom it trusts for all the rewards which truth and devotion can hope for. . . . .

I would not debase you more than your conduct has done, and therefore would not be brought to see you by the persuasions of any one but yourself. Feel, if you can, the obligations you owe to a person, who, in granting your request, does it in a way that cannot depress you, when you appear before her, with a sense of being indebted to any but yourself and her, for the favor of conversing with her.

I am, Sir,
Your humble servant,

P. Neville.

LADY NOEL TO MRS. WALPOLE.
LETTER 82. NOEL-CASTLE.

May my Emma's happiness be as durable as it is perfect, and make
Rose-Court a second Eden, blooming with every joy in the frosty air
of the north! . . . . .

From the *infirmary* I was carried to the gay scenes they have had
lately at the Grove. I found an invitation, when I came home from
you, to attend Sally Glanville, who would not put on the bridal attire
until I should be there. Young Bridges, whose *penchant* I so early
saw, having been accepted of, was, with my uncle's help, able to
secure a settlement for her; and with the consent of all parties they
were married a fortnight ago. They have taken a neat house, between
my uncle's and Mr. Glanville's, where they may live very prettily on
their present fortune, which, though but a middling one, will maintain them very well. I am extremely rejoiced that this good girl has
been so lucky.

Pray, will Miss Neville vouchsafe to take Colonel Sutton now? I
want to hear the conclusion of Walpole's plot against her. These men
are always willing to assist one another against us: we are the enemies
they attack; the most upright of them hold, that in love and war,
stratagems are allowable; yet they exclaim at the least detection of
hypocrisy in us. We are to be guileless, that they may be at greater
liberty to impose upon us. Upon my word, this is not very creditable
for the plotters: methinks there would be more dexterity in their
foiling us in an equal struggle, than in their taking us by ambus-
cade.—But what am I saying? I should not permit such accusations to
come from me: I have never been sensible of any art, but that of
pleasing, in my Charles; and I should take my opinions of the others
from him, but Lady Wilmington from disappointment, and Kitty
Bishop from being satirical, have given me some very unfavorable
thoughts of the generality of mankind, and I have been foolish
enough to reveal them now: I could find in my heart to retract, was
it not for blotting out so many lines of my letter, which would give
it such a slovenly look, that I should write it all over again, and that
I have not time to do this post.

My sister Wilmington and I have been disputing which would be
preferable, the losing of a lover from his baseness, or from his death.
She would chuse the last, were she put to her option; whilst my
cowardly spirit would rather bear with the loss of his heart than of his
life. She says, that her tears could flow upon his bier without reproach; that she could think of him without being lowered in her
own esteem; could fancy him the inspector of her actions, the invis-
ible agent who would direct her steps, and exult in her merit; whose
soul would be her object of love, and to whose recollection she
should be constant.

I, on the other hand, talk of the horrors which his very perfections would occasion when he was snatched from me; the desperation of an irrevocable end of all my fond expectations, and the dark melancholy which this would create: whereas the falsehood which mortified my pride would lessen the passion which was slighted, and, after having surmounted the *shock*, the mind would return to its natural ease: the storm abated once, the calm that succeeded would be more certain, and the purchase of experience would make some compensation for the pain: I should stand a better chance of being *easy* the rest of my life, from the hard lesson I had been taught, and might know, that she who does not depend upon a mortal shall not be deceived.—We each supported our thesis with great *elocution*, but neither of the disputants was to be drawn from her own.—Miss Neville now, I should imagine, might decide with the tone of a love-casuist, and let us abide by her determination.— Julia does not quite agree to this: she declares, that, had my Lord died when she was opposing her mother for him, she should have been far happier than in supporting his indifference. I cannot think so; for her imagination would have tormented her forever with his image, embellished with every amiable quality; and she would have pined in endless grief for him; whereas now she is every day becoming less sensible of his neglect: but she may indeed speak more knowingly upon this, than can

Your

F. Noel.

MRS. WALPOLE TO LADY NOEL.
LETTER 83. ROSE-COURT.

"Who shall decide when *doctors* disagree?" Which shall we give the prize to, where the controversy has been so equally supported? I should vote with you, but that does not finish it at all. It is the particular opinion of each one who is to chuse, not the real merit or demerit of the subjects, that can be ascertained by it.

Miss Neville, in the plenitude of her joy, from the reconciliation that has been brought about, with great labor, between her and Colonel Sutton, was not so impartial an arbitrator as you should have had. When I put it to her, she said laughingly, "Tell Lady Noel, that there are more arguments on her side than on Lady Wilmington's; that death leaves no consolation; but that there is a pleasure in *forgiving* the faults of a lover, which makes one forget they have suffered from them."—Her's are really such; for she is not to be guessed at for the same love-lorn Priscy, who looked like a spectre, and appeared to *accept*, not to *enjoy* life.—She now skims along blithe as a bird, and has more vivid hues in her complexion than all Warren's cosmetics could give.—There is not such a beautifier as content.———"Roses will bloom, where there's peace in the breast."

The Colonel came down as soon as he heard of her being in our neighborhood; but being told of her objection to seeing him, he wrote the evening he arrived, and sent it by our footman, to prevent her being prepossessed against it. The letter had been directed and sealed by me. Her answer, which did not come until the next day, gave him much *discomfiture*: he read, and knit his brows, as if it was some sharp rebuke he had had. He put it up, walked out, stood long over the edge of the pond in the garden, as if he had taken it for the *Leucadian rock*, the leap for despairing lovers to take; but thinking, as all wise men should, that it was time enough to die when he could live no longer, or very possibly being struck with his person which the liquid mirror reflected, he might gain new courage to assay the heart again which that fine figure had once found vulnerable; he went up to his desk, and wrote a second letter. When he came back to us, he looked so *woe-worn*, that Mr. Walpole, in perfect pity to him, could not jest with his usual lightness, but comforted him by saying, "He had too much regard for Miss Neville, to think she could refuse to see any gentleman who had asked her permission to visit her."— "But I am not to be classed with others, Walpole: She makes now the most unkind distinctions between me and the rest of the world.— I am a *betrayer*, who should by her account, be treated with the greatest severity.—I must not hope to be admitted to see her."

"If she once comes to rail at you," replied his friend (well read in the characters of women) "she will not long be unaccessible. Had she returned your epistle unopened, or even unread, supposing she had been misled by the method of conveyance to break the seal, I should have advised you to have raised the siege, in your own phrase, and to have abandoned the impregnable fortress; but if the foe parleys, she will capitulate, or I am no *general—admirer* of your sex, my love," said he, turning to me.

These assurances had no great sway with Colonel Sutton, who was in and out of the doors, up and down stairs, forty times in the day. Priscy would be won with difficulty, and did not send any billet-doux until she had taken time to digest all he had written to her: then came this desired grant, which was to heal all wounds. He staid not to give her space for recalling it, if she had been desirous of doing it, but went off directly to Rye-Farm; though Mr. Walpole, by way of teasing him, pulled him back once to tell him he would ruin all by his haste; that, if he made her wait a little, it would whet her desire of seeing him, and make his appearance more welcome: he shook off his hold, and hastened out of the house.

His reception was not such as he had wished for; he was not in spirits when he came home: but he did not blab a word of what had passed. He kept on visiting there for ten days, when Miss Neville came to see me, and owned honestly, that, after raising herself to such a height above him, she did not well understand how she could come down to treat upon an equal footing with him. It was palpable, that she would not long be distressed about this. He, all humble and respectful, left her in no incertitude about his having the justest sense of his error; whilst his assiduity and passionate tenderness for her assured her of his present regard.—A week or two completed the courtship. When all was agreed upon the evening before they were to be married, he gave her a paper, which he begged she would present to Mrs. Wentworth, and which made over to her Miss Neville's fortune, her own having been partly spent during Mr. Wentworth's life. This was liberality as unexpected as welcome to his Priscy, who had been afraid of her sister's being hurt by the division of the money; as withdrawing five thousand pounds from their stock would have reduced hers to a very narrow compass. She is to live with them, at Colonel Sutton's own request. The hymeneal rites being performed, they left the country—are to pass the ensuing winter in London then to go to reside at Isleworth, where he has a charming villa.—This is no bad winding up of *their romance*, for methinks they seldom carry the story beyond the conclusion of the marriage; a sly insinuation, perhaps, that there ends all *the love* of the adventurous pairs who had run through such hazardous encounters for each other before they had been secured by the Gordian knot, and obliged to abide by one another for the rest of their lives.

I have returned you the news of Priscy's wedding for yours of Miss Glanville's, whose luck I was vastly pleased to hear of.

Lady Wilmington should not have much weight with you: you know that you yourself said, the match, which took place through her *stubbornness* and his *covetousness*, did not foretell any great felicity. Had she not been hood-winked by her own perverseness, she might have seen how *tepid* the heart was which at his age could love gold.—I think her situation exceedingly to be dreaded, but she herself not so pitiable as many women would be. Her capriciousness would have made her uneasy with any companion; and her having such an one to persecute with it, is not amiss.

How frequently have I known what has been deemed *good-nature*, to be nothing more than an insensibility of temper! Which making men totally unconcerned about the accidents that happen, they preserve all their equanimity when warmer souls would be enraged: such are usually the Stoics we see in the world; for without religion (which few of them have) there is no curbing impatience. . . .

Kitty has indulged herself in uttering every thought that passes in her mind, and is such a wag withall, that she is still less to be minded when she talks of mankind.—You and I, my dear Fanny, should be their champions against these two accusers, for we have found them guiltless of all they have laid to their charge.—Your Noel is not less worthy of your partiality, than is my Walpole of that of

Your

Emma Walpole.

MISS BISHOP TO MRS. WALPOLE.
LETTER 84. BURTON.

I may now expect to be treated with indulgence, since my dearest Emma has left the *elegiacs*, and can smile at the quaint conceits which I indite.—My gaiety has actually been raised to its topmost pitch since I have heard of your happiness;—every nook has rung with my noise. My brother, who has been too long absent to remember that I always had much of the boisterous in me, now draws in his chin, and reads me lectures upon the impropriety of my *excessive vivacity*, which is very repugnant to his *sober sadness*.—There must be something in the tour, which forces young men to emulate the gravity of their grandfathers. William is no *Maccaroni*, but he is *tristful* enough to suit their plan: or very likely he seems solemn to me only; for he is commonly named as an agreeable youth, out of my company. He is rather too sentimental for me, and now and then arrives at *pomposity* from his great exactitude in fitting his language to his stories.—Lady Catharine is proud of him: my father sees himself renewed in him, and grows young when he is recounting the feats of his son, who really has, like a true and liege knight, *comported* himself very honorably, if his tutor and his friend are to be credited; but one may praise himself in commending him, and the other may not have solidity enough to judge of him: however, he is, *en verité*, a very good son and a very *careful* brother.

The dialogue I am going to give you will inform you, better than any thing I say besides, of this last. I shall not mention the names of the two who held it, after every sentence—*so said he*, and *thus said I*: —but you will know the speakers by the tenor of it.

I was stroking my paroquet, and teaching it some words a few weeks ago, when William brought in his friend, Lord Beaumont, who travelled with him, and who is the repository in which all his thoughts are stored up for the use of both. The Viscount is as like him in his manner, as another brother could have been; but he is better humored, and can bear a joke. After his introduction, he was continually coming down to us, to stay three or four days at a time.

I saw nothing particular in this; but some time after, when I was left alone with William one morning he begun, after a roundabout way, to ask me some questions—as thus:

"Pray, Kitty, have you ever taken any notice of Lord Beaumont's coming here?"

"No, if *you mean* as to the number of times, I protest I have kept no reckoning; but I have been observant enough to know when he has come or gone away so as to do the civil thing."

"You might have supposed I did not mean any such nonsense."

"Well then, tell me plainly what you do; for I am no conjuror to find out men's thoughts."

"Have you then seen nothing in his behaviour that could speak for him?"

"Nothing more than in other people's—he has not been so queer as to make me think him crazy, nor so wise as to make me think him a Solomon. He has been good-humoured, and, if not jocose, he has not quarreled with me for being so. His *dress*, I recollect now, once drew my eye; and I was just going to tell him, he had a very handsome *waistcoat* on, but that I thought England rather too cold a climate to go without a *coat*—when, fortunately looking a little closer, I found out the dapper skirts, which I had not been able to see at first."

"Heavens! How ridiculous to talk at this rate!—Lord Beaumont, let me acquaint you, is no fool, nor shall he be used as one by you."

"Did I not say just now, that I had not been very observant of him? So that I am obliged to you for your information—I might else have *mistaken* him—But what does all this tend to?"

"Why, I was *commissioned* by him to speak to you—"

"Is he to pay you so much *per cent* for your words, that you have given me this long preface to the business?"

"Insupportable flippancy!—Kitty, you fancy yourself a wit, but you are devilishly deceived: you talk fast, and laugh loud; but shallow waters make most sound, and empty heads most noise."

"These are judicious observations—pray, did you hear them on this side, or on the other side of the Alps?—You are a great proficient in similes—do you take Mr. Bayes' advice, and make one when you are *surprised* always."

"To talk to you is loss of time; I shall never spend mine so unprofitably."—(He was going, but I would not part in anger.)

"Come, my choleric brother, let us understand each other better: I will be silent, if you will be concise; but you must come to the point, or I will not answer for myself.—Now, dear William, do not be ill-natured, for I have no gall; I am a pigeon for that. I have always been used to make free with my betters; so that you cannot break me all at once of this *flippancy*, as you term it—but who knows how I may be *amended* by your conversation? Tell me what Lord Beaumont *commissioned* you to say—I will take that time to breathe a little."

"You will sneer probably at him for loving you?"

"I don't know what I might do, was I to hear him make love for himself; but, as *you* are his *ambassador*, I dare not, for fear you should be affronted."

"Answer me, Kitty; is it affectation, or insensibility, that makes you so careless about him?"

"Both, William—I *affect* to despise admiration—I am *insensible* to the passion he feels."—(I spoke with a broad grin: this stirred up his bile again.)

"Trifler!—You cannot be serious."

"Then love is an antidote to mirth: disclaim it then, and the *peer* of the woeful countenance may find out another Dulcinea as soon as he will."

My brother took up a book, and would not talk more to me. I called Favori to come and commune with me, that I might not be reduced to mere soliloquy: the dog fawned upon me; but, as he could not speak, I soon left him, and took up my guitar, to which I hummed *Maudit amour*, then *Le jour du mariage est le tombeau de l'amour*. I had strummed myself almost into the dumps, and might have had recourse to a dirge, by way of solemn harmony, had not my mother come in, and by her facetiousness and pleasantry raised my spirits again. I related to her all our *squabble:* she called William testy, and me *bizarre;* but after the *boy* had quitted us, she enquired whether I really chose to have Lord Beaumont or not, as he would not be disagreeable either to her, or Mr. Bishop. I made no objection; and in some days after, *the lover* came down: we were left together: he seated himself by me, hummed, looked upon the carpet, then walked towards the window, and said something that he had *said* upon first taking the view, but which he repeated now, for want of other discourse. After a dozen *hems*, half a score *haws*, and shewing his white teeth in attempting to speak, he found his words more fluent, and made his mind known to me. I imagine there never is any thing very *extraordinary* in this sort of oration: I declare there was not in this, at least. After this, my Lord is considered as one of ourselves—he is for ever near me: it is somewhat *gênant* to be so constantly attended by the same man; and I sometimes have tried to escape from his watchfulness. Favori barked at him yesterday, when he wanted to snatch a nosegay out of my hands: I told him it was because he could not bear to see any *puppy*, but himself, caressed by me. He was unresolved how to take my compliment until my brother, in high choler, swore he would not bear such insults tamely. My Lord then laughed off the speech, and this did him more service with me than seven years of servitude. I am not clear that he is all that *youthful ladies* "fancy when they love;" but he is quiet and unassuming, makes generous offers, and is so ready to applaud me, that I never finish a period, without crying, "*Hey, Beaumont!*"—William may advise himself hoarse; a man *in love* is not to be helped by it; and as long as I please to rally, so long will his friend bear with it.

I often talk of going down to Rose-Court for a few weeks, as I have no thoughts of marrying for some months; yet, if I come, I shall bring with me the train of my attendants—Lord Beaumont to gallant me, my sage brother to reprove me, my dog to follow me, and the paroquet to entertain Bel and myself.

You know now the whole *scheme of my lottery*—I shall be more likely to raise provisions by it, in Yorkshire, than money, I doubt: but at the worst, to make money, I may shew my lover for a *monkey*; Favori for *le chien savant*; the talking bird for a *phoenix*; William and myself, as two personages who have sailed round the world in quest of rarities, and come back to *astonish* our countrymen with strange sights! Curiosity, I guess, is as prevalent in your latitude, as it is elsewhere; and we shall, without fail, gather as much renown, as any adventurers who have been celebrated.

Adieu, Walpole, and you must believe me
Yours sincerely,

Catharine Bishop.

*[Here several letters are omitted,
as they contained nothing interesting or new.]*

MR. WALPOLE TO COL. SUTTON.
LETTER 85. ROSE-COURT.

Short has been, my dear Sutton, the peace I boasted. The means by which I found it, are now the disturbers of it. My Emma, who is all the most unreasonable could desire—my Bel, the finest child that father could wish for—these dear paragons of virtue and goodness, who should have been my greatest comforts, are now my bitterest pangs. I behold my wife deprived of a thousand things agreeable if not essential to her, in a situation that requires more than ordinary helps to make her easy and safe. Her health, delicate as it has always been, and the bleak north wind ready to pierce through the house, and from its roughness threatening her weak chest with new complaints, makes me every hour more alarmed about her. I had been promised an appointment in one of the new-settled islands by Lord————: I had reserved this as a security against the wants of my

family; and when I found Mrs. Walpole demanded more than our
wrecked fortune could give, I wrote to his Lordship, without saying
any thing of it to her, designing to go over myself, and to support
her in London, where she would be better assisted by the salary
which my place would give. I was answered, that the appointment
had passed, and that I might take possession of it when I liked. My
Emma was with me when I got this letter—I read it to her—she
clung about me, beseeching me to stay, or to let her go with me, for
she should not outlive my absence—I could not refuse her what she
begged with such ardor, but which to comply with was not to be
soon adjusted—to stay and see her perish, was death to me—to take
her through all the dangers of such a voyage, as much distressed me.
She still importuned me to say what I should do, and to make her
satisfied; for going abroad, or staying in Yorkshire with me, would be
just the same to her; she disliked nothing, but being severed from
me. I asked her whether it was possible for me to remain an indifferent spectator of her sufferings; and whether my absence would not be
preferable to our starving together, if I staid?—What chimerical fears
are these, my dearest Mr. Walpole! answered she: would you realize
misery, by leaving me, to prevent artificial indigence?—Are we not
rich in peace? And what is there wanting, to make our lives glide
with tranquil happiness, more than what we enjoy? I pray to heaven,
every hour, for a continuance of this placidity: it is the state I have
always most envied; and would you rob me of it? Have you ever seen
discontent lowering in my looks, since you have returned to me? Why
will you now force it on me? The luxuries of the Asiatics would be
freely exchanged by me for the delights of this retirement. I find no
deficiency in our income; it supplies us with simple aliments, and
raiment adapted to our wishes. In you I find a refuge against every
harm; but if you desire more pomp and wealth, let me share your
toil, and your company will make me fancy there are charms in those
words, which I never before discovered.

I strained the sweet seraph to my throbbing heart, bid her talk
on, and I should no longer recollect that I could be uneasy. But as I
did not positively say how I had determined about her, she began to
entertain some suspicion of my going off without any more notice
being taken of it; and the first time she missed me for a few hours, I
found her, at my coming back, with the deepest anxiety depicted on
her intelligent countenance, and her eyes still humid: this has made
her since keep a sort of guard upon me, which when I saw, I gave
her the firmest promise of not going without her. But, my beloved,
added I, can you venture to go such a voyage at this time? Will you
be able to undergo the hardships and horrors of it? And what can be
done with Bel?

"O, as for her," cried she, "it will not incommode her in the
least to be at sea; she is of an age not to feel any inconvenience from

it; and I have not *terrors* to apprehend. The same Providence that watches over us here, will be there. I ask for its protection with the most assured confidence in it; for it is as benevolent as powerful, and does not disregard the humble suppliant."

There is no opposing truths from such lips; and as I could not, without doing violence to her and myself, leave her behind me, I must perforce risque my whole hope at once, and embark, with her and my daughter, for the new world. Sutton, you can tell how rived my heart must be by this scheme; it is ready to give way, when I think over the hazards those two are to run: yet we must do something; for my extravagance has left so small a matter for their wants, that it cannot administer enough even for my moderate Emma, though she would make me think she has plenty for all her *wishes*. She enjoys *tranquil* pleasures, and can be content—but, George, the wasteful spoiler—the unthinking dissipater of her fortune—he can know none. I grieve momently with the idea of her wanting something, which we cannot procure her; and what she names *artificial indigence*, is *realized* indeed with me.

In six weeks, at most, we must quit England. We must go to London for two or three days, in our way to Portsmouth. I shall see you, my friend; I shall converse with you, probably for the last. But why make you suffer any of the troubles which fill the soul of William Walpole?

COL. SUTTON TO W. WALPOLE, ESQ.
LETTER 86.

You have injured our league, my dear, high-minded Walpole; but refusing to accept of my assistance in redressing your affairs; you have made a breach in the covenant of friendship; and if you were not already unhappy, I should be tempted to abandon you for your obstinacy in rejecting my offers.

Mrs. Sutton expects you and Mrs. Walpole will be with us during your stay in town, as the house in Portman-Square will not be aired. I do not love to add to your dejection, but I should mention my opinion to you about your voyage: it does not appear to me likely to answer the purpose: the new islands may be very promising; but it's a great while before they can be flourishing, and it is from this only that you can be enriched: it takes time to bring every settlement to maturity: numbers have been shipped off, who have not found the *golden dreams*, they went with, made out on their arrival. You are not necessitated to seek *your bread*; you might wait at least until some months hence, when, if you have a son, you will be able to cut down timber enough to pay off all your incumbrances: but you have not patience to stay for any thing; the minute you wish you must be gratified. If Mrs. Walpole should have another girl, then really you might be in haste to make some provision for them: but be quiet until that is determined, and in the mean while bring her and Bel. to us, where they will be out of reach of the rough breath of Boreas, and well attended to. Priscy and Mrs. Wentworth are excellent nurses. If this is to be disregarded, as all my proffers have been by you, I shall not so easily forgive it, as you will disoblige three of your sincerest friends by it: so be no longer refractory.

Who do you think I saw the other day, but Mrs. Bromley? I went into the chapel at———, where I was told I should hear a famous Methodist preacher, who was in the midst of his *furious* exhortation, ranting away like a daemoniac. I was not long taken up with him, you may imagine; but throwing my eyes about to see the congregation in a snug feat I perceive the now demure widow, turning up her *piercers* to the ceiling, and distorting her face with all the grimace of a fanatic. I could scarcely persuade myself that it was she, until I saw her *frized* out about the head, and uniting all the *prophane* vanities of a worldling to the *sanctified* convulsions of the *children of new grace:*—no one but herself, I knew, could be so contradictory. This is a good finishing to such a part as she has acted in life. A termagant may make a *perfect* saint, where violence is merit.

Adieu; be more compliant, and know to be always
Yours,
George Sutton.

MR. WALPOLE TO COLONEL SUTTON.
LETTER 87. ROSE-COURT.

I will not exasperate you with saying what had been my answer to your last, since I can now, my dear Sutton, stay at home and see my Emma blaze in her own lustre again. But good fortune makes me more incoherent than all our misfortunes did. I am inebriated with joy, and cannot tell where to commence my narrative; but take it piece-meal then.

We had actually packed up every thing, and had fixed on Wednesday for setting out from hence on our migration. Emma showed not the smallest reluctance; but I cast many a wishful look at every thing about me, which increased in my esteem the nearer I was to leaving them. Sunday passed, and no change came; but on Monday noon I received the following information.

"Sir,

Mr. Savage has by his will bequeathed you the bulk of his fortune, which by what I can learn does not fall short of a *plum*, placed in the different funds of England. I am nominated joint executor with you to discharge a few trifling debts and legacies out of it: and as soon as you can act, I shall be ready to help in fulfilling the will of my late worthy friend.

I am, Sir,
Your humble servant,

Martin Allgood.

I have not had so agreeable a correspondent for some time as this Mr. Allgood. His late worthy friend, and my uncle, was my mother's third brother, and her favorite. He was brought up in the city, where his industry soon raised him to be of some note amongst the merchants. He had an only son, who about two months ago broke his neck by a fall from his horse: but he was a very fine lad, and the doating-piece of his poor father, who used to be very kind to me when I was at school, and having a country box about seven or eight miles from town, would take me there on Sundays with him. He did not love my father; but for his good Annabella, she and every child of hers were dear to him. When she died, he had no intercourse with me: I had not seen him for several years; when, after I came from my travels, I called upon him: he had thought himself neglected by me, and had abated much of his regard for me by that time. I still continued to visit him, and took great notice of young Savage, which rekindled some latent sparks of his kindness again. He advanced a sum for me when I was in need of one at my first setting out in dissipation; but finding me too *expensive*, he refused to answer any more of my draughts. This made a coolness between us; but on hearing of his son's accident, I found all my wrath give way to my compassion, and I wrote him a letter of condolance, which one of his clerks answered, informing me that his master had never held up his head since young Mr. Savage's death, but that he had been very sensible of my remembrance; that he was then supposed to be dieing. My heart was affected at the situation of this good man, and I could have wished to have been with him, but there was no means of getting to him then.

My sensations were problematical upon the receipt of this news: I was sorry for the sufferings which had brought me these riches; yet I could not regret so much as I should have done, when I found myself relieved by them from so many dreadful chagrins. My wife's humane heart was not divided by any selfish comfort; she shed tears over the father and his son, and I believe would have compounded with poverty, could she have recalled them to life.

Our London journey will not be postponed beyond the end of this week. We shall meet, my dearest Sutton, with much more glee than has been felt this age by

Your ever affectionate friend,

William Walpole

Mrs. Walpole to Lady Noel.
Letter 88. Portman-Square.

Events as unexpected as unwished for, my dear Fanny, have brought your Emma from her retreat, where use and reflexion had made her feel that thorough contempt for fortune, which all who desire to be happy should possess. It will, I trust, make me know too how to use the affluence which is again fallen to my share.—A large legacy has restored Mr. Walpole to his primitive ease: he has learnt in adversity to regulate his passions:—no longer that captious humorist, who kept me in awe, he is gentle, and always approving:—his love still undiminished; but it is governed by his good sense now, not by his whims, as at first.

I find myself as if transplanted into a new soil here; the novelty of every object strikes me with a sort of surprise: whole streets have been added, and the old ones are so transformed, from paving and lighting anew, that they are not to be known again. But this is nothing strange to you, who have been so lately here.

The Bishops are in town: Kitty drags about her *captive* to every place. I enquired when she intended to be married: she says, not until the marriage-act is repealed, and that she can be wedded when and where she pleases, for she hates restraint of any kind. My Lord smirks at her drollery; but he will not be long pleased if she keeps her resolution; for he is an *inamorato*, literally speaking. She too is not entirely free from the *pleasing pain*, though it has not yet robbed her of any bloom or gaiety: she laughs even at her lover when any of his actions are at all ridiculous; it would be well if she did not often make them so by her manner of drawing them.

Her volubility of speech makes her lover often hurt before she means to ridicule him; but, as soon as he begins to show himself at all afraid of her, she never spares him; for she looks upon this as a declaration of war on his side, and will not be *dared* by him. I wondered that she could try to expose his imperfections, as she professed to love him. "I am not," replied she, "one of those blind fools who can discern no failings in those they like; and as I do not expect others should be less perspicacious, I let them see that I am as much so as they are. Lord Beaumont is a very good creature; but he has some dark spots in him as well as the sun, and I must not be so unfriendly as not to point them out to him.—He has a propensity to *foppishness*, which I must cure: the extreme of fashion comes within the verge of ridicule, and this is all I employ: I cannot discard a man because his coat is shorter than another's, or because his hat is less; but I can satirise him for it."

I could not subscribe to *these articles*; but, as he is not mine, I need not dispute them with this volatile talker, who is not to be argued with from reason.

I should have begun this with more weighty subjects than the quarrels of lovers; I should have told my Fanny, that Lord and Lady Clarendon have been reconciled, and are both mended by the reflexions they have made during their separation. The day or two after we came up, we had spent the day in Burton-Street; and when we had got home, seeing several visiting cards lying on the table, I went to it, and read over the names on many of them. Taking up one, I saw hers on it. I cannot define to you what I felt on finding her among my visitors. Mr. Walpole was by me, and had riveted his eyes upon me, whilst I had been perusing these tickets: he could not but observe my emotion when I held that.—"What is there in Lady Clarendon's name, my dear Emma," interrogated he, "which is so ungrateful to you?—You are alternatively red and pale, as if it contained some noxious quality in it." I remained in speechless suspense, not being fixed in what I should say upon it—when he enfolded me in his arms, and pressing my face to his—"Do not, my love," proceeded he, "endeavour to hide from me your having heard the reports which the malicious world invented about his unhappy women and men. The effect they have had upon you is too obvious; but in it I find new proofs of your love, and I am vain of them. But, believe me, the story is as false as it is scandalous. Lady Clarendon has been aspersed from conjectures groundless as the malice of the town generally is against the beauteous. She has been injured on my account, and therefore I think myself bound to make all the reparation I can to her; and I should be glad if you would countenance her visiting here; for when she is seen to be intimate with my wife, the world will be inclined to acquit her of ever being too much so with me." I should not have merited the confidence of my husband, had I hesitated about this: I was pleased to have him so desirous of repairing the giddiness which had been hurtful to her, and went the next evening to return her visit.—She was at home, and Lady Surry with her: she was confused at my first coming in; but immediately getting over it, she came up, and, with affability unusual in her formerly, welcomed me to London and thanked me for this early visit. Lady

Surry looked more than she chose to say, but it was all favorable to me. When I found them so ready to meet my advances towards intimacy, I spoke of the pleasure I should take in being much with them: Lady Clarendon protested she would not be backward in coming to me.—I thought she never was so perfectly handsome as she was then. I could think of nothing but "Soft, modest, melancholy, female, fair:" haughtiness was all subdued, and her diffidence aided every charm about her. I told Mr. Walpole at my return, that, if I had any thing to fear from him, I should fancy her a more dangerous rival now than ever she had been.—He defied her power.

The morning after, I had an invitation to an assembly at Lady Surry's, and many excuses for its not having been sent before, as it was to be given three days after. In the interim I agreed to call on Lady Clarendon in Wimpole-Street (where she took a house to be near her family) and to go in with her: accordingly we were announced together, to the visible astonishment of many there, who had not supposed we should have been so sociable with each other. This was a signal of our not being at enmity: we made our appearance in many private companies always together. She was rather scrupulous of going in public, as she had never been since their parting; but I prevailed on her to go with me to the Pantheon some time after: she was dressed in virgin white and might at such a place well have passed for the Goddess of Chastity, so timid and so pure did she look. We had not walked about long when I distinguished Lord Clarendon, at some distance, taking a survey of our party, which was made up of Lord and Lady Surry, his own Lady, the Bishops, and Suttons, Mr. Walpole, and myself. I leaned upon my husband's arm, and on the other side of me was Lady Clarendon. Admire at my humility, in having such a beauty so near me. I was amazed at it myself when I thought of it: but I wished to attract no eyes but those whose tender admiration I was sure of; these were my Walpole's, which did not once wander from me. I was soon fatigued, and we got seats; but the others, not being so easily satisfied with what they had seen, left Lady Clarendon and me, to go to some other part of the building: she was sitting by me in close conversation when my Lord passed by, and again eyed us. I thought it best *not to stare* him out of a bow, as he might have been distressed how to have saluted my neighbour: this made me seem not to have observed him; but she could not so well conceal her agitation on their meeting: he walked away, as if to avoid being noticed by her; but he never ceased following us whenever we stirred. . . .

We had seen the marble of Italy surpassed here by composition. The next day we were to see ingenuity carried farther, and to view life and motion given to animals and insects by the dexterity of Mr. Cox, whose museum our set was to visit. Here Lord Clarendon, as if impelled by the same inclination, met us at the door, and was huddled in with our company, as if he had been one of it: he just moved his hat, and separated as soon as we got into the room.—— On the Saturday night next, Lady Clarendon and I went to the opera by ourselves: her Lord was directly under us; he looked up, considered for a little space, then went out: presently our box was opened, and we were surprised at seeing him come into it. He accosted his consort with—"Am I so hateful to Lady Clarendon, that she will not even look at me when we meet?"

"She avoids you, my Lord," answered she tremulously, "because she thought herself *hateful* to you."—"We have deceived each other then, Madam; and if your Ladyship will let me speak with you, I hope we may come to a better understanding."—She told him this was no place for coming to an *ecclairicissement*, but———"You will give me the honor of attending you at your own house then?" said he, before she could finish her sentence.—He did not solicit in vain: the *honor* of waiting upon her was allowed him, and the pacification was quicky concluded between them. They are now as united as people can be; she has given over flirting, and he cannot be jealous. You would imagine I had bestowed the greatest favor on them both, they are so grateful for the service my friendship has rendered them. Mr. Walpole too acknowledges much obligation to me for my acquiescence with his will, in being so much about with her, and thereby helping to disperse the calumnies which had been raised of her.

I have now done with raking, until six weeks or two months are over. I expected you and Sir Charles would have been in town ere this. I sent to Albemarle-Street to enquire yesterday, and hear you will not be up these ten days. I wish to have my Fanny with me when I am taken ill; and you must not exceed that time, or you will not be so useful to

Your affectionate
Emma Walpole.

MR. WALPOLE TO LADY NOEL.
LETTER 89. PORTMAN-SQUARE.

Emma was sorry, my dear Lady Noel, that she could not stay for your Ladyship's coming up; but the forward boy would not be kept back, though he was promised to be received soon after his entrance into the world by your fair hands. He will be more gallant when he has some time in it. My charming Emma is safe, and in great joy on the birth of an heir.—I am more pleased on her account than on his, though few sons were more wished for than he has been by me.

You must come directly to us, for he waits for your Ladyship to answer for his being a Christian, and to instruct him better in what he owes to you.

Noel and Charles, I know, must move whenever you please to direct them: you will have no hindrance then, *mia bellissima*, in coming to

Your impatient friends,

E. and W. Walpole.

The End.

Collation of 1773 and 1784 Editions

ITEMS IN PARENTHESES INDICATE discrepancies between the two 1773 London editions of *Emma*: one at the University of Chicago library, and the other, at the British Library (consulted from a microfilm copy at Michigan State University, East Lansing).

54	humor (1:4)/humour (1:6)	59	*per sempre* (1:27)/per sempre
54	*advice* (1:5)/advice (1:6)	60	*rather foolish* (1:35)/*rather*
54	*beaux* (1:6)/beaux (1:7)		foolish (1:21)
55	kept it a distance (1:9)/	61	honor (1:35)/honour
	kept it at a distance (1:8)		(1:21)
55	*most agreeable* (1:8)/most	62	*peace of mind* (1:42)/peace
	agreeable (1:10)		of mind (1:24)
55	*quite so* (1:11)/quite so (1:10)	62	Milfield (1:43)/*Milfield*
56	*nonage* (1:16)/nonage (1:12)		(1:25)
56	*dotage* (1:16)/dotage (1:12)	63	*oracle style* (1:45)/oracle
56	*peculiar* (1:16)/peculiar (1:12)		style (1:25)
56	*satisfaction* (1:17)/satisfaction	63	*journeying* (1:46)/journeying
	(1:12)		(1:26)
57	*gaieté* (1:19)/gaieté (1:13)	63	*prudence* (1:46)/prudence
57	her sex (1:21)/our sex (1:14)		(1:26)
58	*inamorato* (1:22)/inamarato	63	attraction. [9] (1:47)/
	(1:15)		attraction. . . . (1:26)
58	*flutter* (1:22)/flutter (1:15)	63	*formalities* (1:48)/formali-
58	*la belle Emma* (1:22)/la		ties (1:27)
	belle Emma (1:15)	63	attend her . . . So (1:48)/
58	*her way* (1:22)/her way (1:15)		attend her. So now (1:27)

63   *whims* (1:49)/whims (1:27)

64   Spring-park (1:49)/Spring-
Park (1:27)

64   Maitresse du Chateau
(1:49)/Maitresse de Cha-
teau (1:27)

64   Sunbury. (1:50)/*Sunbury.*
(1:28)

64   *your friend* (1:52)/your
friend (1:29)

65   humor (1:54)/humour
(1:30)

65   self-conceit (1:57)/self
conceit (1:31)

66   The Grove (1:58)/*The
Grove* (1:31)

66   *goblin;* (1:59)/goblin,
(1:32)

66   *frightful tales* (1:59)/
frightful tales (1:32)

66   Sunbury (1:61)/*Sunbury*
(1:33)

66   *It feeds,* (1:61)/It feeds,
(1:33)

67   *resentment* . . . (1:65)/
resentment———(1:34)

67   professions: (1:65)/profes-
sion: (1:35)

67   pavilion (1:67)/pavilion
(1:36)

68   *that* pain (1:67)/that pain
(1:36)

68   *by you* (1:68)/by you
(1:36)

68   *your friends* (1:68)/your
friends (1:36)

68   *compassion.—*(1:69)/
compassion.—(1:36)

68   contempt . . . (1:69)/
contempt———(1:36)

68   cannot . . . (1:70)/cannot—
———(1:37)

68   Walpole . . . (1:71)/
Walpole———(1:37)

68   surprise (1:71)/surprize
(1:37)

69   subject . . . (1:72)/subject—
———(1:38)

69   sigh . . . (1:73)/sigh (1:38)

69   *him* (1:73)/him (1:38)

69   pavilion (1:73)/pavilion
(1:39)

69   room; (1:75)/room: (1:39)

69   happiness . . . (1:76)/
happiness———(1:40)

70   with . . . (1:78)/with———
(1:41)

70   *shock* (1:79)/shock (1:41)

70   *comedy of the* Pavilion
(1:79)/*comedy of the
Pavillion* (1:41)

70   passed . . . (1:79)/passed—
———(1:41)

70   rest:—this (1:79)/rest: this
(1:41)

70   *your leading* (1:80)/your
leading (1:41)

70   *delightful* (1:80)/delightful
(1:41)

70   counsel (1:81)/council
(1:42)

70   *years of discretion* (1:81)/
years of discretion (1:42)

71   Sunbury (1:82)/*Sunbury*
(1:42)

71   failings . . . (1:83)/failings—
———(1:43)

71   *heiress* (1:86)/heiress (1:44)

71   *daughter* (1:86)/daughter
(1:44)

72   so near to it, that (1:88)/so
near to it that (1:45)

72   hope . . . (1:89)/hope———
(1:45)

72 raptures . . . (1:90)/rap-
tures———(1:46)

73 suspicions . . . (1:90)/
suspicions.———(1:47)

73 . . . She saw (1:94)/———
She saw (1:48)

73 me . . . (1:96)/me. (1:48)

73 Russian Service (1:96)/
Russian Service (1:48)

73 pavilion (1:96)/pavilion
(1:49)

74 *jealous* (1:97)/jealous (1:49)

74 The Grove. (1:98)/*The
Grove.* (1:50)

75 profession . . . (1:101)/
profession—

75 Sunbury. (1:103)/[No
place] (1:52)

75 concealed . . . (1:103)/
concealed——— (1:52)

75 *minds* (1:106)/minds
(1:53)

76 *scraps* (1:107)/scraps
(1:54)

76 those.———(1:107)/those.
(1:54)

76 *unfortunates* (1:107)/
unfortunates (1:54)

76 *discernment* (1:108)/
discernment (1:54)

76 money . . . (1:110)/money
———(1:55)

76 *Fanny's* fears, (1:110)/
Fanny's fears (1:55)

77 *my folly* (1:112)/my folly
(1:56)

77 words . . . (1:113)/words—
——(1:56)

77 both . . . (1:114)/both———
—(1:57)

77 capable . . . (1:115)/ca-
pable——— (1:57)

77 "nothing (1:115)/'nothing
(1:57)

78 cause . . . (1:116)/cause———
—(1:58)

78 honor (1:117)/honour
(1:58)

78 gone): (1:117)/gone:)
(1:58)

78 it. (1:117)/it.———(1:58)

78 *real honor* (1:118)/real
honor (1:58)

78 this.——— (1:121)/this.
(1:60)

79 situated . . . (1:122)/
situated.—(1:60)

79 despairs! . . . (1:122)/
despairs!——— (1:60)

79 *Spring-Park* (1:123)/Spring-
Park (1:61)

79 me . . . (1:123)/me———
(1:61)

79 since? . . . (1:61)/since?———
— (1:61)

79 smiles: happy Sutton! . . .
(1:124)/smiles; happy
Sutton!——— (1:61)

79 *my flirts* (1:124)/my flirts
(1:61)

79 *spirit* (1:125)/spirit
(1:61)

79 *sociable* (1:125)/sociable
(1:62)

79 *agreeable* (1:125)/agreeable
(1:62)

80 Villars . . . (1:126)/Villars
——— (1:62)

80 *heart,* (1:127)/heart
(1:63)

80 *of sorts* (1:128)/of sorts
(1:63)

80 kind . . . (1:129)/kind.———
—(1:63)

80 *fatiguing* (1:131)/fatiguing (1:64)

80 *promise* (1:131)/promise (1:64)

80 her . . . (1:131)/ her ——— (1:64)

81 rival . . . (1:132)/rival——— (1:64)

81 *fall from favor* (1:132)/fall from favor (1:65)

81 good-humor (1:132)/good-humour (1:65)

81 yours (1:133)/your's (1:65)

81 Sunbury. (1:133)/*Sunbury.* (1:65)

81 her! . . . (1:134)/her!——— (1:66)

81 history . . . (1:134)/history———(1:66)

81 joy . . . (1:135)/joy——— (1:66)

82 hope:—you (1:136)/ hope:you (1:67)

82 refractory?" (1:138)/ refractory?' (1:67)

82 composed.——— (1:138)/ composed———(1:67)

82 me . . . (1:140)/me——— (1:68)

82 *worst* (1:140)/worst (1:68)

82 "Do (1:140)/'Do (1:68)

83 sensibility.——— (1:142)/ sensibility. It (1:69)

83 . . . (1:142)/ . . . (1:69)

83 tenderness—I (1:143)/ tenderness. I (1:69)

83 me . . . (1:146)/me.— (1:71)

83 pleasure.———There (1:146)/pleasure. There (1:71)

84 command . . . (1:147)/ command.— (1:71)

84 strength . . . (1:147)/ strength.— (1:71)

84 *drops,* (1:149)/ drops (1:72)

84 The Grove. (1:150)/*The Grove.* (1:73)

85 destiny . . . (1:152)/destiny.— (1:74)

85 prosperity . . . (1:153)/ prosperity.——— (1:74)

85 alive . . . . . . (1:155)/alive.——— (1:75)

85 yours . . . (1:156)/yours. (1:75)

85 Bond-Street (1:157)/ *Bond-Street* (1:76)

86 deceived . . . (1:157)/ deceived.——— (1:76)

86 (an happiness) an an happiness (1:157)/ an happiness (1:76)

86 me . . . (1:157)/me. (1:76)

86 *on the wings of love* (1:158)/on the wings of love (1:76)

86 the inn (1:158)/thee inn (1:77)

86 *O yes* (1:159)/ O yes (1:77)

86 "Well (1:159)/'Well (1:77)

86 *only* (1:160)/only (1:77)

86 *particular* (1:160)/particular (1:77)

86 *It* (1:160)/It (1:77)

87 ill-humor, (1:161)/ ill humour, (1:78)

87 me." ——— (1:162)/ me.'——— (1:78)

87 *a story* (1:163)/a story (1:78)

87 Some (1:163)/"Some (1:79)

87 (Percy's) Percys, (1:164)/
    Percy's, (1:79)

87 *is at all* (1:165)/ is at all
    (1:79)

87 *bloody hand* (1:165)/bloody
    hand (1:80)

87 (Pooh!) *pooh!* (1:106)/
    pooh! (1:80)

88 *urgent business,* (1:167)/
    urgent business (1:80)

88 *fine gentleman,* (1:167)/fine
    gentleman (1:80)

88 *so happy.* (1:167)/so happy
    (1:80)

88 *tender.'* (1:168)/tender
    (1:81)

88 *antiquated* (1:168)/anti-
    quated (1:81)

88 *indignation* (1:168)/
    indignation (1:81)

88 (he) *he* (1:169)/he (1:81)

88 (decamped...) *decamped...*
    (1:169)/decamped. (1:81)

88 *fracas* (1:170)/fracas (1:82)

88 greater ... (1:171)/
    greater.——— (1:82)

89 *your sentiments,* (1:173)/
    your sentiments, (1:83)

89 object: (1:174)/object
    (1:83)

89 company.—You (1:174)/
    company. You (1:84)

89 *You saw!* (1:175)/You saw!
    (1:84)

89 *not* see (1:175)/not see (1:84)

90 resentment ... (1:179)/
    resentment.——— (1:85)

90 *some absurd* (1:180)/some
    absurd (1:86)

90 *sees* (1:181)/sees (1:86)

90 *clear-sighted* (1:181)/clear-
    sighted (1:86)

90 *desperate action* (1:181)/
    desperate action (1:87)

90 her ... (1:181)/her———
    (1:87)

91 Spring-Park. (1:182)/
    Spring-Park (1:87)

91 *British Colonel* (1:183)/
    British Colonel (1:88)

91 her power of doing mis-
    chief, (1:185)/her power of
    doing mischief, (1:88)

91 retreat ... (1:185)/retreat—
    ——— (1:88)

91 *my way* (1:186)/my way
    (1:89)

91 *feel* (1:186)/feel (1:89)

92 disappointments, (1:187)/
    disappointments, (1:89)

92 *the tribe* (1:187)/the tribe
    (1:90)

92 Sunbury (1:188)/*Sunbury*
    (1:90)

92 *prudential* (1:189)/pruden-
    tial (1:90)

92 me! ... (1:190)/me!———
    (1:91)

92 person.———Though
    (1:190)/person. Though
    (1:91)

92 *recovery,* (1:190)/recovery
    (1:91)

92 more ... (1:190)/more———
    — (1:91)

92 *refinements* (1:191)/
    refinements (1:91)

93 *gay* (1:191)/gay (1:91)

93 *niceness* (1:191)/niceness.
    (1:91)

93 *singularities,* (1:191)/
    singularities; (1:92)

93 *delicacy,* (1:193)/delicacy,
    (1:92)

93   *curious* (1:193)/curious
     (1:92)
93   *oddities* (1:194)/oddities
     (1:92)
93   wish'd ". . . (1:195)/
     wish'd."——— (1:93)
94   me-every (1:196)/me; every
     (1:94)
94   danger.—Why (1:196)/
     danger. Why (1:94)
94   his?—But (1:196)/his? But
     (1:94)
94   stroke!—But (1:197)/
     stroke! But (1:94)
94   moves.—He (1:197)/moves.
     He (1:94)
94   me—I (1:197)/me; I (1:94)
94   summons.***********
     (1:197)/summons . . . (no
     asterisks)(1:94)
94   had . . . O (1:198)/had.——
     —O (1:95)
94   intreaties . . . "Have
     (1:198)/intreaties———
     Have (1:95)
94   quotation marks on left
     column (1:198)/ no
     quotation marks on left
     column (1:95)
94   dishonor? (1:199)/
     dishonour? (1:95)
95   *another* (1:202)/another
     (1:96)
95   "It is well (1:203)/It is
     well (1:97)
95   dependence (1:204)/
     dependance (1:97)
95   time" (1:205)/time." (1:98)
95   request . . . (1:205)/re-
     quest.— (1:98)
96   *have* loved! (1:206)/have
     loved! (1:98)

96   obeyed!—"Your (1:206)/
     obeyed! "your (1:98)
96   *particular,* (1:207)/particu-
     lar; (1:99)
96   wretched . . . .Mr. (1:208)/
     wretched.—Mr. (1:99)
96   dependence (1:209)/
     dependance (1:100)
96   another . . . (1:209)/
     another———(1:100)
97   judgement (1:212)/judg-
     ment (1:101)
97   *my father happy* (1:212)/my
     father happy: (1:101)
97   *him* (1:212)/him (1:101)
97   *concealment* (1:213)/
     concealment (1:102)
97   raised . . . (1:214)/ raised.—
     —— (1:102)
97   Burton (1:215)/*Burton.*
     (1:102)
97   of (1:215)/ of of (1:102)
97   *causes,* (1:216)/causes;
     (1:103)
98   *effects.* (1:216)/effects
     (1:103)
98   that . . . (1:221)/that.—
     (1:105)
99   *humanity* (1:221)/humanity
     (1:105)
99   *inflammable,* (1:222)/
     inflammable, (1:105)
99   Yours, (1:223)/Your's,
     (1:106)
99   self-examination (1:225)/
     self examination (1:106)
99   *him* (1:226)/ him (1:107)
99   (earth! . . .) earth . . .
     (1:226)/earth!———
     (1:107)
100 his.—Generous, (1:226)/
     his—Generous, (1:107)

100 it.—I (1:226)/it.—I (1:107)
100 *self,* (1:229)/ self, (1:108)
100 *greatness* (1:230)/ greatness (1:109)
100 world . . . (1:230)/world— (1:109)
101 *your impatience* (1:232)/ your impatience (1:110)
101 *Mrs. Walpole* (1:233)/Mrs. Walpole (1:110)
101 *dull* (2:133)/dull (1:111)
102 *that day* (1:236)/ that day (1:112)
102 *too serious* (1:237)/too serious (1:112)
102 Burton. (1:239)/*Burton.* (1:113)
103 *my husband* (1:240)/my husband (1:115)
104 "My dear Mr. (1:246)/ My dear Mr. (1:116)
104 Quotes in left margin (1:246)/ No quotes in margin (1:116)
104 tears... (1:247)/tears———— She (1:117)
104 *his* (1:249)/his (1:118)
104 *her father* (1:249)/her father (1:118)
104 *friends* (1:250)/friends (1:118)
105 *the sort* (1:250)/the sort (1:118)
105 *real* friend (1:250)/real friend (1:118)
105 Spring-Park (1:251)/*Spring-Park* (1:119)
105 sorrow . . . (1:253)/sor- row———— (1:120)
105 *civil* (1:254)/civil (1:120)
105 *high merit* (1:254)/high merit (1:120)

106 (Bond-Street) *Bond-Street* (1:255)/Bond-Street. (1:120)
106 *once* (1:255)/once (1:121)
106 do, (1:258)/do; (1:122)
106 behavior (1:258)/ behaviour (1:122)
107 *my gratitude* (1:262)/ my gratitude (1:124)
107 coquettry (1:262)/coquetry (1:124)
107 *loving* (1:262)/loving (1:124)
108 *my esteem* (1:265)/my esteem (1:125)
108 (her) *her,* (1:265)/ her, (1:125)
108 *she* (1:266)/she (1:126)
109 *her friend* (1:270)/her friend (1:128)
109 *reasons* (1:271)/reasons (1:128)
109 *enquirer* (1:271)/enquirer (1:129)
109 *sagacious* (1:272)/sagacious (1:129)
110 lovers! .. (1:274)/lovers!— (1:129)
111 The Grove. (2:1)/*The Grove.* (1:131)
111 prospects.... (2:2)/pros- pects— (1:131)
111 affected. (2:3)/affected; (1:132)
111 *prejudices* (2:5)/*prejudice* (1:133)
111 offence (2:5)/offenee (1:133) (error in 1784)
112 *unsullied virtue* (2:7)/ unsullied virtue (1:133)
112 this: (2:7)/this; (1:134)
112 there.———— (2:8)/there ———— (1:134)

112 *your friend,* (2:9)/your
    friend, (1:135)
112 *willingness,* (2:9)/willingness
    (1:135)
113 but, (2:10)/but (1:135)
113 *Fairy* (2:13)/Fairy (1:137)
113 *best* (2:15)/ best (1:138)
113 heart? . . . (2:15)/heart?—
    (1:138)
114 *ancients,* (2:15)/ancients,
    (1:138)
114 *we* (2:16)/we (1:138)
114 Burton Street. (2:17)/
    Bruton Street (1:139)
114 companion? (2:18)/com-
    panion! (1:140)
114 inspire . . . (2:19)/inspire—
    —— (1:140)
115 *in duty* (2:19)/in duty
    (1:140)
115 *polite age* (2:20)/polite age
    (1:140)
115 *you* (2:21)/you (1:141)
115 of *ton* (2:21)/the *ton*
    (1:141)
115 *highest* (2:21)/highest
    (1:141)
115 *his friend* (2:21)/his friend
    (1:141)
115 *provided* (2:23)/provided
    (1:142)
116 *country cousins* (2:24)/
    country cousins (1:142)
116 *still* (2:24)/still (1:142)
116 *complain,* (2:26)/complain,
    (1:143)
116 *gay,* (2:27)/gay, (1:144)
116 *good* (2:27)/good (1:144)
117 pattern (2:28)/ PATTERN
    (1:145)
117 fairest (2:29)/FAIREST
    (1:145)

117 noblest (2:29)/NOBLEST
    (1:145)
117 among (2:29)/Among
    (1:145)
117 /Rutland, a Leinster, a
    Temple, an Antrim, a
    Carrick, a Moira, an Arran,
    a Charlemont, a
    Mountgarret, a
    Kingsborough, a Lissord,
    and innumerable others
    whose BEAUTY adds the
    highest LUSTRE (2:145) a
    Portland, a Manchester, a
    Buccleugh, a Thanet, an
    Abingdon, more than one
    Spencer, a Delaware, a
    Torrington, a Wenman, and
    innumerable others, whose
    beauty adds the highest
    lustre to their prudence
    (2:29)
117 minds (1:29) MINDS
    (2:145)
117 spleen . . . [9](1:30)/
    spleen——— (1:145)
117 *chimney corner* (2:31)/
    chimney corner (1:146)
117 xxxiii (2:31)/xxxiv (1:146)
117 *words* (2:32)/words
    (1:146)
117 *esteem* (2:32); esteem
    (1:146)
117 expression (2:32)/expres-
    sions (1:146)
118 *Walpole* (2:32)/Walpole
    (1:147)
118 *my eyes* (2:33)/my eyes
    (1:147)
118 *live* (2:33)/live (1:147)
118 *danger* (2:34)/danger
    (1:147)

118 *common-sense style* (2:34)/ common-sense style (1:147)

118 *admires* (2:35)/admires (1:148)

118 *jealous* (2:35)/jealous (1:148)

118 *bustler* (2:35)/bustler (1:148)

118 *friend* (2:35)/friend (1:148)

119 *natural* (2:37)/natural (1:149)

119 conquest . . . (2:39)/ conquest——— (1:150)

119 wonder? . . . (2:40)/won-der?——— (1:150)

119 *him* (2:41)/him (1:151)

119 *bustler* (2:41)/bustler (1:151)

120 *affects* (2:44)/ affects (1:152)

121 one—*failing* (2:46)/one, failing (1:154)

121 absence; (2:48)/absence? (1:154)

121 *loving* (2:48)/loving (1:155)

121 considerable; (2:49)/ considerate: (1:155)

121 *she is in love with him* (2:49)/She is in love with him (1:155)

122 *ensnare me* (2:50)/ensnare me (1:156)

122 *intended* (2:51)/intended (1:156)

122 *my nicety* (2:53)/my nicety (1:157)

122 *particularly* (2:54)/particu-larly (1:158)

122 one; (2:54)/one? (1:158)

122 hers, (2:55)/her, (1:55)

122 *vain* (2:55)/vain (1:158)

122 (ill-humor) ill humour (2:56)/ill-humor (1:158)

123 (Sir) sir (2:57)/SIR (1:159)

123 *Madam* (2:58)/MADAM; (1:159)

123 manner. (2:59)/ manner, (1:160)

124 (*undress*) undress (2:60)/ undress (1:160)

124 Ma'am (2:60)/Madam (1:160)

124 her: (2:60)/her; (1:161

124 *insinuation* (2:61)/insinua-tion (1:161)

124 *disappointment* (2:61)/ disappointment (1:161)

124 *some* (2:61)/some (1:161)

124 William Walpole (2:62)/W. Walpole (1:162)

124 (Bond-Street) Bond Street (2:62)/*Bond Street* (1:162)

124 *hit-or-miss* (2:64)/hit-or-miss (1:162)

124 who, not (2:64)/who not (1:162)

125 *disquietude* (2:64)/disqui-etude (1:163)

125 *obliged* (2:64)/obliged (1:163)

125 *you* (2:65)/you (1:163)

125 *civil* (2:65)/civil (1:163)

125 though, not (2:65)/though not (1:163)

125 after, (2:65)/after (1:163)

125 *loving* (2:65)/loving (1:163)

125 Nature (2:66)/nature (1:163)

125 *that scene* (2:66)/that scene (1:164)

125 (won't) *wo'n't* (2:67)/won't (1:164)

125   *life* ... (2:67)/life.———
         (1:164)
125   *some* (2:68)/some (1:164)
125   *particular* (2:68)/particular
         (1:164)
125   *expected* (2:68)/expected
         (1:165)
125   encouragement: (2:69)/
         encouragement; (1:165)
126   *wantons,* (2:69)/wantons.
         (1:169)
126   The Grove (2:70)/*The*
         Grove (1:165)
126   *haste* (2:71)/haste (1:166)
126   *my reign* (2:71)/my reign
         (1:166).
126   *civil things (2:72)/*civil
         things (1:167)
126   *humbled* (2:73)/humbled
         (1:167)
127   *a look* (2:74)/a look (1:168)
127   *kind* (2:75)/kind (1:163)
127   *elected* (2:76)/elected
         (1:163)
127   *modernised* (2:77)/
         modernised (1:169)
127   *made happy* (2:77)/made
         happy (1:169)
127   *real* (2:78)/real (1:169)
128   *last letter but one* (2:78)/
         last letter but one (1:169)
128   *family* (2:81)/family
         (1:171)
128   good-natured (2:81)/good
         natured (1:171)
128   *insensible* (2:82)/insensible
         (1:171)
129   *loved* (2:82)/loved (1:172)
129   *that light* (2:82)/that light
         (1:172)
129   contemplate (2:83)/
         comtemplate (1:172)

129   *wish* (2:84)/wish (1:172)
129   *marplot* (2:84)/marplot
         (1:172)
129   *priding* (2:85)/priding
         (1:173)
129   *refinement* (2:85)/
         refinement (1:173)
130   Spring-Park (2:87)/*Spring-*
         Park (1:174)
130   ! Well (2:87)/! well
         (1:174)
130   lover ... (2:87)/lover———
         (1:174)
130   love ... (2:90)/love.———
         (1:176)
130   *head* (2:91)/head (1:176)
130   (his) *his* (2:94)/his (1:177)
131   *smallest* (2:95)/smallest
         (1:178)
132   *now* (2:96)/now (1:178)
132   *you* (2:96)/you (1:178)
132   *the first visit* (2:96)/the first
         visit (1:178)
132   *prescribed* (2:97)/prescribed
         (1:179)
132   receptions ... (2:97)/
         receptions———(1:179)
132   her ... (2:98)/her———
         (1:179)
132   humor (2:98)/humour
         (1:179)
132   *The Grove* (2:98)/The
         Grove (1:180)
132   *captives* (2:99)/captives
         (1:180)
132   *female vanity* (2:99)/female
         vanity (1:180)
132   *pride* (2:99)/pride (1:180)
132   *presents* (2:99)/presents
         (1:180)
132   *seeming* (2:100)/seeming
         (1:181)

132 *his friends* (2:101)/his
friends (1:181)
132 *at this* (2:104)/at this
(1:182)
133 *vulgar prejudices* (2:105)/
vulgar prejudices (1:183)
133 *loves* (2:105)/loves (1:183)
133 *above* (2:105)/above
(1:183)
134 *vulgar prejudices* (2:105)/
vulgar prejudices (1:183)
134 *trifle* (2:105)/trifle (1:183)
134 *improper* (2:106)/improper
(1:183)
134 *quarrelsome* (2:107)/
quarrelsome (1:184)
134 *mild and patient* (2:107)/
mild and patient (1:184)
134 *wish* (2:108)/wish. (1:184)
134 *curious* (2:109)/curious
(1:185)
135 *faults* (2:110)/faults
(1:186)
135 me . . . (2:112)/me———
(1:186)
135 benefitting (2:112)/
benefiting (1:187)
135 Sunday Morning (2:112)/
Sunday Morning (1:187)
135 *my glass* (2:113)/my glass
(1:187)
135 nap; (2:113)/nap: (1:187)
136 *again* (2:114)/again
(1:187)
136 *offended* (2:114)/offended
(1:187)
136 Noel-Castle (2:116)/Noel
Castle (1:189)
136 *business* (2:117)/business
(1:189)
136 home: (2:117)/home;
(1:189)

136 head-ach (2:117)/heid-ach
(1:189)
136 off (2:117)/of (1:189)
(error in 1784)
136 named . . . (2:117)/named
——— (1:189)
136 *tartness* (2:117)/tartness
(1:189)
136 have: (2:117)/have; (1:189)
137 *this dispute* (2:118)/this
dispute (1:190)
137 *contradict* (2:118)/contra-
dict (1:190)
137 Spring-Park (2:119)/Spring-
Park (1:190) (No italics in
either; an exception)
137 *flourishing* (2:119)/
flourishing (1:190)
137 *Noel-Castle* (2:119)/Noel
Castle (1:190)
137 *assistance* (2:120)/assistance
(1:191)
137 Sayer (the (2:121)/Sayer,
(the (1:191)
137 *situation* (2:121)/situation
(1:191)
137 *poring over* (2:121)/poring
over (1:191)
137 *wise* (2:121)/wise (1:191)
137 *verbose* (2:121)/verbose
(1:192)
138 *friends* (2:122)/friends
(1:192)
138 *wishes* (2:122)/wishes (1:192)
138 *sentiments* (2:123)/senti-
ments (1:192)
138 wife. Are (2:123)/wife:—
Are (1:192)
138 *my sage* (2:123)/ my sage
(1:192)
138 caviling (2:123)/ Cavilling
(1:192)

138   *piously* (2:123)/piously (1:192)

138   *your spouse* (2:123)/your spouse (1:193)

138   *mixed* (2:124)/mixed (1:193)

138   *excluding us* (2:124)/ excluding us (1:193)

138   *heirs* (2:124)/heirs (1:193)

138   *passive-obedience* (2:125)/ passive obedience (1:193)

138   *in love* (2:125)/in love (1:193)

138   *glory* (2:125)/glory (1:193)

138   *patroness* (2:125)/patroness (1:193)

138   passion . . . (2:126)/pas-sion——— (1:194)

139   *intruders* (2:127)/intruders (1:194)

139   awkwardnesses, (2:127)/ awkwardness, (1:194)

139   *them off* (2:127)/*them* off (1:194)

139   *libertine* (2:129)/libertine (1:196)

139   *fight* (2:130)/fight (1:196)

140   exacts (2:131)/acts (1:196)

140   *rude* (2:132)/rude (1:197)

140   well-bred; (2:133)/well-bred (1:197)

140   *obstinate* (2:133)/obstinate (1:197)

140   *tractable* (2:134)/tractable (1:197)

140   *une nouvelle epouse* (2:133)/ une nouvelle epouse (1:198)

140   *best* (2:134)/best (1:198)

140   *flirt* (2:135)/flirt (1:198)

141   *fashionable* (2:137)/fashion-able (1:199)

141   *highest respect* (2:139)/ highest respect (1:200)

141   (tendernesses) *tenderness* (2:139)/tendernesses (1:200)

141   *you* yawn (2:140)/you yawn (1:201)

141   Spring-Park (2:140)/*Spring-Park* (1:201)

141   *longed* (2:140)/longed (1:201)

142   longer . . . (2:141)/longer ——— (1:201)

142   brother. (2:142)/brother. ——— (1:202)

142   *my shade* (2:142)/my shade (1:202)

142   name.— (2:143)/name:— (1:202)

142   (him . . .) him . . . (2:147)/ him——— (1:204)

143   (Wednesday) *Wednesday* (2:147)/ Wednesday (1:204)

145   temper: (2:153)/temper, (1:208)

145   *afraid* (2:154)/afraid (1:208)

145   counsel (2:154)/councel (1:208)

145   *adviser* (2:154)/adviser (1:208)

147   *fatal secret* (2:154)/*fatal* secret (1:209)

147   *our* affections (2:158)/our affections (1:210)

147   *theirs* (2:158)/theirs (1:210)

147   *habit* (2:159)/habit (1:210)

147   *really* (2:159)/really (1:210)

147   (Noel Castle) *Noel-Castle.* (2:161)/Noel Castle (1:211)

147 (*Platonic* scheme) *platonic scheme* (2:161)/ *Platonic scheme* (1:212)

148 *wishing.* (2:163)/wishing. (1:213)

148 *brooding over* (2:164)/ brooding over (1:213)

148 (sermonizing) *sermonising* (2:166)/sermonising (1:214)

149 *crazing cares* (2:168)/ crazing cares (1:215)

149 *constancy* (2:168)/constancy (1:215)

149 *loved for ever* (2:168)/loved for ever (1:215)

149 (flirt) *flirt—* (2:168)/flirt— (1:215)

149 heart: (2:168)/heart; (1:215)

149 *whimperer* (2:169)/ whimperer (1:216)

149 *venerate* (2:169)/venerate (1:216)

150 *delectable flirt* (2:170)/ delectable flirt (1:216)

150 character . . . (2:170)/ character.— (1:216)

150 *me* (2:171)/me (1:217)

150 *vis* (2:172)/vis (1:217)

150 *nonsense agreeably* (2:172)/ nonsense agreeably (1:217)

150 *les yeux doux* (2:172)/les yeuz doux (1:217)

150 *eleve* (2:172)/eleve (1:217)

150 *pastor fido* (2:174)/*pastor fido* (1:218)

150 (*please*) please.— (2:174)/ please.— (1:218)

150 *snappish* (2:174)/ snappish (1:218)

150 (aversion) *aversion* . . . (2:175)/aversion—(1:218)

151 *slighted* (2:176)/slighted (1:219)

151 *thanked* (2:177)/thanked (1:220)

151 *chaunted* (2:177)/chaunted (1:220)

151 *oddity* (2:177)/oddity (1:220)

151 *oddity* (2:178)/oddity (1:220)

151 *quote* . . . (2:178)/quote— (1:220)

151 hearing; (2:179)/hearing: (1:221)

152 least . . . (2:179)/least— (1:221)

152 *Edward* (2:180)/Edward (1:221)

152 *agreeable* (2:180)/agreeable (1:221)

152 *handsome* (2:180)/hand-some (1:221)

152 *me* . . . (2:180)/me——— (1:221)

152 *patience* (2:181)/patience (1:222)

152 misery . . . (2:183)/misery— —— (1:223)

153 *prudent* (2:184)/prudent (1:223)

153 *that* (2:184)/that (1:224)

153 *taste* (2:185)/taste (1:224)

153 loved . . . (2:187)/loved— (1:225)

154 person . . . That (2:190)/ person. That (1:226)

154 *extraordinary* (2:190)/ extraordinary (1:226)

154 *Colonel Sutton* (2:190)/ Colonel Sutton (1:226)

154 mistress!— (2:190)/ mistress! (1:226)

158 *Villars (2:206)/*Villars (2:10)
158 *fine gentlemen* (2:206)/fine gentleman (2:10)
158 Duc, Marquis (2:206)/Duc Marquis (2:10)
158 *only* death (2:207)/only death (2:10)
158 *sport of nature* (2:207)/ sport of nature (2:10)
158 *its* designs (2:207)/its designs (2:10)
158 *common* (2:209)/common (2:11)
158 *like* (2:208)/like (2:11)
158 ease . . . (2:209)/ease (2:11)
158 *setting my cap* (2:209)/ setting my cap (2:11)
158 *twin soul* (2:209)/twin soul (2:11/12)
158 *the destiny (2:209)/* the destiny (2:12)
158 *Ganges shore!* (2:209)/ Ganges shore! (2:12)
158 *hints* . . . (2:209)/hints—— — (2:12)
158 *man of quality* (2:209)/man of quality (2:12)
158 *Maccaroni.*—— (2:210)/ Macaroni.—— (2:12)
159 Lisle. (2:212)/*Lisle.* (2:13)
160 *true martial* (2:14)/true martial (2:14)
160 *admired* (2:214)/admired (2:14)
160 *admire* (2:214)/admire (2:14)
160 *travels* (2:215)/travels (2:14)
160 *narrow* (2:215)/narrow (2:14)
160 score . . . (2:215)/score—— — (2:15)

160 *Parisian* (2:216)/Parisian (2:15)
160 Aix la Chapelle (2:217)/*Aix la Chapelle* (2:16)
161 dejection . . . (2:220)/ dejection—— (2:17)
161 came; and (2:221)/came and (2:18)
162 (you."—) you." . . . (2:224)/you."— (2:19)
162 (quiet:) quit: (2:224)/quiet; (2:19)
162 mind . . . (2:226)/mind— (2:20)
162 brought-to-bed (2:226)/ brought to bed (2:20)
163 more." . . . (2:228)/ more."— (2:19)
163 fury.—We (2:230)/fury— we (2:20)
163 know . . . (2:231)/know. (2:20)
164 treatment." . . . (2:232)/ treatment."— (2:21)
164 intellects.— (2:232)/ intellects . . . (2:21)
164 it." . . . (2:233)/it."—— (2:22)
164 catch" . . . (2:233)/catch"— (2:22)
164 you . . . (2:235)/you— (2:23)
164 you . . . (2:235)/you— (2:23)
164 undeceived." . . . (2:235)/ undeceived."— (2:25)
164 minutes . . . (2:236)/ minutes— (2:23)
164 alacrity . . . (2:236)/alac- rity— (2:23)
165 frightfull (2:236)/frightful (2:23)

165 (harassed) harrassed
(2:237)/ harassed (2:24)

165 engagement . . . (2:241)/
engagement— (2:26)

166 reflections (2:241)/
reflexions (2:26)

166 *reflections* (2:242)/reflexions
(2:26)

166 *refusal* (2:242)/refusal
(2:26)

166 you! . . . (2:243)/you!———
(2:27)

166 *my* heroism (2:243)/my
heroism (2:27)

166 *your daughter* (2:243)/your
daughter (2:27)

166 *my wife* (2:243)/my wife

166 angel! . . . (2:244)/angel!—
——(2:27)

166 I resigned *my love* to *your
duty* (2:249)/I resigned my
love to your duty (2:27)

166 you . . . (2:245)/you—
(2:27)

167 *always* (2:249)/always
(2:30)

168 *your* (2:251)/your (2:31)

168 *her* (2:251)/her (2:31)

168 happen . . . (2:252)/hap-
pen— (2:31)

169 XLIX. (2:254)/XLX. (2:32)

169 *affect* (2:255)/ affect
(2:33)

169 *solicitude* (2:255)/solicitude
(2:33)

169 *relapsing* (2:256)/relapsing
(2:33)

170 *obstacle* (2:259)/obstacle
(2:35)

170 *cause* (2:261)/cause (2:36)

170 me." . . . (2:261)/me."—
(2:36)

170 time; (2:261)/time: (2:36)

170 *His memory* (2:262)/His
memory (2:36)

171 *delicacy* (2:263)/delicacy
(2:37)

171 *delicacy* (2:264)/delicacy
(2:37)

171 *wiser* (2:264)/wiser (2:37)

171 *witlings* (2:264)/witlings
(2:37)

171 *Prejudices* (2:264)/Preju-
dices (2:37)

171 *humanity* (2:264)/humanity
(2:37)

171 *highly polished* (2:265)/
highly polished (2:37)

171 *deference* to *the fair*
(2:265)/deference to the
fair (2:38)

171 *whistling* (2:265)/whistling
(2:38)

171 *wind* (2:265)/ wind (2:38)

171 *responded* (2:265)/re-
sponded (2:38)

171 par; (2:266)/par: (2:38)

171 her . . . (2:266)/her—
(2:38)

171 Now," (2:266)/Now."
(2:38)

171 *delicacy* (2:266)/delicacy
(2:38)

171 *hurting* (2:267)/hurting
(2:38)

171 *delicacy:* (2:267)/delicacy:
(2:39)

171 humorist." . . . (2:267)/
humorist."— (2:39)

171 affliction . . . (2:268)/
affliction— (2:39)

172 *her* (2:268)/her (2:39)

172 interviews . . . (2:291)/
interviews.——— (2:40)

173 can ... (2:273)/can———
     (2:41)
173 *My wife* (2:273)/My wife
     (2:41)
173 Death ... (2:273)/death
     (2:42)
173 *coldness (2:273)*/coldness
     (2:42)
173 *conceal one* (2:274)/conceal
     one (2:42)
174 amuses me ... (2:279)/
     amuses me——— (2:44)
175 *one!* (2:284)/one! (2:47)
176 *the will* (2:286)/the will
     (2:48)
176 *they gave me* (2:290)/they
     gave me (2:50)
177 (entreaty) intreaty (2:291)/
     entreaty (2:51)
177 after ... (2:293)/after———
     (2:52)
178 worst ... (2:295)/worst
     — (2:53)
173 Albemarle Street (3:1)/
     Albemarle-Street (2:53)
179 *robust* (3:1)/robust (2:54)
179 *advised,* (3:4)/advised,
     (2:55)
179 imprisonment. (3:4)/
     imprisonment! (2:55)
179 *truant* (3:4)/truant (2:55)
179 *honor* (3:5)/honor (2:55)
180 *unlimited* Loo (3:6)/
     unlimited Loo (2:55)
180 *prudent* (3:6)/prudent
     (2:56)
180 *constant* (3:6)/constant
     (2:56)
180 *fear* (3:6)/fear (2:56)
180 *silly* (3:7)/silly (2:56)
180 censure ... (3:7)/censure.—
     (2:56)

180 Park ... (3:8)/Park— (2:57)
180 *impassable barriers* (3:8)/
     impasable barrier (2:57)
181 *your* (3:10)/your (2:58)
181 tea-table (3:11)/ tea table
     (2:58)
181 best-natured (3:11)/best-
     natured (2:58)
181 Walpole ... (3:11)/
     Walpole——— (2:59)
181 day-light (3:12)/day light
     (2:59)
181 woman ... (3:12)/woman
     ——— (2:59)
181 *poor husband's* (3:13)/poor
     husband's (2:59)
182 *my friends* (3:14)/my
     friends (2:60)
182 *anecdote* (3:14)/anecdote
     (2:60)
182 entertain ... (3:14)/
     entertain——— (2:60)
182 *failings* (3:14)/failings
     (2:60)
182 *my pride* (3:15)/my pride
     (2:60)
182 *advice* (3:15)/advice (2:60)
182 *idiot*(3:15)/idiot (2:60)
182 *example* (3:16)/example
     (2:61)
182 *misrepresentation, accidental
     meetings* (3:17)/misrepre-
     sentation, accidental meet-
     ings (2:61)
182 *helps* (3:17)/helps (2:61)
182 *innocent* (3:17)/innocent
     (2:61)
183 *rival* (3:18)/rival (2:62)
183 conduct ... I (3:20)/
     conduct———I (2:63)
183 Portman-Square (3:20)/
     Portman Square (2:63)

183 *common gallantry* (3:21)/
common gallantry (2:64)

183 flirtation . . . (3:22)/
flirtation——— (2:64)

184 quitted .... (3:22)/quit-
ted——— (2:64)

184 *loyalty* (3:24)/loyalty (2:65)

184 *ill luck* (3:26)/ill luck (2:66)

184 her . . . (3:26)/her.———
(2:66)

184 *amicable* (3:27)/amicable
(2:67)

185 *a Diana* (3:29)/a Diana
(2:68)

185 *me . . . (3:30)*/me———
(2:68)

185 *I* (3:31)/I (2:69)

185 *innocent* (3:39)/innocent
(2:73)

186 (innocent) *the shade* (3:40)/
the shade (2:73)

188 *smarter* (3:40)/smarter
(2:73)

188 *select* (3:40)/select (2:73)

188 *flirt* (3:42)/flirt (2:74)

188 *love* (3:42)/love (2:74)

188 misused . . . (3:42)/mis-
used——— (2:74)

188 *garb* (3:43)/garb (2:75)

189 misery . . . (3:45)/misery
——— (2:76)

189 it . . . (3:47)/it——— (2:77)

189 *folly* (3:47)/folly (2:77)

190 *mean* (3:49)/mean (2:78)

190 *story* (3:49)/story (2:78)

190 *all* (3:50)/all (2:78)

190 Albemarle-Street (3:51)/
Albemarle-Street (2:79)

190 *croaking* (3:52)/croaking
(2:79)

190 *surprising* (3:52)/surprising
(2:79)

190 *love* (3:52)/love (2:79)

190 *love* (3:52)/love (2:80)

191 *public spiritedness* (3:52)/
public-spiritedness (2:80)

191 *her or him* (3:53)/her or
him (2:80)

191 *surmise* (3:53)/surmise
(2:80)

191 candidate . . . (3:54)/
candidate——— (2:81)

191 *good-nature* (3:55)/good-
nature (2:81)

191 *persecution* (3:55)/persecu-
tion (2:81)

191 *forget* (3:55)/forget (2:81)

191 *good idea* (3:56)/good idea
(2:82)

191 *love-matches* (3:57)/love-
matches (2:82)

191 *that* (3:57)/that (3:82)

192 *cestus* (3:58)/cestus (3:82)

192 *fickleness* (3:58)/fickleness
(3:83)

192 *failings* (3:58)/failings
(3:83)

192 *humors* (3:58)/humors
(3:83)

192 *her* (3:59)/her (3:83)

192 *good-nature* (3:59)/good
nature (3:83)

192 *charms* (3:59)/charms
(3:83)

193 *price* (3:61)/price (2:84)

193 *pledging* (3:62)/pledging
(2:85)

193 *oppose me* (3:63)/oppose me
(2:85)

193 *staunchest* (3:63)/staunchest
(2:85)

193 *secured* (3:63)/secured (2:85)

193 *the Nabob* (3:64)/the
Nabob (2:86)

193 *eclipsed* (3:65)/eclipsed
(2:86)

193 more . . . (3:65)/more———
(2:87)

194 *lost* (3:65)/lost (2:87)

194 . . . *prior (3:67)/*———prior
(2:87)

194 *honest* (3:68)/honest (2:88)

194 *debts of honor* (2:68)/debts
of honor (2:88)

194 *scum of the earth* (3:68)/
scum of the earth (2:89)

195 *gain* (3:70)/gain (2:89)

195 *finesse* (3:70)/finesse (2:89)

195 *honors* (3:70)/honors
(2:90)

195 *Hygeia* (3:72)/Hygeia
(2:90)

195 *mischances,* (3:73)/mis-
chances (2:93)

195 *kings* (3:73)/kings (2:93)

195 *knaves* (3:73)/knaves (2:93)

195 *shuffling* (3:73)/shuffling
(2:93)

195 *dealing* (3:73)/dealing
(2:93)

196 *diversion* (3:74)/diversion
(2:93)

196 *tempter* (3:75)/tempter
(2:94)

196 *general* (3:75)/general (2:94)

196 *individuals* (3:75)/individu-
als (2:94)

196 Spring-Park (3:76)/*Spring-
Park* (2:94)

197 . . . This (3:78)/—This
(2:95)

197 contempt! . . . (3:79)/
contempt!— (2:96)

197 *place* (3:79)/place (2:96)

197 *seeming* (3:80)/seeming
(2:96)

197 *feeling* (3:80)/feeling (2:96)

198 Rose-Court (3:83)/*Rose-
Court* (2:98)

198 completed (3:87)/
compleated (2:100)

199 who, satisfied (3:88)/who
satisfied (2:100)

199 rooms; (3:88)/rooms; (2:101)

199 garden. . . . (3:89)/garden—
—— (2:101)

199 *colour of my fate* (3:91)/
colour of my fate (2:102)

200 (would) *would* (3:92)/
would (2:103)

200 *lessening* (3:93)/lessening
(2:103)

200 *hardened* (3:94)/hardened
(2:104)

200 Rose-Court (3:96)/*Rose-
Court* (2:105)

201 Spring-Park (3:96)/Spring
Park (2:105)

201 *opinion* (3:96)/opinion
(2:105)

201 *chuse* (3:96)/chuse (2:105)

201 *most dreary of regions*
(3:97)/most dreary of
regions (2:105)

201 *darksome abode* (3:97)/
darksome abode (2:105)

203 *practical preacher* (3:106)/
practical preacher (2:110)

203 Charleses (3:107)/Charles's
(2:111)

203 *adventures,* (3:107)/
adventures, (2:111)

203 *hates* (3:108)/hates (2:111)

203 *loves* (3:108)/loves (2:111)

203 *agreed* (3:108)/agreed
(2:111)

203 *flouting* (3:108)/flouting
(2:111)

204 *tenderness* (3:112)/tenderness (2:113)

204 *managing* (3:112)/managing (2:113)

205 *good-nature* (3:114)/goodnature (2:114)

205 *weakness* (3:114)/weakness (2:114)

205 *girlishly* (3:114)/girlishly (2:115)

206 *indifference or insults* (3:116)/indifference or insults (2:115)

206 *you* (3:118)/you (2:116)

206 *partial* (3:119)/partial (2:117)

206 *it . . .* (3:120)/it——— (2:118)

207 neighbours (3:122)/neigbours (2:119)

208 *the friends* (3:127)/the friends (2:121)

208 great." . . . (3:130)/great."— (2:123)

209 *almost* pretty (3:136)/almost pretty (2:125)

209 *almost* sensible (3:136)/almost sensible(2:125)

209 *almost* agreeable (3:136)/almost agreeable (2:125)

210 *an objection* (3:138)/an objection (2:126)

210 even when the (3:138/9)/blot out (2:126)

210 *her* (3:139)/her (2:127)

211 *your honor* (3:142)/your honor (2:128)

212 else . . . (3:148)/else——— (2:131)

212 trip . . . (3:150)/trip——— (2:132)

213 shrieked out; (3:152)/shrieked out, (2:133)

213 been over; (3:153)/been over, (2:134)

213 then wrote, (3:154)/then wrote (2:134)

213 *manes* (3:154)/manes (2:134)

213 malediction, (3:154)/malediction (2:134)

213 family: (3:155)/family; (2:134)

213 made in her; (3:155)/made in her: (2:135)

213 is sensible, (3:156)/is sensible (2:135)

213 (such an) *such an* (3:156)/suchan (2:135)

214 you adieu.
Yours always, (sep. line) (3:157)/you adieu. Yours Always, (2:135)

214 *fickle kind* (3:158)/fickle kind (2:136)

214 *long enough* (3:158)/long enough (2:136)

214 the vice (3:158)/thevice (2:136)

214 with sickness . . . (3:159)/with sickness———(2:137)

215 this offer *now* (3:160)/this offer now (2:137)

215 *charity* (3:160)/charity (2:137)

215 still weeping: (3:161)/still weeping. (2:137)

215 *attachments* (3:162)/attachments (2:138)

215 (relied on) *relied on . . .* (3:163)/relied on——— (2:138)

216 treachery: (3:165)/treachery, (2:139)

216 *honor* (3:169)/honor (2:149)

217 happiness" . . . (3:171)/
happiness"——— (2:142)
217 *forget,* (3:172)/forget,
(2:142)
217 Rye-Farm . . . (3:172)/Rye-
Farm——— (2:143)
217 For." . . . (3:173)/for."—
(2:143)
217 my soul was contracted
(3:173)/my soul *was*
contracted (2:143)
217 time,. . (3:173)/time, (2:143)
217 probity. . (3:175)/probity
——— (2:144)
218 *deceive* (3:175)/deceive
(2:144)
218 (pardonable) *pardon-
able* . . . (3:175)/pardon-
able——— (2:144)
218 (me, Fanny) to me; Fanny;
(3:177)/to me, Fanny;
(2:145)
218 soon . . . (3:178)/soon—
(2:145)
219 *your fortitude* (3:179)/your
fortitude (2:146)
219 (verbatim) *verbatim*
(3:181)/verbatim (2:147)
219 *sure* (3:182)/sure (2:147)
219 little . . . (3:182)/little.———
(2:148)
220 *Champagne* (3:183)/
Champagne (2:148)
220 *designed* (3:185)/designed
(2:149)
220 *reason* and *philosophy*
(3:185)/reason and philosophy (2:149)
220 argueing (3:185)/arguing
(2:149)
220 *integrity* (3:186)/integrity
(2:149)

220 *my friend* (3:188)/my
friend (2:150)
221 Rose-Court (3:189)/*Rose-
Court* (2:151)
221 *reserve* and *respect* (3:190)
/reserve and respect
(2:151/2)
221 *intimacy* (3:190)/intimacy
(2:152)
221 *hanger-on* (3:190)/hanger-
on (2:152)
221 neglected; (3:190)/ne-
glected: (2:152)
221 *lower* (3:190)/lower (2:152)
221 *poor* (3:190)/poor (2:152)
221 Heavens (3:190)/Heaven
(2:152)
221 *my circumstances* (3:190)/
my circumstances (2:152)
221 *a friend* . . . (3:191)/a
friend——— (2:152)
221 *Pride* (3:191)/Pride (2:152)
221 *littleness* (3:191)/littleness
(2:152)
221 *giving* (3:191)/giving
(2:152)
221 *take* (3:191)/take (2:152)
221 yet afar off (3:192)/yet far
of (2:153)
221 *expectations* (3:192)/
expectations (2:153)
222 *your pity* (3:192)/your pity
(2:153)
222 *full cup* (3:192-3)/full cup
(2:153)
222 *oblige* (3:193)/oblige
(2:153)
222 (her dissolution) *her
dissolution* . . . (3:194)/her
dissolution——— (2:154)
222 *her Fanny* (3:194)/her
Fanny (2:154)

222 *heart* (3:194)/heart (2:154)

222 *lungs* (3:194)/lungs (2:154)

222 free (3:195)/freee (2:154)

223 infant . . . (3:196)/infant—
——(2:155)

223 *love* (3:197)/love (2:155)

223 *violence* (3:198)/violence
(2:156)

223 *I* (3:199)/I (2:157)

223 (blest—) blest.— —
(3:200)/blest.——(2:157)

223 Rose-Court, Tuesday
(3:201)/*Rose-Court,* Tuesday (2:157)

223 , longer, (3:201)/ , longer
(2:158)

224 *yet* (3:201)/yet (2:158)

224 *my* (3:203)/my (2:159)

224 stately dome (3:204)/stately
doom (2:159)

225 driven by *me* (3:204)/
driven by me (2:159)

225 *Pappa* (3:205)/Pappa
(2:159)

225 go to her— (3:206)/go to
her— — (2:160)

225 last sigh— (3:207)/last
sigh— — — (2:160)

225 Sidney's death— (3:207)/
Sidney's death— — (2:161)

225 He *will not* (3:207)/He
will not (2:161)

225 did I say?— (3:207)/did I
say?— —

225 *cannot* (3:207)/cannot
(2:161)

225 perhaps— (3:207)/per-
haps— — (2:161)

225 carried to him!— (3:207)/
carried to him!— — (2:161)

225 imprisonment— (3:208)/
imprisonment— — (2:161)

226 she had had: (3:210)/she
had: (2:162)

226 to-morrow (3:211)/to
morrow (2:162)

226 To-morrow (3:211)/To
morrow (2:163)

226 as good." . . . (3:213)/as
good."— — (2:163)

227 away . . . (3:214)/away.— —
(2:164)

227 was come: (3:215)/was
come; (2:164)

227 murder." . . . (3:216)/
murder."——— (2:165)

227 feels!" . . . (3:217)/feels!"—
—— (2:165)

228 (best-beloved) *best-beloved*
(3:219)/best-beloved
(2:167)

228 Rose-Court (3:220)/*Rose-
Court* (2:167)

228 afflictions? . . . (3:220)/
afflictions?——— (2:167)

228 hearing me . . . (3:223)/
hearing me.——— (2:168)

229 to me to-day (3:223)/to
me to day (2:169)

229 Rose-Court (3:224)/*Rose-
Court* (2:169)

229 ever affectionate (3:224)/
ever affectionate, (2:169)

229 *divine* (3:224)/divine
(2:169)

229 *talked of you* (3:225)/talked
of you (2:169)

229 *my love* (3:225)/my love
(2:169)

229 *properly* (3:225)/properly
(2:170)

229 *forms* (3:225)/forms (2:170)

229 *feelings* (3:225)/feelings
(2:170)

229 *need* (3:226)/need (2:170)
230 oracle . . . (3:226)/oracle.—
     —— (2:170)
230 contradict (3:229)/
     cuntradict (2:172)
231 my Emma's (3:231)/*my
     EMMA'S* (2:172)
231 *system* (3:231)/system
     (2:173)
231 *of her* . . . (3:232)/of her—
     —— (2:173)
232 tale . . . (3:235)/tale——
     —— (2:175)
232 happy. (3:235)/happy
     (2:175)
232 Rose-Court (3:235)/*Rose-
     Court* (2:175)
232 *your* (3:237)/your (2:176)
232 see me . . . (3:235)/see
     me—— (2:176)
233 Rye-Farm (3:239)/*Rye-
     Farm* (2:17)
233 *perfectly womanish* (3:240)/
     perfectly womanish (2:177)
233 *defence* (3:240)/defence
     (2:177)
233 *days* (3:241)/days (2:178)
233 *sincere* (3:241)/sincere
     (2:178)
233 *affectionate* (3:241)/
     affectionate (2:178)
233 *Inflexibility* (3:242)/
     Inflexibility (2:178)
234 *unhappy* (3:243)/unhappy
     (2:179)
234 *our attachment* (3:244)/our
     attachment (2:179)
234 *choice* (3:244)/choice (2:179)
234 Rose-Court (3:246)/*Rose-
     Court* (2:180)
235 *injured* (3:247)/injured
     (2:181)

235 *your own experience*
     (3:247)/your own experi-
     ence (2:181)
235 *obdurate purpose* (3:248)/
     obdurate purpose (2:181)
235 see (3:249)/se. (2:182)
235 me: (3:249)/me; (2:182)
235 you; (3:251)/you: (2:183)
236 *mutability* (3:251)/mutabil-
     ity (2:183)
236 a lover, (3:251)/a lover
     (2:183)
236 *Principle* (3:251)/Principle
     (2:183)
236 *attachment* (3:252)/
     attachment (2:183)
236 *not vindictive* (3:252)/not
     vindictive (2:183)
236 penitent? . . . (3:253)/
     penitent?—— (2:184)
236 *my power* (3:253)/my
     power (2:184)
236 *vermilion* (3:253)/vermil-
     lion (2:184)
236 *betrayer* (3:253)/betrayer
     (2:184)
236 Rye-Farm (3:255)/*Rye-
     Farm* (2:185)
236 *ambition* (3:255)/ambition
     (2:185)
237 importunity; (3:256)/
     importunity: (2:185)
237 hope for . . . (3:259)/hope
     for ——— (2:187)
238 Noel-Castle (3:268)/*Noel-
     Castle* (2:187)
238 north! . . . (3:260)/north!—
     —— (2:187)
238 *infirmary* (3:260)/infirmary
     (2:187)
238 against her. (3:262)/against
     her (2:188)

238 *pleasing* (3:263)/pleasing
(2:189)

239 *shock* (3:265)/shock (2:190)

239 *easy* (3:265)/easy (2:190)

239 *elocution* (3:266)/elocution
(2:190)

239 can Your (3:267)/can Your
(2:191) (line break after
"can" in 1773)

239 Rose-Court (3:267)/*Rose-
Court* (2:191)

239 *forgiving* (3:268)/forgiving
(2:191)

240 *accept* (3:269)/accept (2:192)

240 *enjoy* (3:269)/enjoy (2:192)

240 *discomfiture* (3:269)/
discomfiture (2:192)

240 *Leucadian rock* (3:270)/
LEUCADIAN ROCK
(2:192)

240 ———-*admirer* (3:272)/—
——admirer (2:193)

241 *their romance* (3:275)/their
romance (2:195)

241 *the love* (3:275)/the love
(2:195)

241 *stubbornness* (3:276)/
stubbornness (2:195)

241 *covetousness* (3:276)/
covetousness (2:195)

241 *good-nature* (3:277)/good-
nature (2:196)

241 happen, they (3:277)/
happen. they (2:196)

241 impatience . . . (3:278)/
impatience——— (2:196)

242 Burton (3:279)/*Burton*
(2:197)

242 *excessive vivacity* (3:280)/
excessive vivacity (2:197)

242 *sober sadness*(3:280)/sober
sadness (2:197)

243 *Maccaroni* (3:280)/Maca-
roni (2:197)

243 *tristful* (3:280)/tristful
(2:197)

243 *pomposity* (3:280)/pompos-
ity (2:197)

243 (Catharine) *Catharine
(3:280)*/Catherine (2:197)

243 *comported* (3:281)/com-
ported (2:198)

243 *careful* (3:281)/careful
(2:198)

243 *dress* (3:284)/dress (2:199)

243 *waistcoat* (3:284)/waistcoat
(2:199)

243 *coat* (3:284)/coat (2:199)

243 *mistaken* (3:285)/mistaken
(2:200)

243 *commissioned* (3:285)/
commissioned (2:200)

243 *surprised* (3:286)/surprised
(2:200)

243 *flippancy* (3:286)/flippancy
(2:201)

243 *amended* (3:287)/amended
(2:201)

244 *commissioned* (3:287)/
commissioned (2:201)

244 as *you* are (3:287)/as you
are (2:201)

244 *ambassador* (3:287)/
ambassador (2:201)

244 *affect* (3:287)/affect (2:201)

244 *insensible* (3:287)/insensible
(2:201)

244 "Trifler!— — (3:288)/
"Trifler!——— (2:201)

244 *squabble* (3:289)/squabble
(2:202)

244 *boy* (3:289)/boy (2:202)

244 I made (3:289)/I mad
(2:202)

244 *the lover* (3:289)/the lover (2:202)

244 *extraordinary* (3:290)/ extraordinary (2:202)

244 *youthful ladies* (3:291)/ youthful ladies (2:203)

244 *Hey, Beaumont* (3:291)/ Hey, Beaumont (2:203)

245 *in love* (3:291)/in love (2:203)

245 *scheme of my lottery* (3:292)/scheme of my lottery (2:203)

245 *monkey* (3:292)/monkey (2:203)

245 *savant* (3:292)/savant (2:204)

245 *astonish* (3:293)/astonish (2:204)

245 Rose-Court (3:294)/*Rose-Court* (2:204)

246 to make her (3:295)/ to mak her (2:205)

247 "O, (3:300)/"O (2:207)

247 *terrors* (3:300)/terrors (2:207)

247 heart (3:301)/breast (2:208)

247 *wishes* (3:301)/wishes (2:208)

247 *tranquil* (3:301)/tranquil (2:208)

247 *artificial indigence* (3:301)/ artificial indigence (2:208)

247 *realised* (3:301)/realised (2:208)

247 (William Walpole?) WILL-IAM WALPOLE? (3:302)/ WILLIAM WALPOLE. (2:208)

247 promising; (3:303)/promising: (2:209)

247 *golden dreams* (3:304)/ golden dreams (2:209)

247 *your bread* (3:304)/your bread (2:209)

248 *furious* (3:305)/furious (2:210)

248 *piercers* (3:305)/piercers (2:210)

248 *frized* (3:306)/frized (2:210)

248 *prophane* (3:306)/ prophane (2:210)

248 *sanctified* (3:306)/sanctified (2:210)

248 *children of new grace:* (3:306)/children of new grace (2:210)

248 *perfect* (3:306)/perfect (2:210)

248 Rose-Court. *(3:307)/Rose-Court* (2:210)

249 (Allgood) ALLGOOD." (3:308)/ALLGOOD. (2:212)

249 *expensive* (3:111)/expensive (2:213)

249 riches; (3:312)/riches: (2:213)

249 divided (3:312)/divested (2:213)

249 comfort; (3:312)/comfort: (2:213)

250 Portman Square (3:313)/ *Portman Square* (2:214)

250 *captive* (3:315)/captive (2:215)

250 *pleasing pain* (3:315)/ pleasing pain (2:215)

250 *dared* (3:316)/dared (2:215)

251 *foppishness* (3:317)/ foppishness (2:216)

251 *these articles* (3:317)/these
     articles (2:216)
252 *not to stare* (3:324)/not to
     stare (2:220)
253 (tired) stirred . . . (3:325)/
     stirred——— (2:220)
253 us; (3:326)/his (2:220)

253 *hateful* (3:326)/hateful
     (2:221)
253 *honor* (3:327)/ honor (2:221)
253 Portman-Square (3:329)/
     Portman-Square (2:222)
254 (The End) THE END
     (3:330)/*FINIS.* (2:223)

Appendix 2

Collation of 1773 and 1787 Editions

ITEMS IN PARENTHESES INDICATE discrepancies between the two 1773 London editions of _Emma_: one at the University of Chicago library, and the other, at the British Library (consulted from a microfilm copy).

54   Woman of Fashion (1:4)/ woman of fashion (1:2)

54   humor (1:4) /humour (1:2)

54   employment, (1:7)/employ- ment (1:4)

55   From the SAME to the SAME (1:8)/ FROM THE SAME TO THE SAME (1:4)

55   Sunbury (1:8)/SUNBURY (1:5)

55   Dullness (1:9)/dullness (1:5)

55   vogue (1:9)/vouge (1:6)

55   tho' (1:9)/though (1:6)

55   you, that (1:10)/you that (1:6)

55   gentlman, of whom (1:10)/ gentleman of whom (1:6)

55   myself; which (1:12)/ myself, which (1:7)

56   hearts; and (1:16)/hearts, and (1:10)

57   bred (1:20)/Bred (1:13)

57   female; if (1:21)/female. If (1:13)

58   hers, (1:22)/her's, (1:13)

58   striking; but (1:22)/striking, but (1:14)

58   liked,or (1:24)/liked or (1:14)

58   Best Sort of Woman (1:25)/best sort of woman (1:15)

58   my word, the (1:25)/my word the (1:15)

58   makes, by so doing, (1:25)/makes by so doing (1:15)

58   which would enslave (1:25)/ that would enslave (1:15)

58   with, before I attach myself to her: her soul (1:26)/ with; her soul (1:15)

59 Lady's orders (1:27)/lady's orders (1:16)

59 voice, on his entering (1:29)/voice on his (1:17)

59 friend, to whose (1:29)/ friend to whose (1:18)

59 adventures, which from his profession he has (1:30)/adventures which, from his profession he has (1:18)

60 me; that I am (1:31)/ me;Bthat I am (1:18)

60 about: he pretends (1:31)/ about. He pretends (1:19)

60 hung his dog, and broke his pipe, (1:33)/ hung his dog and broke his pipe (1:20)

60 when, on (1:35)/when on (1:21)

61 us, than, (1:36)/us than, (1:21)

61 by fortune would (1:37)/by Fortune would (1:22)

61 Inexorable Tyrant (1:38)/ inexorable tyrant (1:22)

61 the Bar; (1:39)/the bar; (1:23)

62 Vernon, are to be (1:41)/ Vernon are to be (1:24)

62 yourself however, (1:42)/ yourself, however (1:25)

63 (*prudence is amply*) prudence is amply (1:46)/ in prudence, is (1:26)

63 heart is (1:47)/ heart, is (1:28)

63 story, I have (1:48)/ storyBI have (1:28)

64 Spring-park (1:49)/Spring Park (1:29)

64 lot, being a good partner; I own that (1:50)/ lot; being a good partner, I (1:30) (error in 1787).

66 weighs down his spirit. (1:60)/ weihs down his spirits. (1:36)

67 indisposition, to attend, (1:63)/indisposition to attend, (1:38)

67 ********** (1:23)/*(1:21)

67 1 line centered "Beyond 'tis agony (1:66)/ 2 lines centered "Bliss goes but to a certain bound; Beyond 'tis agony (1:40)

68 Contempt. . . . . . . (7 periods) /contempt! . . . . . . (6 periods, exclamation point)

69 thus.—— (1:74)/thus—— (1:44)

69 I had soon (1:75)/I soon ran the length (1:44)

70 point, wherein (1:78)/point wherein (1:46)

70 sure, I (1:85)/sure I (1:50)

71 journey, which (1:85)/ journey which (1:50)

72 bedside (1:87)/ bed-side (1:51)

72 sentiments; but (1:89)/ sentiments, but (1:52)

72 sick room should (1:90)/ sick room, should (1:53)

73 following, (1:93)/following (1:54)

73 Russian Service (1:96)/ Russian service (1:56)

73 Knowing that, if (1:96)/ Knowing that if (1:56)

76 *unfortunates* 1:107)/ *unfortunate* (1:62)

76 class a tear (1:107)/ class, a tear (1:62)

77 unhappy.—I (1:113)/ unhappy. I (1:65)

77 capable . . . Taking (1:115)/ capable. Taking me (1:66)

78 me;—but remember (1:117)/ me; but remember, (1:67)

78 *honor* I depend (1:117)/ on your honour I depend (1:67)

78 , acquainting him; that (1:120) / , acquainting him that (1:68)

79 : could I give (1:115)/ :—could I give (a rare exception to the general rule of more hypens and ellipses in 1773 edition) (1:68)

79 the unfortunate, but (1:121)/the unfortunate; but (1:69)

79 worth, not to prize it highly.BIs (1:121)/worth not to prize it highly. Is (1:70)

79 . . . Comfort (1:122)/ . . . Comfort (1:70)

79 lover, who (1:122)/ lover who (1:70)

79 despairs! . . . (1:122)/ despairs!C(1:70)

79 me!—my flirts forsake me . . But (1:123)/me! My flirts forsake me . . But (1:70)

79 . . . (1:124)/ . . . (1:71)

79 Sutton! . . . I (1:124)/ Sutton! . . . I (1:71)

79 evening, that (1:125)/ evening that (1:71)

79 *agreeable* meeting (1:125)/ agreeable meeting (1:72)

80 form; when (1:129)/form, when (1:74)

80 down, near (1:130)/ down near (1:74)

81 ladies cause (1:132)/ ladies' cause (1:75)

81 sustained!-Sidney (1:134)/ sustained! Sidney (1:76)

82 happy!—Tears (1:137)/ happy. Tears (1:78)

82 my Emma; (1:137)/My Emma; (1:78)

82 refractory?"— (1:138)/ refractory?— (1:78)

83 a path, to which (1:142)/ a path to which (1:80)

83 connexion (1:145)/connection (1:82)

84 strength . . . (1:147)/ strength . . . (1:83)

84 to, not because I can talk like him; but being actuated . . . (1:150)/ to; not because I can talk like him, but being actuated . . . (1:85)

85 destiny (1:152)/destiny . . . (1:86)

85 evil;" (1:153)/a great evil," (1:87)

85 peace, than (1:154)/ peace than (1:87)

86 glad of the meeting (1:158)/ glad of meeting (1:90)

87 loth (1:162)/loath (1:91)

87 narrative. (1:163)/narrative:—(1:12)

87 Miss Courtney, being expected. —You (1:164)/ Courtney being expected. You (1:92)

88 Then (1:166)/on. Then,
(1:92)

88 *honorable* (1:169)/
honourable (1:95)

88 coquette (1:171)/coquet
(1:96)

88 Reflexion (1:171)/
Reflection (1:96)

90 other. —These (1:177)/
other. These (1:99)

91 Spring-Park. (1:182)/Spring
Park. (1:102)

91 *British Colonel.* I (1:183)/
British Colonel. I (1:102)

91 favor (1:185)/favour (1:104)

92 *the tribe* (1:187)/the tribe
(1:105)

92 ... (1:190)/ ... (1:107)

93 *delicacy.* (1:193)/delicacy.
(1:108)

93 At the conclusion of this,
the coach (1:194)/At the
conclusion of this the coach
(1:108)

93 frequent calls (1:194)/at
calls (1:109)

93 (past) pass'd sorrows
(1:195)/passed sorrows
(1:109)

93 wish'd." (1:195)/wished."
(1:109)

94 I saw pleasure (1:196)/BI
saw pleasure (1:112)

95 request ... (1:205)/re-
quest ... (1:115)

96 mentioned, (1:207)/
mentioned; (1:115) [>Fa-
ther encourages her to lie
about Walpole]

96 wonder, perhaps, that
(1:208)/wonder perhaps
that (1:116)

96 me, as (1:209)/me with
(1:116)

96 point, (1:210)/point
(1:210)

96 him; and (1:210)/him: and
(1:117)

96 declaring, that (1:211)/
declaring that (1:117)

96 Walpole; (1:211)/Walpole
(1:118)

97 (No) no, (1:213) /no;
(1:118)

103 passed (1:213)/past (1:119)
(1787 error)

97 justice. —I (1:213)/justice.
I dare (1:119)

98 mouth:' (1:217)/mouth."
(1:121)

98 hence: (1:217)/hence. (1:121)

98 countenance, that (1:218)/
countenance; (1:121)

98 (infancy) in fancy; (1:218)/
infancy, (1:121)

98 steps!— (1:219)/steps.—
(1:122)

98 respectable (1:219)/
,respectable (1:122)

98 dieing (1:221)/dying
(1:123)

99 so low and dejected,
(1:221)/so low and so
dejected, (1:123)

99 *dismals.* (1:202)/dismals:
(1:123)

99 progress in love (1:202)/
progress of love (1:123)

99 *inflammable,* (1:202)/
inflammable, (1:123)

100 —I could (1:227)/I could
(1:126)

100 dieing, (1:227)/dying,
(1:127)

102 aspect (1:236)/,aspect (1:132)
102 pests. —That (1:238)/That (1:133)
103 immediately called (1:243)/ immediate called (1:136)
105 your players (1:252)/our players (1:142)
106 you *felt* as if *I* (1:257)/you felt as if I (1:144)
106 sister's (1:259)/sisters' (1:146) (1787 error)
107 coquettry: superior (1:262)/coquettry.Superior (1:147)
107 Harriet, (1:262)/ —Harriet, (1:147)
107 (as I conjectured) had, (1:262) /as I conjectured, had (1:147)
107 —I no longer (1:263)/I no longer (1:147)
107 prattler.—In (1:263)/ prattler. In (1:148)
107 drawn in, by (1:264)/ drawn in by (1:148)
107 snares, (1:264)/snares (1:148)
108 correspondence: my head (1:265)/correspondence: my head (1:149)
108 Siren, (1:266)/siren (1:149)
108 scheme; (1:266)/Scheme, (1:149)
108 Sphynx, (1:266)/sphinx, (1:150)
109 Carleton, (1:272)/Carlton, (1:153)
111 or dignify (2:5)/and dignify (1:157)
112 her; (2:6)/her, (1:158)
112 approbation; (2:7)/approbation? (1:158)

112 adultery! (2:7)/adultery? (1:158)
112 action; (2:7)/action?(1:158)
112 Men naturally inconstant are (2:7)/Men, naturally inconstant, are (1:158)
112 have taught (2:9)/had taught (1:160)
112 him, (2:10)/him; (1:160)
113 Spring-Park (2:11)/Spring Park (1:161)
113 quantity (2:13)/quantity (1:162)
114 (Bel.had) Bel. had (2:15)/ Bel had (1:163)
114 park (2:15)/Park (1:163)
114 universe: (2:17)/universe; (1:165)
114 fluency; (2:18)/fluency! (1:165)
115 whim! (2:19)/whim (1:165)
115 them; (2:19)/them! (1:166)
115 *polite age* (2:20)/polite age (1:166)
115 him that, (2:20)/him, that (1:166)
115 *you* (2:20)/you (1:167)
115 and, if (2:22)/ and if (1:167)
115 *honest woman* (2:22)/honest woman (1:167)
115 *judiciously* term (2:22)/ judiciously term (1:167)
115 Legislators (2:22)/legislators' (1:167)
115 *honorable order*, (2:22)/ honorable order, (1:168)
115 *insipids,* (2:22)/insipids, (1:168)
115 *provided* for, (2:23)/ provided for (1:168)

115 manner (2:23)/manner, (1:160)

116 you, (2:23)/you both, (1:160) [1787 edition is correct]

116 (2:24) *gay*, though the *good*; (2:24)/ gay, though the good (1:168) [slash?]

116 (*complain*, Kitty) complain, Kitty (2:26)/complain, Kitty (1:170)

116 You own, that (2:25)/You own that (1:170)

116 *complain* (2:26)/complain (1:170)

116 Cousin, imagine (2:27)/ cousin, imagine (1:171)

116 *gay*, if (2:27)/gay, if (1:171)

116 *good* with (2:27)/good with (1:171)

117 First Female (2:28)/first female (1:172)

117 morose moralists, (2:29) / morose moralists (1:172)

117 youth as deserving as (2:30)/youth, as deserving as (1:173)

117 as happy (2:31)/has happy (1:173); (1787 error)

118 here, the rest (2:33)/here; the rest (1:175)

118 refusal. —He (2:36)/refusal. He (1:177)

119 on humanity, (2:37)/to humanity, (1:177)

119 dear Madam, (2:40)/my dear madam, (1:178)

119 observing, that, if I was (2:40)/ observing that if I was (1:179)

120 Spring-Park. (2:41)/ SPRING PARK. (1:180)

120 do: he (2:42)/do; he (1:180)

120 Spring-Park, (2:43)/Spring Park, (1:181)

120 humor (2:44)/humour (1:181)

122 it): (2:52)/it:) (1:186)

122 rigor; (2:53)/rigor: (1:186)

122 censorious; (2:54)/censori-ous; (1:187)

125 temper, (2:64)/temper (1:193)

125 *obliged* to (2:64)/obliged to (1:193)

125 *you* as (2:65)/you as (1:193)

125 *civil* (2:65)/civil (1:193)

125 self-love, soon appeased you (2:65)/self love, appeased you (1:193)

125 *loving* (2:65)/loving (1:193)

125 passion: (2:66)/passions: (1:193)

125 *that scene*; (2:66)/that scene; (1:194)

125 *sulkiness*; (2:67)/sulkiness, (1:194)

125 won't (2:67)/will not (1:194)

125 . . . (6) (2:67)/ . . . (10) (1:194)

125 *expected* (2:68)/expected (1:195)

126 *wantons* (2:69)/wantons (1:195)

126 dear friend, (2:70)/my friend, (1:196)

126 *haste* (2:71)/haste (1:196)

126 *my reign.* (2:71)/my reign. (1:196)

126 *civil things,* (2:72)/civil things, (1:197)

126 ease, (2:73)/case, (1:197)

126 *kind* (2:75)/kind (1:198)

127 Barons (2:77)/Barons' (1:199)

127 *made happy* (2:77)/made happy (1:200)

127 *real* (2:78)/real (1:200)

128 friendship.— (2:79)/ friendship. He (1:201)

128 though (2:79)/ tho' (1:201)

129 *marplot* (2:84)/*Marplot* (1:203)

129 thro' (2:85)/through (1:204)

130 allays. (2:88)/alloys. (1:206); (changed word; 1787 error)

130 *ordinaire* (2:90)/ *ordinaire,* (1:206)

130 for).—(2:91)/for.)— (1:208)

131 Spring-Park (2:93)/Spring Park (1:209)

132 humor, (2:98)/humour, (1:212)

132 good-humor (2:100)/good humour (1:214)

133 *seeming* impatience (2:100)/ *seeming impatience* (1:214)

134 (good-humour) good-humor (2:107)/good humour (1:218)

135 honor (2:110)/honour (1:219)

135 up, to (2:110)/up to (1:220)

137 Spring-Park. (2:129)/Spring Park. (1:231)

140 *obey* no longer (2:131)/*obey,* no longer (1:231)

140 *rude* (2:132)/rude (1:233)

140 *obstinate* (2:133)/obstinate (1:233)

140 *tractable* (2:133)/tractable (1:234)

140 *best* (2:134)/best (1:234)

140 *flirt* (2:135)/ flirt (1:234)

140 you, (2:135)/you (1:234)

141 High-life (2:137)/high-life (1:236)

141 (graceful) gracefull (2:137)/ graceful (1:236)

141 *fashionable* (2:137)/fashion- able (1:236)

141 *highest respect,* (2:139)/ highest respect, (1:237)

142 *you* yawn (2:140)/*you yawn* (1:237)

142 . . . (2:141)/ . . . (1:238)

142 agreeable, on (2:141)/ aggreeable on (1:238)

142 me, to beg (2:143)/me to beg (1:238)

142 towards him (2:143)/ toward him (1:239)

143 matter? (2:145)/matter! (1:241)

143 crime, in (2:147)/crime in (1:242)

144 honor." (2:152)/honour." (1:245)

144 nice, nay, sometimes, even (2:152)/nice, nay, even (1:245)

144 humor; (2:152)/humour; (1:245)

145 him, (2:152)/him; (1:245)

145 thwart you, (2:154)/thwart you; (1:246)

148 humor: (2:162)/humour (2:3)

149 placed in (2:170)/placed upon (2:8)

150 a morning (2:172)/the
morning (2:10)

152 (spleen-wort) Spleen-wort
(2:179)/spleen wort (2:14)

152 (*la bella Ceutrina*) La Bella
Centrina (2:180)/ La Bella
Centrina (2:14)

152 *patience* (2:181)/patience
(2:16)

152 ("the Feeling of another's
woe, the Unfeeling for his
own") "the Feeling for
another's woe, the unfeeling
for his own," (2:183)/ "the
feeling for another's woe,
the unfeeling for his own."
(2:17)

153 *prudent* a choice (2:184)/
prudent a choice (2:17)

153 *that* only (2:184)/ that
only (2:18)

153 *taste* (2:185)/taste (2:18)

153 better (2:186)/bettter
(2:18) (1787 error)

153 can't (2:187)/cannot (2:19)

154 honor (2:188)/honour
(2:20)

154 Neville I (2:188)/Neville, I
(2:20)

154 *Colonel Sutton* (2:190)/
Colonel Sutton (2:21)

154 AFTER (2:190)/After
(2:21)

154 *intruded* (2:191)/intruded
(2:21)

154 , which, from (2:191)/
,which from (2:22)

154 ... (2:191)/ ... (2:22)

154 *your heart,* (2:192)/ your
heart, (2:22)

154 *justice,* (2:192) /justice,
(2:22)

155 by *you* (2:193)/by you
(2:22)

155 your *suspicions* (2:193)/your
suspicions (2:23)

155 *indifferent* (2:194)/indiffer-
ent (2:23)

155 *unwelcome,* (2:194)/
unwelcome (2:23)

155 (you) *you* (2:194)/you
(2:23)

155 *you* were too (2:194)/you
were too (2:23)

155 *mutual* (2:196)/mutual
(2:24)

156 (In con.) In Continuation
(2:198)/IN CONT. (2:26)

156 ear of Phoebus (2:198)/car
of Phoebus (2:26) (1787
edition corrects 1773)

158 stand; (2:207)/stand: (2:31)

158 *man of quality* (2:209)/*men
of quality* (2:33)

159 me! (2:210)/me; (2:33)

161 it?" (2:219)/it." (2:39)

163 We went on (2:230)/He
went on (2:230)

163 into his study, (2:231)/in
his study, (2:46)

164 ... (2:233)/ ... (2:47)

164 be, (2:234)/be (2:48)

164 (said he, sobbing audibly)
(2:235)/said he, sobbing
audibly, (2:48)

164 laid on (2:236)/laid in
(2:49)

165 frightfull (2:236)/frightful
(2:49)

165 come very (2:237)/came
very (2:49)

165 This is but the fifth
(2:237)/This is the fifth
day (2:49)

165 out-lived (2:239)/outlived (2:50)

165 honors (2:240)/honours (2:31)

169 Aix.—(2:254)/Aix! (2:60)

169 *affect/solicitude* (2:255)/ affect/solicitude (2:60)

169 *relapsing* (2:256)/relapsing (2:61)

169 negotiate (2:256)/negociate (2:61)

170 *obstacle* (2:259)/obstacle (2:62)

170 effect of a bewildered imagination (2:259)/affect of a bewildered imagination (2:63) 244 you; (2:259)/ you, (2:63)

170 heaven (2:260)/Heaven (2:63)

170 me." . . . (2:261)/me." (2:64)

170 *His memory,* (2:262)/ His memory, (2:64)

170 do, Kitty (2:262)/do Kitty (2:64)

170 wife, because (2:263)/wife because (2:65)

171 *delicacy.* (2:263)/delicacy (2:65)

171 reason; (2:264)/reason (2:66)

171 *humanity* (2:264)/humanity (2:66)

171 *highly polished,* (2:265)/ highly polished (2:66)

171 *deference* (2:265)/deference (2:66)

171 *the fair* (2:265)/the fair (2:66)

171 *whistling* (2:265)/whistling (2:66)

171 *wind* (2:265)/wind (2:66)

171 *responded* (2:265)/re-sponded (2:66)

171 *delicacy:* (2:266)/delicacy: (2:67)

172 . . . (2:268)/ . . . (2:67)

172 *her,* (2:268)/her, (2:68)

172 her (2:271)/her (2:69)

172 . . . (2:271)/ . . . (2:69)

172 returned, holding (2:271)/ returned holding (2:69)

172 face, (2:271)/face; (2:271)

173 Portman-Square (2:273)/ Portman-Square (2:71)

173 hands— (2:274)/hands;— (2:71)

173 fondness!– (2:275)/fond-ness! I (2:71)

174 Spring-Park (2:293)/Spring Park (2:84)

177 vivacity as (2:294)/vivacity, as (2:84)

177 alas! (2:294)/alas: (2:84)

179 world, to (3:2)/world to (2:86)

179 Virtue enables (3:2)/virtue enables (2:86)

179 it (3:2)/ is (2:86) (error in 1787)

179 *advised,* in (3:4)/advised, in (2:87)

179 *genteel* crowd (3:4)/genteel crowd (2:87)

179 (Berkeley Berkley-square, (3:4)/Berkley-square, (2:87)

179 (*honor*) honor (3:5)/honour (2:88)

180 Walpole, Lord (3:5)/ Walpole, and Lord (2:88)

180 *unlimited* (3:6)/unlimited (2:88)

180 *constant* (3:6)/constant (2:84)

180 *silly* (3:7)/silly (2:89)
180 (*impassable barriers*)
impassable barriers, (3:8)
/impassable barriers
(2:90)
180 (your)*your* (3:10)/your
(2:91)
181 *poor husband's,* (3:13)/poor
husband's (2:92)
182 entertain . . . You (3:14)/
entertain. You (2:94)
182 Lady Clarendon or he
(3:16)/Lady Clarendon, or
he, (2:95)
182 (*innocent*) innocent, (3:17)/
innocent, (2:96)
183 (teaze) teize (3:19)/teaze
(2:97)
184 its pleasures (3:22)/it's
pleasures (2:99)
184 humor (3:23)/humour
(2:99)
184 styled (3:23)/stiled (2:100)
184 (Bishop in England)
bishop in England (3:24)/
Bishop, in England
(2:100)
184 spot, as (3:25)/spot as
(2:100)
185 (motley) motly (3:27)/
motley throng (2:102)
185 I was told by every body of
this separation (3:31)/I was
told of this separation
(2:104)
187 Spring-Park, (3:38)/Spring
Park, (2:108)
189 in, go (3:47)/in; go
(2:112)
189 and like the honey be
(3:47)/and, like the honey,
be (2:114)

190 tattling Friendship (3:49)/
tattling, Friendship (2:115)
190 honor (3:49)/honour
(2:115)
191 humorsome (3:55)/
humoursome (2:119)
191 friends repugnance (3:56)
/friends' repugnance
(2:120)
191 *that* seems (3:57)/that
seems (2:120)
192 God of love (3:58)/God of
Love (2:121)
192 *humors,* (3:58)/humours,
(2:121)
193 *price.* (3:61)/price. (2:123)
193 house. (3:61)/House.
(2:124)
193 it an (3:62)/it, an (2:124)
193 East-Indian (3:62)/East
Indian (2:124)
193 *lacs of rupees;* (3:62)/*lacks
of rupees;* (2:124)
193 *pledging* (3:62)/pledging
(2:124)
193 drinking, (3:62)/drinking;
(2:124)
193 Town-hall, (3:63)/town-
hall, (2:124)
193 *oppose me.* (3:63)/oppose
me. (2:124)
193 *staunchest* (3:63)/staunchest
(2:124)
193 *secured* (3:63)/secured
(2:125)
193 *the Nabob* (3:64)/the *Nabob*
(2:125)
193 solace: (3:64)/solace;
(2:125)
193 bett: (3:64)/bet: (2:125)
193 ominous (3:65)/ominious
(2:125) [error in 1787]

193 *eclipsed*, (3:65)/ eclipsed, (2:126)

194 *could* bestow (3:66)/ could bestow (2:127) (error in 1787)

194 ... (3:67)/ ... (2:127)

194 mischief into another (3:67) /mischief to another (2:128)

194 sharpers (3:68)/sharper's (2:128)

194 *honest* (3:68)/honest (2:128)

194 ranks (3:68)/rank (2:128)

194 *debts of honor* (3:69)/debts of honour (2:129)

194 hand, as (3:69)/hand as (2:129)

194 *scum of the earth* (3:69)/ scum of the earth (2:129)

195 where (3:69)/were (error) (2:129) (error in 1787)

195 contagious (that (3:70)/ contagious, (that (2:129)

195 *gain*; (3:70)/gain; (2:129)

195 *honors* (3:71)/honours (2:130)

195 mankind does (3:73)/ mankind, does (2:131)

195 one, (3:73)/one; (2:131)

195 *dealing* (3:73)/dealing (2:131)

195 herd, (3:73)/heard (2:131)

196 *tempter* (3:75)/tempter (2:132)

196 *general* (3:75)/general (2:132)

196 *individuals* (3:75)/individuals (2:132)

196 *excuse* (3:75)/excuse (2:132)

196 (London) london, (3:77)/ London; (2:133)

197 (Can I) can I (3:79)/Can I (2:135)

197 (Did the) did the (3:79)/ Did the (2:135)

197 —Something (3:80)/ Something (2:135)

197 (Bel. Will) Bel.will (3:80)/ Bel will (2:135)

197 Spring-Park (3:81)/Spring Park (2:136)

197 it caused him: (3:82)/it has caused him: (2:137)

198 Rose-Court (3:83)/ROSE COURT (2:138)

198 Spring-Park (3:83)/Spring-Park (2:138)

198 time (3:87)/Time (2:87)

199 Spring-Park (3:90)/Spring Park (2:142)

200 (north one) north, one (3:92)/North, one (2:144)

200 Rose-Court (3:92)/Rose Court (2:144)

200 Noel-Castle (3:93)/Noel Castle (2:144)

200 so; (3:95)/so: (2:145)

200 Bel. (3:95)/Bel (2:146)

200 her, as soon (3:95)/her as soon (2:146)

200 Rose-Court (3:95)/Rose Court (2:146)

202 extremely, (3:101)/extremely; (2:150)

202 (today) to day, and (3:103)/to-day; and (2:151)

202 favors.—(3:103)/favours.— (2:151)

203 Rose-Court (3:105)/Rose Court (2:152)

204 Manners and (3:109)/ Manners, and (2:155)

205 she still went (3:114)/she
     went on (2:158)
206 *you*; (3:118)/you; (2:161)
207 (hers.) hers; (3:118)/hers!
     (2:161)
206 (staid,) staid. (3:119)/staid;
     (2:161)
206 *partial* (3:119)/partial
     (2:161)
206 providence! (3:119)/
     Providence! (2:162)
206 (Christian,) christian
     (3:120)/Christian (2:162)
206 favor (3:120)/favour
     (2:162)
206 it . . . (3:120)/it . . . (2:162)
206 beauty, (3:122)/beauty;
     (2:163)
207 recommended (3:123)/
     recommend (2:104)
207 preferred (3:124)/prefered
     (2:164)
207 our childhood (3:126)/her
     childhood (2:165)
208 *the friends* (3:127)/the
     friends (2:166)
208 two: (3:127)/two; (2:166)
208 "My dear, (3:128)/ My
     dear, (2:166)
209 Styled (3:132)/stiled
     (2:169)
209 "gibes and jokes" (3:135)/
     'gibes and jokes' (2:170)
209 others; (3:136)/others
     (2:171)
209 vices, (3:136)/vices; (2:171)
209 characters, for (3:137)/
     characters; for (2:171)
210 vivacity when (3:137)/
     vivacity, when (2:171)
210 (Church) church. I
     (3:138)/Church, I (2:171)

210 surprise (3:138)/surprize
     (2:172)
210 intentions, (3:139)/inten-
     tions (2:173)
210 sister indeed (3:140)/sister,
     indeed! (2:173)
210 (purpose) purport. (3:141)/
     purport; (2:173)
210 honor (3:141)/honour
     (2:173)
211 (*honor*) honor (3:142)/
     honour (2:174)
211 there; (3:143)/there,
     (2:175)
211 favorable (3:146)/favourable
     (2:176)
212 prize! (3:147)/prize?
     (2:177)
212 her, after (3:150)/her after
     (2:179)
213 post-man's (3:152)/
     postman's (2:180)
213 came; I (3:152)/came. I
     (2:180)
213 to-bed (3:154)/to bed
     (2:181)
214 is inconstancy (3:157)/Is
     inconstancy (2:183)
214 Does absence (3:158)/ —
     Does absence (2:184)
214 (*fickle kind*) fickle kind;
     (3:158)/fickle kind! (2:158)
214 (Noel Castle) *Noel-Castle*
     (3:158)/ Noel-Castle
     (2:184)
214 one; (3:158)/one: (2:184)
214 name, every (3:159)/
     name;every (2:184)
214 (fine,) fine. (3:159)/fine
     (2:184)
214 fears; and (3:159)/fears!
     and (2:184)

214 misery. (3:159)/misery: (2:185)
214 sentiments, (3:160)/ sentiment, (2:185)
215 sufficions (3:161)/suffisions (2:186)
215 overcharged (3:161)/over- charged (2:186)
215 jilted than (3:162)/jilted, than (2:186)
215 it, but (3:165)/ it; but (2:188)
216 him, (3:166)/him; (2:188)
216 in, myself (3:167)/in myself. (2:189) (1787 is correct)
216 *honor*; (3:169) /honour; (2:190)
216 crimes, and (3:170)/crimes; and (2:190)
216 them it (3:170)/them, it (2:190)
217 *forget*, we (3:172)/forget, we (2:192)
217 *my soul was contracted* (3:173)/my soul was contracted (2:192)
217 inconstancy in the light of a foible (3:174)/constancy in the light of a foible (2:193) 312 Sovereign who (3:174)/ Sovereign, who (2:173)
217 probity . . . (3:175)/probity. (2:193)
218 *deceive* us. (3:175)/deceive us, (2:193)
218 pardonable . . . I (3:175)/ pardonable. I (2:194)
218 one, though (3:176)/one; though (2:194)
218 *bon mot* (3:176)/*bon mot*, (2:194)

219 (my Fanny) me; Fanny; (3:177)/ me, Fanny; (2:194) (1787 correct)
219 is: (3:177)/is; (2:195)
219 friends, their (3:178)/ friends; their (2:195)
219 innuendoes (3:180)/ inuendoes (2:196)
219 petty prince. (3:180)/petty Prince. (2:196)
219 Spring-Park (3:180)/Spring Park (2:197)
219 late, but (3:181)/late; but (2:197)
219 Walpole; (3:181)/Walpole: (2:197)
219 Portman-Square: (3:181)/ Portman-square: (2:197)
219 master. 'Sir (3:182)/master. 'Sir (2:197)
219 here." —So (3:182)/here.' So (2:197)
219 intrusion than (3:182)/ intrusion, than (2:198)
219 tradesmen's (3:182)/ tradesman's (2:198)
219 little . . . (3:183)/ little . . . (2:198)
219 petulance, "When (3:183)/ petulance; 'When (2:198)
220 (argueing) argueing (3:185)/arguing (2:199)
220 which is that (3:185)/which is, that (2:199)
220 (legerdemain) leger-demain (3:186)/legerdemain (2:200)
220 Col. (3:187)/Colonel (2:200)
221 fate (3:189)/Fate. (2:202)
221 allies; the (3:189)/allies. The (2:202)

221 *lower* than (3:190)/lower than (2:202)

221 wondered at that (3:191)/ wondered at, that (2:203)

222 favors (3:192)/favours; (2:204)

222 her room (3:194)/the room, (2:206)

222 hope, that it (3:195)/hope that it (2:207)

223 good than (3:196)/good, than (2:207)

224 . . . (9) (3:196)/ . . . (8) (2:208)

224 distress! (3:203)/distress? (2:212)

224 she who (3:204)/she, who (2:212)

224 favorite dog (3:204)/ favourite dog (2:213)

225 lying (3:207)/laying (2:214)

226 honor (3:210)/honour (2:216)

226 informed, that (3:211)/ informed that (2:217)

226 eyelids, (3:211)/eye-lids (2:217)

226 I should disturb their ashes with my cries (3:212)/ omitted in 1787 (2:218) (error in 1787)

227 myself. –But, (3:214)/ myself. But, (2:219)

227 touch.—"My (3:215)/ touch.—My (2:220)

227 murder." . . . (3:216)/ murder." (2:220)

227 dieing (3:217)/dying (2:221)

228 Bel. (3:219)/Bel (2:222)

228 afflictions? . . . (3:220)/ afflictions?— (2:223)

228 Fanny, (3:220)/Fanny; (2:223)

228 pappa, (3:221)/papa, (2:223)

229 and on (3:223)/and, on (2:225)

230 flattering.—Had (3:228)/ flattering. Had (2:228)

230 dieing (3:230)/dying (2:229)

230 reflected, that (3:230)/ reflected that (2:229)

231 vengeance: (3:230)/vengeance; (2:229)

231 reflexion (3:231)/reflection (2:230)

231 arrant sot, (3:231) /errant sot, (2:230)

232 failing; (3:236)/failings; (2:233)

232 favor (3:236)/favour (2:233)

232 : in (3:237)/ —in (2:234)

232 not write my defence (3:237)/not write, my defence. (2:234)

232 Rye-Farm (3:238)/Rye Farm (2:234)

232 me . . . Repeal, (3:238)/ me. Repeal (2:234)

232 *trait* (3:238)/trait (2:234)

232 Rye-Farm (3:239)/RYE FARM (2:236)

233 *perfectly womanish* (3:240)/ perfectly womanish (2:236)

233 *defence,* (3:240)/defence, (2:236)

233 Rye-Farm (3:240)/Rye Farm (2:236)

233 *days* (3:241)/days (2:237)

233 indifference, and (3:241)/ indifference; and, (2:237)

233 *sincere, or affectionate;* (3:241)/sincere, or affectionate, (2:237)
233 man (3:242)/man (2:237)
234 *unhappy:* (3:243)/unhappy: (2:238)
234 myself, (3:243)/myself; (2:238)
234 *our attachment,* (3:244)/ our attachment, (2:238)
234 *choice* (3:244)/choice (2:239)
234 affronted, (3:245)/affronted;(2:239)
234 (fact,) fact; and (3:245)/ fact; and (2:239)
234 PRISCILLA NEVILLE (3:245)/ P. Neville (2:239)
234 (woman to) women to (3:246)/woman, to (2:240)
234 error, which (3:246)/error which (2:240)
235 *injured* (3:247)/injured (2:240)
235 pity, (3:247)/Pity, (2:241)
235 reflexion (3:250)/reflection (2:242)
235 precision; (3:250)/precision: (2:242)
235 regard—Consent (3:251)/ regard. Consent (2:243)
236 *mutability* (3:251)/mutability (2:243)
236 *attachment* (3:252)/ attachment (2:243)
236 *not vindictive,* (3:252)/not vindictive, (2:243)
236 *my power* (3:253)/my power (2:244)
236 *betrayer* (3:253)/betrayer (2:244)

236 favor, (3:254)/favour, (2:245)
236 Letter 81 (3:254)/LETTER 80 (2:245)
236 Rye-Farm (3:255)/RYE FARM (2:246)
237 favor (3:255)/favour (2:246)
237 man, who (3:257)/man who (2:247)
237 imbecillity (3:257)/imbecility (2:247)
238 . . . (3:259)/ . . . (2:248)
238 favor (3:260)/favour (2:248)
238 Rose-Court (3:260)/Rose Court (2:249)
238 parties (3:261)/parties, (2:249)
239 mortal shall (3:265)/mortal, shall (2:252)
239 labor, (3:268)/labour (2:254)
240 content.—(3:269)/Content.—(2:255)
240 Rye-Farm (3:273)/Rye Farm (2:257)
241 foretell (3:276)/foretel (2:259)
241 withall, (3:278)/withal, (2:260)
242 (honorably) 281 honrably (3:281)/honourably (2:262)
242 humored, (3:282)/ humoured, (2:262)
243 him? (3:284)/him, (2:264)
243 similes (3:286)/similies (2:265)
243 Bayes' (3:286)/Bayes's (2:265)
243 always." (3:286)/always?" (2:265) (not a question; error in 1787)

244 (squabble) squabble:
(3:289)/squabble; (2:266)
245 unassuming, (3:291)/
unassuming; (2:268)
245 Rose-Court (3:292)/Rose
Court (2:268)
245 Note: Letters 82, 84, 73
are in the wrong order in
the 1787 edition (2:268)
246 (ardor) arodor, (3:296) /
ardour, (2:271)
246 (realize) realise (3:297)/
realize (2:272)
246 wanting, (3:297)/ wanting
(2:272)
246 (Why) why (3:298)/Why
(2:272)
246 retirement. (3:298)/
retirement: (2:272)
247 since keep (3:299)/since,
keep (2:273)
247 new world (3:300)/New
World (2:273)
247 see you, my friend (3:302)/
see my friend (2:374)
247 flourishing, (3:303)/
flourishing; (2:275)
248 mean while bring her and
Bel. (3:304)/ mean time
bring Bel and her (2:276)
248 teacher (3:305)/preacher
(2:276) (error in 1773)

248 *sanctified* (3:306)/sanctified
(2:277)
249 favorite (3:309)/favourite
(2:279)
249 horse: (3:309)/horse; (2:279)
249 dieing (3:311)/dying
(2:280)
250 fortune, which (3:313)/
fortune which (2:282)
250 too (3:313)/too, (2:282)
250 passions: —no (3:314)/
passions: no (2:282)
250 : —no (3:314)/:no (2:282)
250 : marriage-act (3:315)/
marriage act (2:283)
250 repealed, (3:315)/ repealed;
(2:283)
251 Burton-Street (3:318)/
Bruton-street (2:285)
251 (visitors) visiters (3:318)/
visitors (2:285) (error in
1773)
251 love," proceeded (3:319)/
love, proceeded (2:285)
251 "endeavour (3:319)/
endeavour (2:285)
252 favorable (3:321)/favourable
(2:286)
252 (after, I) after I (3:322)/
after I (2:287)
252 honor (3:327)/honour
(2:290)

Appendix 3

Poems by Lady Georgiana;
with one poem by David Garrick

"THE BUTTERFLY"
GEORGIANA

A child was holding to the Light
A butterfly of colours bright.
With joy its speckled beautys spyd
And Hues with Triumph; gladly cry'd

"I like the spots of pink and Gold
your pretty wings I like to hold
Your various Streaks I love to see
And mean that you should live with me."

HAMET

"Alas" the Butterfly replied
["]You sadly pinch my tender side
And would you like a giant's hold
Shouldst this yr little form enfold.
O quickly let me fly away
To flutter in the warmth of day"

GEORGIANA

The Child good natur'd; let it go
And saw it sailing, to and fro',
And thus imbib'd a maxim true,
As to oneself; to others do.

MAY 1787: POEM BY LADY GEORGIANA TO HER FATHER

If e'er Sincerity inscribed the Stone
Giving the Dead no Minds but their own
Behold it here—this Verse with Sculptures aid
Records the debt by Love to Duty Paid
That Strangers & posterity may know
How pure a Spirit warm'd the dust below
For they who felt the Virtues of his life
Whether the Orphan Friend or Child or Wife
Need not the poets or the Sculptors art
To wake[n] the feelings of a grateful heart
Their love their grief his honours best proclaim
The Crowning Monuments of Spencer's fame.

"THE TABLE"

Of all the Fancied Wants of Life
The greatest part are Fable
But one important one there is
And that Want—is a Table—

When ev'ry Luxury is found
That to contrive you're able
How can these Dainties be enjoy'd
Unless you have a Table—

When Stormy Clouds invest the Sky
And all around looks Sable
A quiet Rubber's a resource
But not without a Table—

If land Disputes or Politicks
should make your House a Babel
Your elbows still may grant repose
If you can get a Table—

When others various Plans pursue
In House or Fields or Stable
With Writing I am well content
Could I but have a Table—

From Aldwich then to Bagnor line
As fast as you are able
For there you certainly may find
That sure thing, call'd a Table—

UPON MR. G—BEING ASK'D WHY HE DID NOT WRITE
SOMETHING UPON THE DUCHESS OF DEVONSHIRE'S ILLNESS, 1778;
BY DAVID GARRICK

When to the Fever's rage, which Art defies,
Georgiana's Charms become the Prey,
When the Mother Ev'ry Virtue sigh's,
And Ling'ring Hope still keeps away:
Shall you alone not feel the gen'ral Woe,
Nor sing the Beauties you adore?
Your Sorrow should in Elegy o'erflow,
And open all it's Tragic Store.

Still Mute my Friend? —Alas!— No measur'd Strain,
No Mimic Grief my heart shall wrong;
Let Heav'n but give _Her_ to this World again,
I'll Join the _Universal_ Song.

DG

Notes

Dedication. *Lady Camden*. Elizabeth, daughter and eventually sole heir of Nicholas Jeffreys, married Charles Pratt, first earl of Camden (1714–1794), on October 4, 1749; she died on December 10, 1779. Charles Pratt was a British jurist (*Cockaygne's Peerage* 500). "Appointed (1761) chief justice of the Court of Common Pleas, he earned wide popularity as a result of his ruling in Entick v. Carrington (1763), where he pronounced against the legality of the general warrant under which John Wilkes was prosecuted. He became lord chancellor in 1766, but his constant denunciation of the government's policy toward the American colonists and opposition to the taxes imposed on them resulted in his dismissal (1770). He served as president of the council under the marquess of Rockingham (1782–83) and under William Pitt (1784–94). In 1786 he was created Earl Camden. His lifelong fight against the existing definition of libel culminated in the passage of Fox's Libel Act of 1792. Camden's son, John Jeffreys Pratt, 2d Earl and 1st Marquess Camden, 1759–1840, was lord lieutenant of Ireland (1794–98). His repressive policies there were a major factor in the outbreak of the 1798 revolution. He later served as secretary of war (1804–5) and president of the council (1805–6 and 1807–12). He was created marquess in 1812" (*Columbia Encyclopedia*, 1994). The elder Lord and Lady Camden appear in Hannah More's letters and attended the trial of the duchess of Beaufort. Lord Camden apparently had an affair with Lady Fitzgerald; the duchess of Devonshire also attended this trial.

    p. 56. "how he passes the 'time there'"; see letter 1.

    p. 58. " I am not in haste to wed," Walpole states: Alexander Radcliffe (fl. 1669–1696), "Phillis to Demophoon," *Ovid Travestie, A Burlesque Upon Ovid's Epistles*, quoted in *The Works of Alexander Radcliffe (1696)*, with an introduction by Ken Robinson (New York: Scholars' Facsimiles and Reprints, 1981), p. 12. "I wish to God that very day we met,/that into Gaol I had been thrown for debt:/Then if I'd ask'd the Question—you'd have said/Thank you, forsooth, I'm not in haste to Wed." The quotation is also relevant to Emma, who might not have married Walpole had she known he would abandon her when she became pregnant and leave her to raise her child in squalor. Shakespeare makes use of the phrase twice in *Taming of the Shrew*. Petruchio (Katharina's suitor) says, "My businesse asketh haste, /And everre day I cannot come to woo" (1:i); Katharina says, in Act 3: "Who woo'd in haste and means to wed at leisure" (3:2:8–10). Obviously, Emma is the opposite of Katharina.

p. 55. "Cotillons and Allemands"; two late eighteenth century dances. A cotillon is a name given to several French dances, sometimes used instead of the term quadrilles (*OED*). An allemande is a name given to various German dances. The gentleman turns his partner, as in American square or country dancing; an allemande can be done with either hand, with the "left hand around with your corner" figure; Handel wrote several of these (*OED*). "These outlandish heathen Allemandes and Cotillons are quite beyond me!" a character says in Sheridan's *Rivals* (III, v). Georgiana was a patroness of dance in eighteenth-century England in whose honor Gaetano Apollino Baldassare Vestris (1729–1808) introduced the Devonshire minuet.

p. 59. Sunbury is in Dorsetshire, a county in southwestern England, bordered by the English Channel (south); the counties of Devon and Hampshire (West and East), and by Somerset and Wiltshire (north) (in Dorsetshire, see p. 59); other locations in the novel include Newark, in the county of Nottinghamshire, central England. Burton, The Grove, Spring Park, Milfield are unspecified, but Rose-Court is in Yorkshire.

p. 61. "Euphemia," wife of Justin I. Euphemia, was the daughter of the Eastern Roman Emperor Marcian and wife of the Western Roman Emperor Anthemius.

p. 63. "the sweet variety that's in her": The phrase, "sweet variety," appears in a number of poems, of which the following, from Granville's "The Progress of Beauty" is only one example: "some yield, some suffer Rapes, Invaded, or deceiv'd, not one escapes/The Wife, tho' a bright Goddess, thus gives place / To mortal Concubines of fresh Embrace;/By such Examples were we taught to see/The Life and Soul of Love, is sweet Variety"; see George Granville, "The Progress of Beauty," *The Genuine Works in Verse and Prose of G. G. Lord Lansdowne*, 2 vols. (London, 1732), ln. 45, quoted in Alexander Chalmers, ed. *The Works of The English Poets* (London, 1810), v. 11, pp. 1–56.

p. 66. "keep it as a match for the Lacedemonian if—which has maintained an unrivaled glory among the Laconic answers." "Very concise and pithy. A Spartan was called a Lacon from Laconia, the land in which he dwelt. The Spartans were noted for their brusque and sententious speech. When Philip of Macedon wrote to the Spartan magistrates, 'If I enter Laconia, I will level Lacedæmon to the ground,' the ephors wrote word back the single word, '*If*'" (*Brewer's* 587).

p. 66. "What an enemy to beauty is sorrow! *It feeds*, 'like a worm in the bud,' on the damask cheek of Sidney": "She never told her love, But let concealment, like a worm i' the bud,/Feed on her damask cheek," Viola says in Shakespeare's *Twelfth Night* (2.4.110–120). Viola, disguised as Cesario, speaks to Orsino; her comment applies to a woman's love, but is attributed to a man,

Augustus Sidney, whose love for Emma goes unspoken. *Emma*'s mixing of gender roles is similar to *Twelfth Night* in other ways as well. Just as Olivia finds Cesario's flattery more attractive than Orsino's forceful sensuality, Emma finds Augustus Sidney's softness and sensibility more appealing than William Walpole's *hauteur.*

p. 67. "Bliss goes but to a certain bound; beyond 'tis agony": From the last stanza of Fanny Greville's "Prayer for Indifference": "Far as distress the soul can wound, /'Tis pain in each degree: /'Tis bliss but to a certain bound,/Beyond 'tis agony."

> I ask no kind return of love,
> No tempting charm to please;
> Far from the heart those gifts remove,
> That sighs for peace and ease.
>
> Nor peace nor ease the heart can know,
> that, like the needle true,
> Turns at the touch of joy or woe,
> But, turning, trembles too.
>
> Far as distress the soul can wound,
> 'Tis pain in each degree:
> 'Tis bliss but to a certain bound,
> Beyond is agony.

Quoted in Sir Arthur Quiller-Couch, ed., *The Oxford Book of English Verse, 1250–1918* (New York: Oxford UP, 1940), #489, p. 566.

p. 68. "Echo": she detained Juno through her conversation, allowing Juno's husband to pursue a nymph; Juno punished Echo by forcing her to repeat the last line she heard. "The tongue that made a fool of me will shortly/Have shorter use, the voice be brief hereafter" (Ovid's *Metamorphoses*, Book 3:lns. 365–368). Echo's difficulty in pursuing Narcissus recalls Emma's miscommunications with Augustus Sidney.

p. 69. "a large dose of hartshorn drops" (ammonium carbonicum); used as a remedy for fainting or hysteria, sometimes administered during a woman's pregnancy in the eighteenth century. Clarissa takes hartshorn upon arriving in London in Samuel Richardson's novel (388).

p. 79. "a subscription assembly": a party paid for by contributing members (*OED*).

p. 89. "nor have I 'aught extenuated, or set down aught in malice' ": "Speak of me as I am; nothing extenuate,/Nor set down aught in malice" (*Othello* 5.2.343).

p. 93. "It is a consummation devoutly to be wish'd." . . . :"The heart-ache and the thousand natural shocks / That flesh is heir to: 'tis a consummation/ Devoutly to be wished" (*Hamlet* 3.1. 60–64).

p. 98. "Sidney is gone to Russia, to seek 'the bubble Reputation even in a cannon's mouth' ": "Seeking the bubble reputation/Even in a cannon's mouth"

(Shakespeare, *ASYL*, 2.7.152). The same quotation appears in Sarah Scott's *Millenium Hall* (114); later in that novel, Lord Edward throws himself into battle in a moment of romantic despair that resembles Augustus Sidney's: "Weary of life, since I could not possess her, in whom all my joys, all the wishes of my soul were centered, I seized every occasion of exposing myself to the enemy's sword" (114). In Scott's novel, Mrs. Trentham contrasts military bravery with the risk women took on marrying unfeeling husbands like William Walpole: "to face the enemy's cannon appears to me a less effort of courage, than to put our happiness into the hands of a person, who perhaps will not once reflect on the importance of the trust committed to his or her care" (164).

p. 98 A Benedict: *MSND.* p. 109

"Dined at Boodle's": Founded in 1764 by William Almack and named after its manager, Boodle's was frequented by country gentlemen but also by Edward Gibbon, William Wilberforce, Beau Brummell, and the Duke of Wellington. The club originally met at Almack's in Pall Mall. In 1783, it moved to its location in St. James, which was designed by John Crunden in 1775 for the Savoir Vivre Club [*The London Encyclopedia*].

p. 115. "wedlock does not lay any restraint on the parties engaged in it." In *The Sylph*, Lady Besford notes that women in late eighteenth-century England were not responsible to their husbands after they provide them with a male heir.

p. 115. "such a *sottise*": foolishness, silliness, nonsense; a stupid, blundering, or imbecilic act *(Larousse's)*.

p. 117. "a Portland, a Manchester, a Buccleugh, a Thanet, an Abingdon, a Spencer, a Delawarr, a Torington, a Wenman." These references further tie this anonymous novel to Georgiana, Duchess of Devonshire for its celebration of Whig politicians and their wives, many of whom were connected to the Spencer and Cavendish families. She begins her list with William Cavendish, third duke of Portland (1738–1809), an English statesman who entered Lord Rockingham's cabinet in 1765, and succeeded him as leader of the Whig party. He was prime minister on two occasions (April to December 1783, and 1807–1809). He served as home secretary under Pitt, and oversaw Irish affairs (1794–1801), which helped make his reputation. The other male figures are as follows: **Edward Montagu**, second Earl of Manchester (1602–1671), who was known as Viscount Mandeville. He sided with the popular party and led the Puritans in the Upper House and was charged by the King (January 3, 1642), along with five other members of the House of Commons, with entertaining traitorous designs. He served under Essex at Edgehill; Cromwell later accused him of military incompetence in the House of Commons and deprived Manchester of his command (1645); The Scott family possessed **Buccleuch** in Selkirkshire in 1415; they were a great Scottish Border family whose descendents include Sir Walter Scot, who fought for James II at Arkinholm against the Douglases (1455) and descendents, one of whom (1490–1522) fought at Flodden (1513), Melrose (1526), Ancrum (1544) and Pinkie (1547), and in 1552 was slain in a street fray at edinburgh by Kerr of Cessford. The **third duke of Buccleuch** (1746–1812) was an agriculturalist; **Lord Thanet** was a visitor to Devonshire House at least as early as 1786 (Foreman 184); his full name is Sackville Tufton, ninth earl of Thanet;

Thomas West De la Warr, twelfth baron (1577–1618), was imprisoned for complicity in Essex's revolt (1601) and so has some connection to Algernon Sidney (who is recalled through the character of Augustus Sidney); **Lord Abingdon** owned an estate at Cumnor (1763–1795) and large holdings near Oxford; **George Byng, first Viscount Torrington** (1663–1733), English sailor who joined William of Orange (1688) in the cause of the Revolution. Other Byngs in the Devonshire house circle include Frederick "Poodle" Byng (1784–1871), a wit and society dandy; George Byng (1740–1812), fourth Viscount Torrington (1750) who was minister plenipotentiary at Brussells (1783–1792); John Byng (1743–1813) fifth Viscount Torrington (1812) who was an army officer.

The women Lady Georgiana refers to include: Margaret Bentinck, Duchess of Portland (1715–1785), daughter of Edward Harley, second earl of Oxford (1689–1741) and his wife Lady Henrietta (née Cavendish Holles, 1694–1755); she married William, second duke of Portland (1709–1762) in 1734. By the terms of her mother's will she inherited the Cavendish estates, and so brought the Welbeck estate into the Bentinck family. Dorothy Bentinck, Duchess of Portland (1750–1794), the next in line, was the only daughter of William Cavendish, fourth duke of Devonshire. She married William Henry Cavendish Bentinck, third duke of Portland, in 1766.

The 1784 Dublin edition was printed two years after Henry Grattan helped establish an Irish parliament. Apparently a printer substituted the following names for those in the 1773 text: "a Rutland, a Leinster, a Temple, an Antrim, a Carrick, a Moira, an Arran, a Charlemont, a Mountgarret, a Kingsborough, a Lissord, and innumerable others whose BEAUTY adds the highest LUSTRE" (2:145). The Earl of Charlemont was a leading parliamentary reformer for Ireland. The Irish parliament remained independent from Great Britain for two decades until the Act of Union in 1800.

p. 118. "the tapis": carpet, rug, tapestry *(Larousse's)*.

p. 131. *"agremens"*: assent, approval.

p. 131. "then most beauteous, when least adorned": "when unadorned, adorned the most" (James Thomson, *The Seasons: Autumn*, ln. 204).

p. 138. "Wherefore are we born with high souls, but to assert ourselves, shake off this vile obedience they exact, and claim an equal empire o'er the world?": spoken by Calista in Nicholas Rowe's *The Fair Penitent. A Tragedy* (1703), one of the most popular tragedies (after Shakespeare) performed throughout the eighteenth-century. Kitty Bishop's remarks have particular resonance for Emma Walpole's relationship with her father and husband. Nicholas Rowe (1674–1718), poet laureate in 1715, was an ardent Whig; his application of Whig principles to women's rights in *The Fair Penitent* and *Jane Shore* (1714) matches what we know of Lady Georgiana's politics. This same phrase ("Wherefore are we/Born") appears as an epigraph for Mary Robinson's *Thoughts on the Condition of Women, and on the Injustice of Mental Subordination* (1799).

> How hard is the condition of our sex,
> Thro' ev'ry state of life the slaves of man!

In all the dear delightful days of youth
A rigid father dictates to our wills,
And deals out pleasure with a scanty hand.
To his, the tyrant husband's reign succeeds;
Proud with opinion of superior reason,
He holds domestick bus'ness and devotion
All we are capable to know, and shuts us,
Like cloyster'd ideots, from the world's acquaintance,
And all the joys of freedom. Wherefore are we
Born with high souls, but to assert our selves,
Shake off his vile obedience they exact,
And claim an equal empire o'er the world?
                              (*The Fair Penitent,* 3:i.40–53).

p. 138. "I would never take the character of an Orestes from a Pylades."
Pylades assisted Orestes in murdering Aegisthus and Clytemnestra; he afterwards
married Electra, Orestes's sister. "What shall I do, Pylades?" Orestes asks in "The
Libation Bearers," "Be shamed to kill my mother?" (ln. 899). Pylades encourages
Orestes in his act of vengeance. In this novel, with its focus on gender, the phrase
probably means taking a man's reputation from a male friend.

    p. 140. he rules, because she *will* obey:
            She, in obeying, rules as much as he

Unidentified, but echoed in the Epilogue to Vanbrugh's *The Provoked Husband*:
"Nay, she that with a weak man wisely lives,/Will seem t'obey the dire commands she gives/Happy obedience is no more a wonder,/When men are men,
and keep them kindly under" (lns. 16–21, p. 160); see also Alexander Pope,
Moral Essays, Epistle ii, lines 261–262: "She who ne'er answers till a husband
cools,/Or if she rules him, never shows she rules" (John Bartlett, *Familiar
Quotations,* 10th ed. 1919). My thanks to Randi Russert for the Pope reference.

    p. 140. "*cicisbeo,*" the recognized gallant of a woman in Italy, usually in the
late-eighteenth century (*Webster's*). Like the term *macaroni, cicisbeo* reflects the
travels of English tourists where they became impressed by Italian customs.

    p. 142. *camerora major":* head chambermaid.

    p. 149. "I shall never attach myself to a younger brother–they do not inherit
as much as the older ones." In England, unlike France, the older brother inherited the family estate, according to the laws of primogeniture.

    p. 149. "drozener": unidentified.

    p. 152. "spleen-wort": This mock cure for the misogyny of Walpole's guest
is offered, perhaps facetiously, by Kitty Bishop. Spleen-wort was a herb used to
remedy diseases of the spleen (*Webster's*). "Wort enters into the names of numerous herbs, as mug-wort, liver-wort, spleen-wort" (*Brewer's*).

    p. 152. " 'The smoothest course of nature has its pains' ": "The smoothest
course of nature has its pains;/ And truest friends, through error, wound our
rest" (Edward Young, *Night Thoughts,* line 278). Mrs. Walpole quotes Young's
lines to show her sensibility and her need to "arm herself," exercising "patient
and submissive conduct" (152).

p. 152. " 'the Feeling of another's woe, the Unfeeling for his own' "; recalls Pope's "Essay on Man," though the source is probably elsewhere: "Teach me to feel another's woe,/To hide the fault I see: /That mercy I to others show, /That mercy show to me" (6.590.37.148)

p. 156. "Maccaroni": A precious, exquisite young man; a member of a class of traveled young Englishmen of the late eighteenth and early nineteenth centuries that affected foreign ways; a precious affected young man: exquisite, fop, dandy (*Webster's*). In 1760, the Macaroni Club was instituted by a group of Englishmen who had traveled to Europe; Lord Melbourne, Sir Joshua Reynolds, and friends of Thomas Gray were members. They introduced the new Italian food, macaroni, to Almack's and were known for their gambling, drinking, duelling, gambling, and insolence.

p. 156. "lighter than the ear of Phoebus": In the 1787 edition, this phrase is "car of Phoebus," which refers to the phaeton Apollo rides to start the new day, a car that was notoriously light (198); "car" (2:26; 1787) better fits the sense of the passage than "ear" (2:198; 2:6; 1773). To explain the 1773 reference, one might note that Phoebus Apollo's musical gift was legendary; he was also the god of archery, poetry, medicine, prophecy, and the sun. Phoebus Apollo drew sounds from the lyre that Hermes gave him; when he played in Olympus the gods forgot all else (Hamilton, p. 103); the lightness of his ear presumably refers to this musical gift. "How by the shaft of a God . . . What deed of outrage, Phoebus, hast thou done This . . . shall not be lighter, though Aeacus' son . . . less in might/Than was his sire . . . Out through his ear," Homer, *The Iliad, 3:128*; Apollo's ears are contrasted with the "stupid ears" of Midas, whose ears are turned into those of the "slow-going jackass" in Ovid's *Metamorphoses* (11:176–177);

p. 156. "This animated Venus, concluded I, will certainly rival the statue of the Medicis, and give some scope for his admiration": The *Venus de Medicis*, supposedly by Cleomenes of Athens, was dug up in the seventeenth century in the villa of Hadrian, near Tivoli, in eleven pieces. In 1680, it was removed by Cosmo III to the Imperial Gallery at Florence from the Medici Palace in Rome (*Brewer's*).

p. 158. "the dust of Alexander stops a bunghole"; "The noble dust of Alexander the Great now stops a 'barrel-hole' (bunghole)—The imperions of Caesar, now turned to clay, might stop a hole to keep the wind" (*Hamlet*, Act 5.1).

p. 158. "Sieur Perico"; "Fantoccini":

p. 158. *"man of quality"*: a man of fashion.

p. 160. "au comble de ses desirs": at the height of their desires.

p. 160. "Piqued at his disregard to the sex, I twitted him with the great Sully's answer to Henry the Fourth on a similar occasion": This comment does not occur in the four-volume edition of Sully that I have consulted; nor does it appear in reviews of Charlotte Lennox's translation, though Henry's response to Sully's (not Sully's) appears as follows: "I should have been glad," says Henry IV, "if God had sent me a dozen sons; for it would be a great pity that from so grand a stem there should be no shoots" (Sully 3:390).

p. 169. "Catch it ye winds, and bear it on your roseate wings to Aix": unidentified; Aix may refer to "Aachen, or Aix la Chapelle, the favourite city of Charlemagne, where, when he [Charlemagne] died, he was seated, embalmed, on a throne, with the Bible on his lap, his sword (La Joyeuse) by his side, the imperial crown on his head, and his sceptre and shield at his feet. So well had the Egyptians embalmed him, that he seemed only to be asleep" (*Brewer's*).

p. 175. " 'rare are solitary woes, they love a train; they tread each others heels–and make distress, distraction' ": "Rare are solitary woes; They love a train, they tread each other's heel." (Edward Young, *Night Thoughts on Life, Death, and Immortality: in Nine Nights, The Complaint*. 3:63).

p. 180. "*unlimited* Loo": A round card-game played by a varying number of players. The cards in three-card loo have the same value as in whist; in five-card loo the Jack of Clubs ("Pam") is the highest card. A player who fails to take a trick or breaks any of the laws of the game is "looed"—required to pay a certain sum, or "loo," to the pool. "If there is a loo in the last deal of a round, the game continues until there is a hand without a loo. At an unlimited loo each player looed has to put in the amount there was in the pool. But it is generally agreed to *limit* the loo, so that it shall not exceed a certain fixed sum."

Whist is "a game of cards played ordinarily by four persons of whom each two sitting opposite each other are partners, with a pack of fifty-two cards, which are dealt face downward to the players in rotation, so that each has a *hand* of thirteen cards; one of the suits (usually determined by the last card dealt, which is then turned face upwards) is trumps: the players play in rotation, each four successive cards so played constituting a trick in which each player after the leader must follow suit if he holds a card of the suit led. The game dates back to 1663."

Piquet is "a card-game played by two persons with a pack of thirty-two cards (the low cards form the two to the six being excluded) in which points are scored on various groups or combinations of cards, and on tricks. The game dates from 1646" (*OED*).

p. 184. "I shall play the schoolboy, as poor Jaffier says": "I play the boy, and blubber in thy bosom./Oh! I shall drown thee with my sorrows!" (*Venice Preserved*, Act I).

p. 188. "the stews": brothels or slums (*Webster's*).

p. 192. "the temple of Plutus": Plutus, god of Wealth, is a roman allegorical figure wrongly confused with Pluto. The "flame cultivated for the God of Wealth" indicates that Georgiana's allusion is correct.

p. 192. "cestus": the girdle of Venus, which was decorated with every object that could arouse amorous desire; more generally, cestus refers to a girdle or belt, especially as worn by women of ancient Greece (*Webster's*).

p. 193. "Lady Wronghead's fist": Lady Wronghead is the gambling wife of Sir Francis Wronghead in Vanbrugh's *The Provok'd Husband* (1728) who defeats Lady Townly at cards (5:2:50–52). "No, after that horrid bar of my chance, that Lady Wronghead's fatal red fist upon the table, I saw it was impossible ever to win another stake" (5:2:50–52). Peter Dixon annotates this as follows: "Perhaps it was thought to bring the caster bad luck if another player touched the table while play was in progress. Lady Wronghead does not know the etiquette of hazard and blights Lady Townley's game" (Note to 5:2:50–52, p. 132).

p. 193. "Arion would have been beaten, Bucephalus would have lost his spirit, Eclipse himself would have been *eclipsed*": Arion was Hercules's horse, given to Adrastus, formerly the horse of Neptune (*Brewer's*, 132); Bucephelus was a black horse owned by Alexander the Great. "It proved unmanageable until the twelve-year-old Alexander, observing that it shied at its own shadow, turned its head to the sun, soothed, and then mounted it" (Howatson, 102).

p. 194. "So dear a bliss my bosom could not know
When to my raptured bosom I clasp' the maid,
As now her wedded fondness *could* bestow."

Henry James Pye, "Elegy VIII, Written at Ministed in the New Forest, August 24, 1767." The lines from Pye are as follows:

"Yet witness every lawn, and every shade!
So dear a bliss my bosom could not know,
When to my breast I clasp'd the yeilding* maid,
As now her wedded fondness can bestow (line 16, p. 76);

* misquoted, or quoted from memory, in 1773 and 1787 edition.

p. 195. *"Hygeia"*: Hygeia was the goddess of Health, said to be the daughter of Aesculapius. (Hamilton 329).

p. 199. " 'degrees make all things easy' "; stage adaptations of Aphra Behn's *Oroonoko* were more popular than the novel itself. This line appears, identically, in two stage adaptations: John Hawkesworth, *Oroonoko* (1759), 1:2, and Thomas Southerne's *Oroonoko* (1696). "Learn to know it better: So I know, you say, / Degrees make all Things easy. All things shall be easy" (1:2).

p. 199. "The house, even from its resemblance to the *colour of my fate*, has some charms for me; it gives me subject 'for meditation even to madness,' and I indulge myself in it to the full": Iago declared his intention to distort Othello by "Practicing on his peace and quiet/Even to madness" (Shakespeare, *Othello*, 2:1:320). Emma is self-tormenting, though her husband's conduct also plays an Iago-like role. His jealousy of her recalls Othello's for Desdemona.

p. 200. " 'far as distress the soul can wound, 'tis pain in each degree.' ": see annotation for p. 303. Fanny Greville's "Prayer for Indifference."

p. 200. "bantlings": young babies.

p. 201. "her figure was *prevenante* without being fine": becoming, if not beautiful.

p. 204. "unless, like Pygmalion, she could animate the statue by her love": Pygmalion is the male, misogynist sculptor described by Ovid. The allusion is effective, however, for Lord Wilmington, like Pygmalion, does try to shape his young bride, Lady Hamilton, into the perfect model of womanhood.

p. 215. "The already plundered need no robber fear": "Not bound by vows, and unrestrain'd by shame, In sport you break the heart, and rend the fame./ Nor that your art can be successful here./ Th' already plunder'd need no robber fear: /Nor sighs, nor charms, nor flatteries can move,/ Too well secured against a second love." Lady Wortley Montague, "An Answer to a Love-Letter, in Verse," ln. 18, p. 68.

p. 220. "an hydra-woe, as a conceited author calls it": Shelley, "Queen Mab," 5: ln. 196. Pre-1773 source is unidentified. Since a hydra has many tentacles, a hydra woe would be one that has many facets; hydras multiply when their heads are cut off, so a hydra-woe multiplies quickly. In Greek legend, Hydra was the offspring of Typhon and Echidna, a gigantic monster with nine heads (the number varies), the center one immortal. The destruction of Hydra was one of the twelve labors of Heracles, which he accomplished with the assistance of Iolaus. As one head was cut off, two grew in its place; therefore, they finally burned out the roots with firebrands and at last severed the immortal head from the body. The arrows dipped by Heracles in the poisonous blood or gall inflicted fatal wounds (*Britannica* 186).

p. 226. "Tired nature's sweet restorer, balmy sleep": "TIRED nature's sweet restorer, balmy Sleep!" (Edward Young's *Night Thoughts*, ln. 1).

p. 226. " 'The bad, when compared to worse, appear as good' ": "those wicked creatures yet do look well-favoured,/When others are more wicked not being the worst/Stands in some rank of praise" (Shakespeare, *KL*, 2:4:251–253). My thanks to Jennifer Parrott, Matthew Infantino, and Randi Russert for assistance locating this quotation.

p. 228. "Like Romeo, I shall revive, and be an emperor, when she shall breathe new life into me by her kisses": "And breathed such life with kisses in my lips, That I revived, and was an emperor" (Shakespeare, *RJ*, 5:1:9).

p. 228. " 'Paradise has opened in the wild' ": "And Paradise was open'd in the Wild" (Alexander Pope; "Eloise and Abelard," 2:134.300).

p. 230. *"a schismatic":* one who separates from a church or religious communion; nontraditionalist; "Generally speaking, the schismatic does not deny the Faith, just the Church. One of the most infamous schisms was caused by a dispute over the primacy of the pope over the Universal Church, and resulted in the split between the East and West" (*Catholic Encyclopedia*).

p. 231. "The rage of Tisiphone's fury". Tisiphone is one of the Erinyes (the Furies), powerful divinities who personified conscience and punished crimes against kindred blood, especially matricide. Their names were Megaera (jealous), Tisiphone (blood avenger), and Alecto (unceasing in pursuit). They were usually represented as winged women with serpent hair. When called upon to act, they hounded their victims until they died in a furor of madness or torment (*Brewer's* 103; Hamilton, 40). In the myth of Orestes they appear as Clytemnestra's agents of revenge. After Athena absolved Orestes of guilt in the murder of his mother, she gave the Furies a grotto at Athens where they received sacrifices and libations, and became euphemistically known as the Eumenides (kindly ones). See Aeschylus's *The Eumenides*. Walpole imagines himself as the murderer of Emma. See earlier reference to Orestes and Pylades, p. 138, 306.

p. 233. " 'to err, is human; to forgive, divine' ": "To err, is human; to forgive, divine" (Alexander Pope, *Essay on Criticism*, 2: ln. 325).

p. 240. " 'Roses will bloom, where there's peace in the breast' ": from a song sung by Perdita in "Florizel and Perdita," by David Garrick, section 2. "By mode and caprice are the city dames led,/But we, as the children of nature are bred;/By her hand alone, we are painted and dress'd;/ For the roses will bloom, when there's peace in the breast." Perdita is the part Mary Robinson played when the Prince of Wales became infatuated with her. The couple became known as Perdita and Florizel.

I.

Come, come, my good shepherds,
our flocks we must shear;
In your holy-day suits, with your lasses appear:
The happiest of folk, are the guiltless and free,
And who are so guiltless, so happy as we?

II.

We harbour no passions, by luxury taught;
We practice no arts, with hypocrisy fraught;
What we think in our hearts, you may read in our eyes;
For knowing no falsehood, we need no disguise.

III.

By mode and caprice are the city dames led,
But we, as the children of nature are bred;
By her hand alone, we are painted and dress'd;
For the roses will bloom, when there's peace in the breast.

IV.

That giant, ambition, we never can dread:
Our roofs are too low, for so lofty a head;
Content and sweet chearfulness open our door,
They smile with the simple, and feed with the poor.

V.

When love has possess'd us, that love we reveal;
Like the flocks that we feed, are the passions we feel;
So harmless and simple we sport, and we play,
And leave to fine folks to deceive and betray.

David Garrick, "Song in the *Winter's Tale.*"

p. 244. "the *peer* of the woeful countenance may find out another Dulcinea as soon as he will": Don Quixote admired Dulcinea, a peasant girl, whom he transformed through the power of his imagination into an enchanting beauty. See Part 1: chapter 25 of *Don Quixote*, p. 210.

p. 244. *"Le jour du mariage est le tombeau de l'amour"*: a guitar song, like *"Maudit amour,"* which is strummed by Kitty Bishop. The phrase appears in Charles Palissot de Montenoy's (1730–1814) song or poem, "L'heureux mariage": "On dit que le mariage/Est le tombeau de l'amour,/Que jamais dans le menage/

On ne coule d'heureux jours." The line also appears in Richardson's *Clarissa:* "Matrimony indeed, which is the Grave of Love, because it allows of the End of Love" (*Clarissa* 1100).

  p. 244. *"gênant"*: pinching, embarrassing, constraining.

  p. 248. "rough breath of Boreas": God of the north wind in Greek mythology; son of Astraeus, a Titan, and Eos, the morning (*Brewer's* 38).

  p. 250. *"pleasing pain"*: Anne Hunter (fl. 1790), text to Franz Hayden: "Far from this throbbing bosom haste,/Ye doubts, ye fears, that lay it waste;/Dear anxious days of pleasing pain,/Fly never to return again/ But ah, return ye smiling hours,/By careless fancy crown'd with flow'rs;/Come, fairy joys and wishes gay,/And dance in sportive rounds away./So shall the moments gaily glide/O'er various life's tumultuous tide,/Nor sad regrets disturb their course/ To calm oblivion's peaceful source." Another source may be Spenser's *Faerie Queene*: "And painful pleasure turns to pleasing pain"; or Thomas Gray, "The Bard" III. 3, ln. 125–130; in Thomas Gray, *Odes by Mr. Gray*: "The verse adorn again/Fierce War, and faithful Love,/And Truth severe, by fairy Fiction drest./ In buskin'd measures move/Pale Grief, and pleasing Pain."

  p. 252. " 'Soft, modest, melancholy, female, fair' ": "A theme so like thee, a quite lunar theme,/Soft, modest, melancholy, female, fair!" (Edward Young, *Night Thoughts on Life, Death, and Immortality: in Nine Nights, The Complaint*. 3:50–54).

  p. 253. *"ecclairicessement"*: clearing up, explanation; enlightenment; education (*Larousse's* 95).

  p. 253. "raking": misbehaving, with the connotation of libertinism (*OED*).

REFERENCES

Brewer's Concise Dictionary of Phrase and Fable, ed. by Betsy Kirkpatrick. London: Cassell, 1992.

Cervantes, Miguel de, trans. by J. M. Cohen. *Don Quixote*. New York: Penguin, 1950.

Garrick, David. "Song in the *Winter's Tale*." In *The Poetical Works of David Garrick*. 2 vols. 1785. New York: Benjamin Blom, 1968.

Granville, George. "The Progress of Beauty," *The Genuine Works in Verse and Prose of G. G. Lord Lansdowne*, 2 vols. London, 1732. Quoted in Alexander Chalmers, ed., *The Works of the English Poets*. 11 vols. London, 1810, v. 11.

Gray, Thomas. *Odes by Mr. Gray*. Strawberry Hill: R. and J. Dodsley, 1757.

Greville, Fanny. "Prayer for Indifference." *The Oxford Book of English Verse, 1250–1918*, ed. by Sir Arthur Quiller-Couch. New York: Oxford UP, 1940. #489, p. 566.

Hamilton, Edith. *Mythology: Timeless Tales of Gods and Heroes*. New York: Mentor, 1940.

Howatson, Margaret, ed. *The Oxford Companion to Classical Literature*. Oxford: Oxford UP, 1989.

Hunter, Anne. Text to Franz Haydn's "Pleasing Pain." English and Scottish Songs. Paris: Opus 111, 1994. Recorded St. Barnabas Church, London, 1994.

Levy, M. J. ed. *Perdita: The Memoirs of Mary Robinson*. London: Peter Owen, 1994.

Montague, Lady Wortley. "An Answer to a Love-Letter, in Verse," *The Poetical Works of the Right Honourable Lady M—y W—y M—e*. London: Printed for J. Williams [etc.], 1768.

Sully, Maximilien de Bethune, duc de. *Memoirs of the Duke of Sully, prime minister to Henry the Great*. Tr. from the French. Edition: A new ed., rev. and cor.; with additional notes, and an historical introduction, attributed to Sir Walter Scott. 4 vols. London, G. Bell & sons, 1877–1892.

The New Encyclopaedia Britannica, ed. Philip Goetz. 24 vols. 15th edition. Chicago: Encyclopaedia Britannica, Inc. 1988.

Otway, Thomas. *Venice Preserved*, ed. by Malcolm Kelsall. Lincoln: University of Nebraska Press, 1969.

Ovid. *Ovid: Metamorphoses*, trans. by Rolfe Humphries. Bloomington: Indiana UP, 1955.

Palissot de Montenoy, Charles. "L'heureux mariage." Quoted in *Oeuvres de M. Palissot*. 4 vols. Paris: De l'Imprimerie de Monsieur, chez Moutard, 1788.

Pope, Alexander. "Eloise and Abelard." In *The Poems of Alexander Pope*, ed. Maynard Mack et. al. 11 volumes. New Haven: Yale UP, 1969.

———. *Essay on Criticism*. In *The Poems of Alexander Pope*, ed. Maynard Mack et al. 11 volumes. New Haven: Yale UP, 1969.

———. "Moral Essays." In *The Poems of Alexander Pope*, ed. Maynard Mack et al. New Haven: Yale UP, 1969.

Pye, Henry James. "Elegy VIII, Written at Ministed in the New Forest, August 24, 1767." In *Poems on Various Subjects*, by Henry James Pye. 2 volumes. London: John Stockdale, 1787.

Radcliffe, Alexander. "Phillis to Demophoon," *Ovid Travestie, A Burlesque Upon Ovid's Epistles*. In *The Works of Alexander Radcliffe (1696)*, with an introduction by Ken Robinson. New York: Scholars' Facsimiles and Reprints, 1981.

Richardson, Samuel. *Clarissa, or the History of a Young Lady*. 1747–1748, ed. with an introduction and notes by Angus Ross. New York: Penguin, 1985.

Shakespeare, William. *The Complete Works of William* Shakespeare, ed. by David Bevington. 3rd ed. Chicago: Scott, Foresman, 1988.

Vanbrugh, Sir John and Coley Cibber. *The Provoked Husband*, ed. by Peter Dixon. Lincoln: University of Nebraska Press, 1973.

Young, Edward, with illustrations by William Blake. *Night Thoughts* or, *The Complaint and The Consolation*, ed. by Robert Essick and Jenijoy LaBelle, with 43 engravings by William Blake. New York: Dover, 1975.

Index